PAINTING CELIA

MAYA BAIREY

ISBN 979-8-9900655-5-0
Library of Congress Control Number: 2024936528

Published by Lingua Ink Books
Portland, Oregon • linguaink.com

To Peter,
the most important person the world.

CONTENTS

ONE

Selfish? Really?

"We'll have to talk later, Mom." Celia ended the phone call, cutting off her mother mid-objection.

Her fingers trembled, clenching the phone tightly. Nothing made those calls better. Hanging up was getting easier with practice, at least.

What more could she do? She bankrolled her mother's comfortable life and tried to act the part of attentive daughter. It wasn't enough. There was always a new need.

Today's request was a first. Mother wanted her to pay for two friends to join her on a cruise. A cruise! She'd already told her friends it was no problem. Celia explained it was indeed a problem, then braced for the browbeating.

Mom did her shouting, and Celia ended the call once the name-calling started. The usual.

She needed to do something productive, clear her mind.

A spot of grease on the gas range caught her eye and Celia whisked across the kitchen. Heat from the oven had baked it on, but a hard scrubbing won out. The timer showed nearly two hours to go on the ribs slowly roasting inside. Celia watched the number tick down one minute, then two.

But you can afford it, her mother's voice echoed. *How can you be so selfish, Celia Rose?*

Right. Snap out of it!

Was there anything else to clean before Andrew and the rest showed up tonight? A couch pillow at the wrong angle, a teacup to put away, or...a scan of her vast white living space put an end to that hope. Not one item out of place.

She hated that moment each day when she ran out of jobs. Even worse was when it coincided with one of Mom's calls.

Nothing left for her inside, Celia decided to swim. The backyard pool was convenient when all else failed, and gainful exercise could use up a whole hour.

Wrapping her wavy hair into a tawny topknot, Celia slipped out the sliding glass door and padded down the sloped lawn to her pool house. Glossy dust-free shelves stood laden with folded towels and baskets of sunscreen. No tasks to do here either.

She stripped down and draped her clothes on the neat daybed, checking the distant view of downtown Los Angeles through the floor-to-ceiling windows. The air was less smoky today. Wildfire season seemed to be coming to a close. Thank goodness for autumn.

The sun-blocking film on the pool house windows created a faintly-purpled mirror in which she could see herself applying sunscreen.

Not terrible for just past forty. The daily laps were staving off the inevitable sag.

Maybe a cruise would distract Mom from calling so often?

Stop thinking about it! Her mother would have to accept 'no' for once.

Celia stepped from the pool house onto the blazing flagstone pool surround, nude but dutifully protected from the baking sun. Palm trees and pricey greenery hid her yard from the houses perched on either side. Up here in the canyon, everyone could afford to face the city view and not their neighbors.

The soles of her feet burned, and tickles scampered over her skin as the sun dried the fine hairs on her body. This final summer heatwave was lingering. Celia would rather swim at night in the cool darkness, but she didn't get to pick when she needed refuge.

She drew a deep breath.

No thinking about her mother, no thinking about money, no thinking of the hours left to fill today. No thinking at all.

With a grace from long practice, Celia dove into distraction.

• • •

León stood to pace again, covering the same fifteen feet of Andrew's dim apartment. He ran out of space, again, at the window overlooking the courtyard below. The glass blazed with a painful afternoon glare. The shadowed pool, two floors down, could barely be seen.

His own orange-washed reflection looked back at him, clearer than anything outside. Arms crossed, brow furrowed—his father would call him sulky if he saw him now. *¡Tranquilo!* Relax.

León leaned into the reflection, shielding his eyes and pressing his forehead to the hot glass. The sun would slip behind the rooftop any minute now.

The pool below was deserted and still. Who would swim in a courtyard that got shade all afternoon? The dusky water reflected the terra cotta walls in a wonderful mix of colors, blues and oranges blending into a surprising purple. He could match that with a mix of rose violet paint, primary cyan, a little white.

A glance at his shabby boxes of painting gear unpacked in the corner provoked a low grumble. How long until he could spread them out and get to work? Missing opportunities like this hurt.

He looked back down as motion drew his eye. A lone dark-haired toddler stooped in the shallows, rousing waves of reflected color with chubby hands. Someone was watching that kid, right? Oh, there, a bored mother in the shade.

Ah, but look!

The moment was made for a canvas. The orange angles above, cool purpled shadows below, ripples ringing a stray baby patting at the water.

Dammit!

This was why he'd come to LA, to paint colors like this, moments like this. He needed to get unpacked so he didn't miss them. The light down there was already changing.

"Andrew," he called out, getting a noise in response from deeper in the cramped apartment. "What if I don't go out with you tonight? I could get out the small easel and do some painting while you're gone."

"You should meet people out here," came the reply. "And I know you, once that easel's out, it'll stay out. There's just no room."

León scowled again at his useless boxes, an arm's length

away from his bedroll on the couch.

"Just come with me to Celia's tonight," Andrew called. "Tomorrow, I can help you look for an apartment."

León tucked his hair behind an ear, heading back to the couch to sit heavily. He did need Andrew's help.

Andrew came into the front room, tall and lean, running a hand over his freshly shaved head. His clothes were more stylish than usual, a white shirt gleaming against his earthy brown skin, and—dude, cologne? Wasn't this supposed to be a casual backyard barbecue they were going to?

León's scowl deepened. "Do I have to dress up for this?"

"Nah," Andrew grinned. "I just like looking good."

"Your head looks like a big brown egg."

"And you look homeless. I've got another razor if you want to clean up that scruff."

León slouched deeper into the couch, rolling his eyes to the ceiling.

"Come on, this is my crew," Andrew said. "Don't put off meeting them. They're artists too. Trevor can introduce you at like ten galleries."

Well, that would make going worth it.

"You sure he won't mind helping?" León asked. "Didn't he break up with you last year?"

Andrew shook his head as he gathered his phone and wallet. "You're thinking of Tom, and he was earlier. Last year I was dating Celia."

Right. The woman whose house they were going to. Andrew's ability to stay friends with his exes was legendary.

If this Trevor person could introduce him around, he could sell a painting. That would buy some time. León only had enough money to last a few months, and there was no way he'd slink back to New York that quickly.

León smoothed down his rumpled T-shirt. *Tranquilo.*

Fine, he'd meet these friends of Andrew's. And then paint! The buildings and bridges back home had lost their magic, but this new coast had things he'd never seen. If he could just get some space! And a subject. And inspiration. Easy. He had a whole month to discover the right raw, authentic shapes.

"Are you thinking about painting again?" Andrew asked. "Dude. You were more laid back the last time you visited."

León shook his head, finally cracking a smile. "I didn't have deadlines then." He jumped up from the couch again. "Let's get this social shit over with. I'm not changing clothes. Let's just go."

Andrew gave him an easy grin and reached for his car keys.

• • •

Kelsey was first to arrive at Celia's after work, shedding her slim jacket and canary yellow heels, slinging them as usual toward the nearest sofa. "Ten hours in those shoes," she said, nursing one foot, balancing on the other.

Celia closed her eyes, savoring the fuss and disorder. Kelsey always brought a little life into the stale house.

"I am starving, Celia," she sang. She danced in a circle, arms wide, then closed her eyes and followed her nose into the kitchen. "Is that beef I smell?"

"It's just ribs," Celia said, opening the fridge. Kelsey's preferred ginger ales were keeping cold behind the white wine.

"You made all those sides, too," Kelsey said, crowding close behind to peek. "Potato salad? Real coleslaw! So, we're having actual barbecue tonight? I was getting used to curry and French stuff."

"I wanted to keep things simple." Celia closed the door with her elbow, handing the drink off to Kelsey. "Andrew's bringing that guy, remember."

Simple. Ha. It had taken days to assemble this meal. She'd invented ways to fill those empty hours, toasting and hand-grinding spices, mixing vinegars for the right tang. Stupid behind-the-scenes flourishes no genuine cook would bother with. Maybe it would make the food special, though?

No one likes a show-off, Celia Rose.

Kelsey sipped the ginger ale but eyed Celia's tightly wrung fingers. "Honey, relax," she said. "We'll all be here to talk to Andrew's new guy. You can just sit back if you don't want to join in."

Right. Celia shook out her hands. "It's fine," she said. "I'm okay."

Who would be scared of a friend of Andrew's?

Kelsey picked up the platter of ribs to take out back. "The guys will all just talk art anyway."

Celia shook her head. "You saw Trevor's not coming, right? It's just us and Andrew."

Kelsey shrugged. "So, we'll talk about your art list."

The doorbell rang.

"Not my weird list, please," Celia said as she went to answer.

She opened her front door to Andrew's silhouette on her shady front steps, the sun on the trees behind him. Was that...cologne? He'd dressed up, and his gleaming grin widened as he saw her noticing.

"Hey, girl," he said.

She shook her head at him with a faint smile. Charming Andrew forgot he was an ex sometimes.

A few feet behind him, overshadowed in nearly every measure, hovered this New York friend Andrew had brought.

He stood stiffly, hands shoved into the faded pockets of his loose jeans, his lived-in hoodie zipped up despite the heat. Seeing her head turn to him, he lifted his chin, his black eyes brooding and skeptical. Then, sighing, he shook his head faintly as he looked her up and down. Pulling his hands from his pockets, he ran one through unruly shoulder-length black hair and pursed his lips. The other hand he raised in a trifling wave.

Celia froze. React! Be polite!

She took too long. It grew awkward, so she just looked away.

. . .

León eyed the muted woman judging him from the ornate doorway. This was who Andrew had dressed up for? This gray-clad girl?

Something about the way she wavered in the entry, hanging against the door, felt young. On closer look, though, she was a little older than him. A little shorter. Ordinary. He would never have noticed her on the street, honestly.

Her poker face was blankly skilled, though her coppery

skin and tilted eyes told their own story. He watched her solemn gaze take in his half-hearted wave, then glide back to Andrew, expressionless. León almost cracked a smile—it was so silently regal. This little queen.

"Celia, this is León," Andrew said to her, breaking the silence. He turned to León, pointing back. "That's Celia."

"You don't say," León said.

"Come in," she said, fading back into the hall. "We're taking the food out back." Andrew draped an arm around her shoulder and walked with her through the plain entry, León trailing behind.

The hallway opened into a huge combined kitchen and living room, the low sun flooding through a wall of west-facing windows, painting great temporary orange triangles on the bare white interior.

What did this woman have against color? Her house was as unadorned as she was. It felt like a hotel, spacious and manicured but lacking personality.

Andrew picked up a tub of iced bottles from the kitchen island as soon as he reached it, Celia opening the sliding glass door to the backyard for him. There was no standing on ceremony, apparently.

León didn't see anything else to carry out, so just smiled as he passed through the door after Andrew. She glanced outside as he passed, casually skipping the eye contact. Not regal, rude!

He emerged onto a narrow backyard but stopped dead as he saw the bejeweled view.

Jesus!

He held his breath, absorbing the unexpected colors and shapes. A glowing swimming pool hugged a wrought iron fenced retaining wall overlooking a spectacular view of downtown LA. The setting sun, directly before them, bathed the yard in an orange blaze. A low, rectangular pool house made of windows sat to the right, mirroring every color back at him.

This, he could paint. The dusky slopes, that star-strewn city, and the luminous still water under a fiery sunset.

The woman, Celia, passed him to walk down the sloped

lawn. She and Andrew were headed for a heavy table to the left, already laden with covered platters. Behind it sat a gathering of low chairs encircling a rosy brick firepit. A shapely sun-kissed blond awaited them there.

León followed, feeling sulky again. Another painting missed.

Andrew set the drinks tub on the table with a hearty crash of partially melted ice. Then, nodding at the wood stacked ready in the firepit, he glanced at Celia.

"Not enough to do today? Usually, I build that." She shrugged, looking away. With a shake of his head, Andrew pointed at León and the blond woman in turn. "Kelsey, León," he said.

The blond smiled and handed him a cold bottle of beer on her way back up to the house. León sidled out of the way while the others bustled around, bringing out salad bowls and lighting the fire. Everyone knew what to do but him.

He tuned out their fuss and watched the sunset, thumb tapping impatiently against his thigh. On the drive up the canyon, around twisty hairpin roads hemmed on all sides by enigmatic private houses and elaborate gates, the low sun hadn't hit his face once. It was blocked intentionally, he realized.

Hoarding the expensive view. It was immoral.

A lull behind him drew his attention, and he turned to find an empty plate being handed to him by the blond. Kelsey.

"All right!" Andrew said. "Let's see what exotic dish—hey, this is barbecue!"

"Not barbecue," Celia corrected, standing by and watching plates being filled. "It's just ribs cooked in the oven."

"Just, ha!" Andrew said, carrying a plate to a chair by the fire. "Nothing you cook is 'just' anything, girl."

Kelsey followed with her own plate. "You can always count on Celia to out-cook anyone," she lilted.

León saw Celia go still at the end of the table, her eyes darting quietly across the ground. The tension in her shoulders belied that persistent poker face. She didn't like being singled out.

He placed a rib on his plate, then leaned in to her. "What's wrong with showing off anyway?"

She inhaled sharply, snapping to attention, finally meeting his eyes.

He gave her a casual smile and turned to the firepit with his food.

. . .

Plates empty, fire illuminating the little seating area, Celia sat back and tried to be invisible. New people were so hard for her.

"You can meet Trevor next time, León," Andrew promised, peeling the label from his beer bottle. "I wish he'd been here."

Kelsey looked up from where she draped nearly sideways in her chair. "That cologne was probably for him."

Andrew made a face at her as she poked him with an outstretched foot.

"Too bad Trev's off working," he said. "He keeps you too busy to cause trouble."

"Me! You're the one who—" She squealed as Andrew touched her foot with his cold beer.

Celia watched their antics, grateful. Let Andrew and Kelsey provide the entertainment.

León was leaning forward, elbows on knees, head low. The firelight shone off that curtain of dark hair, hiding his face.

How had he known she was worried about showing off earlier? No one else had. If they had, they wouldn't have teased, right?

When León rubbed the back of his neck and looked up, Celia sank back, deeper into the shadows. He tapped Andrew's arm, his face damp and shiny in the firelight.

"Dude," Andrew said, sitting up and leaning toward him. "You feel okay?"

León shook his head. "Where's the bathroom?"

Andrew stood, holding out a hand to his friend and pulling him out of the low chair.

"I'll show you. Anyone need anything from the house?" Andrew didn't wait for an answer but began the walk up the lawn, shepherding León ahead of him.

"Bring my jacket!" Kelsey called.

Celia's gaze followed as the two dimmed into silhouettes against the lit house, one tall and one...stooped over? León didn't just want the restroom, did he? She rose to go after them.

She caught up as Andrew opened the patio door. In the light from the house, León looked pale and sweaty.

"Are you okay?" she asked. He shook his head, arms held low across his stomach. Celia and Andrew exchanged an alarmed look. León's face had turned gray awfully fast.

"I get this sometimes from shellfish," he said, "but...."

Celia's stomach lurched. Shellfish.

"But we ate ribs," Andrew said, watching her. Celia shook off the shock, putting a hand under León's elbow and walking him to the bathroom herself.

"León, there was shrimp in the food tonight. Are you allergic?"

"Not allergic," he muttered. "Later. I'll tell you later." He went in, kneeling on the floor, then kicking feebly at the door until it closed.

Andrew stared at Celia. "There was no shrimp at dinner!"

"There was," she said. "Shrimp stock in the cabbage dressing." Sounds from inside the bathroom got real. "León, do you need 911? An EpiPen or—"

"No," came the muffled answer during a pause. "Not allergic. Go away, okay?"

Kelsey appeared at the back door, eyebrows arched high. Andrew propelled Celia toward her, a hand on her shoulder.

"What is going on?" Kelsey asked.

Andrew ushered both women outside onto the patio. "León's sick. I guess he can't have shellfish."

Celia laced her fingers and tucked them under her chin, eyes wide. "There was shrimp stock in the dressing," she repeated. "I should have told everyone."

This is what came of showing off! People could die from allergies, and she was hiding ingredients in—

Andrew tapped her shoulder. "Don't hog that

responsibility, girl. I should have asked him."

Kelsey pulled out her phone to ask the internet. "Is he allergic?"

"He said no," Andrew told her, looking over her shoulder. A tense minute passed as Kelsey typed and scrolled, her face lit from below by her screen.

"If it's just an intolerance, he should be all right," she said. "The danger is if he gets hives or can't breathe."

"He was just sick to his stomach, I think," Andrew said.

A shaky breath escaped Celia.

"Why don't you two go sit," Andrew said. "He won't want us all hanging around. I'll stay."

Celia pressed her hands against her cheeks. "I shouldn't have gotten fancy with the ingredients."

"Honey, no," Kelsey said. "It was just unfortunate. Come sit down."

"I'll call if we need anything, Celia," Andrew told her.

Celia let herself be led back to the fire but knew she'd be back as soon as Andrew signaled. She could at least get León water, medicine, whatever helped.

She felt like vomiting herself. She'd never poisoned a guest before.

TWO

Squinting against a bright hot light, León awoke in an unfamiliar room, sun pouring onto the bed through a skylight. He blinked, rasping an unshaven cheek off the pillow. Where the hell was he? Not Andrew's, not a hotel or—wait, this was that lady's house. Celia's.

He breathed as last night came back to him. He'd been sick, then Andrew showed him to a dark guest room to lie down for a bit. He must have fallen asleep, and they'd just left him.

León took stock, scooting out of the bleached sunbeam. He'd kicked a blanket mostly off during the night but was fully dressed. His phone was half under the pillow. A bottle of water baked on the nightstand. He hadn't realized how thirsty he was until he saw it there.

On the white dresser sat a precise array of things obviously meant for him. Towels, hair ties, a ridiculous number of medicines, and even a toothbrush new in its packaging. A small garbage bin huddled next to the bed. Someone had thought of everything.

He didn't need all that stuff. He was fine. He wanted to leave.

He texted Andrew, hoping he'd spent the night too, but was told he'd just finished teaching his morning ceramics class. He'd be back at Celia's soonish.

Ugh. Well, how hard could it be to kill time up here?

He huffed a sigh, then paused. Why was he so impatient?

Closing his eyes, he ran through a little mental exercise he used before painting. His art required emotional honesty, so he practiced it. What was he really feeling?

Tranquilo. Stop and be present.

He felt irritated. That usually meant he was fighting himself. On what?

Well, he wasn't actually fine; he was embarrassed. Being

sick at a stranger's house—that was awkward. Weird and intimate. Should he apologize? It wasn't really anyone's fault. Probably he should start taking the shellfish thing more seriously. And Celia, there was no way she could have known.

Okay. It felt embarrassing but was no one's fault. Hopefully, they could just shake hands on it and never bring it up again.

He felt better. He wanted to get moving.

The distant clinking of crockery said León's host was up and about. He ventured out, following the sound.

The kitchen was as stark and bright as the guest room, the few items sitting out as white as the countertops. There were no upper cabinets, and the wall of windows and greenery outside at least softened the room a little.

Celia was on duty at her stove top, standing ready in front of a steaming teapot. She was back to giving him those serious eyes and nothing else. She'd acted human when he got sick. Was that over?

"How are you feeling?" she asked.

He hitched himself up onto a tall stool at a kitchen island wider than a pool table. "Embarrassed about last night," he said, "but not sick anymore."

Her wooden face allowed no reaction. It was strangely irritating.

"I owe you a huge apology," she said, eyes steady.

"You don't, though."

She swallowed, and León eyes followed the motion. As her shoulders inched back and her chin tipped up a fraction, he felt his tension ease. She was good at keeping her face straight, but his craft was seeing bodies, how their shapes and movements told stories. Clearly, she didn't agree with him about the apology.

"I'd rather we just never spoke of it again," he said. When she opened her mouth to counter, he stepped over her. "Andrew says he'll be up here soon."

Silence. She looked distantly through him, once again the little queen. How subtle she was with that dismissal, glazing over as though he wasn't there at all!

He looked her over more closely, noting a faint rosy flush rising on her cheeks, the only color in the white room. Even her clothes were a dark gray. Why all this neutrality? He opened his mouth to ask.

"Tea?" she asked, stepping over him.

Without waiting, she bent to a cabinet in the island, coming up with a cardinal red ceramic teacup. She chose one for herself in royal blue.

Surprising! Andrew had made these vibrant cups. They were clearly his style. What other colorful treasures did she have hidden away?

Celia poured steaming tea, then pushed the red cup across the island to him.

His gaze stole along her arm to the balanced little tableau she made, head bowed over the stove before her, radiant windows at her back, one hand reaching to slide the cup to him. An almost saintly figure, the light behind her a halo, her arm offering a feminine benediction.

She didn't fit, though. There was nothing celestial about her at all. She was roundly mortal, sturdy and dressed in charcoal. Backlit ringlets of sober brown hair were turned to gilt, tendrils brushing her neck. He could imagine leaves twined in it. Her skin was burnished olive, not the bloodless porcelain of a madonna.

The moment fell apart as she turned her face from his scrutiny and straightened a knob on her stove that didn't need it.

He breathed out. Wow.

He had to paint today by whatever means necessary.

Celia's jaw clenched as she forced her gaze back to his and tucked her hands behind her. "I owe you a huge apology," she said again.

Jesus, she had a speech ready! And she intended to give it too. Just look at her. "If I accept your apology, will that move things along?"

She pursed her lips and narrowed her eyes at him. So, she made expressions sometimes?

"I put shrimp stock in the cabbage dressing," she said. "I'd usually use anchovy paste, but I had fresh stock and didn't think. I'm sorry for not warning you. It was irresponsible."

His knee was bouncing. He stilled it and sipped deliberately at the tea. "And what exactly is shrimp stock?"

Her hand stole forward, fingers just touching the stove in front of her. "I simmered shrimp shells and heads," she said, "then strained the liquid to use. It adds more flavor to a dish."

He swallowed. "Shrimp heads. Gross."

"It's a way to use up scraps," she said, showing some legitimate interest for a change. "You make stock from the bits you can't eat, then use it in other dishes. Like, beef bones. People call it bone broth now, but it's just stock."

"You boil the bones?"

"Or feet. Feet are the best."

"Feet!" His stomach stirring, León shifted on the chair and rubbed his forehead. "I want to talk about something else."

Cheeks flushing, she looked around the quiet kitchen as though a new topic would materialize. It kept its secrets. "Is there anything I can get you?" she asked.

"Fresh air."

He jumped down from the stool and found the sliding glass door among the other windows before she could assist, taking a few queasy steps onto her patio. The light breeze against his skin was a relief.

Forget food. Think of something else.

The tall buildings of distant downtown were brighter but harder to see. The magical sunset last night came back to him, the exact oranges and blues vivid in his mind before he realized how mundane this backyard was now. In regular daylight, it was just grass, sloping down to pool and fence and hazy view. That lawn had felt way steeper last night, a dark menacing climb while trying not to retch.

What a range in twelve hours. No wonder he was itching to paint. This yard had moods!

Hmm.

Even if the magic only happened here when the sun was low, there was room in her backyard for an easel. Certainly, more promise here than at Andrew's. It would take a few nights if he could only paint at sunset, but he could capture something real up here.

Celia was following him out, clutching both their teacups. She stopped next to him, looking as he did at the view.

She was hard to read. Why was she so stiff? Maybe she didn't like him. Most people liked him.

He had to ask. He had to paint.

"There is something you could do for me," he said, "if you're really offering."

Her head swiveled to him, her grave eyes meeting his directly. Her hand, holding the tea to him, froze just out of reach.

"Of course I'm offering."

"I'd like to paint that sunset," he said. He motioned at the grass in front of them. "Here, with that view."

Did her face soften just a bit? "You mean, right here?"

She would let him, he could tell. "If you'll let me."

"Of course," she said. "Yes."

"What if it took a few nights?"

"Absolutely."

"This week?"

"Tonight, if you want. It's the least I can do after poisoning you."

Her gaze was still composed, her mouth solemn, but León thought that might be a joke. He smiled in case it was.

She looked down, saw she still held his tea, and extended it again.

He took it, then clinked his cup lightly against the one she held. A small gasp escaped her as the fine ceramics rang together like a tiny bell. Then, wonder of wonders, she gave him a small, shy smile.

A noise at the side of the house made them both look.

"Hey, no one answered the front door," Andrew called, entering through the side gate. He was followed by a lean man a bit older than all of them. "I brought Trevor too."

Trevor was nearly as tall as Andrew, pale-skinned with curly salt-and-pepper hair and stubble. He raised a hand to León in an easy wave but quickly glanced past to Celia, his calm blue eyes studying her through dark-rimmed glasses.

León turned back to see Celia focused on the newcomers, her face alight, relieved smile wide. She sidestepped him and bounded to greet the two men.

León chafed his shoe against the patio, looking back at the view.

• • •

Celia's heart leapt at Andrew's voice. Oh, thank goodness—reinforcements.

"You holding up?" Andrew asked Celia with a kiss on her cheek as soon as she was within reach.

She grasped his open hand and nodded, relieved but guilty. She should be able to manage her anxiety over new people without help.

León approached, crossing his arms as he drew near. He was still staring at her! His sulky dark gaze had made it hard to talk all morning.

"Sorry to miss dinner yesterday," Trevor said, leaning in and hugging her shoulder. "The photo shoot went long last night. Did I miss anything?" His mouth twitched as he tried to hide a smile. Andrew must have told him about the shrimp debacle.

Celia looked up solemnly. "I almost killed a man, Trevor."

He laughed. "I heard."

Andrew threw an arm around León's neck, hauling him into the circle. "He looks fine to me."

León grinned. He wasn't so intimidating next to Andrew.

"Trevor knows of an apartment," Andrew said as he released León. "Want to drive over? You can talk galleries on the way."

"Hell yes!" León said. "Let me grab my stuff." He galloped inside.

"You want to come, Celia?" Trevor asked. She shook her head. "Tired from talking with someone new?"

This time she nodded. "He looks at me. A lot. It's hard to say things when he's staring."

"In a creepy way?" Trevor asked, frowning.

"No, just...focused."

"León's a visual guy," Andrew said. "If he's actually leering, I'll smack him."

What more could she ask for?

"I could have spent the night here too," Andrew said, straight-faced.

"You didn't offer," Celia said, mildly.

Hoodie in hand, León swept outside. "Let's go! That clock is ticking!" He stopped still as all three turned to face him, then actually bounced on the balls of his feet. "But!" he said. "But! Here's the thing. I need to be back here before sunset. Celia's letting me paint her view."

The three men all turned to face Celia. She'd just explained that it was hard when people looked...oh, let them work it out. She schooled her face, wiping away all expression. León's face soured.

"So, I'm driving León's gear up here?" Andrew asked, holding out a hand to Celia. "I'll keep you company while he paints."

She reached to touch his fingers briefly. He'd be inviting everyone else next.

"It's just the easel," León said, pulling on his hoodie. He was going to get hot in that.

"And paint, and brushes, and probably lots more," Trevor grinned.

Andrew rubbed a light sheen from his smooth bronzed head. "Are there ribs left from last night?"

"Not many. I was going to put them in chili. Do you want that?"

"Yes!" Andrew rubbed his hands together happily. "I get dinner and my living room back!" He looked around at her pool house. "Any chance we can leave the easel in there until León gets his own place?"

Celia looked at the small glass-walled building. There was plenty of room inside. Space, she had.

"You could use it yourself to paint when León's not up here," Andrew added, sweetening the deal.

"No, she can't!" León said.

"I have my own!" Celia said at the same time.

León met her eyes over their shared outburst.

"You paint?" he asked, his eyes doing that searching thing again.

Face blank!

Trevor put both hands in his back pockets. "Celia paints, draws, models...."

"It's her art list," Andrew said, as though that clarified matters.

Both men were enjoying León's wide-eyed confusion.

"Fine," León said. "I'll bite. What's an art list?"

Andrew leaned in while Celia clenched her teeth.

"Celia's learning to make every type of art there is," Andrew explained. "She's taken most of the classes at the college by now, right?" He looked at her but didn't wait for a nod. "I met her when she took my ceramics course." He counted on his fingers all the different things Celia had tried. "Poetry, woodcarving, architecture, you name it."

León shook his head, looking like he was waiting for a punchline.

"And she poses," Trevor added. "That's how I met her."

"You cast me off for Kelsey as soon as I introduced you," Celia said.

"She's commercial. I need commercial. You're much better as a life model."

Okay, it was a little funny to see León's doubtful eyebrows keep rising. So, he couldn't see her as someone who posed nude for art classes? Guess he didn't know everything.

"You?" His glance was frankly unbelieving.

"Yes."

He narrowed his eyes at her, nodding slightly. "Why the art list?" he finally asked.

Unexpected question! Celia froze, no answer coming to her. León waited, eyes unwavering, and the pressure to speak built unbearably.

"I don't know," she finally said.

He grinned. "Bullshit." And he kept waiting.

One heartbeat, two. No one had ever asked why.

"I'll tell you later," she said.

Wait, she'd said what?

Andrew gave her a pat, then turned to Trevor. "Let's beat traffic." They began the walk back to the side gate, and León followed after one last smirk at her.

"Hey!" he called from the edge of the lawn. Celia looked up, wary about his capricious enthusiasm. "That chili, can you leave out the feet?"

Andrew hauled him up by the scruff and hustled him through the gate, closing it behind them.

"Man, quit teasing her! Can't you see she's—" Their voices faded.

Finally, a free breath.

She shook out her hands, bent to touch her toes, then looked at the glinting pool. She could swim after she cleaned, exercise away her nervous energy.

Celia gathered the cups and stepped back into her kitchen.

She stopped. One cupboard door was wide open, all of her teacups on show.

León! He was the only one who'd been inside. He'd been snooping! How like a man to sneak a look but forget to close the door behind him.

He pried, he teased, he interrupted. And he stared way too much! What a far cry from her friends, who were polite and gentle with her!

But.

Celia closed the cupboard and set the used cups in the sink.

Andrew and Kelsey and Trevor knew about her art list, asked if she'd made anything good, if she'd enjoyed it. But none had ever asked why she did it. They never pried, waiting for her to be ready to confide.

Was she really going to tell León? He seemed to care about painting. He might understand.

A shiver washed down her and she closed her eyes.

Her dad, looking back from the top of a bridge, holding out a hand. "You don't have to live like that," he said.

She'd been eight when her dad took his life. She hadn't been there, of course, but her imagination had supplied that image, and it stuck.

One of the two safe people in her life went away, and then the second one was no longer safe, crushed by single motherhood and rage, and Celia the only target left.

She'd stopped talking for a year or so. There had been no language for what she felt, so she gave up language, and feelings seeped away the longer they went unexpressed. At first, she was praised for being quiet. Later, when they wanted her to talk, there was a power in not speaking.

The bond between Mom and her in-laws withered. By the time Celia was old enough to have questions about her heritage, she couldn't ask her Filipino grandparents. They'd both passed a few years after their son, and another part of her was erased.

She found ways to cope. Working hard left no room for feelings, so as she grew she worked and eventually started a little business. She could talk to clients like a normal person. She was useful.

When the wealth happened to her, it stripped all challenges from life. What was left to strive for when she could just buy everything? Without work, she was useless. She wasn't equipped for unlimited free time with her thoughts, and her father's gloom crept into her, bringing shame and guilt with it. She searched quietly, desperately, for distraction. Buying Mom a house six hours north took up a year, but even that task ended. Travel killed a lot of time, so she did that.

Then, the Louvre. She'd walked into the rooms of statuary, smooth nude marble bodies standing about like angels in a cemetery, but so alive. She could almost feel the warmth from some of them. She could have pinched their skin, if allowed, and felt it give.

Awe had overwhelmed her. The thoughts and feelings of artists long dead were so strong that she could hear them. That statue of a girl on tiptoe, whispering a secret, its sculptor was telling her about fragility, fear, and hope. It filled her poor, wasting heart.

Maybe art was what she was looking for! This might be her language if she could learn. Could she draw the contours and textures of her story? Dance her body awake? Weave her way backward, cautiously, into frayed feelings?

She dove back into demanding work, making her art list and taking each class, but still failed. She could learn techniques but couldn't put her soul into the material. Her sculptures looked like clay, not flesh. They didn't express her, didn't shout 'Celia' to the world. The darkness crept back, stronger.

Why the art list?

It was that or the bridge.

Her phone chimed, startling Celia back to the present. A call. Mom. It was always her; her friends only texted in their group chat. Celia let it go to voice mail for once.

How long had she been staring at the cups in the sink? Their afterimage swam before her when she closed her eyes.

She couldn't tell León all this. It was too much, and she didn't have the language.

THREE

Andrew insisted on staying when he brought León back to paint in the late afternoon. Dear, dependable Andrew.

"If you want, I'll carry the conversation for you," he said. "There's nothing to worry about. Just tell me what you want to do. Swim? Sit inside?"

León carried his easel through the side gate.

"I think I want to watch him paint," she decided. "I don't need help. You can swim."

Andrew smiled, stripping off his shirt. "Just yell if you want me back."

The yard was again sun-drenched, the hills below gilded. Andrew's cannonball into the pool barely registered against the glare. Celia hovered in the open sliding-glass door, wavering as León set up his easel, silhouetted against the sky and lowering sun.

Should she ask to watch or just sit down? Did he want privacy? A drink, maybe? Should she—good lord, how many questions was she going to ask herself? Move, Celia.

She sat gingerly on the nearest lounge chair, shielding her eyes with one hand, and girded herself. "León?"

His head turned at her voice, his gaze flickering down her bare legs and back up so quickly that she almost missed it.

"Can I watch you paint?"

"Sure," he smiled. "Not back there, though. I don't want to keep looking behind me. Come up here where I can see you." He pointed to the side with a foot, much nearer but where she could still see the canvas.

As she dragged the lounge closer, he set up. Easel, canvas, paints, palette. She sank onto the cushion to sit cross-legged.

León had timed his return well. The late afternoon light was turning golden, blue shadows stretching away from the city view. The harsher orange rays had all but faded, dusk approaching, the light from the pool and city starting to rival the sunset.

Celia kept her eyes on his gold-washed form, eager to see real art being made.

He ducked into the shadow of the canvas, reaching into his pocket and pulling out an elastic band. As he gathered his black hair to tie back, his eyes raised to her, looking up through his lashes.

He was sort of cute, in a scruffy way.

León's expressions weren't hard to read. He pursed his lips slightly, one eyebrow just barely raising. She was being perused, judged. Not in a mean way, but his eye contact was always too direct. Sitting motionless was the only response that came to her, the one that always came to her.

He finished tying his hair, gave her a little nod, and turned back to his canvas. Then he stopped and closed his eyes, a change washing over him. He went quiet, his face relaxed. He actually became still.

Celia held her breath with him.

Then he exhaled, opened his eyes, and began brushing colors on the bare white canvas.

What had that been, that stopping and being quiet? Was it something she could do when trying to make things? Was he just clearing his mind or meditating or—

"No questions?" he asked, glancing at her before looking at the view again.

She stifled a snort. She had so many questions that she couldn't dredge one to the surface, like her tongue was stuck in mud.

He'd stopped looking at her, concentrating on his colors.

Um. "How long will this take you?"

León swept a pool of robin's egg blue across the bottom of the canvas. "Depends on how long it takes to figure out what the painting is about."

About? "Isn't it about the sunset? The skyline?"

"It's inspired by the view," he said, peering closely at various oranges on his palette, "but the painting isn't about the landscape. It's a story."

"What story?"

"I don't know yet. I'm finding out." He held up his brush

to her, amber paint on its bristles like a miniature torch. "These colors are the process. They tell me as I go."

She shook her head. "What does that mean?"

He turned back to paint as he talked. "So, abstract art—all art really, but abstract for sure—is about truth. It could be 'here's a flower,' or it could be more." His motions were quick but practiced. Soothing to watch.

Why was this new to her? She'd checked painting off her list after taking the still life class but hadn't taken other styles into account. Maybe abstract painting was different. Maybe she'd try it.

"Maybe," she ventured, "a flower could be dangerous. Poisonous."

He didn't turn to look, focused on the colors going onto canvas. "It could be. But is that a story?"

"What if you...." This was hard. She'd always had trouble deciding what to draw. "What if something was dying under it?" She saw him wince silently, briefly. "I know, it's cliché. I can understand showing conflict in a still image, but how would you show what came next? The resolution?"

"That's where truth comes in. The painting tells that on its own."

"But how?"

A gleam in his eyes, León paused his work and turned to her. "All right. Say you're painting a flower. Not a poisonous one, just a regular pansy." With his brush, he drew a circle in the air, waiting until she nodded. "It's in a flowerbed against a house. The light is pale and delicate and gray. It's dawn."

She could see what he was describing.

"It's a cool morning, and dew is clinging to its petals, a bit too heavy. The flower is bowed down under the weight. Its stem has little hairs on it. You can sense its thin trembling leaves fluttering in a breeze."

Poor little flower.

"But the sun is coming, as it always comes. That's a truth. The breeze may dry it, the dew might drop away, or the sun will warm it. All the flower has to do is stay strong until then."

Of course. The picture could show the sun coming around

the house, or a tall shadow receding. "I can see that!" she said. "You could show those physical details in one image, but they tell a story. They are a story."

He nodded. "In an abstract painting, you don't show the flower itself. You play with the physical details. The color of the light, the tension in the stem." His eyes stayed with her instead of his work.

His smile was nice.

"If you don't have a story tonight," she finally asked, "how do you know which details to show?"

He stood back to consider her backyard, then the canvas.

"There's the blue pool against the sky's orange. Cool versus warm. Close versus far. This will probably be about contrasts. I still need to find the story, though."

This was fascinating.

"Then the colors," he said. "The pool is aqua and lacy whites. The city is dark purple with spangled oranges. The pool is flat and still, and the city is flickering with small stars."

"Contrasts," she breathed. "All the opposites. I never looked at it that way, and I've looked at this view for six years."

"And that's a contrast, too," he grinned. "Old and new views. All the hidden stories and shapes and colors." He stopped. "Oh."

"What?"

"Hidden." He turned to look around the yard, lowering his tools. "This view is hidden from the road outside." He turned back to the canvas, large gaps of unpainted space awaiting him. "Look, Celia. The white canvas with spots of color. It's your kitchen cabinet with the mugs hidden in it."

He began to paint furiously, with no hesitations.

Six years. She'd gone all the way through her art list, six years of classes, and León saw this magic in her backyard in one day.

He painted in silence as the last of the golden light slipped away, and she watched.

This was art. This was what she had to learn to do. Pluck sights and sounds from life and say...what? She needed a story too. She hated to disturb the whispers of brush marks being made, his economical movements in the cooling blue dusk, but she had to know.

"Where did you learn this?"

He leaned in to inspect a detail. "Art school and practice," he said. "This is how I see things. I have to paint to show people what I'm seeing and thinking." He glanced at her quickly, face indistinct as the sun slipped below the ocean. "You have that art list. You've taken a lot of art classes by now, right?"

"Classes didn't teach me how to do that."

He stepped back and folded a rag around the top of his brush. "Well, they can't. It's unique to each person. You create your own process." He wiped his fingers on the outside of the rag, eyes focused too directly on her again.

"Could I learn how?"

The challenge on his face was clear, even in the dusk. "Why do you want to make art?"

She'd said she would tell him.

"I think art might save me."

"Yeah." He finished wiping his fingers. "Me too."

Bare feet whispered across the lush lawn and Andrew's form emerged from the dark, a wet towel around his shoulders. He shivered visibly as he stepped into the soft glow from the house windows. "It got dark," he said. "You done for today?"

León tossed his paint rag into the box of paints. "I guess. My stuff's wet, though. We can't load your car just yet."

"Can't we keep it in the pool house, Celia?" Andrew asked.

"Of course," she said, rising to pick up a smaller box full of jumbled brushes and palette knives. Both men trailed after her to the pool house.

León nodded at the space and went back for his gear. Andrew stayed to towel off, his bare chest dusky and bronzed under the dim overhead light. Celia scanned the tidy square room, shelves and day bed by the door, huge black windows looking over the city behind her. As León brought in his things, she made space for his smaller boxes on the shelves. The painting was brought in last.

Andrew leaned close and squinted at the unfinished canvas. "What's it about?"

León shrugged. "I'll find out soon enough. Two more nights, at least."

• • •

It wasn't until the men left that the backlash hit.

"Why do you want to make art?" León had asked. A normal question.

There were so many sane answers Celia could have given, but no. Her crazy ass had to dump a weird truth into the conversation. "Art might save me."

Celia heard the melodramatic, laughable, pathetic phrase drumming in her head all night.

It was still there the morning after.

"Art might save me," she mocked under her breath as she made her morning tea, grimacing. How could she say something so cringeworthy? León must think she was off her theatrical rocker. How could she look him in the face again?

What could she possibly need saving from? The wealth, the free time, the utter privilege? People scraped their knuckles bare working for this, and it had fallen in her lap. She didn't earn a living. Funny, that implied living had to be earned, could be deserved.

The thought chased her around the house all day, getting more insistent. She recognized her spiral but was powerless to stop it. Her one chance was to stay too busy to think.

She cleaned her house, scrubbing furiously. Any room, any surface, it didn't matter.

She sidled into her craft room, untouched for the last month but dusted regularly. Nothing to clean here. All her art supplies were conventionally stored in floor-to-ceiling storage units. Everything in her life went behind white cabinet doors.

Get that mess out of sight, Celia Rose!

Her famous art list, written in earnest capitals, hung neatly by the door. She'd poured true hope into this, but every item on the list had been crossed off. Tracing the words with a fingertip was like poking a bruise.

In six years, she'd finished every class at the college. She was out of ideas. Art hadn't saved her.

She didn't want to tell her friends. They'd ask what was next.

She closed her eyes tight. A leaden knot sat in her chest, and she didn't know how to budge it.

Wondering if swimming would help but knowing it was too late to stop her gloom, she drifted out to the pool house to look at León's painting. Unfinished, but already better than anything she could ever do. Expressive. Colorful.

She would never squeeze something like that out of her cold little heart.

The painting on its easel looked at home here. She'd always thought the pool house would make a good studio. It was partly why she'd bought this too-big house. She'd intended to work through her art list out here but had ended up turning a spare bedroom into the craft room.

Don't take up so much space, Celia Rose!

Could she clean out here?

Her eye fell on the daybed, its head near the main door. She patted the thick, orange-striped cushion, watching for dust, but no cloud rose. She settled for scrubbing the tiny bathroom and the little drinks fridge, then scrounged up a lesser-used table lamp from her house to put near the daybed. The overhead light had felt dim when putting away León's things last night.

In the area near the big windows, overlooking the pool and view, she swept and mopped. The windows were tall, but she was able to give them a good cleaning with a step ladder.

There. Space, light, amenities. A room for creation—for a real artist. Not her.

Making up pointless tasks was exhausting.

Celia sat down on the daybed, like a doll tossed there, waiting for someone to come play with it.

You don't have to live like that.

She was losing the battle today.

She went to lie in her bed, pretending to read. She napped off and on and tried not to think.

When she heard León arrive hours later, she got up and waved at him through the sliding glass door but retreated immediately back to bed. He'd probably be relieved she wasn't bothering him with stupid questions.

She was ridiculous, selfish, talentless...a waste of space. Why did she think she needed a talent when she had nothing to say?

She burrowed into her bed in the dark and closed her eyes, giving in to her nightmare insides. An unpredictable looming judgment pricked at her, finished sentences for her. Be mature. Be useful. *Just be normal, Celia Rose!*

Well, here she was, all grown up. Dad was gone forever, Mom banished hundreds of miles north. Celia could disappear too, who would notice? Even her friends didn't know her. She had them fooled into thinking she was a regular person. If they knew she was this worthless inside, they'd leave too.

No one was better for her being here. There was nothing the world needed Celia for. Others could give away money better. Others could cook better. Others could make art.

Art might save her. Ha! The art list had been a distraction, a diversion, a delay. It had come to a ragged end, and there was no use clutching at it. She'd hoped...couldn't there be one original thing inside her? One thing only she had? Something she could put into art and say *see, I deserve to be here too.*

She gave up. The evidence of failures piled around her, the slaps and welts of wooden spoons, the dirty spite with which she'd given up language.

You don't have to live like this, Dad said. He stretched out a hand from the bridge.

There was peace in giving up the fight, lying still, and being worthless. She could lie here until she ran out of air and light. She could follow him. What else was left to try?

"Celia? You here?"

Andrew! Back to pick up León already? He'd come in the back door.

She sat up in bed and brushed her hair quickly with her fingers. He poked his head into her bedroom to see her in the rumpled bed, curtains drawn.

"Celia." He frowned. "Are you having a bad day?"

She nodded, caught.

Andrew had seen this before. He came in and sat on the bed, enfolding her in a hug. She let him.

It lasted a long time.

He finally patted her shoulder gently. "You're supposed to call me when this starts, remember? We made a deal." She nodded again, like a child. "Well, I know now. Okay if I sit with you for a while?"

"Okay," she whispered.

He kicked off his shoes and climbed onto the bed with her. He sat up against the headboard, arms wide. Celia leaned into his chest, her eyes burning. She'd have to go back to trying now. His strong, brown arms closed around her, and she made an effort to back out of her hopeless place.

Quit the self-pity, Celia Rose.

"You know I like you, right?" he asked. "You know you're important?"

Sweet Andrew. He knew the antidote. What would it be like to feel like him, generous, accepting everyone at face value? Dating him had been so easy. Low stakes, casual intimacy, fondness but no love to mess things up. Who knew why he hadn't walked away after the romance ran dry.

"You want to tell me what started it?" he asked.

She released a shuddery breath. "It's over," she finally said. "The art list is done." There. She'd admitted it.

"Really?" he asked, stroking her shoulder. "You've taken every class?"

"Every one. And I was awful at them all."

He leaned his head against hers. "Aw, you were just new to it. Art takes practice." His voice rumbled in his chest against her cheek. "What did you like best?"

She didn't want solutions, but he was trying to help. "Posing, maybe," she said slowly. "I was a part of other people making good art."

"You are an excellent life model," he said, a smile in his voice. "Remember the sculpture of mine you posed for last term? I'm firing the final piece now. If it survives, I can show you this week."

Artists always ended up talking about their work, even the sweet ones who meant well. What would it be like to have something of her own to talk about?

Andrew rubbed a gentle hand up and down her arm. "You don't have to limit yourself to the college, you know. This is LA. There are artists everywhere who need to earn a living. You could get private instruction. If you want to keep going on the list, keep going."

She sighed heavily. Meeting new people one-on-one? She was bad at that too.

Andrew reached up to ruffle her hair. "Let's eat something, then get in the pool. That sometimes helps, right? The sun's probably down by now. It'll be cooler out."

Celia let him lead her around, taking fruit and cheese from the fridge and going outside into the dusk. León had already put away his easel. His shadow moved in the pool house. Andrew made a beeline for it.

Oh no.

She didn't want to see León after saying what she'd said.

Andrew didn't give her a choice, pulling her by the hand right into the pool house.

León was in the bathroom, cleaning his brushes. "Oh, hey," he said. "Is it okay if I clean these here? I'll fix any mess I make."

Was he acting like she hadn't been awkward yesterday?

Andrew sat on the daybed to take his shoes off, looking around. "It's different in here."

"Not much," she said. "I added a lamp."

Andrew stood to grab his swim trunks from the drying rack he'd laid them on the day before, unzipping his pants without regard to who was in the room. León caught Celia's eye and grinned, giving Andrew a meaningful side glance.

He was going to ignore what she'd said!

He straightened from the sink, approaching her with dripping brushes, but she wasn't ready to be talked to. Celia retreated to the door, still holding Andrew's forgotten plate of cheese. "I'll just...."

Andrew was pulling his pants down as she slipped out.

She escaped to the very edge of the yard, between the pool and the wrought iron fence that ran along the top of the retaining wall. The canyon fell away below her, smelling of sage, the distant yips of coyotes a familiar greeting.

She'd made it through again. She still felt the weight of her failures, but Andrew had helped. If nothing else, she had to act normally so he didn't worry.

Maybe she would look for private art teachers. Poetry, maybe. That didn't need a lot of equipment, and throwing away a lousy poem was easier than some of the other awful artworks she'd made.

"Absolutely not!"

Celia jumped as León's voice, raised and strident, pierced the serene backyard.

"No way in hell!"

He was shouting in the pool house! An old panic began rising. Andrew's voice could be heard, low and placating, but she couldn't make out the words.

Silence. It drew out.

Andrew came out to the pool, looking ordinary in his swim trunks. He wasn't agitated or worried. Her heart began to beat again.

"What was that?" she asked.

He waved a hand back at the door dismissively and grinned at her. "I'm a genius, is all."

"It didn't sound...."

Andrew came close and reached for her free hand, a relaxed smile spreading across his face. For someone who'd just been yelled at, he looked awfully pleased with himself.

"Celia. León needs a place to stay, and you have that pool house. You could let him stay there in exchange for painting lessons."

The evening went suddenly cold. Sharing her backyard? Someone living here? She barely knew León! No way in hell.

"Absolutely not!" she said.

Andrew just grinned wider.

FOUR

León checked the sun's angle as Andrew drove slowly from traffic light to traffic light. Hours to go before the next sunset. Hurry up and wait. He caught his thumbs tapping against his thighs again and stilled them.

The delays were killing him.

If it wasn't LA traffic eating up time, it was apartment managers who didn't call back or Andrew's damn social life.

His thumbs again...ah, whatever, let them tap.

A dismal, misshapen feeling kept beating around his head, looking for a way in. The painting had taken a wrong turn, it whispered. The truth and the story hadn't made it onto canvas. It was New York all over again.

There was no choice but to try again, but his deal with Celia was for this one painting. Andrew's place was still too small, and the apartment search going nowhere. He'd thought his New York budget would go further out here, but no.

And instead of helping, here was Andrew, dragging him out for happy hour, of all things. Drinks were an indulgence he couldn't afford. He didn't have the time. Hell, he didn't have the cash.

Still, as Andrew pulled into a parking lot, León tried to calm himself. He wasn't sulky. His problems were his own. If he had to chit-chat for a few hours before sunset, he'd do it nicely.

The bar was high-ceilinged and airy, arched windows spilling golden sun onto brick walls and brass fixtures. Broad-leafed tropical plants waved on the crimson walls at classic intervals. León followed Andrew's navy-blue shoulders into cool, dim interiors smelling of pine and citrus.

Celia would be here. Could he talk her into a few more nights? She might let him, though he couldn't pay her back.

Andrew's bright idea from last night was still rattling around his head too. Yes, he could desperately use the pool house. But he didn't know how to teach, had no time to waste on giving lessons, and Celia was far too wooden to paint from the heart.

Also, he'd heard her say no. She didn't want him there.

"Why'd we come here instead of going to Celia's?" León asked. "Is she tired of us hanging in her backyard?"

"We're giving her a break from hosting," Andrew said, not breaking stride. "She likes this place."

In a private brick-lined corner, they found Trevor sitting at a polished wooden table, Celia already across from him. Trevor's ocean-blue shirt was a relief, a pop of cool color in this otherwise red and gold edifice. The inaudible talk at the table halted as Andrew swanned up. In a smooth motion, he scooted across the bench next to Trevor and dropped an arm around his shoulder.

"Can I come fishing with you next time?" he asked. "I need a vacation."

Andrew, fishing? Being quiet, outdoors, for more than five minutes? That was a joke, right?

Trevor rolled his eyes with a smile but leaned into Andrew's embrace. "You can come any time," he said, "but I'm not driving you back when you miss civilization the first night."

"When's your next trip?" Andrew asked him, giving his shoulder a squeeze.

León turned his attention to Celia.

She glanced into the drink cupped between her hands. Back to avoiding eye contact, were we? Jesus, that was an annoying habit! He pulled out the seat at the end of the table, furthest from her, his fingers on the chair blotched with shades of green paint.

Look at her, wearing some brown thing that blended right into the wall. She'd picked the one chair that avoided the yellow light spilling from the pendant above the table. Her turned-down face was worn, shadows under her eyes and lines framing her mouth.

She'd seemed interested in painting that first night but hadn't come out since. Was she sick, maybe?

Kelsey fluttered up, claiming the last chair and littering her keys, phone, and purse across the table. Why did women always carry so much? She brightened the table, though, her cream blouse and honey-colored hair giving the golden pendant something to light up.

For a second, the colors swam before León's eyes. Kelsey in yellow, the little lamp in her orbit, matching her glow. Trevor and Andrew to the right, blue and navy shirts pooling together in cool contrast to the overwhelming red brick background. And Celia, sepia, fading into the brick and wood.

Andrew twirled a finger above his head, signaling a round for the table to a server beyond the two women. Kelsey turned to specify a ginger ale, loudly, and the moment of colors faded.

"Is Charlie coming?" Trevor asked as Kelsey turned back.

"Ugh, no," she said with a grimace.

"You two broke up again?" Andrew asked.

She shrugged. "Probably. Let's talk about something else."

A gleam lit Andrew's face as he leaned in under the pendant. "I got my piece for the exhibition fired. No cracks in her." He winked at Celia for some reason.

"Her?" Kelsey asked.

"A nude torso, female, about two feet high." Andrew's hands raised to inscribe the height and curves. "The glaze came out beautifully too. Bronzes and greens, just like our Celia."

Ah! León looked Celia over quickly. Bronze, yes, her hair and skin had that burnished coppery light, then the olive undertones...good eye, Andrew.

Celia's shadowed face turned to the light of the table. "The figurine I posed for? I thought you were making a small one, like...." She raised a hand above the table about half a foot.

"The studies were smaller," Andrew said. "I needed to work up to the big piece. Good thing the firing went well. I couldn't do another in five weeks."

"That reminds me, León," Trevor said, leaning over Andrew. "I called the gallery, the one holding the exhibition next month. They said to bring you in to talk about showing in it."

León jumped out of his chair, nearly knocking a tray of

drinks from the approaching server's grasp. He could have leapt on the table and crowed.

"Ha, yes!" He could sell his work at an exhibition!

Sparkling glasses, clear and clinking with ice, were set down by the server in front of all but Kelsey. The alcohol smell was unpleasantly strong, with more citrus and pine.

"What did you order?" León asked, sitting back down.

"Gin," Andrew said. "That's what they serve here. It's a gin bar." Trevor and Andrew grinned as León wrinkled his nose. "You're what, thirty-five? It's time to acquire some grown-up tastes. Like decent alcohol."

"Blue cheese," Trevor offered. "Sashimi."

Kelsey leaned in. "Oysters."

"No shellfish," Celia warned from her corner.

Andrew laughed. "No shellfish!"

"I eat blue cheese," León said.

Kelsey tittered into her soda, setting it down with a light slosh. Andrew swirled his glass, the tinkling ice louder in the conversation's lull.

"León," Trevor said as he leaned back, "tell us how you and Andrew met."

"Ah." León lightly drummed fingers on the table as he raised his glass for a sip, eyeing Andrew over the rim. Andrew smirked back. "We met in art school. He stole my girl."

Andrew shrugged as his friends chuckled.

"She wasn't officially mine," León continued. "We were just hooking up. But here came this tall, dark senior swooping in, and that was that."

Trevor stirred his drink. "He stole a boyfriend from me once."

"Ah, come on," Andrew broke in. "I never actually stole anyone. People, they go where they want."

"Anyway," León said, "he was so nice about it, we just became friends." He looked around the table. "I suppose he's dated all of you at some time?"

A laugh went around as everyone turned to Celia, who raised her hand diffidently.

"Just me," she said.

Kelsey leaned closer to León. "Did you ever date Andrew?"

León shook his head. "Not my type," he said. "Plus, my dad would have killed me. *Machismo*, you know."

Trevor nodded. "I hear that." He hitched a thumb at himself. "Mormon."

Kelsey sat up straight and grabbed at her phone. "Trevor, that reminds me, I need to show you this." She was scrolling as soon as the screen lit up. "Celia, will you switch seats?"

Silently, Celia stood. Kelsey switched to the far chair, leaving Celia to sit next to León.

"Now I can see you," León said.

She hesitated, then sat wordlessly as León picked up his glass. He shook it, surprised to find only ice.

Celia pushed her glass to him. "I didn't drink any."

León accepted it. Gin wasn't that bad, actually.

Andrew stood partway, peering at the dim bar. "Hold up, I know that woman over there. Be right back." On his way past, he leaned down to plant a kiss on Celia's head. "Talk a little, girl."

"Girl," she muttered. "I'm two years older."

León watched her sigh, then sit taller in her chair. Look at her, bracing to follow instructions.

Why was she so reluctant to unbend? She couldn't just enjoy time with friends? He didn't feel like it either, but he'd made an effort. What was her story?

The sunny luster of the lamp hit her cheekbones as she lifted her chin, tension faintly cording her neck. A server walked briskly past their table, leaving tendrils of her hair fluttering in the breeze. A composition started blooming in the back of his mind.

"Andrew says," she began, then halted. Her napkin wasn't aligned to the edge of the table and apparently needed fixing.

León waited, eyebrows raised. A charming smile to help her relax. A sip of the drink to show he was relaxed too.

She looked up. "He says you're just thinking of paintings when you stare at me. At people."

He sputtered but avoided choking on his drink.

"Yeah," he said, dabbing around with his own napkin.

"Sometimes. Sorry. I don't mean to stare."

It was hard not seeing paintings in this dramatic light, though. The gold brought out those bronze tones in her skin.

She tucked her hair behind an ear, eyes lowering to the table. "If I accept your apology, will you stop looking so hard now?"

He laughed, turning his eyes up to the ceiling. Really? She was asking him to not look at her? Celia's relieved breath was faint but audible confirmation.

His gaze wandered to Kelsey and Trevor, heads down over her phone, then to the chaotic, distant bar.

"Hell," he said, leaning in, eyes still averted. "Look at Andrew over there." He felt her turn in her chair.

Andrew was getting a phone number from a woman at the bar.

"I hope he doesn't bring her home," León said. "I end up hanging out by the bodega for hours."

Celia turned back, her gentle voice close. "Oh no."

He sat back and drank again. Having a conversation without looking at her was a handicap. But, at least it made her talk—she couldn't just make those big serious eyes at everything.

Delays and handicaps and fading paintings. He had to make something good happen! Time to butter her up a little and work around to letting him paint longer.

He set the drink back down, looking into it. "You haven't been around," he said. "Everything good?"

Her stillness and silence started to become an answer, but as he opened his mouth, she swept her napkin tightly into her lap and spoke.

"Good. Yes." He heard a quick determined-sounding breath. "Getting out and socializing. It's good."

He rubbed fingers over his mouth, hopefully concealing his smile. Man, she really hated socializing.

"How is the painting?" she asked quickly.

Well.

He ran a hand through his hair, still looking down at the table. He had to ask the right way.

"This is weird now," she said. "It's okay to look at me, sometimes."

That would help. Gladly, León looked up at her earnest eyes, the amber light turning them a mossy gray-green he could match with cadmium yellow and—wait. Don't.

"I'm about done with the painting," he admitted. "I thought I might ask for a few more nights, though. This one isn't grabbing me, you know?"

Her brows lowered in sympathy as she nodded. Either his charm was working, or she felt familiar enough to show expressions. Good.

"You ever look at art, and it really grabs you?" he asked.

"Yes," she said at once. "In Paris, once." Her eyes were wide, the napkin crushed in a fist in her lap.

"This painting just didn't get there. If I can try one more time...."

Her utter focus on him was gratifying.

"I only have a few months to succeed out here," he continued. "I have to keep trying. The next painting might be the one that saves me from going back."

Her quiet little gasp surprised and delighted him. Look at that spark in her! She got it! She was hanging on his words like—

"Do you want to move into my pool house?"

Jesus.

No. But yes.

He watched crimson bloom across her chest, her neck, her cheeks.

It would solve so many of his problems.

"In exchange," he said, thumb tapping against his thigh, "I give you painting lessons. Like Andrew said. Right?"

She placed her hands over her hot cheeks, then pulled them back to look at her palms as if confused about where the heat had come from.

"How many lessons, though? How often?" he asked.

She covered her mouth with her fingertips and frowned at the tabletop.

"Celia?"

40

Her half-dazed eyes finally returned to his, a smile beginning to play at her lips. She lowered her hand. "Is twice a week too much?"

He slowly shook his head. "That's not bad."

The pool house. It had that little bed, a bathroom, and a tiny fridge. He could paint near the window overlooking the city view. And the price—he couldn't pass it up.

He leaned in. "I'll need privacy sometimes, a lot of times, to concentrate on my work."

"I can give you privacy," she said, crossing her arms in her lap and holding her elbows.

Her smile was nice.

She leaned forward to meet him. "You should know, Andrew and the rest, they all come over to eat once or twice a week."

In unison, they glanced over to Kelsey and Trevor.

Both were staring back at them, mouths open. Andrew leaned on the wall just behind Kelsey, arms crossed over his chest, smug as all hell.

"What?" León asked.

Without turning her head or closing her mouth, Kelsey elbowed Trevor.

"Celia is usually...more reserved," he said.

León turned to look at Celia again. No way could she possibly be 'more reserved.'

Her gaze darted around the eyes on her, a blush once again setting her cheeks alight.

"Surprise," she said softly.

• • •

It was a wobblier crew that emerged from the bar into the late-afternoon heat. Trevor accepted a ride from Kelsey while Andrew announced he'd be going back in. Celia would drive León back to his place to start packing. She still sported bright red cheeks despite not having sipped a single drink.

Andrew encouraged Celia to go get her car and bring it to the entry. León, he stopped from accompanying her.

With an amused grin, Andrew stepped up to look León over, straightening imaginary lapels on León's hoodie and giving him a sharpish pat on the cheek.

"Finally moving out of Papa's place," he teased. "Good luck."

León rolled his eyes but couldn't stop smiling. A place to paint!

"Just one thing," Andrew said, his smile fading. "I want you to be nice to Celia."

Uh, insulting! "Of course, I'm going to be nice to her! Why would you say something like that?"

"You can be pushy, León," Andrew said. "Don't take advantage of her, okay?"

León's throat tightened, but he stood taller, meeting Andrew's eyes. "Why don't you tell the little queen to be nice to me?"

"She doesn't need telling." Smiling again, Andrew held out a hand. When León grasped it, he was hauled in for a hug. León squirmed out of the embrace as Celia pulled up.

"Don't worry, we're going to get along, *Papa*," León said, getting in and closing the door harder than he intended.

Andrew stooped to look in, and León watched the window roll down on its own. Oh, of course, Celia had control buttons. That gin may have been stronger than he thought.

"I'll be texting you, girl," Andrew said across him. Celia nodded, eyes tinged with warmth, and they drove off.

"Andrew is being freaking fatherly today," León complained.

She nodded but kept her eyes doggedly on the road. Was she back to avoiding eye contact? Already? He could make her talk, say something obnoxious she couldn't resist answering. Or, he could be nice to her.

Nicely, León looked everywhere but at Celia. The car interior was immaculate, just like her house. It was an older car, a Lexus. Upscale but not new. It smelled faintly of vanilla.

Ah, screw being quiet. He was too happy.

"I thought you might be sick," León said. "You didn't come out to talk painting yesterday."

The blush on her cheeks just wasn't going away!

"I had a lot of cooking to do," she clearly lied. "Cleaning. Things."

Wait.

Part of her clicked into place.

"You clean, you boil feet to stretch food," León said. "You're no trust fund baby, are you?" If she didn't grow up rich... "Did you win the lottery or something?"

"Sort of."

He waited for more, rude or not.

"Bitcoin," she explained. "I had some. A few hundred."

Oh, Bitcoin. Whatever that was. It made some people wealthy, but that was all León knew about it. "Do you, like, buy them?"

She shook her head, turning onto the straight sunny boulevard to Andrew's. "A client where I worked paid me in Bitcoin," she said. "He thought it would replace the dollar, paid everyone in it if they let him. It was only worth about two thousand dollars, back then. And I kept it."

Look at her, chatting away! "It went up?"

"Way up," she admitted.

"Where did you work that clients paid you in Bitcoins?"

"Charity organizing," she said. "I didn't run one, I helped people start them."

Keeping her talking was fun. "Was it rewarding?"

"No," she said, slowing at an intersection. "Rich people start charities to hide money, and poor people lose what they have, trying to keep one going."

So, she did have a little bite to her! "Dang, Celia, that's a little cynical."

She gave him a sideways glance. Eye contact! "It's the nicest way I can say it. Charities are just about moving money place to place."

"Some do good things, surely." León slowly shook his head. "Money solves a lot of problems."

"Not real problems," she said quietly. "It can't buy talent. It can't make art."

"Oh yes, it can," León said, sitting up. "It buys time! Artists need that more than anything. Time to learn and to practice." He looked across at her, thumb tapping on his thigh again. He felt pleasantly dizzy from the gin. "You're giving me the time I need. I appreciate that."

Her face when she turned to him...her creased brow eased, eyes softening with wary hope. Two! Two expressions!

"And you'll help me?" she asked. "You'll show me how to paint like you?"

He smiled. "I'll do my best. I've never taught anyone."

"When?"

"Give me a couple of days to move and settle in?" She nodded. "Tuesday, then."

FIVE

The bang of the side gate told her it had begun. León was moving his stuff in.

Celia leaned against the wall in her hallway, arms crossed, hanging back to peek at León and Andrew as they carried boxes into the pool house. The coolness of the wall against her temple steadied her bones with its solid support. Her home, her bastion, wasn't changing. Just her backyard.

She wasn't freaked out. This was fine. She'd invited him.

The faint rumble of the sliding door on the pool house punctuated every trip the men made. Big canvases walked into the pool house, seemingly on their own, backs turned toward her so she couldn't see if they were painted or bare.

He would teach her how to paint.

A smile sneaked past her misgivings, faintly touching her lips.

Even though it was scary, I invited him. Good for me.

She turned and slipped back into the seclusion of her bedroom. There was no reason to hover while they worked.

Good or not, it felt weird. Maybe she'd stay indoors until she toughened up and got used to the weight of eyes on her from this new direction. It would be hard to find time to swim, but León wouldn't be here every minute, right?

She just needed to stay busy. Was there anything to do until Tuesday? A drawer that needed organizing, a rug to be cleaned, or...why was there never anything to do in this house?

Cooking was tempting, but they could see her in the kitchen if they looked. Besides, she had only herself to feed until mid-week. She needed something to lock her away in a room for days.

She'd just have to clean something that didn't need it. Something big. A whole room, probably. Her craft room would do. She hadn't gone through it in a month, anyway.

The floor-to-ceiling reorganization took her through the

first night and into the next evening.

Her mother called twice, deflating her with complaints, but she used her tools to forget—label maker, drawer dividers, little white hooks one could hang anything from.

The third morning dawned.

Tuesday.

Common, ordinary Tuesday. Celia drank tea, watched Kelsey and Andrew exchange gifs in the group chat, and stiffly tamped down her anticipation each time it flared up. Except for neglected cups of tea going cold and her phone screen blanking out when she stared too long, it was just another day.

She didn't dare care about this. She didn't dare not care.

Poor León, coming in to teach her when she was wound tight.

She'd already laid her supplies out very carefully in the craft room, prepared with acrylic paint from other projects, a tabletop easel, and a stack of cheap painter boards. She'd opened a fresh pack of brushes. Two water glasses, in case one got dirty quickly, some rags from the bin.

She cooked to distract herself. Potato soup was quick to throw together and easy to leave on a simmer.

Staring into the pot of soup got old too.

Fine.

She stole into the craft room, admitting her impatience. It was early—but not too early—to practice. She could at least show León that she knew how to mix colors.

She settled on painting an apple. Her gradients and shading weren't flawless, but they were precise. It was very round, red, with a shadow on one side and a highlight on the other, just like she'd made in her beginner class. The apple didn't look much like art.

She probably shouldn't have her hopes up like this.

She brushed off the depressing thoughts her basic apple had engendered. This could be the baseline, something to measure her new skills against. It had a place if only to show how much improvement she made in the future. And she would! She was ready to learn.

Celia vowed to put herself fully in León's hands.

She heard the sliding door open at noon and stuffed her excitement down as hard as possible so he wouldn't know how ridiculous she was.

"I'm in here," she called. The room seemed smaller, the walls leaning in at her. Oh lord, this was it. She wasn't ready.

He followed her voice into the craft room. "You have a space to paint in here? Oh, good."

She turned to respond.

Oh my.

No hoodie for once. His worn white pants and shirt were covered in smudges of every color. His hair was tied back, but locks had come loose and been thoughtlessly pushed behind an ear. He had an orange paint smudge on his temple and yellow on his neck. He looked like a real artist.

This was a mistake. She'd be wasting his time. He'd be judging her amateur attempts with professional eyes.

Those eyes were as dark and eager as ever, scanning the supplies she'd prepared, her washable clothes, her face. He'd shaved at some point, but new black stubble framed an easy, cheerful smile.

She swallowed hard instead of smiling back and saw his expression falter.

"Okay," he said. "You're nervous. That's fine. We'll use that."

How could he tell things like that? Could everyone tell, and just not say anything?

"I'm not nervous," she said. "And how would we use it?" She picked up a long-handled paintbrush to turn in her hands.

León chuckled. "My dad used to come into my room and yell at me when I had trouble painting. On purpose. All so I could paint about the injustice of tyrannical fathers."

"That sounds awful."

"It worked, though. Strong emotions are easier to paint."

He looked past her at her apple. "I see you know some basics. We're not doing technique today, though. We're going to paint a story, not objects."

She was never going to be able to do that.

At her silence, he reached out and gave the end of her

paintbrush a playful tug. His hands had paint on them, too, orange and amber. Celia saw with surprise that she had red paint across her own knuckle.

She would try. She had to.

She stepped aside and let him approach her supplies.

He started filling her palette with colors in quick, practiced motions. He handed her a brush, then stepped back, letting her approach the fresh canvas board. Then, backing off, he stood a short way behind her. Maybe a little too close.

"You're nervous. Excited."

She took a deep breath, looking at the canvas and not at him.

"Yes," she admitted. It was hard to say.

"It's a good strong emotion. Which of those colors seems the most nervous to you?"

She looked at her palette, feeling a tiny bit of panic rise. What color represented nerves?

"Faster, Celia," he barked quietly.

His near voice made her jump. She pointed at the yellow.

"Why yellow?" he asked.

"Lightning is yellow, that's like being nervous."

"Lightning is usually blue and white in nature. It's only yellow in kids' drawings."

She hesitated, then pointed to the blue. "So, blue?"

"Why blue?"

"Because you...."

"Close your eyes," he said. Celia complied. "How does your body feel right now?"

Feel? Lord, she was failing at everything he asked. "I'm not sure how to answer."

"Hot? Cold? How do your hands feel?"

"My hands? They're normal. Maybe a little cold?"

She could hear him move behind her, then felt fingers on her wrist. She opened her eyes to stare straight ahead, trying to not stiffen up.

"You feel a little hot, a little damp," he said.

"So...red?"

He chuckled behind her. "We've got work to do here," he

said, removing his hand. "Okay. Let's start at the absolute beginning. You're going to paint yourself on the canvas, but all you can do is make colored lines."

His hand reached toward her canvas board, the only part of him visible from behind her, describing in the air what he wanted her to do.

"The lines can go up and down, side to side, curved or angled, but no objects, no circles or squares. Pick any color, no judgment, and make a line to represent you at this moment."

Deep breath. Red was the last color mentioned, so she went with it. A little hot, a little damp. A single straight line, up and down, in red.

"Good. That's you, right here, right now. Clean the brush, please." She followed the direction. "Now, let's make your line nervous. Pick another color. Yellow is fine, whatever color you feel is best."

She hesitated, then went for the blue. He'd said blue for lightning. She felt rather than heard him sigh faintly behind her.

"Let's make a nervous line," he directed. Celia hovered the brush near the canvas but went utterly blank. "Do you feel nervous in your whole body, alongside the red line? Does it cut across your line? Does it zig zag? Is it a lot of little lines?"

The last one sounded the closest to what she imagined nervous might look like. She painted shorter blue lines, cutting across the red line, slanted upwards.

"Now we're getting somewhere," he said, voice warmer. "See how nervous might look? Cutting into you? It breaks up your shape, like feeling nervous can break up your body."

Relief. He approved.

What next? She waited, but he left her hanging, saying nothing. The tip of her brush trembled, and she focused on stilling it as the silence grew uncomfortable. What was he expecting from her?

"What should I do?" she finally asked.

His voice behind her was calm, giving no clues. "What feels right?"

Hell.

She cleaned the brush, stalling. What felt right? What did that even mean? With no cues about what else to do to her line, she slowly mixed an orange and drew another straight line to the left of the red one.

"And what is that?" he asked.

"You," she explained. "You're making me nervous standing back there, so I put you in it."

"Why am I orange?"

Um. "It's the opposite of blue."

"And why am I the opposite color from nervous?" His voice sounded amused.

"You're not supposed to make me nervous," she explained. "I mean, I should be the opposite of nervous because you're trying to help me."

"Actually, I'm purposely trying to keep you a little nervous."

Like he had to try.

"Well, then...I'm red, and you're a person, so you're orange, which has red in it."

"You're getting literal again."

Ugh! Without cleaning her brush, she dipped into the black and painted a thick line across the top of the orange.

He chuckled behind her. "What's that strong line about?"

She breathed out hard. "I ruined it."

"No," he said low, leaning in, "you painted that for a reason. That's good! So, why?"

"I...." Why had she done it? "I don't understand what you want, so I crossed you out."

He laughed. He wasn't mad?

"That's legit!" he said. "That could be fear, or frustration, or anger at me for not being clear."

Fear, maybe. She didn't do anger.

"Are you still red?" he prompted. "Do you have other colors?"

She motioned as though she'd clean the brush again, then changed her mind and added a black line near a blue one, crossing her.

"I'm crossing myself out for not getting this."

"Sure, frustration can be in more than one place."

She drew a breath, cleaned her brush, and chose a yellow, stroking it over the orange just to the side.

"I'm yellow now too?"

"You're encouraging me, it makes me less nervous. So, you're not as scary."

"And why yellow?"

"I like yellow."

He laughed, and a slight chuckle rose up in her too. This wasn't remotely like her old classes, but she could begin to see what he was expecting.

He finally came to her side and took the brush and palette from her. "Look at what you did. You told a story on the canvas about emotions."

She looked at her rudimentary primary colors. It looked like a child's drawing. Worse even. Just lines.

She glanced sideways at him, and he flashed a reassuring smile.

"Okay," he said, "it's not going into a gallery, but the important thing is what it represents. Especially this." He pointed at the black. "That was spontaneous expression. That's a good thing."

She smiled weakly.

"This is your study," he continued. "You made a sketch of where the painting might go. I will interpret your sketch using technique, so you can see what it might look like complete. If it were me painting it, of course. Your style will be different."

He put another canvas board on the easel from the stack she had ready, then cleaned her palette knife. He quickly mixed colors and swiped a slightly curved slash of red down the board, another one in orange and yellow, then added teal and charcoal slashes going upwards across them.

The difference was astounding.

"But it's so professional!" she said. "That could be a real painting. Almost like Japanese calligraphy."

"Does it look nervous?" She shrugged weakly. "What might you think it represents?"

"Energy? Movement?" she ventured.

He leaned in. "Calm energy?"

"No, not calm. Definitely not calm."

He set down the tools, turning to look at her. "You just made your first abstract painting, telling a story about emotions you felt."

"Well, you did."

He shook his head, tucking loose hair behind his ear again. A smudge of red was added to the orange already there.

"I just interpreted your story," he said. "You'll get to that stage soon enough. For now, let this sink in a bit. Think it over."

She looked up at the clock, shocked to see how much time had passed. It had seemed like minutes. Done already? It had been hard, but she liked it. She wanted more.

. . .

León smiled at the dismay painted so blatantly across her face. Expressions! She'd done better with those than he expected.

She was obviously practiced at keeping her face still and slipping into shadows, but her body reacted against her will. He'd quite enjoyed all her tiny gasps and shivers as she painted, keyed up and distressed. The delicate rosy flushes along her neck as she struggled to put those feelings into the brush were enchanting.

He'd enjoyed the lesson more than her—that was clear. He'd give her a break.

"Should we switch gears? You've been nervous for long enough. What if we try recognizing emotions?"

She stiffened immediately. That social anxiety of hers must be hell.

What relaxed her? He thought back. Drinks. Food.

"But first," he said, "I'm a little hungry. Do you have anything made?"

She turned to him and melted, simple and artless, every tense line softening in subtle relief. The sight was fascinating. Her face tipped up to his, baring her neck just the slightest bit. It transformed her.

"Do you like potato soup?" she asked.

He grinned and held out a hand toward the door.

The process of serving the food calmed her. She was much more relaxed by the time they each had a hot cup of soup before them, sitting at her kitchen island on the tall stools. He asked how she'd made the soup, meaning to disarm her, but her enthusiasm about the process beguiled him instead. She glowed as she explained.

No wonder she liked feeding everyone when they came over. All that planning and skill, genuinely enjoyed, needed to be shared. She acted like she rarely got the chance.

"Okay," he said, pushing away his empty cup. "I'm not thrilled there are feet in there, but it tastes good."

Her smile was nearly merry.

"Thank you," she said, twisting her fingers together, looking down at them in her lap. "You're being very nice."

"All a part of the service."

She didn't look back up. "No, I mean being kind, asking to eat. You didn't have to do that."

Kind? His own cheeks felt a little warm. "Well. You were sort of wound up, weren't you?" She nodded. "You spend a lot of time wound up, I think."

Her shoulders tensed, but she looked up at him. Her face was slipping back to serious.

"I do okay," she said.

He shook his head. "I want to teach you something I do. It can help."

Her shoulders straightened, at once eager and tense. "Help paint?"

"Help everything. Here, stand up."

As she stood, he reached out, positioning them across from each other, one arm's length away. He dropped his hand, took a deep breath, closed his eyes, and went still. Finally, he exhaled, and his shoulders dropped.

"You did this the other night," she said, voice soft. "Before you started painting."

"I do it a lot," he agreed. "Now, follow along. Close your eyes. Relax. *Tranquila.*"

"What does that mean?"

He peeked through slitted lids, checking what she was doing. Her eyes were closed, her shoulders down, but she wasn't trying. "It means 'be calm.'"

Her brow furrowed, not tense but concentrating. Jesus, no one should have to work so hard just to feel! In his family, emotions had been so rampant that the struggle was to keep them from boiling over.

"Think of a calm place," he said. "Do you have one?"

Her brows furrowed in thought. "Floating in the pool at night, I guess?"

"You swim at night?"

"Sometimes."

Getting off track. "Fine. Imagine you're in the pool. How does that feel?"

"I...." Light anxiety crossed her face, and she stopped.

Great. Celia needed to be led step by step. "I'll help. You're floating. It's dark. You're alone."

Her face softened. When concentrating on a task, her defenses seemed to fall away. It soothed his irritation. Maybe she could do this.

"How do you feel? Warm or cold?" he asked quietly.

"Warm."

"What do you hear?"

"The water, lapping."

He paused to let her really imagine it, watching to see how long she could go before thinking. When she fidgeted, he leaned in.

"Is there a scent?"

Her face lifted lightly. "Chaparral."

"What do you see?"

"Stars. Palm trees."

"Your breaths are slow," he said softly. "Your heart is quiet." She nodded, lips barely parting. "Do you feel—"

Her phone chimed.

She startled along with him, opening her eyes and pulling the phone from her pocket. Without looking, she rejected the call and put the phone on the counter.

"Sorry," she said.

"It's fine. Shake it off. We'll—"

The phone sounded again, louder now that it was out.

"Do you need to take that?"

She looked down, away, jaw tight. "Sorry. One minute."

Her fingers moved over the phone, and she retired with it toward the couches.

"What?" she answered. "I know. I know. The mechanic's number is in the binder I made you. Did you call them?"

Too bad about the distraction. She'd been getting the hang of it.

"They'll pick the car up and bring you a loaner, Mom. It's all covered."

She'd turned partly away, phone hidden from him, but a bright red spot bloomed on her near cheek.

"I am helping! This is what the binder is for. You just call."

Her breath came faster, and a muscle in her jaw jumped as she ground her teeth. There was no way she could miss these signs of emotion in her body! León grinned, stepping closer.

As she turned glassy eyes to him, he patted his cheeks, then pointed to her.

"Red," he mouthed happily.

She stared, bewildered.

"Hot," he whispered, touching the back of his fingers briefly to her cheek.

Mouth falling open, she touched where his fingers had brushed. Then, she lowered the phone slowly.

"Just feel it," he whispered, his hands gently rising and falling with her breaths. Her rapt hazel eyes didn't close. He exhaled and lowered his shoulders.

"*Tranquila,*" she whispered back, then copied him. Her breathing slowed, and her cheeks faded. As her eyes softened, another of those shy, pretty smiles slipped out.

"Celia Rose!" The voice from the phone was audible to both. She stiffened again and raised the phone back to her ear.

Damn, she'd been getting it.

"Oh no," she said, her voice suddenly anxious. "LA is too long of a drive for you. And I have other plans." She frowned ferociously. "I'm going out of town for a few weeks."

She was?

"No, I'll be forty-two." Her face was aflame again. "Forty-two, Mom."

She'd never sounded so assertive in front of him. Nice to see she had it in her.

"You can try, but I don't think there's cell service where I'm going."

Maybe he shouldn't be standing here listening.

"I *will* have a great time. Goodbye!"

Celia ended the call, breathing hard, then turned wild eyes back to him.

"What are you feeling right now?" he asked, elated for her.

She scanned the room, round eyes searching as she ignored his question.

Maybe now wasn't the time. "I'm sorry," he said. "You were on the phone. I just got excited."

Shaking her head, she closed her eyes, her hands clenching tight. Her face drained of expression, going wooden.

Ah, that was too bad.

"I should get some cleaning done," she said.

He nodded, seeing the familiar blankness solidify its hold on her.

"I've got laundry, I think," she said. Her eyes were shuttered, shoulders as tense as he'd ever seen. "Do you have any clothes you'd like washed?"

Really? One distracting phone call and she was back to her poker face? Teaching her to paint was going to be a slog, worse than he thought. He didn't have time to break through all that armor.

"No, I'm good," he said. "See you in a few days, I guess."

He left her standing where she was.

SIX

She was cooking again.

León tried to avoid watching Celia across the backyard but often forgot. The pool house was dimly lit compared to that blazing white house of hers, his little glass box dwarfed by the wall of windows across her space. His eyes were naturally drawn there. At night, he could see her walking about, rarely still. She spent hours standing at that stove, chopping and stirring.

She was in pale sweats and a T-shirt tonight, her hair pulled back. Maybe she was getting more comfortable about him being out here. It was probably weird to have him in line of sight. Not that he was looking!

He was thinking about a painting. Yes. A satin nocturne in night-washed greens, tropical shapes lurking, the leaves backlit by a jewel box of brilliant...gleaming...nope. This wasn't true inspiration. He was just looking up at the house instead of his canvas, avoiding work.

He'd holed up in the pool house for three days straight, painting yet another storyless mess of colors. At this rate, he'd have exactly zero good paintings for the exhibit. Way to start a career on a new coast, showing work you don't believe in!

He was going to have to emerge for food soon. Andrew and the rest were coming tomorrow night, but León had finished the last of his cold pizza this morning.

Maybe it would save time if he went up to the house real quick? She'd offered food before. What was Celia cooking?

"Want some squash curry?" she asked when he knocked on the back door. He wasn't sure until the fragrance hit him.

"Oh my god!" The whole house smelled of roasted spices and tangy sweetness. "I absolutely want some."

Her shy smile as she ladled him a small bowl was nice to see, though she kept her face down. She'd been cleaning, he saw now. The knees of her sweats were dirty. How? There wasn't a smudge in the whole place, let alone actual dirt.

He offered to take the food back to the pool house, but she served him at the kitchen island and began asking questions as though he were a guest. Did he need towels? Should she turn off the pool lighting at dusk? Was he warm enough?

He agreed to take more bedding to quiet her. He scraped up the last of his curry, spicy and sweet and savory, as she went to collect blankets. Jumping down and following, he stopped at the hallway entrance, glancing into the dim craft room.

Hey, she'd been practicing.

Canvas boards sat in the shadows, all with a red vertical line in the middle. Celia, with varied colors coalescing around her. What feelings had she been trying to paint?

Many had a solid black shape at the top, a horizontal line, an arch above, and bars connecting them. A bridge. Looked like someone had an idea!

She emerged into the bright hall again, nearly hidden behind an armful of striped blankets, then stopped as she saw him looking into the craft room. He ducked his head, rubbing the back of his neck.

"Thanks for these," he said, moving forward to take the bedding. "And for the food."

"It'll taste better tomorrow," she said, fidgeting. "You know everyone's coming over?"

He nodded, and she went to open the sliding door.

"Um," she said as he edged out sideways. "I asked about towels because you keep hanging one on the pool house door. Does that mean you need more?"

He gave her a grin. "No. That means I'm working. Do not enter."

"Oh," she said. "Of course."

"Text if you need to come in, though. It's still your place."

She nodded solemnly as he left.

• • •

Celia hadn't been exaggerating about her food. The curry did taste better the next day. Andrew and the rest demolished the meal around the firepit, joking and laughing. Celia didn't lean back into the shadows as much but didn't join in their high spirits.

León's face smoldered at her in the firelight, frowning every time the group laughed, and she didn't. He was sitting across from her, for once, not jumping out of his chair every few minutes. Still, his knee bounced, and he turned his fork over and over in his hands, the silver flash bouncing onto her rhythmically.

Why was he annoyed? What had she done?

She was quick to follow Andrew and Trevor into the house when they carried dishes up for her.

"So," Trevor said, "how are lessons from the new tenant?"

She decided to be charitable. Her practice hadn't gone well, but she'd learned a little.

"We've only had the one, but I think it went okay. You were telling me about putting emotions into art, but he's showing me the steps. Slowly. Here, wait." She went to get the painting León had made of her little emotional story. Both Andrew and Trevor gathered to look.

"You painted this?"

"León did, but the lines and colors were from me." Finally, having a painting she was partially responsible for sparked her excitement. "Can you tell what it is?"

Trevor smiled. "Abstract art isn't objects you identify. It's ideas. But I will say this is two figures, one in motion, maybe running away?"

Andrew nodded.

"Definitely motion. Running toward? The blue lines have energy, and the yellow line here is like stability. So, is this one León?" He pointed to the energetic line.

Celia laughed. "Nope! I'm the one with energy this time."

It was funny to see her friends bemused. She wasn't always predictable!

• • •

"Celia's right," Kelsey said, waving her phone toward the house. She didn't seem to put it down often. She was draped sideways in her chair again, looking over her feet at León.

He turned from the house and raised eyebrows at her. He

didn't know what to make of Kelsey yet. She acted chirpy and affected, but no one treated her that way.

"You look at her a lot," she said.

León snorted. "I look at everything."

"Not me." The firelight illuminated her amused smile.

Oh, it was like that? "I'm not here to look at girls. I'm here to work."

"We're not girls."

He leaned forward, elbows on his knees. "You mean Celia's still thinking I look at her too much?"

"She mentioned it. We all got used to not making eye contact when she's quiet, but you're new."

"That's just weird," he said. "You guys are all friends, but you can't look at her?"

Kelsey sat up a bit, tugging her top back into place. "She wasn't always that way. She's so much fun, really. She's just in a rough place right now."

"Right now," he repeated, looking back at the house. "How long have you known her?"

"Oh, it's been years," Kelsey said. "Before the money. She was at a club, and I got her to buy tickets to my concert. After that, we just started talking and got along."

"You play music? Or sing?" Andrew had said his friends were artists, but not what Kelsey actually made.

"Oh no," she laughed. "I was just pushing tickets. It's what I did before I started at *La Creche*."

"What's that?"

"The clothing store I work at. Melrose. Fancy-ass clothes that cost more than my rent."

That did not sound like art. "Why were you pushing tickets, then?"

"Promotion. I was a street team kid." His face must have shown his confusion because she laughed again. "You know, hired by whatever company. We'd dress up and go into clubs to get people to buy a brand of vodka or talk about sneakers."

Oh, he'd seen that in New York. Years and years ago.

"It was so fun," she said, "but I aged out of it. No one believes you're cool if you're over thirty."

"Andrew said you were an artist, though," León said.

"Only sort of. I model for Trevor, and I'm picking up some photography tips from him." She waved her phone again. "The shop can be boring, so sometimes I style the mannequins and take pictures, and the social media guy posts some of them for the store."

"Well, that's art." Sort of. He wouldn't judge, though.

"Nah, it's promotion. I just like buzz. It's fun when someone comes in asking about something I shot."

"Modeling is an art."

She nodded. "I guess. Trevor and I get each other. His paying gigs have cast models, but I sometimes help on his personal projects."

León remembered an earlier conversation. "Celia said he dropped her after she introduced you."

"Nah," she said, "he still shoots her sometimes. She's better for fine art, though. She used to pose at the college all the time. She's good."

But how? She was so inexpressive! "I have a hard time picturing her doing that."

"Doing that well, you mean." Kelsey didn't pull punches, apparently. She swiped on her phone. "Look."

She scrolled for quite a while, then handed the phone to León. Trevor's Instagram.

The photo was moody, the background a black unlit studio, a snowy white figure in the center, mid-pirouette. Celia. She wore slim white pants and a gauzy white button-up shirt tied at the waist. Her hair was longer, her face obscured, but definitely her.

"Nice tits," he said.

Kelsey grimaced. "Really, dude?"

Well, they were pretty obvious, the spotlight from the side outlining her breasts under the shirt. Her nipples were dark shadows pushing against the fabric.

"Keep scrolling," she said.

He swiped on the photos. Same shoot, different poses. Celia bent at the waist, fingers splayed around her calves. Celia, on tiptoe, stretching tall but hands behind her head, elbows akimbo. Celia hunkered down, knees spread wide, her hands clasped and dangling between them. She was smiling in that one. Pretty.

She really could pose! She looked like she was in motion but was actually holding complicated postures. That took strength. Her angles were well-considered, meeting the camera with no foreshortened shoulders or feet disappearing behind the other.

She didn't look like a dancer or a professional model, someone who'd studied how to point a toe or extend an arm. Instead, she looked authentic and natural, like she'd been candidly caught standing that way.

It reminded him of their painting lesson. Her body gave her away, expressing things she thought she was hiding. Truth seeped out of her naturally, and the lack of filter kept it pure. The turn of her waist in the first picture was tender and raw, honest—

"All right, quit staring." Kelsey reached for her phone.

León frowned. "I was just—"

"I know, looking."

. . .

The day of the second lesson dawned. Celia turned her phone off first thing. No interruptions today.

When she heard León enter, she was reading in her bedroom, lying on her stomach across the bed. Nonchalant. She heard him moving around, looking in the craft room across from her bedroom, then he poked his head in her open doorway. She looked up as though she hadn't heard him.

"Oh, hey," she said. What a farce.

He held up a laundry bag. "Can I wash these while we paint?"

She jumped up, glad to be able to start with something she knew how to do. "Sure, I'll show you."

The clothes started in the washer, she looked at him almost bashfully. His look at her was sharper.

"What are you feeling right now?" he asked.

Unexpected question! Somehow, her tongue ran away. "Nothing. Embarrassed. Nervous."

He smiled, taking the sting out of barking at her. "Why?"

Well. She was trying to get better at this, right?

"It's new. I want to learn fast and get better at it. I'm excited about it, but I feel silly."

He grinned. "If you enjoy it, why not be excited? But let's get going. This might be quick today. I'm going to that gallery with Trevor later."

She didn't feel deflated at all. This was just a lesson. She already knew she was too excited. She breathed slowly to calm herself.

They moved to the craft room, where she again had supplies set out casually. Her experimental canvases were put away, and she picked up a brush, itching to find out if her practice had been worth it.

"Actually," he said, "we're doing something different today. I'm going to paint first."

But she'd had a plan!

"You do life modeling, right?" he asked. She nodded. "Let's do a little of that. I'm going to name an emotion, and you're going to model it for me. First, I'll capture some lines, then we'll identify why certain shapes show emotions."

She felt her cheeks getting hot again.

His face clouded, then cleared. "Oh. Clothes on, of course."

"Of course." She moved uneasily further into the room as he put some black on the palette, addressing the canvas board.

"Let's do sadness. How would you pose for that?"

She chose to sit on the floor, one knee up across her body, and sank her head onto it. Her arm lay limply at her side, trailing onto the ground.

"That's good," he said. "Really good."

"Thanks," she said, her voice muffled.

The quiet sounds of brush on canvas came to her, but she concentrated on her task. Sadness, Celia. Pretend. Do what sad people do.

"Come see," he said, far sooner than she expected.

She stood and became herself again, quiet and composed. León gave her a questioning sidelong glance as she walked back. Why?

She came to look and was astonished. It was her! The bare black lines were practically a caricature—every minute detail definitely her, despite being so simple. He was so talented. She'd never achieve this level of painting, not ever.

She sneaked a look at him and caught him doing the same.

Back to the canvas! "Is this what you meant by painting lines last time?"

He shifted to his other foot beside her.

"No, you did exactly as I asked then. This is a figure study, different from what we did." He looked at the canvas, shaking his head slightly. "I was going to give you some pointers about expressing emotion physically, but you don't need them."

He exhaled hard. Was he unhappy about that?

"Okay. It's your turn," he said. "I'll watch, and you copy this study. Just do the lines the same way as I did."

Yeah, right. "I'm not as good as you, León. I can't replicate that."

"Humor me."

She gave it a shot, aware of him judging her the whole time. The brush trembled in her fingers a little. He shook his head as the line of black wavered.

"Here, this is an old trick." He turned the canvas upside down, so the lines lost human meanings and looked more random. "Now, paint that pose again, down here. Paint exactly what you see."

She gave it another shot, a little less nervous this time. When she finished, León reversed the canvas again, and she was surprised to see how much closer she'd gotten. Her little figure actually looked sad.

"Why has no teacher ever shown me that?" she asked. "That's amazing."

"I guess it depends on the teacher. Some just teach things like shading and musculature. We've got to work on your visual honesty. Emotions don't come from shading. They come from the human body, the heart, the sensations you get when you feel them."

He pointed to the line he'd painted of her arm, trailing to the ground.

"This line is numb, hopeless, empty. It's frail. Weak. You held the pose beautifully. Did you feel sad when you did it?"

She shook her head. "Not really. I sort of imagine things, a story where I would feel the way I'm supposed to."

He scowled faintly. What was she doing wrong?

He cleared his throat. "Your first try with the brush," he said, "you were aware of how an arm should look. You made it heavier here at the top, which makes it look tense. The elbow is bent a little more. It gives it more purpose and less weakness. But on your second try, you just painted with your eyes. You didn't make an arm. You made the line."

She saw what he meant. But... "How do I use this in a real painting? I'm just copying you."

"For now. But we'll practice painting what you see, not what you think you see. And then we'll talk about what you really saw and why it works."

It was all so abstract, though he made it sound reasonable. He was challenging what she thought painting was. Something to practice! Wheels turned in her head, taking in the new rules.

"How do you feel right now?" he asked. Celia turned to face him, a little startled to find him focused on her with those dark eyes again, his body turned to her, his head lowered to make direct eye contact.

"Excited," she admitted. "It's new."

"How does 'excited' make your body feel?"

She closed her eyes without him asking. "Interested. I want to try—"

"No, in your body, your heart, your fingers."

She hesitated, trying to get to where he was aiming her. The silence went on too long.

"Your breathing is faster," he prompted. "Your neck is hot." She raised a hand to feel it. He was right. How did he know?

She shivered and opened her eyes to his.

"I feel it," she breathed, surprised. "How do I paint it?"

"Colors, lines, shapes. What comes to your mind?" She started considering. What was the correct answer? "Quick!" he barked.

She jumped. "Orange. Wavy lines. Small waves. Not like fire, like...."

"Don't think of an analogy. Feel it." He reached out and grasped her wrist, feeling the pulse there. For once, she didn't stiffen up.

"Fluttering lines," she said, set upon her task. "Pale bubbles rising, tiny ones. Movement, expanding over the whole canvas."

He smiled proudly. "You're starting to get how feelings can translate visually."

"Can I write this down?" she asked.

He laughed, releasing her wrist. "Sure. Are you going to try to paint it?"

"Do you want me to?"

"It's your feeling. You decide."

She grinned. "I guess it depends on if I get any homework. Maybe I'll try it. Maybe I'll try other feelings too." She went to a side table to write down the words she'd listed. He stayed to look at the quick line study he'd made.

"Just remember to paint when you feel it," he said. "You can't force it." He bent to look closer at his little study. "When you want to paint something, you'll know."

She wrote silently behind him, jotting down everything she could remember, closing her eyes to recall more clearly. The physical feelings had been faint and subtle.

She was so accustomed to feeling nothing that she had to concentrate, but she could practice. If she could force emotions, like with a scary movie or sad song, she could practice alone. But she could also try to practice in real life. Surely there would be opportunities.

When she turned, he was still studying the figure. And frowning! Celia's fledgling emotions drained away in response.

"Is something wrong?"

He exhaled, a scowl still twisting his mouth. Then he tried to relax, soothing himself, calming his features. She brightened, knowing that technique now.

"I should go," he said. "I know this was short, but you made a big breakthrough there. It's a good place to stop."

Oh.

He picked up the canvas board as if to take it with him. Then he set it back down just as quickly.

"I'll be busy this week," he said. "I'll see you in a few days, I guess."

He was already heading for the door.

"León, wait!" He paused impatiently. "Sometimes, I get bored with my usual stuff. Is there maybe some exercise I could do then?"

He still looked a little irritated, his eyebrows lowered.

"Paint boredom."

She stared as he stalked out.

SEVEN

León stomped back to the pool house, angrily shutting down visions of smooth coppery angles.

He did not want to paint Celia!

Treading carefully around her anxious moods, seeing her timid doe eyes raised to him like he knew all the answers—she was too much work. Besides, teaching her took enough of his time. And even that was a risk! If he stepped wrong, and he would eventually, she could kick him out. She was trouble he couldn't afford.

He closed the door behind him, a towel hung on the outside latch, and went straight to his latest painting, up against the tall windows overlooking Los Angeles.

It was shit.

He'd tried to show the majesty of the steel beehives in the distance, golden reflections bouncing around the basin, but the feeling wasn't there. Somehow it just showed distance and isolation. Why?

He had to scrap this one too. He might as well be Celia trying to paint.

All right, he was grumpy because his paintings weren't going well. He was distracted. He kept feeling Celia rattling around in that stark house, painting her repressed little apples.

Maybe going to the exhibition space with Trevor later today would clear his head.

Chafing at his lack of direction, he paced. He had the time. Why couldn't he use it right? Maybe he should try floating in the pool at night like Celia, meditating or whatever. He hadn't actually seen her out there once. Probably avoiding it because of him.

Why did she have to keep popping into his head?

Fine! He'd draw her! Maybe that would exorcize her and he could move on to something he actually wanted to do.

Today's study of her was a starting place, but not what he

should sketch. She was better in motion. The openness when she relaxed and turned to him during the first lesson—that had been a good moment.

He pulled out a pad and charcoal and tried to recall how she'd looked when he suggested she feed him. Her shoulders had relaxed. Her face had tipped up to his, baring her neck just the slightest bit. That slight turn, calmness in her lines, openness, warmth.

He couldn't perfectly draw it, but at least he was working. He tore the page off and tried again.

By the time Trevor texted to say he was on his way to pick them up, he'd made at least ten sketches. They were close, but none were right. His frustration was back.

Wait, 'them?' Was Celia coming too? Why?

León made an effort to clean himself up. He was meeting potential exhibitors. He ought to look less scruffy. He shaved around his facial hair and pulled on a beanie. He wore his one blazer over a dark T-shirt. He really needed to get some nicer clothes.

He grabbed the printed sample cards of his work and went out through the side gate to await Trevor.

Celia came out the front door right as León reached the driveway. She was wearing a belted brown knit dress that reminded him of Andrew's vision of her in bronze. Whatever. She looked okay.

She wasn't going to speak, just shifting her weight from foot to foot and looking warily at the trees across the road.

"You're coming too?" he finally asked.

She reached to fidget with her necklace but didn't turn to him. "Trevor asked me an hour ago."

"Why?"

Her whole body went still, and she turned stony eyes on him. "Why not?"

That dismissive way she could stare through him!

"*Con permiso, mi reina,*" he muttered, looking away as though watching for Trevor's car.

"'Excuse you'...what?"

Oh, she understood some Spanish? Well, it was LA.

"Excuse me, queen," he clarified, his voice sharper than he intended. He waited for a return challenge, but she only looked away.

Tires crunched on gravel as Trevor's car came around the hairpin turn before her driveway. Thank god. Celia got in the passenger seat without a word. León sat in the back behind her, where he couldn't see her.

"Glad you came out, Celia," Trevor said. "I think you'll like this gallery."

If she replied, León couldn't hear her. "What's this showing like?" he asked. "Is it juried?"

"No," Trevor said, "just one curator. It's going to be a pretty big event."

The car's tight turns swayed León to the side, where he could just see Celia's face, staring straight ahead.

"It's multimedia," Trevor continued, "covering several large rooms, with a gala on opening night. The works will only be up for two weeks, but there ought to be some deep pockets there the first night. Plenty of collectors."

"You think I have a chance to get in?" León asked.

"Your work is good, and New York always has cachet," Trevor said. "I'm just introducing you, though. Knowing the right people pays off. Andrew could network, but he seems content to teach. Not me. I'm going to have them calling me for work rather than having to hustle for it."

"They already call you, Trevor," Celia said.

"Bigger people. Vogue is going to call me," he said confidently.

The gallery wasn't far by LA standards, and Trevor dominated the conversation as they navigated traffic, naming people it would be handy to meet. León asked questions about framing and catalog requirements. Celia contributed nothing.

Trevor summed up the location as they drove through. They were between the Arts District and Boyle Heights neighborhood, straddling a boundary of the urban renewal battle. Handy for pulling from both populaces, León figured. The artists could ride the bus from the cheap side, and the rich could drive from wherever they lived. Up in the canyons, apparently.

70

The gallery was similar to that gin bar, a cavernous converted warehouse. A brilliant forest of ceiling fixtures pointed at mostly-bare brick walls. Pieces had come down in preparation for new ones coming.

As they waited for the curator, León watched Celia's gaze wander around the space. Although she couldn't stop fiddling with her necklace, she was wearing that deadpan mask she wore around people she didn't know. Irritating!

A notice near the front desk advertised the upcoming exhibition, with "Last Chance" printed across it. Celia motioned at it, turning away to Trevor.

"They're closing?"

"Oh, yeah. They've done well here, but there's been opposition from the neighborhood to galleries in the area. Gentrification, you know. They've been renovating a smaller gallery downtown."

"Is that why this show only runs for two weeks?" León asked, crowding forward, back into her line of sight.

"Yeah. They'll have a longer one in their new space right away, but this show will be big. They have the whole space to fill."

Celia's gaze wandered over the brick walls and lofty ceilings. León watched her eyes try to light up, but get snuffed out by that damn control of hers.

"Hard to believe they'd let go of such a cool space," she said.

The curator appeared, and Trevor made introductions. Celia listened sedately as León listed showings he'd had in New York and produced the sample cards of his best paintings. She was handed a few as they were passed around, a gentle blush rising on her chest, but her face was like stone.

Why had she even come?

Her prim silence was infuriating. She was so appealing when she opened up. She would have charmed this curator without saying a word. Instead, she looked at his cards blankly, even though he could see small telltale signs of interest. Was she even aware she was stuffing the feelings down?

To learn to paint, she'd have to break through that reserve.

León was politely invited to join the exhibition. They had space for three paintings and gave him the delivery date. He did his genuine best to respond enthusiastically. This did matter to his career.

Trevor and the curator began discussing an artist they both knew, and though León knew he should join in, he couldn't concentrate with Celia bottling up reactions right in front of him. He bowed out of the conversation and took her by the elbow, walking her to the few hanging artworks.

"Tell me what you think of this painting," he said, biting off the words.

That at least got an expression out of her, if only the usual doe-eyed trepidation.

"It's nice," she said, wary.

"No feelings about it, then?"

She glanced wistfully back at Trevor, then faced down the painting.

It was shades of white with a stripe of yellow running horizontally across it about two-thirds of the way up. Organic, like marble with a vein of gold. Simple.

"It's cold," she said. "Subtle. It looks like stone. The gold up high looks top-heavy, like the bottom half is too fragile to hold it up."

He wasn't letting her get away with that. "None of those words describe feelings."

"I don't know, then!" she hissed, shaking her elbow loose from his hand.

He shook his head. "Maybe this one is a bit advanced."

"And I'm not," she finished for him. "Fine, what does it make you feel?"

"Optimism," he said firmly. "That shock of yellow through the neutral whites and grays is like a burst of joy, like seeing someone you love come through a door. I feel calm, relaxed, balanced, then excited because that burst of unexpected happiness interrupts the peace."

She stared at him. "That's the story?" Her eyes turned upon it again, doubt written across her face.

"The artist may have meant something else," León said,

"but that's the feeling I get. The viewer is an active participant in art. As long as I feel something, it doesn't matter what it is. But good painters, yes, they can communicate something specific."

She shook her head, her brow furrowing. He moved her to the next one.

This one should be easier since it had a recognizable object. It was broad swipes of grays, darker at their edges, creating a mosaic look. The geometric shapes combined into the form of a chair. León instantly saw a kaleidoscopic view of reality, a mundane object viewed through a shattered lens. He felt intrigued, with a childlike curiosity about what else one could see through this new prism.

"What do you see? What does this make you feel?" He watched her face as she struggled to perform the task.

"Tiles. A mosaic. Um, it's comforting?"

She was trying so hard. "Why comforting?"

"Because it broke, but the pieces are glued back together stronger. It'll be okay."

Good girl. Seeing something he hadn't didn't make her wrong. It just mattered that she'd found an emotion in it.

Her eyes on his were both frightened and relieved, waiting to hear that she'd done well. He turned to her.

"How do you feel right now, not about the painting, but just in your body?"

"Worried. I don't know if I got it right."

"No, in your body."

She closed her eyes. Seeing her soften eased León's temper.

"Heart is beating faster," she said. "And I feel jumpy, too much energy."

"Good. You're getting better at this."

Relief flooded her, the tension leaving her shoulders, her face thawing with the warmth he'd been waiting for. She opened her eyes again and inhaled sharply, suddenly realizing how near he stood. She stole back a step.

"Let's do another," he said.

She stiffened instantly. Dammit!

"What is it?" he asked.

"What is what?"

"You, tensing up for no reason. We're just looking at art."

She frowned. "I'm not tense."

"You're lying," he snapped.

Her eyes flared with hurt.

Well, she had to hear it! "If you're not honest about your emotions, at least with yourself, none of this will work. None of this—" he waved a hand at the paintings, "will make sense because honesty is the only thing that matters here! You have to put honest emotions into the painting, and the viewer has to be honest about what feelings they get. That's the connection, the whole point!"

"Let go!" she growled.

He looked down and found he'd grabbed her elbow again, so released her with an exasperated noise. Her fierce little face was proof that his words were getting through, at least!

"This locking away of emotions you do," he bristled, "I can't tell if it's on purpose. It's hurting you. It's stopping you from being...being pretty, being real!"

"Pretty!" Her cheeks flamed.

"Not pretty. Human, genuine. You have no idea how different you look when you're being honest and open. It's night and day!"

She lifted her chin and stepped back, putting a cold distance between them. He saw the shutters go down over her face, literally saw it.

"Our arrangement was painting lessons. That's all! If learning how to feel out loud is part of painting, fine! But it's nothing to you if I'm pretty doing it. I'm trying!"

She wasn't hearing him.

"I know you're trying," he said, lowering his voice. "I didn't say that right. I'm sorry. It's not your appearance I mean. I can see the tension when you're nervous, and when you say you're not nervous, that's not true."

Her eyes flashed, her chin lifted defiantly. "You think that's better? You're still calling me a liar."

"I mean...be honest. Just be more honest!"

"The opposite of a liar?"

Jesus, the edge in her voice! His hand flew wide again, and she flinched. "I don't mean you're deliberately lying! Or maybe you are. What do I know?"

He hadn't meant to shout, but she'd raised her voice first! Did she want to learn from him or not?

Trevor materialized between them.

"Hey, guys," he said quietly. "Um, what's happening here?"

León opened his mouth to tell him, then clamped it shut. Damn.

Celia shot Trevor a glance but quickly turned her flushed and angry glare back to León. Their breaths came hard, and León realized his hands were balled into painful fists. Dogged, he returned her glower, his own face hot.

She had to understand what he was telling her. He couldn't work with her as she was.

"Yeah," Trevor said slowly. "So, let's go, then."

Celia turned on her heel for the door, head held insultingly high. *¡Reina!* León paced after.

The car ride was silent and tense. Trevor met León's hard eyes in the rearview mirror too often.

"I'm not sure what you two were arguing about," he finally said, "but you weren't loud, not until the end. I don't think anyone noticed."

"We weren't arguing," Celia said through tight lips.

"We were, too," León replied. "Be honest."

And that was the end of the conversation.

León exited the car as soon as it stopped at Celia's, gave Trevor a wave that potentially meant thank you, then slammed the car door and stalked into the backyard.

As he closed the side gate, he heard Trevor, faint but clear. "Are you okay? Is this not going well?"

León stopped. What would she answer?

"I made him mad somehow," she said. "I'm not learning fast enough, I think."

"You don't have to let him stay," Trevor said. "He can always go back to Andrew."

Oh no, he couldn't! León reopened the gate, then froze.

Celia was out of the car, bending down to talk through the window. That knit dress hugged the backs of her thighs, and all he could see for a moment was that lovely line down her back, hugging the lush curve of her backside, then sneaking back low under her leg. It begged to be drawn.

His breath caught in his throat.

He turned at once, heart pounding, and stomped to the pool house before they saw him. Okay. Okay, maybe he had some inspiration going here.

Hell. He might want to paint Celia.

EIGHT

The firepit crackled and spit behind her, Celia's shadow falling across the food table. Andrew, Trevor, and Kelsey chatted in their chairs, still eating. Andrew had refused to let her cook for her own birthday, bringing tamales from a place he knew. Kelsey brought cake. Trevor brought beer. Cooking was usually all she contributed. What was there to do now?

She fussed with napkins in the dark, then looked across the glowing pool to the pool house. Light shone dimly behind the lowered shades, but no shadows moved inside.

In her cardigan pocket, her phone dinged. The group chat. She pulled it out to read a text from Andrew telling León to come out.

"Celia, come sit down," Kelsey called from behind her.

León had locked himself down after their fight. He'd pulled the shades and left the towel hanging on the pool house door, which was perfectly fine with her. Let him sulk. Celia hoped he was very happy, working on his art without the strain of trying to teach her.

She turned and drifted back to her friends. Kelsey had insisted she take the best chair, looking over the fire at the city view. She couldn't lean back into the shadows in this one. Pulling her sweater cuffs down over her hands, she sat, exposed.

"What kind of music do you want, Celia?" Trevor was selecting a playlist on his phone. She shrugged.

"Relax, girl," Andrew said, reaching to hand her a beer and a wrapped tamale. She held them in her lap, hoping the smile she gave him looked more genuine than it felt.

"I'm okay," she said. She was! It was just harder to cram everything down lately. Dumb painter and his dumb lessons.

Kelsey slouched in her chair, curling her bare toes over the edge of the firepit brick, concentrating on balancing her ginger ale on her stomach. Trevor's music started.

Celia almost missed the sound of the pool house door sliding open. Almost. Stock still, she looked covertly sideways to see.

León's dark figure approached, briefly lit by the aqua pool lights as he passed it, then flaring into gilt as he came into the circle around the fire. He was in his smudged painting clothes, hair loose. His eyes raked Celia, then turned to Andrew.

"Hey," he said. "I can't stay."

"Aw, come on, man," Andrew complained. "I've barely seen you lately."

"At least have some cake," Kelsey said.

León's brow knotted, and he turned to look at the food table. The decorated cake drew him closer. Then, bending to read the writing on it in the firelight, he snorted.

"Of course," he said flatly, then stalked back to the pool house.

"Not real social, is he?" Trevor asked.

Andrew began peeling the label off his beer bottle, sprawling in his chair nearly as low as Kelsey. "He's like this when he has trouble painting."

Celia set the beer and food on the arm of her chair and pulled her sweater tighter around her. She had trouble painting too, but was still polite.

"Is he making anything good, Celia?" Kelsey asked.

"I haven't been in to see."

The sliding door on the pool house grated again, but she didn't look, eyes staring through the fire.

Something touched her head, and she jumped, her hand flying up to feel something weightless and fluttery.

A...hat? A paper hat?

León stood over her as she took it off to see. He'd cut paper into a wild fringe and folded it around a disposable bowl.

"I couldn't paint it," he said. "It would have taken too long to dry." He took it from her hands and set it back on her head. "I didn't know it was your birthday. You never said."

León aimed a scowl at Andrew, who grinned crookedly and spread his hands. "Read the group chat sometimes."

León's black eyes snapped back to Celia. So, he was still

annoyed with her? Was it because she'd talked back in the gallery?

"Are you enjoying yourself?" he asked.

She held the hat on her head to look up at him. His face, seen through the silly fringe, was hard-edged in the flickering firelight.

"Yes," she glared. What did he care, anyway?

He raised fingers to the hat, pushing aside the fringe that hid her eyes. "That's not true, is it?"

"Man..." Andrew started. Celia looked around hopefully, but he said no more.

"It's a thing we're doing," León said, still poised above her. "Emotional honesty. Or else she'll never paint."

Andrew and Trevor exchanged frowning glances. Kelsey turned to sit sideways in her chair, watching. No one was going to rescue her here.

Celia swallowed and gave it a shot. "I'm embarrassed that everyone's making a fuss."

"Why?"

"I guess I'm not sure what I'm supposed to do."

"Let's ask them."

Trust León to make this happen out loud! Andrew swallowed some beer as León raised his eyebrows at him.

"You don't have to do anything," Andrew said. "We just want to celebrate. We like you."

Trevor fell under León's gaze next.

"You are doing something. You're hosting us again. Only you didn't get to cook this time."

Kelsey didn't wait for León. "We want to enjoy your birthday too. Let us."

León's head swiveled back to Celia.

"That's one for no expectations, two 'you already are doing somethings.' How do you feel about that?"

She narrowed her eyes at him. He wasn't going to let it go.

"Better," she said, "but annoyed that you're making everyone talk about it."

He finally smiled. "Good girl."

"And don't patronize me." She took off his stupid hat.

"I meant it," León said. "That was some good truth. Anyway, you're supposed to squirm on your birthday. That's half the fun for everyone else."

Oh. Thanks so much, everyone.

Kelsey laughed. "That's true," she said. "Here, presents will make you feel better." She pulled a small package from her capacious purse, handing it across. "Happy birthday."

The gift was a delicate necklace with a jeweled painter's palette hanging from it. Celia threaded the loose clasp under her hair, then ducked her chin, trying to fasten the tiny ends. León leaned in to help, not asking. His fingers, when they brushed her neck, had rough traces of dried paint on them that tickled her skin.

She let him fasten the clasp. Telling him no was futile.

Finally, he crossed to the last open chair. So, he was joining them.

"Here," Trevor said, handing around another package. It was flat, maybe a book. But no, it was a framed photo of Celia and Kelsey from a punk-themed shoot he'd done with them years ago. Celia had to smile at the fishnets, boots, and wild hair, their thinner faces harshly lit under an iron bridge.

"Finally, art to hang on your walls," León commented.

She shot him a sour look across the fire. He was stiff-backed, thumb tapping on the sides his thigh.

Andrew took his time getting up to retrieve his bag, looking satisfied with himself, as usual. The heavy duffel clinked lightly when he set it down in front of his chair. Ceramics.

He began setting out forms wrapped in miles of paper on the edge of the firepit surround, four small ones and one about two feet tall.

"Okay," he prefaced. "The big one is simply to show off. But, Celia, you can choose which of the smaller ones you want to keep." He ceremoniously unwrapped the large one, then turned it to catch the firelight. Everyone leaned in as one.

It was his bronze and green sculpture, a nude torso. The glaze looked liquid in the firelight, slick and rich. It was a celebration of motion and delicacy, the curves unapologetic.

"Oh, Andrew," Celia said, "it's gorgeous." She shook her head, heat on her cheeks. "I don't look like that."

"Yes, you do. I just found your best angles." He began unwrapping one of the smaller packages. "These are the studies. You choose one. Happy birthday and thank you for posing."

Gradually, smaller sisters of the large sculpture came out to sit near the fire. Celia picked up each to look them over, then handed them to Kelsey, who passed them around further. Fuss was made over Andrew's workmanship. Trust him to give himself a gift at the same time.

Celia chose her statue, cradling it in her lap. León drew her eye again. He was turning one figure over in his hands, scowling. Still annoyed for no reason. He looked up, catching her watching him, and stood.

"I've got to get back to painting. I'm not ready for the exhibition."

Kelsey and Andrew groaned.

"You work too much," Kelsey complained. "Hang out, I brought a card game." León shuddered, and she laughed. "More players, more fun."

He shook his head, stepping over their feet to get around the firepit. "Andrew, come with me? I want to show you something." He still had the ceramic figure in his hand and gave it to Andrew, who rose and followed him into the dark.

Celia finally lifted her beer to her lips. Fine. Let him go back to sulking so she could enjoy herself.

• • •

Once inside the pool house, León held his hand out for the figure again. Andrew handed it over, puzzled.

"I don't really have anything to show you," León said. "I just wanted to ask, can I keep this one for a while?"

"Why?"

Why?

He'd hoped that not seeing Celia for a few days would kill his thoughts about painting her. It hadn't worked in the least. Her face had gleamed in the firelight like just-forged copper, her apprehensive huddle inside that oversized sweater telling a story he could capture in burnt sienna and cadmium reds and yellows.

Those uncertain hazel eyes of hers sparked something unkind in him, and he knew better than to mix inspiration with complication. But, maybe he could scratch his itch another way.

"I want to paint a few studies of the statue," León said. "The shapes are really...honest."

Andrew grinned. "Sure, man. You know, she'll sit for you if you ask."

León shook his head. "Just studies, that's all. It's your work. I want to try out some lines without, you know, bringing her in."

Andrew looked at him thoughtfully. León tried to rein in his expressions, aiming at casual and noncommittal, but swallowed uneasily.

"Did you...improve on this?"

Andrew's eyebrows shot up. "You asking if that's really what she looks like naked?"

León exhaled hard. Of course, he would find this funny.

"You're into her!" Andrew grinned.

"I am not!" León said. "Oh hell, call it curiosity. You dated her. I bet you could do her from memory anyway."

"My memory's not that good. It needs refreshing sometimes."

León ignored that. "There's nothing to paint up here," he said. "I just want to know if I can keep this for a week or so."

"Yeah, yeah, it's fine. So, you're definitely not into her."

"Hell no."

Andrew shrugged. "Okay then. But are you actually going to start now? Why not sit out with us? You used to be more social."

"No time."

"If you say so. Beat that deadline, man," Andrew teased with a grin on his way back out.

León set the nude on the bedside table, then sat on the cot to inspect it. Gently, he reached out and turned it slowly, watching the light from his one lamp bounce off of the glazed organic curves, highlighting different angles and shadows. It was a fine piece of work. For once, he wasn't stuck searching for a subject to paint. He still needed a story, but he was closer.

• • •

The fire burned low.

Unable to get anyone interested in her card game, Kelsey gave up and began showing Celia some photos she'd taken. Andrew and Trevor started leaning toward each other, talking about their exhibition pieces. Celia considered getting out her 'excitement' painting to show she could do work too, but it wasn't good enough. It sucked being the one talentless person in the group.

You're just useless, Celia Rose.

Ugh, that foul voice in her head again? She hadn't heard it for a while, not since she lied to Mom about going out of town. It had been a vacation, after all, from the calls.

Wait. *Tranquila.* It had helped her that day.

She imagined floating in the pool at night. She hadn't floated for so long, not since León moved in. She missed it.

Dark, calm, tranquil. Celia took slow and easy breaths, feeling her heartbeat slow. It was working.

And next... 'What are you feeling?' Pride that I remembered this trick. 'No, in your body?'

She smiled suddenly, realizing she was conversing with León in her imagination, and he was still pushing her.

She looked up to the pool house. He'd come out for such a brief time tonight.

"Hey, you're ignoring me."

Kelsey was never shy about saying what she thought. Well, why rely on León for pushing? Kelsey was here. She was her friend, and she was honest. Safer than León, to tell the truth.

Celia took a deep breath. "Kelsey...I feel happy that you're here. Thanks for coming."

Kelsey's mouth fell open, then she reached out to touch Celia's arm. "I'm happy to be here," she said. "You know, I don't think I've ever heard you say something sappy like that."

Celia looked down at her hands in her lap. "It feels weird to say out loud, but it's true."

Kelsey leaned closer, over the arm of her chair.

"This is León's work, isn't it?" she asked. "I gotta know, why are you listening to him? I've known you for like ten years. You barely know him."

"It's my lessons. He says I have to be honest about feelings, or I can't paint."

"Is that working?"

"A little," Celia admitted. "It's embarrassing. I wish people could understand without me having to say it. Like, you see me smile, so you know I'm happy."

Kelsey laughed. "It's different when you say it, though."

"Scary."

"Maybe. But, you might want to kiss someone or you might say, 'I want to kiss you.' Totally different."

Celia nodded slowly. Huh.

"If you say it," Kelsey continued, "the other person gets to respond. Maybe they want to kiss you too. Plus, they know you want it bad enough to say it out loud. I guess, saying it is an invitation to the other person to react."

Celia kept nodding but felt her throat tighten. Kelsey was right; having feelings was only the first step. Dealing with the other person's reaction was the terrifying part.

Kelsey gave her a shrewd look. "I always thought you were just private, but now that I'm seeing León hound you, I'm realizing you don't mean to be, do you?"

Celia tensed. Be honest. "I'm too afraid to say things out loud, sometimes."

"And all this time, I thought you just didn't want to." Kelsey smiled. "Honey, I could have helped. You know me. I'm safe to practice on." She looked over at Andrew and Trevor, deep in discussion. "You can trust them too. You could try honesty on Andrew. He's always chill."

Celia laughed. "With Andrew? You know where connecting with him can land me. Though, he doesn't ask about staying the night as much as he used to."

Kelsey nodded toward the two men, absorbed in their talk. "Actually, I think that's why."

Celia kept her face carefully neutral until she could lean

closer to her friend. "You mean, Andrew and Trevor...together?"

"I've been noticing for a while. They have chemistry."

"Hmm." Celia could see it, actually.

Kelsey leaned in even closer. "You know who else has chemistry?"

"Who?"

"You and León."

Celia's face flamed instantly. Good thing it was dark.

"Yeah, no," she countered. "He was nice at first, but now he's either shouting at me or locked up in the pool house."

Kelsey waved her hand at the chair León had been sitting in. "When you're both in the same place, you always face each other. I've been watching it. It's funny."

"I'm sure that's not true," Celia objected.

"He pays way more attention to you than anyone else."

Celia shook her head. "He's always mad, though."

Kelsey grinned. "In movies, if they fight, they're in love!"

Celia had to laugh along with Kelsey. This was no movie!

"What's so funny over there?" Andrew called, drawn to the laughter as his conversation with Trevor concluded.

"I'm telling her León likes her," Kelsey explained, "but she doesn't believe me."

"León likes her fine," Andrew said, rising from his chair. "And so do I, and so does Trevor, and so do you. Let's eat cake! Let's spank her for her birthday!"

"Don't you dare!" Celia cried.

Kelsey's beautiful cake was demolished, mostly by Andrew. As the fire died to embers, Celia began collecting the beer bottles, exhausted from being the center of attention for too long. It was a sign they all knew.

Trevor helped her take dishes to the kitchen while Andrew and Kelsey straightened the backyard. Andrew had to carefully rewrap his little sculptures as well.

"You and Andrew had plenty to talk about," she told Trevor as they cleared the kitchen. She managed to catch a blush on his cheek. Maybe, then.

"Just art, the same as always," he said, offhand.

Kelsey and Andrew came in—she carrying a bag of trash, and he, his bag and large sculpture. He set them all carefully on the kitchen island.

"Kelsey," Trevor said, "I'm parked behind you. You'll have to go before I can."

"I'm ready."

The two of them hugged Celia, wished her a happy birthday one last time, and left together. Andrew eyed the last piece of cake, still out.

"How can you eat more?" Celia said.

"Sometimes I'm not finished when I think I'm finished," he said, giving her a look she knew very well.

"Ah."

He moved in closer to her, warm brown arms stealing around her waist. "We could make this a really happy birthday."

Well. It did feel good to be held after being alone so much lately. "Happy for whom?"

"Both of us." Emboldened, he pressed his luck with a quick kiss. "It's been a while. I could remind you what you're missing."

"No one's missing anything," she smiled. "I'm just convenient."

"So am I. Do you have anything better on offer tonight? You know it'll be nice."

Sweet Andrew with his one-track mind. Celia felt no electricity, but the brush of his cheek past hers recalled warm, familiar nights. They had laughed together, nude, soaking in touch and darkness. She hadn't felt as safe and wanted in a long time.

Why not?

She kissed him back lightly, having to stand on her toes to reach. An image of León rose in her mind. Would he notice Andrew had stayed? Well, what did that matter? She had a history with Andrew, and it was her birthday. She could treat herself if she wanted.

Andrew's hands roamed a little further down onto her hips.

"I won't even ask for breakfast, Celia, promise."

"You don't have to talk me into it. Yes."

He picked her up with arms back around her waist, kissing her neck, tickling her where he knew she liked it. "Maybe you'll get those birthday spankings after all."

She laughed and squirmed in his arms. "Oh, no, I won't!" she said. "Here, put me down. Let's get the lights."

He helped her shut down the house, knowing as well as she did which low lights to leave on. The cake and sculpture they left out, shutting the bedroom door behind them.

NINE

Andrew's loving was practiced, familiar, and it felt wonderful to be touched after so long. He was generous in bed, as he always had been. His sensitive brown hands slipped around her curves as though she were clay, his velvet murmurs urged and enveloped and celebrated.

However, the beer, food, and sex had him deeply asleep after an hour. Celia lay awake, skin sweaty and muscles pleasantly sore. Her bed felt too hot, her head too full now that she had time to think back over the evening.

Opening up with Kelsey felt good. Why had she avoided it? Why had she picked friends who let her stay locked up out of respect? León may be blunt about things, but he was good for her. A catalyst. A friend. She was learning more than painting, definitely.

Being honest with herself felt good too. When Andrew hinted at staying over, he took her 'no' with his usual good humor. She rarely considered that she might enjoy having him stay. Tonight she'd done what she felt like doing; León would be proud that she'd let her feelings guide her. Well, it wasn't really his business, but she could be vague and not give specifics. He'd be pleased with her progress.

Wide awake, Celia gently slipped from the bed. Andrew would sleep like a rock, but she'd get a drink of water or maybe step outside to cool off.

• • •

León tipped his head back and closed his eyes. Completed studies littered the daybed around him, maybe twenty charcoal sketches, attempts at replicating the organic curve that had fired his imagination. Andrew's little sculpture had done its job.

It was the arch of the back, he'd discovered—right where her hip swelled into that curve of her waist, flowing over her ribcage and up.

He'd gotten the curve onto canvas, though. Where the painting would go next, he didn't know. The arch itself was the crucial shape. He looked at it again, scrolling up like the stem of a wine glass flowing to the bowl, a tendril of smoke curling lazily to the ceiling. It could be anything as long as he captured the line.

He turned the statue again, viewing the front. Maybe that curve under the ribs, that shape just at the front of her hip. That one had potential too. He picked up the charcoal again.

• • •

Celia opened the sliding door of the house, the mild air refreshing her sweaty skin. She left the door open to let the house breathe in some of the coolness.

She'd pulled on her robe but hadn't bothered dressing. She wouldn't be outside long. After checking that the fire was out, she walked to the pool's edge, looking over the city lights, sipping her glass of cold water.

She felt good, unafraid for once to think instead of keeping busy. Just standing, being, feeling better than she had in days. León was right: if one paid attention to one's body, actual sensations accompanied feelings. She'd ignored them for so long that the warmth and lightness inside her were a surprise.

Maybe she would get into the pool and float for a little while.

She turned her head to look at the house. No lights shone other than the usual low ones in the living room. Andrew would sleep until morning. He knew her bed; he was comfortable there.

Turning the other way to view the pool house, Celia saw the lamp shining behind the shades but no shadows, no movement. León was either absorbed or asleep.

He kept himself closeted inside much more than she'd expected. Was he happy when he was inside, creating? How did he feel when he made real art? He'd said the whole point was honesty between the painter and the viewer. But how did one paint honesty? How could it be drawn, or sculpted, or sung?

León had praised what he called her emotional story, her silly childlike lines of color. How could she do it again, better?

What truth did she have to tell?

The question stumped her. He'd stopped helping her right when she was beginning to understand.

She decided to get in the pool. She could think there, maybe figure it out on her own this time. She dropped her robe on a chair and walked to the pool steps, the gentle breeze on her nude body refreshing and familiar.

It was almost a shame to disturb the mirror finish of the water, but ruffling it was one of her favorite parts. A chill enveloped her body as she went deeper, but only at first. The water spread out from her body in expanding waves, rippling softly against the tiled walls. It was beautiful, standing at the center of a web of waving lights.

If she was going to figure anything out, it'd be here, now, after a night of small successes. She turned to float on her back, letting her mind clear. What was an honest thing she wanted to tell someone?

I'm here. See me. Except...that's scary. I'm afraid to be seen. Be gentle.

These were all truths someone else must have felt before. Everyone in the world had, surely. But how could you draw that? Paint that? How did you say that without clichés?

If she could put herself into art, maybe she wouldn't have to risk saying things to people. She could just let them look at the art and know her. She didn't even have to be in the same room. It would be the ideal way to express herself if she could just figure out how.

Her mind drifted along with her body. The water lapped at her, both cold and warm, her back insulated and buoyed, her front chilled by the night air. The contrast raised goosebumps. She existed right now in this wandering place between the water and the stars, feeling them both. It felt lovely.

Maybe she could paint water. Floating. Existing. A leaf on water. Light on water.

She only had to illustrate the feeling of being. Easy.

• • •

León set down his charcoal and rubbed his eyes. The second curve battering around his head refused to go onto paper right. He needed a break.

Lights from the pool were wavering gently across the ceiling. Usually, the still pool glowed steadily, but the wind sometimes gave him this little light show as the surface ruffled. He could step out and get some air, maybe sit at the firepit in the dark and feel the breeze.

Sliding the door open, he froze, arrested. Glimmering in the pool in front of him was the curve he'd seen in his head.

Celia! Jesus. Look at her.

She floated on her back, nude, eyes closed, arms out to her sides. Her arms—they made the difference. In the statue, they were raised. Here, her shoulders were relaxed and supported by the water. That curve at her ribs rounded into a fuller, more graceful arch. It was the shape.

Her shoulders, the gentle angle where they met her neck...another curve started speaking to him. Then more of them. Her hip, her wrist...he had to paint this.

Transfixed, he didn't leave the doorway. Instead, he drank in the fascinating shapes, the rippling aqua light washing over her, dappled touches of orange barely reaching her from the house. The water echoing her shape in organic sweeps of gossamer light and shadow. The serenity of her quiet aimless drift.

Goosebumps flooded his body as her hand lifted to gently drag fingertips through the surface of the water, rousing waves of reflected color.

It broke the spell.

She'd been pure organic shapes until she acted, and suddenly she was real. The scene had a story. Her private moment was no longer private. Any second now, she'd move, turn, flee. She floated in that instant before discovery, naively still before facing this threat of...what? Exposure? Shame?

Her vulnerability struck him in the chest. He had to paint this, tell this story.

He tried to burn the sight of her into his mind before this miracle slipped away.

. . .

Celia let her mind float along with her body, imagining the lines she might paint. She could be blue this time, curved. No more straight red lines, no bridge. Turquoise circles, teal scallops, aqua crescents.

Oh, the moon! She smiled to herself.

A crescent moon reflected in blue water. Celestial for Celia. Finally, an idea! Sure, it was a little dumb, but she had to start somewhere.

The breeze whispered over her, making her shiver and her nipples harden painfully. She felt relaxed and revived, but discomfort began distracting her. It was time to go inside. That warm bed with Andrew to snuggle against would feel wonderful. She'd be able to sleep now.

She turned over and slipped under the water's surface, aiming for the shallow side of the pool. Her hair flowed back, and she came up near the stairs, gasping for a fresh breath.

As the water streamed from her face, she opened her eyes to see León frozen in the doorway, his eyes fixed on her, one hand holding the door. Her mouth flew open, but she didn't make a sound.

For a long moment, they stared at each other in silence. The water stilled as her movement stopped, calming into quiet waves. Then she shivered involuntarily as the cold struck her again. The water beading on her shoulders felt icy in the faint breeze.

"I'm getting out of the pool," she said softly.

• • •

León flinched as the real world abruptly snapped back into focus.

He ducked into the pool house and then right back out. He didn't even know why he'd gone in. It was a little late to disappear inside.

"My robe," she said. "On the chair. Will you get it?"

He peered toward the pool's edge until a darker shadow on one chair became evident. Numbly, he retrieved the robe and took it to the pool stairs, holding it open for her.

She waded to him, water streaming off in chilly runnels as she emerged. Looking only at her face, he laid it around her shoulders, then moved aside. Her teeth chattered as she ascended, pulling the robe closed, not bothering to put her arms into the sleeves.

For another moment, they just stood there, looking at each other.

León's head was still full of curves and tranquility and exposure, envisioning how to embody her moment on canvas.

He realized suddenly where they were, that she was real, chilled and bewildered in front of him. She would speak. She might be mad. He had to save what he could of what was in his head.

"Give me a minute, please," he implored. He rushed into the pool house, leaving her standing in cold shock.

• • •

What was happening? What did León mean, 'give him a minute?'

She hadn't expected him there. Had he been watching her? Intruding on her private moment? But why?

She should go, disappear, dry off, wrap a towel around her hair, and warm up next to Andrew.

Instead, she followed León.

He was sitting on the daybed with his pad and charcoal, frantically sketching. Two loose pages were already on the floor next to him, and as she entered, he pulled off another and laid it atop them. He continued pulling the charcoal across the page in long mad strokes.

"Why—"

"Wait, please," he begged.

Was this how real art happened? Was she finally seeing it? He didn't look happy.

After six pages, his shoulders relaxed, his hand stilled. Finally, he turned his eyes to her as she stood in the doorway, shivering and dripping.

"I'm sorry. I saw lights from the pool, I didn't think it might be you." He rose to whisk a towel from the shelves nearby and hand it to her. "Your hair, it's still dripping. You look cold." As she wrapped it around her head, he stacked his sketches carefully on the nearest easel. She finally put her arms into the sleeves of the wet robe as he sat.

"I'm going inside," she said. But after a moment, she

moved to sit on the bed next to him.

He took a deep breath, then exhaled heavily.

"I didn't mean to intrude. I promise I just saw a painting." He waved a hand toward the easel. The top sketch was just shapes, but she could see a nude floating in the water, defined in graceful, strong, sweeping lines. It was good, like his caricature studies of her posing before.

"I didn't think you'd notice me out there," she said.

He turned his face to her, then ducked his head. He looked down at his hands, clasped together, elbows on his knees.

"I didn't mean to intrude," he repeated. "I just went to look, then...the shapes. I needed to get them down."

She looked back at the sketches, then dropped her eyes to the rest of his pages and work scattered on the floor. Wait, one of Andrew's small sculptures was sitting on the table directly in front of them. What? She shivered, feeling a flutter in her stomach.

Her eyes went up to the canvas right behind the sculpture. The black line was unmistakable—her body was painted on the raw linen. She felt a hum of alarm deep inside.

"What is going on here?"

"Inspiration," he said. "I swear. I'm not being creepy. I'm not spying or thinking anything. I just got inspired by this curve here." He turned the sculpture away and traced a finger down it. It was the same as on the canvas. "Then I saw you out there. It's good. It'll make a painting."

Celia didn't spend time with artists without learning about inspiration. She'd seen them stop mid-stride to try and capture it. He was inspired by her?

"I could have just posed, you know."

"I think you have to now."

She sat up straighter. "Have to?"

"Well," he said, "if you want to see it finished."

"No one's asked if I do."

"Will you, then? It's going to be good. I can feel it." He turned his head to stare at the sketched lines intently. "The water, you, so honest and unguarded, and that line—"

"Wait. I was out there trying to find my own inspiration."

The import finally struck her. "I was going to paint something about floating in water! You're stealing it from me?"

He whipped his face back to hers, hair flying.

"Stealing!"

"You were teaching me, but now you're going to use me as a subject? Do you have to take my idea for yourself?"

• • •

León leapt to his feet at the accusation, wounded. "You don't own the idea! If I don't paint it—"

She stood as well, eyes flashing. He faltered, her uncontrolled glare unexpectedly distracting.

"You're going to make a much better one than I can," she cried. "Why should I even bother now?"

Her face was fierce, wet ringlets trembling, lips pale with cold. But she wasn't hiding. She was unrestrained. He couldn't resist.

"What emotion are you feeling right now?" Her eyes widened. "Right now!"

She shook her head in disbelief. "Anger!"

"No, that's not it. Deeper." He saw the struggle on her face, eyes lowering as she tried to feel inside. Then she looked back up, surprise on her face.

"It's none of your damn business!"

She stalked out, back to the house. He followed. He had to.

"Celia, wait!" She was already at the open door. "Please." She turned to decline but stopped when she saw his face.

"What."

"I'm not using you," he pleaded, "but I can't not paint this. It'll be in my head until I do. I won't be able to do anything else until I get it out."

She turned away, but he laid a hand on the door jamb, blocking her path. She had to listen! She settled for turning her face from him, chin lowered.

"León, I'm cold."

"Please pose."

"León."

"Celia, what can I do? I can make this up to you somehow.

I'll work with you after, do more lessons. We'll get you painting too. It'll be different. Yours will be good."

He was pulling out every excuse he could think of. She had to agree.

. . .

Celia felt embarrassed for him, negotiating like a child begging for a treat. Leaning back against the door frame, she clutched her robe closed. She'd stopped dripping but was still cold. A shiver ran through her as he moved in closer, eyes on hers, willing her to agree.

"That was my time for my own thoughts," she said. "You want to show everyone."

"I do, but it won't be like that," he said. "When you see, you'll understand. It won't be you. It'll be abstract, anonymous." He bit his lip, holding his breath.

"I thought I was alone!" She heard her voice raising and lowered it to a whisper on the last word. Alone? No need to wake Andrew. This was complicated enough.

"Celia, that's the point. You with your guard down, it's beautiful. Please."

He swayed closer, determined eyes still focused on hers. The pressure she felt to give in ran deep.

She wavered, and he saw. Eyes narrowing, he let his hand slip down the door frame, and she couldn't help the gasp that escaped her.

For a moment, she thought he was reaching for her and felt more thrill than fear. The shock of it! Her heart was pounding, her skin tingling where she'd anticipated his touch. His arrogant pressure was...exciting? That couldn't be right.

The surprising response in her body snuffed out her defense. She was already accustomed to giving in to his will, had been practicing for weeks. Why bother fighting him? He'd paint it even if she said no.

. . .

He saw her capitulate. Shoulders softening from defiance to resignation, eyes lowering, the subtle tilt of her head in concession. He wanted to paint that change too, capture the transition from stiff to submissive. He could paint a whole series of her.

"I'll do it," she said. "I'll pose."

She was so fully his in that moment that he raised a hand to trace her skin. He trailed her collarbone thoughtfully with a finger, seeing brush strokes in his mind. This delicate surrender limned in a pale and fragile yellow against a field of warm colors, umbers and golds. This was the second painting.

The soft light from inside the house fell across the angles of her neck, barely highlighting the warm lines and shadowed planes. His fingertip wandered to her throat, thinking of the exact color right there on her skin.

"Beautiful," he murmured. Her breaths were coming quicker, the pulse visibly beating in the hollow of her neck. The closer he looked at her, the more he realized he'd missed. Her lines were perfect. He wanted to see more, inspect her in a low light.

His gaze traveled up to her lips.

"Celia," he said. The revelation of her was overwhelming.

"León," she whispered, "I can't."

His eyes snapped back to her face. "Can't what?"

Their position finally dawned on him. He'd backed her up against the door frame, wet robe clutched to her, towel still wound atop her head. Her eyes looked up at him, liquid and bright, full of soft distress. He'd felt quite possessive then, touching her like he owned the lines of her. But she wasn't his—he'd barely gotten her to agree to pose.

Painting. This was about the painting. He could draw art out of her, but she had to agree to help. This wasn't the right way. He stepped back, lowering his hand.

"I'm sorry," he said. "I got a little caught up." He rubbed the back of his neck, trying to break the spell. "I'll go. It's just the painting."

"Just the painting," she repeated, shivering.

León shook his head, trying to come back to himself.

"In the morning, okay? Can you sit tomorrow?"

She nodded mutely, eyes wide. He noticed his breaths were coming faster too. He'd gotten too engrossed in seeing her. It was excitement over the series he could make.

"This will work out," he said. "You'll see. I can do it."

• • •

She wondered who he was trying to convince. He said he was leaving but stayed. What was he waiting for? For a moment, she'd thought he was about to kiss her. Her stomach fluttered at the thought.

She remembered Andrew, her friend, his friend, lying naked in the next room. She couldn't kiss another man with one in her bed already. That wasn't her.

She straightened, pulling the robe even tighter over her neck. León watched her hide herself, disappointment in his face melting into resolve.

"Right. Good night." And with that, he turned and strode from the doorway.

She watched him retreat, mouth open. So, his onslaught really was just about getting her to pose? He could have refused to leave, kissed her like he'd been so clearly considering. She would have let him. She shouldn't, but she would have.

Indignant, she closed the door.

That man! Why was she always one step behind him? He'd spied on her, chased her, made her agree to pose, and now she was regretting him not acting even more badly?

She could never figure out what to expect from him. Sometimes kind, then sarcastic or annoyed. Tonight he'd been intense, nearly possessive. It was like he'd suddenly discovered her, though she'd been here the whole time.

Being seen. She'd thought so hard about that earlier. Tonight, he'd seen her. Was he going to act differently now? Every day he was different. Why try to guess how he'd be tomorrow?

The uncertainty was tiring. Being seen by León was intense. He seemed to strip her down to parts he could put on a canvas. Should she show him the rest, the parts that didn't curve or reflect light? Would he want to see it?

She sighed. Feeling things was even more exhausting than hiding from them.

She went quietly into the bedroom.

Andrew was sound asleep with no idea of all the activity

that night. He'd have been sorry to miss the drama, she thought with a wan smile. He stirred as she climbed back under the covers and hauled her close under his heavy warm arm.

"Happy birthday," he murmured as he captured her again. He sleepily kissed her cheek, then neck. It felt as comforting as she'd imagined earlier. Andrew was a safe place, a warm, enthusiastic, loving friend, but just a friend. She'd never felt the urge to be seen by him, and he'd never truly put in the effort.

She'd tell Andrew tomorrow that this had definitely been the last time. No more benefits other than friendship. Whether it was with León or not, Celia wanted more.

Ten

Andrew woke her with kisses, the sun through the skylight already traveling toward the bed. They'd slept late! She realized he was angling for an encore and hastily claimed a need for the bathroom. Inside, she threw on underwear, sweats, and a tank top from the hamper, forgoing a bra. The tank was tight enough for now.

"Aw, I was just kidding, girl," he said as she came out. He pulled on his pants from last night.

"Unless I was into it."

"Well, obviously." He grinned.

"It's not my birthday anymore. Come on, I'll make you waffles."

He swatted her playfully on the behind as she tried to dodge, giggling.

They tumbled out of the bedroom together, him shirtless, her hair tousled. Standing at the kitchen island, looking at the large sculpture Andrew had left there last night, stood León.

He paled as he took them in.

Oh no. No.

"Hey, León," Andrew said. "Want waffles?"

León looked back and forth at them, denial written across him, then settled on Celia. His face drained of expression. Stiffly, he raised the cup of tea in his hand.

"Just came in to see when Celia can sit today. After breakfast?"

She nodded mutely. She'd been doing that a lot around him lately. He left without another sound, and Andrew exhaled.

"He didn't expect me," he grinned.

"No, I don't think he did."

"I think I forgot to mention that we sometimes still...."

Still. Andrew really ought to be past tense by now. They'd been lazy about it.

"Yeah," she said. "Hey, about that."

He raised his eyebrows, then tilted his head and sighed. He knew her well.

"I think it's time to pull the plug on this, Andrew. I like it!" she hastened to say as he opened his mouth to speak. "I just think we're not moving onto new things because we're okay with the old ones."

He sat down at the island, not arguing. He'd looked more surprised when she agreed last night. "You have a new thing in mind?" he asked.

"Not really. Not yet. But I will one day."

He pushed around the salt and pepper shakers, pouting a little.

She reached out to touch the photo from Trevor, still sitting on the counter. "I think you do, though."

"I do?" He looked up and noticed her hand on the frame. His eyes got serious very quickly. "Oh."

"Maybe you two...?"

He fiddled with the salt, not looking at her. "I don't know. Maybe. I don't know."

"You're not going to find out if you can stay here when you're lonely."

His mouth quirked into a crooked smile. "Oh, I can do both."

She smiled back. "I can't."

"So, there is someone?" he asked.

"No. Maybe. I don't know."

"León?"

Her eyebrows shot up. "Why does everyone keep saying that? Just because he's staying out there?"

"His face just now," Andrew asserted. "When he gets all poker-faced, he's hiding something. He hasn't made any moves?"

She instantly flashed back on León last night, one fingertip tracing her skin, murmuring 'beautiful.' She felt her face flame.

"He did!" Andrew said. "I didn't know. He told me last night he wasn't interested in you. I wouldn't have asked to stay if he'd said otherwise."

Celia looked at him, stricken. "I'm posing for him, that's all."

"We'll see." He sighed. "I figured this was coming, but not because of León." He touched his sculpture, then looked back at Celia. "I'll skip breakfast if that's okay with you. But I'm going to check with León on the way out. Make sure we're cool."

"Don't say anything, please," she urged. "About me, I mean."

"I'll just check that he and I are good," he said. "I'll leave anything else to you."

He went to put his shirt on, wrapped his sculpture carefully, and hefted his bag. Then, with one last kiss, a little wistful, he was out.

• • •

"Hey," Andrew called as he opened the pool house door.

León huffed quietly. He stood near the southern windows, frowning at a canvas but not painting. Andrew came to look too. The paint was wet and incomplete, but base layers of blues and greens and purples showed the direction it would take. A bold black line curled up, across the colors.

Andrew looked carefully. "You've seen her doing her night swimming thing."

Obviously. Andrew didn't have to rub in how well he knew her. He'd just seen that for himself.

Andrew turned to look at some nearby sketches, also of Celia. "She's a good model. I tried to tell you."

León frowned. He'd been doing it all morning. All week.

Andrew looked directly at León. "You know, last night you said you weren't into her."

"I'm not."

"Then you don't mind that I spent the night."

"Nope."

"You should know—"

León cut him off with a glare. "I'm not interested in her that way. I don't need to know anything."

Andrew met his eyes, then shrugged, taking León at his word.

"Good luck," he said a little pointedly.

León finally smiled a little, sheepish, and touched his friend on the arm. Andrew smiled back. They'd be okay.

As Andrew left, León went back to staring through his canvas.

It was better that she and Andrew were still an item. He was embarrassed to remember his behavior last night. Watching her swim nude without her knowing. Chasing her down to demand she sit for him. Backing her up against the door, touching her without asking. She'd told him more than once that she was cold and wanted to go, but he'd badgered her. He owed her an apology.

Andrew had been lying in her bed while he pestered her.

He'd thought about her all night, the sight of her so vulnerable in the water. He hadn't tried to stop the memory—he needed it fresh. He'd been up painting at dawn.

It was good that she was with Andrew. It took the whole sexual chemistry thing off the table. It was a common problem between artists and their models. Seeing them nude, obsessing over the details of their bodies, the tension you needed to keep things dynamic...it sometimes devolved into sex. It was a human reaction, after all. No one needed that complication here.

It had been a surprise, though, seeing them come out of the bedroom. An unpleasant one. For a moment, he'd felt betrayed. She was his! Not personally, but her body was his to paint. Obviously, that wasn't true, but for a moment, he'd forgotten.

It was great that she and Andrew were together. It'd keep him focused on the painting.

He heard a knock and steeled himself. Apology first, then work.

• • •

Celia entered, nervous about which León awaited her.

She hadn't changed her clothes. No way did she want him thinking she'd cleaned up for him. As she walked from the dim interior into the light from the large windows, she could see his face get blacker with each step.

He was back to irritable, apparently.

"I need to apologize to you," he gritted out.

He what?

"No," she said. "I said you could come in any time. I'm sorry that Andrew and I surprised you."

He scowled fiercely. "Not about that. I don't care about that."

"Oh."

"I apologize for watching you last night. I should have left."

"Well, yes," she agreed slowly. "You should have. But I understand about inspiration."

"Do you?" His expression eased a fraction.

"Not personally, not yet," she amended. "But I know artists. I get what happened."

"Okay. Thanks. And," León said, swallowing, "I apologize for chasing you down and bugging you to sit for me." When she tried to shake her head, dismissing him, he cut her off. "You kept saying you wanted to go, but I didn't listen."

"I said I was cold," she replied.

His eyes fell, his face finally looking as though he was sorry. "And I apologize for touching you without asking."

But she hadn't minded. It had been natural in the moment. Still, when he put it that way, he had a point.

"It won't happen again," he said.

Oh.

For a moment, their eyes met, both with faces as carefully blank as unpainted canvases.

He looked away to start straightening his brushes. "I'd like to get the shapes right now," he said, "but the light's wrong for final work. Would you sit again tonight, out by the pool, so I could get the colors?"

"I can do that."

"Thanks. For now, could we put you...." He looked around at the floor-to-ceiling windows, flooded with morning light, then looked to the pool. "If we lay you here, on the floor, I could move back here. That's about the same angle as the pool. We'll put down some blankets so it's more comfortable."

"All right."

"You can leave on underwear if you want. I just need shapes." He began pulling blankets and pillows off his bed and laying them on the floor. She began undressing.

She sneaked a few looks toward him as he worked. He moved quickly, impatiently, but his face was like stone. Usually, she could see exactly what he was thinking, his expressive brows and mouth giving away everything. However, Andrew had said he only looked impassive when he was hiding something.

He finished laying out blankets and stood by his easel with pillows in his hands to cushion and prop her up where needed. He didn't turn his head as she got down on the floor.

Bare except for her underwear, she stretched out on her back, raising enough to lean on her elbows, waiting for him to direct her.

• • •

Her underwear was pink.

León snapped his eyes to the canvas. He'd thought for a second she was fully nude, reclining on his bedding in the sun. His mouth was dry, his heart pounding. Damn. Come on, he'd worked with nude models since art school.

He had to look back to give direction.

Wow. The sight of her.

The sun was golden and fragile, with that gentleness you only got in the mornings. It reflected off her skin, rounding the curves away from the window with dark gold shadows, the parts of her near the window glowing. Her skin was warm and softly textured. The fine hairs on her arms burned like filaments. A long stripe of sun running down her thigh made a beautiful line he'd need to capture, but not for this blue painting.

Okay. Get it together.

"Could you lay back like you were last night, please? Arms out to your side." She did so. "Your right leg bent a little at the knee, please." The left leg had that glorious stripe of sun, the other a shadow that mirrored it, hinting at roundness and motion. "Arch your back just the smallest bit." It made her look more as though she were floating. "Head back, please. A little less. Okay, hold that."

He approached with the pillows, tucking one under her knee to help support it. His eyes met hers, asking silently if it was comfortable, and she nodded. He bent closer to push one under her arched back, having to tuck it firmly when it bunched against the blanket. The back of his hand brushed against her skin, and he clenched his jaw.

The final pillow went under her neck and shoulders, helping to support her arched neck. The line of her bared throat made him swallow hard. He studiously avoided looking elsewhere.

"Good?"

"I'm fine."

At least one of them was.

He went back to his easel. *Tranquilo.* Breathe.

Come on, relax.

No use. The tumult inside him refused to be stamped out, so he just focused on building an impression of her in paint.

León worked furiously, grimly, layering shadows of shapes onto the canvas, painting with his eye instead of his head as he'd taught her. Much of it would be covered by vibrant colors later, but the shadows were the foundation that would give the painting depth.

Eventually, his motions slowed. He needed to move on to colors but couldn't until they recreated this setup tonight. But, he didn't want to stop now! The way she glistened in the sun, a sheen of perspiration on her chest—oh.

"Getting hot?" he asked. He glanced at his phone nearby. Thirty minutes, he'd painted. He hadn't even enjoyed it.

"A little warm," she said, her throat tight.

"Let's break."

He walked away, but his eyes stayed drawn to her as she slowly relaxed out of the pose. Watching as tension melted out of her was irresistible.

Clothes! Give her some clothes.

Her tank top landed on her shoulder when he tossed it at her. She pulled it on, the sun glowing through the pale khaki fabric as she stretched it over her.

Wiping her forehead with a hand, she clambered off his blankets and went to sit on the bed, the only seating area in the shade.

She looked across the room at the canvas on the easel. Did she see where it was going? It was raw and unfinished, layered with shadowy abstracts of a woman's form. Weightless respite. Naiveté.

"That's what you saw last night?" she asked.

"It's got a way to go."

She fanned herself. Water! He pulled cold bottles from the fridge and strode closer to hand her one, then leaned back against the shelves across from the daybed, crossing one ankle over the other. Casual.

He watched as she pulled up her feet to sit cross-legged and opened her water. Jesus.

Pink underwear, for god's sake. The only piece of clothing she owned that wasn't brown or gray, probably.

"It's just impressions," she said, waving her water at the easel. "I mean, just shapes."

Discuss the painting.

"You see it, right?" he asked. "I'm trying to capture the idea. Not, you know, you."

Her knees were shades darker than the rest of her. Too much time cleaning? Should he hint at that in the painting? It was a part of her story.

"I do see it," she said, lifting the water to her lips, then lowering it with a glint in her eyes. "If it were a painting of me, I'd just be a red line."

He finally smiled for the first time today. "I guess."

Look at her, relaxing, making jokes! Sitting there cross-legged on his bed, wearing only underwear and a tank top, the hand holding her water lowering to her side. She lifted the other hand to comb back hair clinging damply to her neck. A peek of loosely creased stomach appeared as the tank top inched up.

She was all contrasts! Rough pointed knees and soft curvy midriff, shielded by crossed limbs but untroubled by her near nudity. Triangles, arcs, circles—

"I might try a blue line in tomorrow's lesson," she said, her eyes amused over the bottle as she finally took a drink.

Tomorrow? But he needed to work! "Yeah," he said. "Hey, about that."

Mid-sip, her eyebrows raised at him.

"I was thinking about yellow. I mean, a yellow painting. Another one. Of you."

"Oh. You mean, right after this one?"

He scuffed a shoe, shifting his weight against the shelves. Celia's shoulders were drooping already.

"The exhibition is not many weeks away," he said, "and I need more good paintings by then. If I'm already thinking of another, I could do a series. If you'll pose."

That amber vision from last night, her close-up capitulation...that memory would stay vivid, waiting as he worked through this blue inspiration.

He crossed his arms. "Is that okay with you? Would you help me until then, and we concentrate on lessons after?"

She nodded slowly, her mouth turning down. "I can wait, I guess. If you need my help."

Well, he really owed her now. Face lowered, he smiled ruefully up at her. "I better create something good."

"You're determined. You work hard. You'll do it." She looked again at the unfinished painting, face wistful. "Maybe I can learn by being a part of the process."

He finally took a drink, relief welling up in him. Space, time, and inspiration! He'd been so worried a key piece wouldn't show up.

"You're integral to this," he said. "You inspired the story, then posed." He looked down and chuckled. "Andrew kept telling me how well you sat. He was right. I'll have to name the series after you if that's okay."

She inhaled and looked away, trying to go pokerfaced but cheeks flushing.

"Celia," he said, warningly but with a smile in his voice.

She looked back at him. "Fine," she conceded, lips curving up. "I feel happy about that. Flattered."

She may be turning pink, but her shoulders weren't tensing like they usually did. She was getting better at admitting to feelings, or at least more comfortable around him. She leaned forward, face turned up to him, the light tank top gapping away from her tanned skin. She was playing with that necklace Kelsey had given her, her voice soft. He raised a hand to scratch an itch on his own neck.

"What?" she asked.

He blinked. "What do you mean, what?"

"Why are you glaring at me like that? What did I do?"

He ran his hand through his hair. He'd stopped listening to her at some point, lost in his own thoughts.

"I'm not being present. Give me a second to think." Okay, he was looking at her. For painting! She was getting under his skin, and he didn't like how it made him act. He just wanted so badly to paint her. He was starting to get pushy. Andrew had known, had asked him to be nice to her.

But how could he keep her posing until he'd painted her enough? And how long until it was enough? The yellow painting wouldn't be the last in his head. How could he keep himself from creating around her, turning her until he found all her parts, drew every movement and feeling—

He realized she was still waiting, those damn eyes watching him, brows furrowed. Why did she always look so worried? He was the one under pressure here. He had to think.

"León—"

"Just...wait." He held out a hand to stop her, and stop her it did.

She stood up. "Take all the time you need. I'm going."

"Going! Why?"

Her eyes snapped. "You're not in charge of every conversation we have, you know! You beg me to sit for you, apologize, and then scowl at me the whole morning. You bark at me to say what I feel, then tell me to stop talking. It's rude!"

What? "You asked me—"

"Oh my god, stop talking! You may be an artist, but you're not better than me. You still have to treat people with respect. Maybe I don't know how to talk about my feelings as well as you do, but I'm not stupid!"

"I know that!" he shot back. "You just always look like you're afraid of what I'm going to ask, and it's irritating!"

"And you're always glaring at me like I'm doing something wrong!" She put her hands on her hips, leaning forward at him. "I can learn if you ask questions nicely like you did at first. You're not the boss of every conversation. You want me to pose? Then stop being so...so inconsiderate!"

She stomped out, trying to slam the sliding glass door, but it caught in the frame as she hauled too hard. With an exasperated huff she left it open and stalked away.

León stared in shock, then burst out laughing. She was expressing herself now!

He held his stomach, howling as she climbed the grassy slope, those swaying pink underwear a perfect punchline. She failed to slam the slider to her house too, and her indignant squeak doubled him over. A moment later, as he convulsed, a door slammed from inside, loud enough that he could hear it. She'd found one that made noise!

He wiped his eyes, gasping. Jesus, he'd needed that laugh.

He sighed deeply. It actually wasn't funny at all. Just the sight of her trying to slam the door in her underwear, it had been too much. All the emotional ups and downs and lack of sleep had to come out somehow. He shook his head, kicking at her sweatpants on his floor, then walked over to his painting. He was going to have to apologize much better this time. He sort of wanted to paint her mad, though.

Okay. Okay, *Tranquilo.* Think.

She wasn't wrong. He'd been acting high-handed. He liked that she wasn't going to let him push her around. He hadn't intended to test her limits, but if he was being honest, he'd done it anyway.

And as long as he was being honest with himself—which he clearly needed to do—he had to face something else. This wasn't just about painting, and he wasn't glad she was with Andrew. That was straight bullshit.

When he saw her swimming last night, he'd been thinking of a painting, but not this morning. Today, he'd been irritated because what he wanted was to join her on those damn blankets.

That, he'd be keeping to himself.

He couldn't paint more until tonight, so filled the crawling time with fantastic plans for the 'Celia' series in his head. He'd already started her in blues. An angry depiction in reds seemed inevitable now. The obvious continuation was a rainbow of paintings. Yellow submission, her face turned up to him like a sunflower. A blithely nude Celia dancing in a field of green grass, maybe. Celia in orange, reclining in dawn light with that gleaming stripe down her leg. Purple, Celia draped in shadowed and moody shades of dusk. The stories would reveal themselves as they painted.

By sunset, his eagerness was unbearable. He paced the pool house, thumbs tapping against his thighs, but Celia didn't come out. She didn't answer his texts either. This apology would have to be stepped up.

He dressed in his nicest clothes, realizing again that he needed some actual nice clothes. He picked flowers from her yard and knocked on her sliding glass door.

She came into view, dressed again in gray. She looked at him blankly, then turned to walk back into her bedroom.

Fine.

He pulled up a chair next to the glass, sat down, and waited.

ELEVEN

Celia was done talking to that infuriating man. At least for today. Maybe tomorrow too.

His appearance at her back door, dressed in his blazer and carrying flowers, was preposterous. How many apologies must she accept in one day?

She retreated to her room to read. When León knocked again after a few pages, she started a loud playlist on her phone.

He'd give up. Not talking was her damn specialty.

The chapter's end blindly reached, she peeked to make sure he'd left. Still there! He'd turned the chair to watch the dying sunset, the bright lights of her living room illuminating his dark hair, curling up at the ends against his shoulders.

He wasn't getting the message. Celia marched over to knock on the glass. The quick turn of his head sent his hair flying.

"What are you doing?" she asked through the glass.

"I'm here to apologize." He held up the flowers.

"You did that this morning. I'm not talking to you again today."

He raised his chin. "I'm not going anywhere."

She turned on her heel and returned to her room, heart pounding.

He could sit there all night if he wanted. She had her book and her phone. She'd fall asleep comfortably, and he could sit and think about what an ass he'd been. It was nothing to her.

The knocking started again after a while. His muffled voice was audible even through the glass and the music.

"Celia, let's talk, please."

Absolutely not.

He kept knocking. "I'll just listen, I won't talk."

Step in the right direction, but no.

"You're right about everything."

Definitely getting better.

"I'm going to sit here all night, Celia!"

Good.

If she went out, it'd be a win for him. She waited silently, superior. Her outburst earlier embarrassed her, but shutting people out? Oh, she could do that.

Unbidden, she relived the same thing running through her head all day. León, glaring as she posed this morning, ogling her like she couldn't tell he was doing it. Then, talking down to her after! It was so unfair. So rude. So arrogant.

A shiver ran through her as she pictured him scowling down at her.

Okay, it was sort of hot. Maybe she'd wanted him to give in, lunging onto her with the passion he so clearly held back. But still!

Four more songs played before she looked again. Still there, sitting in the full dark, only the back of his bowed head visible. It was more siege than apology. What did you call a person under siege? A hostage? She looked it up on her phone, but couldn't find the right word.

A faint tapping sound started repeating in the living room, like he was rocking gently against the slider. He wasn't actually trying to open the door, right? When the sound stopped, she peeked again.

What was....

That...that brat had painted on her glass doors! Big white letters that he must have done backward so she could read them.

I WAS WRONG

I'LL DO BETTER

ONE MORE CHANCE

PLEASE

That paint had better come off!

She tore open the door to find him standing there with paint and brush still in hand. He'd dripped some on her patio too! His face was a mix of expectation and wariness and pleasure and not nearly enough contrition.

The cocky bastard!

"You are proving me right," she spat. "You're still trying

to control the conversation! I say I'm done, and you camp out here for a few hours?"

He opened his mouth to speak, but she wasn't finished. "No means no! I shouldn't have to tell you that!"

She could literally see the wheels turning as he sought a justification but failed.

His posture caved, his eyes stricken. He looked so ashamed that she had to suppress an urge to relent. After a taut moment, he simply nodded and left to go to the pool house.

Celia spun to inspect the paint. Who'd asked for big gestures? Had she been unclear that she didn't want to talk?

He didn't have to look so beaten just now. Unless...was she blowing things out of proportion?

You're always overreacting, Celia Rose.

Shaking her head, she went inside. He could clean the window himself—to her standards.

Aware that he could see her from the pool house but wanting to take back her space, Celia paced. Living room to kitchen. Kitchen to living room.

She'd never seen him cowed like that. Happy or mad, he was always confident. Had she been too hard on him? He'd been trying to apologize for what felt like hours. He was wrong, but he'd tried, and now she'd just made him feel bad too.

You say you're sorry, Celia Rose!

Ugh, Mom's voice in her head again? She'd been doing better since lying her way out of the calls.

León was an artist, temperamental, expressing himself, feeling out loud. That was what she wanted in life. How could she fault him for doing it?

Fine. She was trying to get better at this. What was she feeling right now?

Guilty.

She turned to look back at the door.

I WAS WRONG

I'LL DO BETTER

ONE MORE CHANCE

PLEASE

She texted him.

He knocked on the door moments after she hit send, and she let him in. She'd practically worked herself up to apologize to him, but he beat her to it.

"Celia, I'm sorry. Truly sorry. I'll listen more, I won't get carried away. I—" He paused, eyes widening, and clapped a hand to his mouth. It tugged a small smile out of her.

"León," she said, shaking her head. "Sit down."

She moved to her place by the stove as he obediently climbed onto a stool, obviously dying to explain but keeping his mouth shut. About time.

She leaned on the countertop, onto her elbows, her hair falling forward. "I'm sorry I yelled at you, but you have to stop bossing me around." His earnest dark eyes weren't quite contrite, but he was at least silent. She took a deep breath. "I'll still pose, but I don't want to stop the lessons."

He nodded eagerly. "That's fair."

"I can only pose for a few hours a day. I want something to work on when you're busy."

"Of course. Yes."

"We start back up tomorrow." She leaned in to make her point.

He nodded again, glancing down at her chest as she leaned forward. Did he think she didn't see things like that? "I promise, Celia," he vowed. "I'll do better."

His relieved grin made her feel better. She'd stood up, and he was okay with it! She wondered how long he would make it before pushing her again.

He leaned onto the island, settling on his elbows like her. "Is it too late to pose tonight?" he asked. "I can't paint anything else until this one is on canvas. Will you?"

She sighed. So, not long then. "Would I need to be in the water?"

"No, next to the pool is fine. It's the lighting I'm after. The colors. I can finish and be ready to concentrate on your lesson tomorrow."

She reached up to tuck her hair behind an ear, checking the clock on the stove. She had hours to go before bedtime anyway. Better to work than to think. She was tired of thinking.

"Okay."

"Can we start now? Please, Celia. If you want to." He reached across the kitchen island to brush back a strand of hair she'd missed.

Her heart leapt at the intimate touch, bounding in a sudden rush of beats, and her startled eyes leapt to his. Cheeks going red, he pulled his hand back.

He swallowed. "Do you want to?"

Heartbeat loud in her ears, she nodded. She did want to. "Go set up. I'll be out in a minute."

His smile lit up his entire face, and he raced for the sliding doors.

Celia exhaled hard. Good lord, León was so confusing! How had she gone from angry to this? His bravado just worked on her. He asked for what he wanted, and she rolled over. Maybe he could teach her how to do that.

She stretched, arms reaching, waist twisting, trying to relieve the tension that had silently built all evening. The stretches warmed her muscles but did little to quiet her still-racing heart. She went to her room and undressed, slipping on her robe.

She was only posing, like this morning. No reason for butterflies. Breathing deeply to calm herself, she went out to the pool.

León had already hauled out his easel and supplies, the blankets and pillows from his bed, and the half-finished painting. He practically skipped as Celia came out to the pool.

"Palette is ready!" he announced.

• • •

León had set up on the narrow flagstones between the pool and the retaining wall overlooking the canyon so that both blue pool lights and orange house lights could reach her as she posed.

Celia slipped off her robe and lay back on the blankets as she had this morning, but fully nude.

He forced a straight face, ignoring the warm lightness coursing through him. That was just relief that he hadn't had to ask her to undress.

Again, he posed her, watching from the vantage of his canvas. Leg slightly bent, back arched, neck back. This time he could judge the light hitting her skin. The image in his head, burned there since first seeing her in the water, was coming back to life. Finally, there she was. Perfect.

He stopped for a moment, struck, staring.

Celia.

Heat sparked under his skin. Every time he looked at her lately, that urge to touch her hit him. He shook his head. He was here to paint. She was here to pose, not to welcome him on those blankets.

Would she, though?

His brow furrowed. When he'd touched her last night, she'd said no. Andrew had been in her bed, twenty feet away.

"León?" she called.

He shook his head again, coming back to the present. The painting. He had to complete it before opening some Pandora's box.

"One second, I'm getting the pillows."

As he had this morning, he kneeled to prop her knee with one cushion. His hand skimmed the small of her back as he slid the second pillow under it.

Impulse overpowered caution. He couldn't help looking over her hipbones, the line of her ribcage, her bare breasts giving in softly to gravity. Her curves made his fingers itch.

He looked away before she opened her eyes to see him staring. It was unprofessional, intrusive. They were friends, but it was still wrong. This entitlement he felt wasn't real.

Well, it was real—it just wasn't based in reality.

He moved to place the third pillow under her neck, tempted to let his fingers graze her there accidentally. Touch her cheek, maybe. His eyes dropped to her mouth.

"Are you comfortable?" he asked softly, still crouched down.

She opened her eyes, looking up into his with a smile. He felt it all the way down his spine.

"It's fine. Not so cold when I'm not wet."

He smiled back. Casual. "I'll try to go fast."

"Do what you need to do."

He swallowed, his eyes flickering to her lips again, then returned to his easel. He clipped a light to his palette so he could use it when needed without ruining his night vision. Then, clearing his mind, he tried to recapture the feelings of the night before.

The serenity, the slow echoes of water expanding from her shape as she floated, the watery turquoise ripples of light that washed over her skin, the golden kisses of light from the house glancing off the peaks of her body.

The calm before the storm.

He exhaled deeply. *Tranquilo.* Gone were the morning's annoyances. It felt right this time.

Finally, *finally*, he started brushing colors onto the canvas. His heart lived in these simple motions. He knew where the colors wanted to be, how they layered. The painting created itself. There was truth here, this vulnerable shape she made. His brush caressed the curves on the canvas as though it was his hands on the woman before him.

The tip of his brush lingered over the spot where her neck met her shoulder. Looking up, León almost expected her to shiver, ticklish.

He tried not to look too often. The urge to finish what his brush started was tempting. He tried to channel the rawness into the paint instead, but he did have to look sometimes. Celia was his model.

His, dammit.

León painted as fast as he dared. If he could put those defenseless shapes on the canvas, stroke after stroke, his hands mastering her shape...

His breaths were coming a bit fast as he finished. There was touching up to complete later, but he'd gotten it. She was captured.

"Celia," he said, clearing his throat as the word came out rougher than expected. "We're done. I hope that wasn't too long."

"Already?" She didn't move, giving him time to be sure.

"Already. You can get up." Again, he hated to see her move

but had to release her.

She slowly sat up. "That wasn't long enough to get cold."

He found her robe and passed it to her, eyes down. Turning his back, he struggled against words that might inflame the moment. Casual.

Instead, he started moving his equipment back inside. The hard-won painting absolutely needed time to dry without the danger of being disturbed.

He set it inside on the easel by his cot, where he could contemplate it. The dim lamp over his bed illuminated it gently. It was good. More than good. Maybe the best thing he'd ever done. The honesty and intimacy he talked about with Celia were there.

He calmed himself, forcing his breathing to return to normal. It was over. He'd gotten his painting without doing something rash.

Outside, he heard a splash in the pool. Head snapping up, he went out to see.

• • •

That had been the edgiest session Celia had ever sat through. The way his whole body tensed when he looked at her! The cords on his forearms tightened, his head lowered, his long fingers stiffened on the paintbrush. He was all coiled energy, almost predatory, threatening to charge if she provoked him.

Maybe she should provoke him.

Her body had thrummed as she lay there, feeling a lovely rush of electricity every time his black eyes raked over her. He'd almost kissed her, once. If he would drop that tight control and kiss her now, she'd welcome him. The idea sent a shiver down the length of her body, nearly disrupting her pose.

Once he'd released her, she sat motionless on the blankets, alive to every movement he made. Repressed energy had welled up unbearably, but she remained still. He'd barely disappeared inside the pool house when she jumped up, shaking her hands to release some of the wild tension. It wasn't nearly enough. The pool in front of her was a familiar solution.

• • •

León came out to see her underwater, the splash from her dive already fading, her shadow streaking toward the far end of the pool. She reached the far end without coming up for air, turning and pushing off while still submerged.

She surfaced in the middle of the rippling pool, stopping to tread water as she gasped for a breath. Water streamed from her as she breathed and moved and found him watching.

The sight of her floored him. Her wide eyes found him as they had last night, just seeing him. Waiting.

She was a goddamn siren.

There was only so much he could take. He was pulling his shirt off before he knew he wanted to. Alarms started going off in his head. This might be a horrible decision. But the way she watched him, expectant, was an invitation. Right?

When he could look again, her eyes were roaming his shoulders and arms. Possible regrets were abandoned. He began unbuttoning his jeans.

• • •

Celia's heart pounded. He was coming to her.

She drank in the sight of him, lit by the wavering aqua light. León was surprisingly fit and lean. His loose casual clothes had hidden strong shoulders and solid biceps. That long dark hair curling up at the ends, what would it look like wet against his neck?

He left on his dark boxer briefs, pushing the jeans past his muscled thighs. And then he was in the water, descending the stairs into the pool.

León waded out, rousing waves, the water rising up his ribs and chest. He stopped, though, where the bottom of the pool began falling away, hesitating before going out deeper.

Beginning to tire of treading water, Celia moved closer, swimming quietly until she could touch the bottom. Shoulders and chest emerging as the slope rose beneath her, she silently invited León to act. Where was all that bravado now?

He seemed too spellbound, watching her approach.

Celia exhaled slowly. Provocation it would be.

She stepped closer yet, the water level falling to her ribs, her wet breasts revealed. He'd seen her bare, but this wasn't posing anymore. This was for him.

He admired her openly, rapt. Glinting water ran off her in rivulets, leaving little droplets clinging to her skin. And then she was within reach, daring him to act.

He didn't resist, closing the small distance between them.

Lit from below by the turquoise glow of the water, he brought dripping hands up to cup her face. His dark eyes had no fight left in them, just want.

He tilted his head, leaned in, and then his lips were on hers.

The water drifted away, the sparkling city, the warm light from the house. All that was left was the stars.

Her whole body sang. León's lips were so soft, their touch gentle on hers, exploring the feel of her for the first time. Then, not gentle. His fingers tightened as his mouth moved on her roughly. Her head swam, wanting even more.

León finally pulled back to look at her, breathing hard. He searched her face with a terrible hope.

She broke into a wide smile.

"Wow," she said softly.

• • •

Satisfaction flooded him. Letting his hands fall from Celia's glowing face, he drank her in, lost. She was bewitching, radiant for him. Just him.

"*Reinita*," he said, a smile finally playing at his lips. A drop of water on her cheek lost its hold and trickled down to her neck. León raised two fingers to trace its path, making her shiver.

A dinging sound, faint but out of place, cut through the moment. León glanced at the pool house. His phone. It dinged again. "That chat of yours," he muttered.

Damn, Andrew. Not now.

He turned his eyes back to the glorious Celia.

Andrew and Celia.

León froze. What was he doing?

He released her, drawing back. His jaw clenched. He shouldn't have let himself get carried away, no matter how much he wanted her.

Celia glanced at the pool house, uneasy. "What is it?"

"Last night, you said no," he said tightly. "You said, 'I can't.' Because Andrew was there, right?"

She nodded, worry starting to stiffen her.

"Why is tonight different?" he asked. León could see her starting to withdraw already, her shoulders tightening, her smile dimming as the openness he found so appealing faded into reserve. But Andrew was a true complication!

Celia's wide eyes searched his. "It was my birthday."

He stared, then chuckled at her unexpected answer. Looking up to the stars, he exhaled heavily. "I picked a hell of a time to ask that, didn't I?"

She held her silence until he looked back. The water around them stilled.

"It's none of my business," he said. "But—"

"It is now," she said.

His hands retreated slowly into the water, weak ripples radiating out to engulf them both. "But," he continued, "everyone said you broke up last year."

"We did," she answered, appeal in her eyes. "We just sometimes, still...you know him."

León sighed.

"But that's over," she insisted. "For good. We agreed yesterday."

León shook his head slowly. "Just yesterday. Maybe this isn't a good idea today." Her disappointment was clear; her shoulders started to droop. "Maybe we should think about this. Do you want to think about this?"

• • •

Celia teetered. Her mind told her to hold back, hide what she wanted. It was safer, and he had denied an interest in her this whole time. If he didn't want her, was she making a fool of herself? She shrank from the risk.

But he did want her, enough that she'd seen him struggle against it. And that feeling when he really saw her...she wanted to take a chance. She couldn't hide forever.

"I'm tired of thinking," she said.

This time it was her dripping hands rising, reaching to

touch wet fingertips to his smooth skin, tender palms sliding behind his neck. That hair was going to get at least a little wet.

She glimpsed a reluctant smile as she leaned in to kiss him. Lightly, softly, she touched her lips to his, her fingers finally threading through that hair she always wanted to touch. When he leaned in again, she let her wet hands roam down his neck and onto his chest, glorying in feeling his breath catch.

His head was shaking, though.

He raised his hands to hers, catching them between their bodies and holding them still. He was stopping her, and she bent her head, conceding. He rested his forehead against hers, both of them panting softly.

The silence drew out. The chill in the air made itself known.

• • •

León struggled to stay motionless, his heart thrumming inside his chest, his body demanding that he just caress her bare shoulder, pull her close to feel her entire soft, warm length against him. One word and she'd be his. But if he kissed her again, he wouldn't stop.

Alone, naked, with more than one bed at hand, the whole night ahead of them? Heaven.

But his entire world was at stake! He'd finally painted her. What if he couldn't paint her after? What if things just went wrong somehow?

"I can't," he said, regretting each syllable.

Her hands, still trapped in his between them, sank in his grasp. Her water-beaded shoulders drooped, but that expressive little chin inched higher. She nodded, eyes closed.

"Let's get out," he said, low. "You're...you're too tempting."

It was an uncomfortable process, leaving the pool while studiously not looking at each other, shivering, her grabbing her robe and him a towel near the door. He'd hung it up to keep her away a few times now.

She joined him there at the pool house doorway, stopping barely within arm's reach. She was a shadow against the bright lights of her house above them, her dewy face barely lit by the pool.

"I'll see you tomorrow for my lesson?" she asked.

"Yes."

There didn't seem to be more to say. Except...she'd started to turn for the house when he grabbed her hand.

"Thank you for accepting my apology. And for posing."

She smiled, but he felt a slight tremble in her.

Jesus. Tell me I'm an idiot, Celia. I'm not the boss of everything. Say you're staying, just walk in to my bed. I'll follow.

Instead, he squeezed her hand and let it go.

"Sleep well, *reinita*."

Her eyes widened. "Good lord, León. How could I?"

She turned and left.

TWELVE

León's first sight upon awakening was Celia in blue.

He'd tossed fitfully all night, submerged in half-sleep, dreaming that she swam circles around him. She was made of living paint, a teasing sprite of liquid curves and lashing waves of blue. The urge to touch her burned in him, but he dared not. His fingers would smear her deep lacings of color.

He awoke at dawn, as usual, to find his canvas shining in the morning light. Dozy and bemused, León breathed in her image—glowing Celia, revealed in luminous hues. His fleeting dreams faded as bright pride swelled. Beaming from his bed, inhabiting every brush stroke, he reveled in the painting's story. The colors were raw, visceral and daring, that all-important curve striking upward, its path true and exquisite through the fluid blues and golds.

It was perfect. The best thing he'd ever done.

He got out of bed and walked closer, in love with the colors in early light.

Her shape floated at peace, vulnerable and authentic as one can only be when alone. It whispered echoes of the womb, relief from fear, trust in support of dark water. It was the most honest image he'd ever painted, and though she was the subject, it came from inside him. He'd felt fragile before, and it could have looked like this.

The top third of the canvas was darker with indigos. A hint of a hovering threat. That sweet faith of hers wouldn't last because disaster lurked. But oh, how precious until then!

What a story. She was wonderful.

He looked up at the house, windows dark, sunlight climbing from behind the roof.

The litany of paintings ran through him again. Yellow, red, green, orange...he'd been seeing stories in her from the first day. Unable to look away, at times. Yes, it was attraction, but more. She was a mirror, showing him truths that he later realized were inside him, ready for his canvas.

Smiling, he basked in the painting again.

What truth was in this for him? Vulnerability, threat...wait.

A chill ran down his back.

Who was under threat here? She was the subject, but it came from inside him.

He froze as the implications sank in. Could he paint a threat to himself without knowing? Why did paintings keep getting away from him? He was failing again!

The lurking shadow in the painting was coming for him, ominous and suddenly terrifying. He looked up at the house again, its dark western windows mirroring the night's end.

He had to get out and think, get away from this painting, from her. Escape.

He quickly dressed, grabbed his phone and wallet, and ordered a ride-share on his way out the side gate.

• • •

Celia awoke to white walls reflecting too much light, her bed stretching too wide for just her. Maybe that would change soon.

León had kissed her.

She hugged her arms around herself, letting herself feel the thrill. Why try to squash her excitement about last night? She felt special when he looked at her, like he genuinely saw and welcomed her. His curiosity about her thoughts and feelings was intoxicating.

Why try to smother the enthusiasm? León encouraged her to be aware of how she felt, and this felt delightful. Celia chose to feel it, hopeful about taking a chance for once. A glance at the clock showed that she had a few hours before noon when León usually came in for lessons. Well, staying busy in the morning was never a challenge.

She hummed in the shower and capered once or twice as she tidied her rooms.

León didn't show up at noon. No text, no appearance at the back door. Maybe he was a late sleeper. She didn't really know.

He would come. He'd promised.

She could always kill time cooking. The gang was coming tomorrow night, so she started a small pork roast braising in the dutch oven with onions and carrots. She smiled as she chopped, determined not to let anything ruin this happy mood.

An hour passed. She texted León. No response.

Feeling uneasy, she checked again that the craft room was ready. She would paint her idea of the moon in water today. Just because León had painted her floating, that didn't mean she couldn't have a different interpretation. A story, she reminded herself with a quick smile.

He'd kissed her. He'd promised to help today.

Celia finally went to the pool house, her buoyancy precarious. She could see his precious blue painting from where she stood, but not well. She didn't want to trespass but finally let her gaze slide to the right, to the daybed. Empty.

He'd left.

Not everything revolves around you, Celia Rose.

So, her day would be the common crawl, the same clock dragging its same recalcitrant hands. The urge to clean hit her. Lord, not again.

She would paint on her own. No waiting around on León! She could make a hundred paintings if she wanted.

She started her own lesson in the craft room. First, *Tranquila*. Second, mix some paint.

She brushed on wavy turquoise and aqua lines that might look watery if one squinted. A crescent moon floating in the middle, not white, because she knew better. She understood its reflection should look broken up, hitting different waves, but the mechanics defeated her. A knot built in her chest, refusing to loosen.

Was it an opalescent moon floating on water? Celestial Celia existing? Not remotely. It was a ridiculous painting, the worst cliché she'd ever seen. She'd never be able to figure this out on her own.

A heavy sigh escaped her. Another painting to stuff into a cupboard. Celia regarded her room with its white cabinets and sensible lighting, her art list supplies tucked away in organized baskets behind tall doors. She hid the clutter of her attempts to find a talent, a voice, all proving she had nothing unique to offer.

You're nothing special, Celia Rose.

Stop thinking like that!

Maybe she should just clean the whole room again, throw out everything. She eyed her practice paintings, stacked on the table next to her, the top one featuring her stupid bridge of black lines. A dull ache formed behind her eyes as she confronted the familiar image.

Apparently that was her only story.

Her dad, looking back from the top of a bridge, holding out a hand.

She stared at the simple arch of the bridge, feeling it mock her crescent moon. The same shape, but so much harder to paint as if it were reflected in a broken surface. No wonder she painted the dumb bridge so often; it was easier.

Why hadn't León been here to help her? His betrayal wrapped around her, cold and constricting.

Why was she always so alone? What was wrong with her? All her life, she'd faced this. Her mother would never stoop to helping her, of course. And Dad had been gone.

The bridge had been easier.

"Oh," she whispered, a raw realization dawning.

Dad could have kept trying, could have protected her from Mom's fists and insults, could have stayed so she didn't have this death hanging over her all her life. A worse betrayal settled in her stomach like a stone.

Her dad, looking back from the top of a bridge, handing something to her.

Shock numbed her, new understanding freezing her in place. She'd never seen it this way before. He...he'd handed her his terrible, black burden. *Here, you carry this now.*

Oh, how could he? It was so unfair!

Tears pricked at the corners of her eyes, the injustice of it all burning as sharply as saltwater on cut skin. Then her heart thudded wildly, her control finally exhausted.

Fuck all of them for failing her! León included!

She'd show them painting!

The small tube of black paint couldn't match her boiling fury. She had more—quarts of glossy black from some pointless project. Muscles tense, her movements jerky with urgency, she knocked over baskets pulling a can from the cupboard.

The lid wouldn't come off, but the spoon in her tea would work. As she pried and mixed, she glared at the empty white wall in front of her.

Fuck this bare blank world, too!

The room shrank as her rage expanded to fill every corner, and she hurled a spoonful of anger into the space before her. Long slashes of black appeared across furniture and wooden floor, wall and ceiling. Breathing got harder, rage burning her face. Who was quiet and responsible now?

Her breath became ragged, her skin prickling with the heat of unleashed anger. Exhilaration sang in her bones as she threw wide slashes straight from the can, ignoring the spoon entirely. She barked a laugh, hair swinging into her face. It didn't matter. She didn't need to see. The paint could land where it wanted.

She shouted with each swing. Screamed.

The paint ran out, and she stood still, panting.

How's that for expressing emotions, León?

The thought pulled the plug on her anger, and her control snapped back into place. Even this she hadn't completely done for herself. A hollow feeling settled in her stomach, the echo of her actions ringing loud in the sudden silence.

Drained, she left the spatters to dry where they landed. At least life triumphed on one wall. At least one couldn't paint clichés when one wasn't even aiming.

What a useless display, Celia Rose.

The aftermath of her outburst left her chilled. Closing the door on the mess, she mechanically washed her hands in the kitchen. Stoic, she pulled the meat from the oven. She cleaned the painted apology off the back doors.

She was pathetic. Good lord, she'd thrown a tantrum.

You're impressing nobody, Celia—

Oh, shut up, Mom!

There must be something better to do than clean, right? Something smarter than her usual response? Andrew, he would talk with her, make her feel better.

But he might tell León she'd called. León would think she was looking for him. As if! She hoped she never saw that liar again!

Kelsey?

She'd been so encouraging when Celia had opened up, however ineptly.

"I'm at work, hon," Kelsey said when she called. "But the shop is super dead today. Come down. I'll pretend to sell you clothes, and we can chat."

• • •

León had asked to be dropped off downtown, homing to the urban center that would feel familiar. It didn't, though. LA buildings were blocks long, the reflected heat arid, sidewalks deserted amid streams of anonymous cars. A tropical ghost town.

Whatever. He walked as he used to in New York.

His best painting was an accident. Celia had shown him something he didn't know he felt and hadn't recognized even as he painted.

This image of vulnerability and threat came from inside him, and if he was painting blindly, he had to confront himself. He couldn't keep finishing work without knowing why it did or didn't speak.

What was the threat?

Long stretches of pavement passed under his feet, fenced parking lots herding him down straight streets.

He missed New York. LA was alien, the streets punctuated with palm trees so tall that their feather-duster tops receded as afterthoughts. Up at Celia's was worse, isolated from even her neighbors, a long drive away from anything. He missed his parents and sisters, cousins and friends and crowds. Was that what was throwing him off?

No, he'd had the same trouble there at the end. He was the problem.

What was he afraid of?

He was afraid of not being able to paint. Well, what if he couldn't? What else would he do? Who would he be?

He'd be nothing. Painting was his whole identity. Without it, he'd be absolutely nothing.

The sharp pang in his heart told him he'd found the threat.

It made no sense. He'd just done outstanding work and should feel encouraged. He could show himself, his parents, and the world that he could succeed at this.

Dad had worked two jobs to pay for his art school. His parents had sacrificed their days and their own hopes, all to improve their children's opportunities. He had to prove it had been worth it.

He couldn't sacrifice too. He couldn't compromise. He couldn't let anything distract him.

He reached a wide intersection, a confluence of estranged air-conditioned cars with tinted windows closed. A bodega beckoned halfway down the block to his right, but he stubbornly chose to cross the street.

Was Celia a distraction or a mirror? God forbid, a muse? León tucked a sweaty lock of hair behind his ear. That woman.

Why her?

She inspired him, no question. He itched to paint her again right now—he had urgent colorful plans. What was it about her? Did they share even one thing in common?

A wide concrete gully yawned under León's straight sidewalk, now a bridge. A laughable trickle of water braided down the middle. They called this a river? It was no Hudson.

Celia kept painting bridges, but not well. She'd have to move on to the next item on her art list. She wouldn't like that.

They had that in common, actually. Looming failure.

He winced.

She didn't even have art to turn to. No wonder she was so wan, drifting quietly through life.

They didn't have any choice here. He had to create well, and here she was to show him the paintings inside him. She wanted a purpose, and here he was, helping her make the art she couldn't. They had to keep going, paint and pose, or come to nothing.

She'd shown him that in the blue painting. They were both vulnerable.

A vibrant mural on a building ahead came into view. They did that right here, the colors reaching up three stories.

He surrendered to the obvious conclusion. Celia was his destination. Dammit, call her what she was. His muse. He'd have to delve much deeper into her truths and humbly admit how they applied to him. He just had to convince her, which wouldn't be easy after running away.

Jesus, she must be furious.

He tried to think of the right words as he took a ride-share back to her place.

He knew he should have answered her text. He'd fumbled that, just like he'd fumbled the kiss last night. She'd seen before he did that they needed to get closer.

How could he top the last apology?

She wasn't at her place when he got back. It surprised him, but what choice did he have except to wait? He sat on the daybed with a sketchpad and charcoal. Maybe he could get in some studies until she returned. He looked up at the empty interior of the house more than he looked at the paper.

• • •

Kelsey jumped up, excited, as Celia entered the empty clothing store on Melrose. The decor was fashionably monochrome and world-wearied, the scent expensive. Celia fit right in.

"Yay!" Kelsey said. "It's been so dead today. I pulled some clothes for you to try."

"I don't really want to buy anything, Kelsey."

"Just look at them. You might."

Well, it was something to do.

Celia followed as Kelsey picked up an armful of knits and started for the dressing rooms. They may as well talk there. The location didn't matter.

"Now," Kelsey said, still excited. "I have thought of you every time I see this dress. Of course, the rest would all look good on you, but please, at least try on this one."

She held up a thin knit dress, soft and luxe. The color was a deep turquoise which instantly put Celia off. She preferred neutrals. She just didn't have the energy to tell Kelsey no.

Slipping into the stall, Celia let the heavy curtain fall behind her. Maybe it'd be easier to admit to her friend what happened today if she didn't have to see her reactions. She began removing her blouse as Kelsey hovered outside.

"All right, spill," Kelsey said. "I can see you're upset. What happened?"

Celia pushed her skirt to the floor, avoiding looking at herself in the mirror. If Kelsey could see she was upset, what was her face doing? She'd tried to look blank.

"I spent the day waiting around for a man who didn't want to be there," she finally said.

"Charlie did that to me once, and I didn't talk to him for two weeks. Who was it?" Kelsey's yellow shoes appeared at the bottom of the curtain. "It was León, wasn't it."

"León." Celia snorted. "It sounds silly to even say it. Why would I wait for that selfish, pushy, arrogant, lying...." She couldn't think of words that were bad enough.

"So, what'd he do?"

The blue dress was so soft Celia considered hugging it like a comforting blanket.

"He said he'd help me paint today, but he just disappeared. I sat around like an idiot for hours."

"Maybe he had to go somewhere."

"He didn't text or call." Celia gathered the hem of the dress to put it on.

"Huh. Did you text him?"

"He left me on read." She pulled the dress over her head and wiggled it into place.

"The bastard."

Celia looked in the mirror finally, tightening the wide belt at the waist. The dress looked okay. But her face, oh no. She looked old. The disappointment had drawn lines on her. Her eyes filled with tears, thankfully blurring the image.

Kelsey must have heard a sniffle. "Oh, honey, oh no." Her shoes danced impatiently outside. "What did he actually do?"

Celia cleared her throat, struggling for control. "He kissed me."

"I knew it!"

"But then he sent me away and disappeared after he promised to be there. I can't believe I waited around like a fool. I don't even like him." The tears were coming harder now, her voice thick.

Kelsey's hand appeared on the edge of the curtain. "Celia?"

Celia reached up and pulled the curtain back, grimacing through the tears as she met her friend's eyes. She'd never cried in front of her. She felt so exposed. But Kelsey stepped in and enfolded her in a hug.

"Aw, honey," she soothed as Celia began crying in earnest. "He doesn't deserve you."

"I do like him," Celia hiccupped. "I thought he'd come."

Kelsey stroked her shoulder. "It's not foolish to wait for someone to show up when they say they will. That's what adults do. He's wrong for not showing up."

Celia was slowly bringing herself back under control. Being hugged helped—it felt good. Kelsey was being so nice.

"He'll come back and be sorry, and I'll let him explain," Celia said, low. "He's always getting his way. He overwhelms me. Yesterday he sat at my door for hours until I let him apologize."

Kelsey reared back to search her friend's tear-stained face. "He what?!"

Celia exhaled heavily. "He brought flowers. He painted an apology on the back doors. I wouldn't talk to him, but he wore me down."

"Wait, you've been having drama like that, and I'm just now hearing about it?" Kelsey bounced, provoked.

"He painted me. And he kissed me in the pool in the dark, and he was jealous of Andrew."

Kelsey's mouth fell open. "Andrew, why?"

"He spent the night. On my birthday."

"Andrew is involved too?! Good god, Celia! You can't leave me out of things like this!"

Celia smiled weakly through the tears. "He said he had to get out of the pool because I was too tempting."

Kelsey let Celia go and fanned herself. "Okay. I would have waited around too."

"But this morning, he just left and never came back."

"He really is a bastard," Kelsey said with a frown. "I didn't realize. The coward."

"What do I do?"

Kelsey finally noticed the dress. It was well-made, graciously hugging Celia's curves, the wide neckline draping delicately just off her shoulders.

"You are going to wear this dress and show him what he missed." She reached up to adjust Celia's black bra straps so they didn't show. "Make him regret it, Celia."

Celia shook her head, unsure.

"Look," Kelsey said, "what do you honestly want?"

Celia wiped at her face, considering. "I wanted art," she sniffed. "I wasn't looking for this."

Kelsey waited as Celia struggled.

"He just...makes me feel things."

THIRTEEN

Uncounted sketches later, León finally saw movement inside Celia's house. She emerged from her entry hall, walking loosely, dropping her purse on the couch. She'd been out socially, it looked like. The turquoise thing she was wearing...wow. Look at those curves, blue like the pool, like his painting.

He had to convince her.

She was going to skewer him, and he deserved it. He walked up to the house, to the slaughter.

She noticed him at the sliding door, illuminated by her interior lights. Her face didn't go blank as it usually did. Instead, her eyebrows lowered, eyes narrowed, cheeks flamed red, mouth flattened to a line. León felt a mixture of pride and worry at her feeling and showing anger. And disgust. Disappointment. Hurt. Uh, not good. He was going to have to work hard to explain.

He looked a plea through the window, shocked when she came to open it rather than disappearing again.

"You stood me up," she said flatly. "Do you have a good reason?"

"Yes and no. Yes. Please let me tell you."

She opened up and waved him in. He was too relieved to wonder why.

She went to lean against the kitchen island in her familiar spot at the stove, but when he walked toward her, she waved him sharply to the other side. Contrite, he went where she pointed but climbed onto his knees in one of the tall stools, leaning his upper body on the island closer to her. She retreated to lean against the sink, keeping distance between them.

He drank in the sight of her. Her skin was smooth and tawny against the turquoise dress, the palette necklace's thin chain draped over her collarbones. She stared at the floor instead of meeting his look, hair pulled back so he could clearly see her cheeks, rosy with pique all the way to her ears.

He felt irrational jealousy toward the person she'd dressed up for. It could have been him.

"You said you'd help me paint today," she said, reaching to straighten the knobs on her stove. "It meant something to me, León."

He hunched into his shoulders, looking up at her. She glared at the stove, refusing to meet his eyes.

"I know," he said, uncomfortably aware that his actions had spoken louder.

"You promised," she said quietly, throat tight.

"I ran away," he admitted, ducking his head to try and catch her eyes. "I'm sorry, Celia. Again. I've been really stupid this week."

"You've got that right." She looked toward the dim hallway, maybe toward escape. "What about me is so scary that you ran away?"

"It's not you," he said, "it's the painting. It scared the hell out of me this morning, and it took a while to figure out why." He frowned, impatient for her to relent and look at him.

"You ran away from your own painting?"

"Yes." He reached out a hand, but she pulled hers back until he withdrew. "Look, I have something big to ask you, and it's too soon, and I don't know how you'll take it."

The knobs on the stove couldn't be straighter, but she went back to aligning them minutely, her knuckles white.

She wasn't going to relent more than this. It was time to ask.

"Do you know what it is to be a muse?"

She finally met his eyes briefly, disgusted. "I'm not dumb."

When she clicked a knob once more, he laid out across the island and impatiently pulled it off. He turned it over and over in his hands as her lips set into a line.

"But do you know about the relationship? It's an artist being inspired by you, using you for their works." He shifted again on the chair, pulling back to sit higher. "Art needs absolute transparency. Truth is hard to see in yourself, so the artist shows the truth of their muse, like holding up a mirror. It needs a lot of trust."

Gently, he set the knob down and slid it silently to her. She didn't acknowledge it. Instead, she leaned against the sink again and crossed her arms. The flush rising up her chest and neck told him she was only acting at being impassive.

"Trust, after today?" she asked. "You can't seriously be asking me to be your muse."

He rubbed the back of his neck. He wasn't asking. She already was.

"I've never had a muse," he said. "It's intimidating. It can go wrong." Leaning toward her again, he tucked his hair behind an ear and took a deep breath. "Even when it works, it can go wrong. Like John and Yoko. Some of his best work was done with her. But he was credited, and she was treated terribly. We got great art out of it, but she bore the cost."

She looked at him fully, finally, rubbing absently at her arms. "And this is how you're selling it to me?"

He didn't mind her sarcasm. She was looking at him, talking with him. He could get through to her. "There's Frida Kahlo and Diego what's-his-name. She painted him a lot. They were together for decades."

"Happily?"

"Okay, not always. You see why I got scared?" He hopped down from the chair with a loud scrape. "The thing is, it's too late. Come on, I can show you."

As he rounded the island, her eyes widened in mistrust. She'd see, though! He could make her understand. He reached out to take her hand, and she fell back another step.

"León, I don't want—"

He grabbed her wrist and gently pulled. "It's important!"

He began towing her, and she followed, not quite unwilling but still holding back.

He dragged her to the pool house, muscling open the sliding glass door and setting her in front of the painting. The lamp by the bed shone too dimly, but he found his clip light near the easel. He shone it on the artwork, the blues glittering like jewels. She would see.

• • •

Celia felt her resistance crack. She'd sworn that this time

he wouldn't break through her guard with his outrageous ideas, but...the painting. She hadn't seen it up close since he finished. She could feel it like the statues in the Louvre. She felt the same flush of recognition, the same understanding of what was being said.

Vulnerability. Her body, floating in flashing water until you looked closer. Made of abstract shapes and shadows, more layered colors than body parts or skin, that one curve he seemed obsessed with as the main feature. The figure was calm, but maybe it shouldn't be. There was a whiff of menace. How had he shown that?

He was good. So good.

He held the light further back. "I realized this morning. Look. See this shadow?" He traced the darker area with a finger. "It's threatening. I thought it was your story, but it's mine."

She followed his gesture but not his meaning.

"It panicked me," he said low. "I don't want to be blind to my own work. But, Celia, it proves that you're my muse. I painted you but accidentally painted me."

Her heartbeat fluttered as he turned to her, flicking off the little light and fidgeting with it nervously in his hand. The low orange light illuminated half of his face, suddenly close to hers. His eyes were nearly black, pinning her in place.

"The truth is," he said, "we're both threatened. I can't fail at painting, and you can't fail at...well, being a part of art. We can succeed if you just agree!"

She eyed him. He believed that?

At her silence, he reached out to grasp her upper arm with his free hand. She tensed, but his fingers were gentle.

"You are already my muse," he insisted.

His fingers tightened. Her whole body flushed awake as he stepped closer.

"Think what we can make," he said. "This painting is just the start. We both need this."

She felt a tremor in his hand, his palm hot on her skin. He believed that.

She finally spoke, but weakly. "What would I have to

actually do? Just pose?"

His chest swelled, anticipation lighting his face. "Posing, yes, but I have to learn you, learn everything you feel. It could take months. Maybe more."

The pressure she felt to say yes! But he'd been right earlier; it was too big, too soon. And all about him, his grand, intense wants!

"Why me?" she stalled.

She realized his breath was coming fast and shallow. Hers too.

"I don't know why," he said. "I just know it's you."

Her body answered with a slow, hot burn.

Her head needed to rule, though. She needed time to think. Telling him everything she felt for months? Was he going to be this mercurial and intense the whole time? Did he even deserve it after today? There were too many questions.

He was waiting impatiently for her assent, breath held. The compulsion she felt to just agree was daunting, but she would not be bullied into this. She would decide for herself.

"Maybe," she finally said.

His eyes widened. "Maybe?"

"I need to think."

He flinched, color draining from his cheeks. "You need to think?!"

He fell back a step, staring at her. His brows lowered, jaw dropping. He was shaking his head, his shoulders squaring to face her.

Careful, her body thrummed. She tensed, poised.

León's hands raised, fingers raking through his hair, but he winced as the clip light still in his hand tangled and caught. With a frustrated cry, he turned and threw the light into the darkness of the pool house. It clattered loudly across the floor.

Celia lurched backward. "Don't!" she gasped.

He turned pained eyes back to her and saw her cower. "You don't understand," he groaned. He wilted in front of her, hanging his head, rubbing a hand over his eyes and forehead.

"León," she breathed.

He took a deep, shuddering breath. He'd clearly thought she would agree. As she watched warily, he moved to the daybed and sank onto it.

"Why do you have to know right now?" she asked, fingers clasped tightly in front of her. "There's time, right?"

He exhaled heavily, running his hands through his hair successfully this time. "I've been searching for this kind of inspiration my whole life," he said. "If you won't help, it's over."

She shook her head, not understanding.

"I'll have to go home," he continued, "find something else to do with my life."

She sidled a step forward, still alert. "I don't see why you'd have to give up painting."

He raised an imploring face to her. "I'm not going to find inspiration like you again. I've been looking!" He pressed his hands against flushed cheeks. "My parents gave me this chance, and I'll fail them. This means everything."

He looked so desolate that she sat next to him gingerly. She never could see someone beaten without wanting to help, and this was...him. León.

"Your parents will still love you, right?" He wouldn't meet her eyes, shoulders hunched, uncharacteristically still. She leaned in. "You're more than just a painter, you're their son. You're kind and thoughtful. You care."

He shook his head silently. Celia still didn't understand his conviction but empathized with his despair. That feeling she recognized.

When she was low, Andrew's antidote was to say he liked her for who she was. She braced herself and tried to find truth for him.

"I would like you even if you didn't paint, León. I'm...I'm sad to see you doubt yourself." Her throat ached from the tension, her hands trembled. The risk of putting this into words! Her whole body quailed, vulnerable. "I like you when you're just you. You're more than a painter to me."

• • •

León hadn't realized how much he'd wanted to hear

that—from anyone—until she said it. Painting was what made him special, excused his worst behavior. Without it, he'd just be lousy, egotistical León.

He really didn't deserve her kindness after today.

Hell, she was telling him her feelings, all on her own, just to make him feel better.

When he still didn't respond, Celia shuddered out a breath, gathered her legs under her, and stood.

Leaving?

He raised his head, reaching for her hand. She paled, eyes flying to his fingers grasping hers, then to his face as he stood up slowly. He didn't let go, his implacable hand gripping hers. No fumbling this time. He stood close, his hand tightening on hers.

"I like you too, Celia," he said low. "Don't go."

Celia's tentative face slowly eased, lips parted, her breaths shallow. Look at her, every tense line softening, a lovely understanding stealing across her face.

Her face lifted to him, and she met his lips with her own.

The soft touch of her mouth stunned him, finality thudding in his chest. This time he knew he was all in. Andrew could go fuck himself. Celia belonged to him.

His other hand lifted to stroke her hair, tucking it back so he could cup her cheek, holding her face to his as his lips tasted hers for the third time. His thumb stroked her cheekbone, feeling her shiver under the touch.

His blood rushed, but time stood still.

She brought up her own hand, sliding it behind his neck. Her fingers tickled, cool and smooth, brushing softly against his skin. She parted her lips to tentatively touch her tongue to his.

Jesus, why had he fought this?

Tightening his grasp, his mouth moved on her roughly, hungrily, his tongue seeking hers.

• • •

Celia reeled, heat radiating through her. He felt so good!

León swayed back just enough to look at her once again. In the low light, his eyes were black with both satisfaction and hunger. His intensity, when focused, hit like a sledgehammer. Celia felt it deep in her chest.

"*Reinita*," he murmured.

Oh, did she like that word. It made her smile.

His crooked smile in return stole her breath. He stepped back long enough to tug his shirt over his head.

How could her heart pound even harder?

His shoulders flexed as he tossed his shirt behind him to the floor. She eagerly took in his warm brown arms, the sensitive hands she'd imagined on her. She shivered.

Eyes roaming lower, she saw those loose jeans, the waistband falling a bit too low on his hips.

She swallowed, her skin anticipating his touch. This was happening.

His breaths were quickening, matching hers. He stepped up to her again, slipping two fingers under the blue-green dress at her shoulder, skimming her skin as he traced the wide neckline to find the single button. His fingers tickled the baby hairs at the back of her neck as he undid it, raising delicious goosebumps. Eyes still on hers, he drew the soft fabric toward him, letting it collapse to her waist.

She undid the belt for him.

His fingers stroked delicately down to her collarbone, his eyes darkening when she inhaled sharply. Each touch burned her skin, and she struggled to remain still, just feeling where he would wander next. His hands arrived at the straps of her bra, and he slid them down her arms to expose her to him.

Breath catching, León took each of her breasts in his hands, lifting them slightly with his palms, brushing his thumbs over her nipples, watching them harden. His lips curved, the desire in his eyes melting her. His hands moved lower, eyes following, skimming down her sides to the dress, hanging to her waist.

One hand found hers, and he lifted it in the air, directing her to turn almost like a dance. With her back to him, he unhooked her bra and tossed it into the darkness, then pushed her dress off her hips to the floor. When she started to turn back, he stopped her.

"Wait," he said, moving closer behind her, face hovering

over her shoulder. "Look."

She followed his gaze past her to the dark window. The low light reflected her murkily, the polarized film tinting her nearly-nude reflection a faint pearly purple. She had only moments to be amused before his hands traveled around her from behind to caress her bare skin.

• • •

She closed her eyes and let her head fall back, but León watched their reflection.

It was another moment he had to remember—to paint. In his arms, Celia was warm flesh and scent and movement. He was free to explore her, the anticipation of it making his head swim. But in the window, he saw a shadowy mirror woman, faintly iridescent and indigo. She was shrouded, unobtainable, beckoning him with welcoming curves he could see his hands roaming, but untouchable.

He finally pressed his length against her from behind, pulling her body to him with one hand on a breast and one on her stomach, starting to slide lower. She inhaled as his fingers inched under the band of her panties and turned her head to his for a kiss. He was still sneaking a look at the reflection, his breath racing.

"León," she murmured. He finally looked at her, the supple human within his reach. "If you are thinking about a painting, so help me god...."

"I'm not," he said. "I mean, I can't help it."

She turned in his arms. "That light is going off."

She left him, going down on one knee on the daybed and stretching to reach the lamp. He had just one second to see her, reaching forward with one arm, one leg stretched back to the floor. What a line, what a pose! Then the light was off, and he could only see her faintly in the reflected aqua light from the pool outside.

In a quick motion, he began unbuttoning his jeans. Celia turned back, standing, watching his fingers, lips parted.

He was done looking. It was time to feel those places his brush had gone first.

• • •

Celia sat back on the bed, the remnants of astonishment transforming into fierce hunger. His eyes were on her body, devouring the places he was about to touch.

When he stepped closer, she helped with his clothes, taking the opportunity to caress that tawny skin on his hips. He trembled, his hands clenched a fraction, but she saw him force himself still while she revealed his stiff erection, then bare thighs. He kicked the jeans completely off and then joined her on the cot, a knee between hers. She leaned back onto her elbows as he pushed gently on her shoulder.

"I've thought so many times about touching you here," he murmured, running his fingers up her side. The curve he found so fascinating. It tickled. Possessive satisfaction flowed in his voice. "Jesus, Celia."

Roughly, he leaned into her, sliding an arm behind her and tilting his head down for another kiss. She couldn't resist running her hands up his back, wanting him just a few inches closer.

His other hand roamed her side and hip, his mouth still on hers. He explored it with his tongue, pressing her back onto the pillow. It was exquisite torture, every fiber in her aflame, demanding more touches, more kisses. She knew from his uneven breathing and the slight tremor in his hands that he was done waiting too. She began drawing him atop her with demanding hands, urging silently that this slow torment give way to action.

He gave in. His weight pressed her down, his hips hard between her legs, his rigid cock hot against her belly.

"León," she pleaded.

He rested his forehead against hers, lips parted, breathing heavy. His weight shifted as he reached down between her to position himself between her wet lips, then slowly pushed in. A fiery shock wave traveled up her entire body. He groaned as she tilted her hips to meet him closer. She clutched his shoulders, pulled his head to her neck, and finally ran her fingers through that mane of sleek black hair.

He slowly stroked out, then back in, pressing hard. Every part of their bodies fit together perfectly. It was mindless, just the joy of touch and pleasure. He was fighting to go slowly, lavishly, but losing the battle as she twisted underneath him, meeting his hips with hers in spontaneous synchronicity, striving against each other but together.

His rhythm was sure, measured, with long slow strokes. Every one raised the stakes, bringing her fractionally closer to ecstasy, her body tenser, whimpers wrung from her throat each time he thrust in. He was slowly fanning the flame in her with every slick movement.

His panting against her neck was rough, small moans starting to tickle against her skin. Sweat was slick between their bodies, the tension increasing until she felt she might snap. His length slid smoothly into her, effortlessly caressing every sensitive spot.

The sensations were peaking, far too overwhelming to resist, unbearable. León's cries matched hers, pushing her further, but his hand finding hers and interlacing their fingers sent her over the edge. She shuddered at that crest, León pausing as she wrestled under him. His hand tightened on hers.

"*Mi cielo,*" he whispered, his throat tight.

The climax faded, leaving behind the sweetest lingering feeling throughout her body. She clutched León to her, fighting to catch her breath.

"More," she whispered. He slowly resumed his motion, shuddering himself. He'd been close, and the pause had strained his control. He moved in her with abandon, making her gasp.

"You're mine," he was whispering, pleading, repeating. "Say it." Her reply was to buck against him, driving him further. He surged into her, clinging fiercely as he rode out his own release. She stroked his dark hair as he panted and whimpered brokenly into her skin. Finally, he quieted, nuzzling and sighing.

"I won't say it," she murmured, "but I'm not mad anymore."

He chuckled, his face still buried in her neck, his hair sticking to her damp cheek.

"You will," he breathed against her.

. . .

The daybed could barely hold them both. León tried to keep his weight off her and, amid caresses and amused wriggling, they found a comfortable spot, entwined closely face to face. It suited him perfectly.

Her face, palely outlined by the watery light, lay inches from his. It was enough, bumping at her gently with his nose, kissing her sweet lips whenever he wanted. Fingers tracing any skin they could reach, they exchanged little nothings that sounded like everythings. His vision wasn't needed here. Her voice could be silent. The whole dusky world was touch and response, wanting and granting.

"What is the word you called me?" she whispered as he teased at her hair with his free hand. "It sounded like my name, but not."

"*Mi cielo*," he murmured back. "It means 'my sky' or 'my heaven.' Celia, *mi cielo*. It fits."

They exchanged their hundredth smiles. Just to feel her move quietly next to him was his heaven.

"*Encantadora musa*," he said softly. When her brows lifted in question, he translated again. "You're my charming muse."

Her sigh was blissful. "Talk to me more," she breathed. "In Spanish." She ran her hand down his back to trace his hip, lovely eyes half closed and content.

She hadn't pushed back. She really was his.

FOURTEEN

Celia heard León knock on her back door at dawn.

She'd gone to her own bed very late, alone, floating up the lawn in a euphoric haze. She couldn't have told even León what she was feeling, her world a feast of jumbled indulgences.

She must have slept in the few hours before he knocked but couldn't have sworn to it.

"You can just come in," she said as she opened the door, feeling strangely shy.

His smile was intimate. "I didn't want to presume."

He then presumed, sliding arms around her waist and pulling her tight for a long kiss. Oh lord.

"The thing is," he said quietly between kisses, "I want to get to work."

She would do anything he wanted.

"I wondered, what if we use your craft room? It has the skylight, but you won't be in direct sun."

"Oh." She dropped her eyes. "Yes, but...well, look." She led him to the door, opening it so he could see the wild paint spatters for himself.

His froze, eyebrows raised. "What happened?"

"I got mad," she said. "I need to clean it up, I guess."

He laughed heartily. "Spontaneous expression in its rawest form. Good for you."

The admiration that softened his voice surprised her. When he reached out to touch his fingertips to hers, she flushed at the gesture.

What a silly mess, Celia Rose.

"What?" León asked.

She blinked. Had she said that out loud? Oh no.

"Uh," she stammered. "Well. My mother called me Celia Rose when I...got in trouble." It was too early to overshare.

León put his arms around her waist, unconcerned. "Celia Rose," he murmured, tilting his head to consider her. "That's way too pretty to scold a girl with."

She smiled weakly.

"We're taking that name back," he said.

It was too early for that, too. She shied away, taking his hand and stepping out of his embrace.

"We could use the other room for painting," she said, leading him further down the hallway to a door near the entry. Inside was a bare room, completely empty, a twin to the craft room.

His mouth fell open at the sight. "I thought this was a closet! You have rooms you never even open?"

She clutched at the doorknob, chest tight. "Some people have too much house."

He walked in, turning around to gauge the space. An identical skylight illuminated it brightly, the sun falling on one wall. The pale caramel wood floor stretched bare, bouncing and warming the light.

"We can work in here? You don't mind? Paint will get on the floors, guaranteed. No amount of drop cloths ever stop it all."

She nodded. "If it'll work for you. It's just sitting here." She looked down, cheeks starting to heat. "Does paint come off of wooden floors? Could I clean the other room?"

"Depends on the paint and the floors. Paint does get into seams in the wood. It might have to be refinished."

She filed that away for later. But, right now—her train of thought was broken by sounds from both of their phones.

"Oh," she said, reminded as she checked the notification.

León's brows furrowed in annoyance as he read his. "I forgot they were all coming tonight."

"If you need to work, we can put them off."

"Well," he said, "It's up to you. I know you can only sit for a few hours, anyway. I can always pick it up after they leave."

As Celia texted the group, he turned in a quick circle, looking at the room again.

"Can I bring my gear in?"

"I'll help."

It didn't take long, the pool house quickly emptying. Celia caught him eyeing her surreptitiously as his possessions filled her empty room. Did he see the implication too? Neither said anything.

While he got ready to start, Celia made tea and sandwiches. He looked at her gratefully when she brought them in.

"Look at you. All I have to do is paint."

"And teach."

"If I can finish these in time, I could make a sale." He grinned, bouncing on the balls of his feet. "I can see each one if I close my eyes, Celia. This'll be worth it, you'll see. Everyone will see."

She handed him his teacup. "It's worth it even if the paintings are no good."

He set the cup down on the chair without looking and pulled her into his arms, brushing his cheek against hers, moving in for a kiss. Her heart pounded. It was still so new.

The momentary silence was sweet.

"This means so much, Celia," he finally murmured. "I'll show you. I'll earn every meal you make for me. Your talents will be part of this, you'll see."

Talents? Making sandwiches? She enjoyed feeding people, but it was hardly art. But posing, supporting an artist's work, maybe that was closer?

León started a purple painting. He wanted her in that long-balanced pose from the night before when she turned off the lamp. "While the memory is fresh," he grinned.

The pose was uncomfortable, but she could hold it for five-minute stretches. An oscillating fan kept her cool even as white sun through the skylight inched closer. The smell of paint wafted to her every time the fan turned.

"Don't you need purple light to paint this?" she asked. She couldn't watch him covertly in this position, but it wouldn't stop her from trying to learn.

"No, this one's more abstract. I need your lines but can supply the colors myself."

She could hear the tinkling sound of him cleaning his brush.

"Although," he said, "it's a little hard from memory."

The tinkling stopped.

"Celia." León cleared his throat, so she looked over, breaking the pose. "I said it's a little hard from memory."

He glanced down, his loose pants doing nothing to hide a clear outline. She snorted, body shaking with suppressed laughter.

When she looked up next, León stood next to her, smug and delighted.

"Definitely time for a break," he said. "Are you sore?"

She nodded, rising to stretch and flex to relieve her joints. He moved behind her to rub her shoulders. She closed her eyes, savoring the new feel of his hands on her skin. As he placed a kiss on the back of her neck, she forgot about the soreness. She'd put up with pain if this was the reward.

"I can work alone for a bit," he said. "Do you want to go cook? Swim? Just relax?"

Well. His consideration for her was sweet. She'd follow his lead.

"I could cook if you really don't need me."

"Go on," he said, planting another gentle kiss on her shoulder. She turned to meet his eyes, loathe to go, but their friends were coming. She'd have to serve something.

She made a fresh corn salad, put yesterday's roast back in the oven to come to temperature before shredding, and started dried chilis and onion on a low boil to make a spicy sauce. It was all simple scratch cooking, only unique because she put in the time. Time was the one thing she had to offer.

Looking at the clock on the stove, though, she realized it was already late afternoon. Hours had flown by today, beyond her notice. Now, that was novel!

When she brought León more tea, he jumped at her entrance. "You walk so quietly!"

It had been a long time since someone had noticed that.

He sniffed at the open door. "What heaven did you make?" he asked, astonished. It was beyond gratifying.

"Pork and chilis."

"When?" He set down his tea untouched, then covered his

paints. "Here, I'll wrap up and we can go to the kitchen." He stepped aside so she could see the painting. "What do you think?"

It was in the same style as the blue painting, with angles and shapes created by layering colors on top of each other. A figure stretched out like a leaping greyhound, attenuated, shadowy. Untouchable, like a ghost. It felt...sad, but not.

"It's beautiful," she said. "I was just turning off a lamp, but this is so graceful."

"It's all you, Celia. The part of you I can't touch yet." He covered his brushes, reached for her, and brought her in for another kiss. "I like the parts of you I can touch. When are they coming?" His hands roamed over her back, igniting that slow fire again.

"Soon. It's after five. They're probably already on their way."

"Where did the time go?" He began kissing her neck, and she trembled at the intimate touches of his lips.

The loose shift dress she'd put on to cook in did nothing to keep his hands from roaming every curve. They started at her hips, then roved around to her backside, pulling her to him. She could just catch the words he growled against her neck.

"*Mi cielo*, come here."

She was more than ready for him, reaching to tickle her fingers up into his hair. It was pulled back into a bun she'd been dying all day to see loosened. She felt him shiver as she pulled the tie free, and his teeth grazed sharply at her neck where it met her shoulder. Before she knew it, he was moving at her, walking her backward, pushing her softly up against the wall.

One of his hands grabbed her wrist, pulling it down from his hair and kissing her fingers. His other lifted to her breast, cupping it roughly through the fabric. "*Mi musa*," he growled, his eyes on hers for just a moment before he bent to her neck again. She felt a deep thrill at his demanding tone. It felt good to be wanted so insistently.

He bit and sucked at her neck, still holding her wrist by

her head. His other hand left her breast to run down her body, fumbling for the hem of her dress.

His mouth on her took all of her attention, almost painful but erotic in its intensity.

"León," she gasped as he bit a little too hard. He growled into her neck but switched to kissing the mark on her neck lightly. His hand finally found her hem and began slipping up under it. He bumped her hips back into the wall with his own, tickling her inner thigh with his fingers. He gave his mark one last kiss and then pulled back to look at it.

"There. You're branded." She gasped as his fingers finally went between her legs. His light touch on her was heavenly.

His eyes were back on hers, a devilish look in them. "I'm going to put that mark in the damn painting," he threatened, low. His fingers slipped between her wet lips, his thumb wandering up to touch right where she wanted it, and she gasped. "You're not untouchable, are you? Everyone who sees that mark will know I made it."

His entitlement was an incredible turn-on somehow. Celia didn't know yet if he meant it personally—he was always talking about painting when he got this way. Breathing hard, she leaned against the wall, pushing her hips into his hand. His eyes were reckless, lips curling into a smile as he watched her reactions.

The doorbell rang. Her eyes flickered to the door, but León ground his hand into her, weakening her knees.

"Early," she gasped.

"I can make you see stars before you open that door," he whispered. He finally released her wrist, only to firmly cup her face, his thumb dragging gently across her lower lip. "You want that?" She nodded mutely, panting lightly as he circled and teased at her with his thumb. "Say you belong to me."

When she hesitated, he slipped a finger inside her. Her eyes closed again, and she leaned her head back against the wall, whimpering softly. He leaned in close, his mouth inches from hers.

The doorbell rang again.

"I'm going to get you to say that," he murmured. His hand

pulled away, then came back with two fingers sliding inside. He kissed her hard, holding her head in place. She moaned into his mouth as he continued moving slickly on her.

"I should just fuck you right here," he breathed. "And you'd let me, wouldn't you?"

She would indeed. She ran a palm down his forearm, holding him to her.

"Hey, are you here?" A voice came from inside the house, making them both jump.

Kelsey. She'd gone around and come in the back door.

León stopped his movements, fingers still inside her, and leaned back just enough to see her face. She saw the disappointment in his, but he paused to see what she wanted.

"One sec, I'm posing," she called out, her voice creaky. "Get a drink." That would keep Kelsey out of the room. She wouldn't even know which room they were in—this one was never used. Celia kept her eyes on León, then felt for his wrist, leading his hand to continue moving. There would be no time for more, but she couldn't let him stop now.

With her free hand, she reached up to that dark hair, running her fingers through it, pulling his head to hers for an impassioned breathless kiss. She could feel his erection hard against her hip, pressing against her as he continued moving his thumb in rough circles. He held her against the wall as she slumped down, leaning her weight into that hand.

The doorbell rang again.

"Get that?" she shouted. León started chuckling against her cheek, then laughing. She gritted her teeth.

"Talk to me," she whispered. He laid his cheek against hers, breath tickling deliciously past her ear as he controlled her with his moving hand.

"My pretty Celia Rose," he whispered. "Do you like it?" She held her breath, her whole body tense, too close to reply. "Do you want it?" His entire body was moving against her, in sync with his hand. "God, I want to take you right here." His growl sent her over the edge, exploding with pleasure. As she trembled and shook, he kissed her deeply, muffling any sounds she made. He read her body so well, knew when to stop moving, and let her feel and experience her release. She wanted to slide down the wall, but he wouldn't let her.

"Good girl," he crooned, stroking her cheek with his thumb. "Celia, my girl." As her breathing started to return to normal, he looked into her eyes again, satisfaction bright in his. "I'm going to get you to say it, you know." His hand dropped to her neck, touching the mark he'd left there, and his lips curled into the wicked smile again.

She drew a deep breath and shook her head to clear it. Her eyes closed.

"I won't," she said quietly but with a smile. He slipped his hand from her and gave her a lingering kiss. Her entire body felt the sweetness.

"We'll see."

A knock sounded from the front door.

"That's all of them," she whispered. In the hallway outside, Andrew's voice could be heard as he went to open the door to Trevor. León brushed gently at her hair, stroking it back into place.

"Why did we waste the day painting? I don't want to stop." He let out his own shaky sigh as he finally stood away from the wall, pulling her with him. Then he grinned. "Your cheeks are scarlet. They're going to know. Want me to go out and say we were painting and that you're getting dressed?"

She nodded, grateful. He ran a hand through his tousled hair, then looked down ruefully. He was obviously hard still.

"I'm going to carry a box out."

They laughed together. Yes, there was no way this wouldn't be obvious to everyone.

He matched action to words, picked up a large box of paints, and held them near his hip, looking nearly natural.

"Ready, *mi cielo?*"

"I...not really."

He eyed her with wicked satisfaction. "Come out when you're ready. I'll give excuses." He left, closing the door behind him. She could hear Andrew greeting him.

She just needed a minute or two to compose herself. Smoothing her hair and dress, she felt her cheeks. They were still hot. She walked to the purple painting, a distraction while she calmed down.

It was her, but not her. It wasn't even a form, just shapes that assembled into a woman when you first looked, then came apart, then back together. He was heartbreakingly talented. She touched the mark on her neck, looking at the spot in the painting he'd have to add it. Would he really?

Why did he want her to say she belonged to him? The thrill when he growled it at her...was possession a turn-on for him, too, or was he teasing? She didn't know him well enough yet.

She finally felt a little calmer and slipped out the door.

Kelsey came over immediately to hand her a drink. She'd clearly been hovering where she could watch the room León had exited.

"I made this for you," she said, "and set out the food. Well, most of it was out already. I wasn't sure what you were going to do with the pork, so I just turned it down." Her eyes were avid, after details.

She wasn't going to get them, not yet. "Thanks," was all Celia said.

Kelsey's eyebrows couldn't get any higher. Just yesterday, she'd been listening to her cry about León, and today they were closeted up, supposedly painting, and coming out all flushed. It was obvious that they'd made up and then some.

Andrew came over and threw an arm around Celia's shoulders. "León's got you sitting for him, huh?" She nodded. "About time. Is he working on that blue one?"

"No, I think that one's done. He's onto purple now."

Trevor joined as well, giving her a hug as Andrew moved back. Everyone had half-smiles on their faces. She hoped they wouldn't say outright what they all seemed to be thinking. Celia looked around for León surreptitiously, but he wasn't in the room.

Kelsey watched knowingly, never subtle. "He left right as you came out," she whispered.

Celia moved resolutely to the kitchen, the group trailing after to gather around the kitchen island. She let them chatter while she quickly shredded a small chunk of the pork and finished her chili sauce. Cooking soothed her, and her friends gave her the space she obviously wanted right now.

Andrew moved to Celia's side of the island. "Trevor says León was pretty snotty the other day. I'll feel bad if I saddled you with an obnoxious tenant."

Celia looked across the island. Trevor and Kelsey were heads down, talking. "He's fine. He's being nice."

Andrew smirked, but kindly. "Putting more moves on you?"

"He's painting me."

He leaned his elbows onto the counter and looked into the drink he held in both hands. "That's quite the mark on your neck."

She reached up to touch it, cheeks suddenly burning. Both Trevor and Kelsey looked up to watch. Okay, so everyone had been waiting for it to be mentioned.

"Yeah, it's...." She had nothing. They'd all guessed anyway. "Okay, yes, it's not a secret or anything."

"It couldn't be," Trevor said with a smile.

Kelsey leaned in. "Did León explain what happened yesterday?"

The two men looked at Kelsey, who obviously had more details than they did.

"Yes." Celia couldn't think of what else to say.

"Did he like the blue dress?"

"He liked it a lot," León's voice answered.

Everyone turned to see León closing the back door behind him, wearing his clean street clothes. He eyed the conclave in the kitchen, Celia covering her neck with one hand.

He walked over behind Celia and put his arms around her from behind in a natural, familiar gesture. Then, casually, he shifted his weight to lean between her and Andrew, who moved over to make room.

Everyone exchanged glances and faint smiles.

"What a shock," Kelsey said dryly.

Trevor leaned on the island. "It is to me. That car ride while you were arguing, oof."

León leaned his chin on Celia's shoulder. "We got past it."

While her friends chuckled, Celia tried to appear at ease. But there didn't seem to be any respite from feelings! She wasn't good at these whipsaw emotions.

The way he claimed her in front of the room, moving Andrew to the side! She basked in the feeling of being wanted, of him asserting his place by her, but there'd been no time to think it over. He'd accomplished it before she'd had a chance to react.

Her thoughts stopped when León subtly pulled her closer to him. Her backside was pressed against his hips, and the intimate touch shot electricity through her. How, when not fifteen minutes ago, she'd been panting and satisfied? Her insides whirled.

Would he want to stay with her tonight, in her bed? They could actually fall asleep there...after. They could wake up together. The suddenness with which he was moving into her life was both euphoric and terrifying.

León laughed over her shoulder at something Trevor had said. Celia realized she'd lost the thread of the conversation. She was still as frozen as she'd ever been, stuck in her thoughts. Sure enough, she looked up to see Kelsey watching her with amusement. Andrew too, who had moved to the other side of the island without her noticing. León had claimed both her body and her space near the stove.

She reveled in it, but it scared her. She wanted time to take it all in.

León leaned forward again to whisper in her ear as the conversation on the other side of the island turned to...something else. She never had picked up the thread.

"Can I stay in the house tonight?" he asked. "I want to be with you."

Pleasure shot through her. She had to turn to whisper back to him, and he loosened his arms around her so she could face him.

"Of course, you can," she whispered back. He smiled broadly, his eyes full of promise for later.

"Damn, the chemistry in this room is getting me hot,"

Andrew complained. "Let's go outside, so if they paw each other, at least it's in the dark, and we can still talk." Everyone laughed except Celia and León, but it was good-natured. Celia let them pick up the food and troop out to the firepit.

León kissed her before letting her move away, then reached up to touch the mark on her neck. He looked so pleased about it. She decided she would like it as well. Being claimed felt too good.

FIFTEEN

Celia stretched out for—hopefully—the last sitting for the purple painting. This pose took significant muscle, balancing on one knee and reaching forward. The pillows under her knee felt thinner every time. He was trying to paint fast for her, aware of her discomfort, but couldn't keep silent for long.

"It's a shame this is in purples," León said, "That pretty gold skin of yours, I wonder if I could even mix the perfect colors."

She held the pose despite the self-conscious delight washing over her.

"Where's your family from?" he asked, hidden behind the canvas. "I'm getting to know you. It's okay to ask that, right?" He liked springing questions on her, she was discovering. She knew what he was really asking with this one.

"It's okay. California," she answered. "And my father was Filipino."

"I wondered," he said. "I was born in New York, but my family's from Puerto Rico." He chuckled. "I've been called Mexican twice out here already."

She concentrated on holding the pose, ignoring her poor knee.

"Have you ever been to the city? New York City, I mean?"

"A few times." It had exhausted her, all the dense crowds. "It's not an easy place for a shy person."

"No, it wouldn't be. So, is it time for a break?"

God yes. She relaxed and took her weight off of her knee.

"Nearly done," he said. "Come look."

She flexed her joints before walking stiffly over.

The tenuous ghostly figure looked done to her. He'd even added that dark spot on her neck.

"Untouchable Celia," he smiled, reaching out to run a finger down her bare arm. She shivered.

"I'm not sure I get it," she said. "I mean, I get having imagination, but you said it's what's inside me, something you can't see or know. Why is it...this?"

"I'm painting the feeling I got then. And I couldn't paint it after I get to know you, right?"

She couldn't paint her own inner self. She couldn't even imagine an image that would be close, but León just charged ahead and made this beautiful vision.

"Are you hungry?" she asked. Cooking, she could do.

"Not for food, *reinita*."

His roguish smile banished her cares and soreness.

• • •

León could not be happier. Celia was perfect. His paintings were perfect. Every hour was perfect!

He woke before the sun every morning in her fluffy cloud of a bed, Celia warm and tranquil beside him, the daybed outside already fading from memory. He couldn't waste time sleeping, waiting as long as he could stand before waking her with quiet morning talk.

They'd paint for an hour, then he'd release her to putter in the house. What she found to clean was beyond him; everything was always spotless, towels laundered, surfaces gleaming. When she called him for breakfast, there were never dirty dishes in the sink.

He reached out to touch her constantly, any time he felt the urge. She was still quiet, but her body told him what she liked. She always welcomed his soft touches. She liked it even more when he was a little rough or possessive, trembling as she looked up with wide, yielding eyes, teasing that she didn't belong to him while her body said the opposite.

He craved the time she'd approach, touching him first, but could never wait long enough. She would, he knew, if he wasn't always there first.

Her lesson was always later, later, but she didn't complain. When Andrew invited himself over, she put him off too. Their perfect days were spent painting.

And then came the nights. The perfect nights.

• • •

With three weeks to go until the exhibition, León was finishing the yellow painting.

"The light and shadow in this one are so sharp," Celia said, feeling the soreness in her neck as she came to look.

He grinned, unable to touch her with paintbrush and palette in hand. "The sight of you in those golden shadows, agreeing to pose...I should have kissed you right then."

She blushed, still somehow able to feel bashful at his declarations. He never seemed to feel embarrassed by them.

"What feelings do you get from it?" he asked. Her lessons kept getting put off, but he still asked that about everything, helping her practice.

The painting was a cubist face in blazing yellows, with slashes of pale light and umber shadows from an unseen spotlight. It was looking up at the viewer, the eyes quietly bold. A hint of insecurity in the foreshortened shoulders and collarbone faded away below. The face said strength, but the posture said submission.

Celia was getting better at interpreting León's work.

"I see caution," she said. "She's pretending to cower."

"Really, pretending?" León glanced over, curious.

Celia stepped back to see the full painting better. "The eyes are sure of themselves," she said, "but everything else is weak. She's pretending to be scared while you're standing over her, but secretly she could mess you up."

He chuckled. "That's almost what I was going for. I was thinking she's challenging you but is fearful underneath, docile. See, her body gives her away."

"I see the opposite," Celia declared. "She's hiding strength, not fear."

León looked at his painting. "Huh."

• • •

León was not a late sleeper, she found. He woke her each morning far too early, with far too much energy. Celia had thought she was a morning person until he began sharing her bed. He liked to gently poke at her until she opened her eyes, and then the talking started.

She awoke to a tickle on her neck. A glimpse toward the ceiling confirmed weak morning light. Was the sun even up yet?

"Someone wants attention," she murmured.

"Me," his voice said next to her. "I do."

She rolled over to face him, seeing dark eyes peeking at her over the white comforter.

"Celia," he asked as she covered a yawn, "have you ever been in a fistfight?"

She was getting used to his constant questions, though how he came up with his random topics was a mystery. Who asked about fights before the sun was up?

Deep down, though, the attention warmed her.

"I have been in a fight, yes. And I won't tell you about it." Before he could protest, she went on the offensive. He liked when she asked questions back, she'd discovered. "Have you ever been arrested?"

"Nope," he said, his eyes almost regretful. She twitched as fingers suddenly ran up her side under the covers, and crinkles at his temples gave away a hidden grin. "Did you like bad boys when you were growing up?"

"Yes, but I never talked to any," she replied. "I stuck to the nice, polite ones."

That spirited smile emerged as he pulled down the comforter and scooted closer. It wasn't fair of him to be charming this early.

What else could she ask?

"Did you like bad girls?"

"All boys like bad girls." He slid one arm over her, snuggling in close, the comforter a cocoon around their shoulders. Could he look more smug? "Would you pretend to be bad for me, *mi cielo*?"

Celia threaded an arm under his to stroke his bare back. "Who says I'd have to pretend? I've been in fights, remember."

He gave her a slow sweet kiss, his loose hair tickling her cheek. His smile as he moved to hover over her was even sweeter. "You're a nice, polite girl, I can tell."

She cocked an eyebrow at him, her smile cryptic. "If you say so. Would you pretend to be a bad boy?"

"Celia, if you asked for it, I'd get arrested."

• • •

With two weeks to go until the exhibition, León started

on a lush painting in celadon green. In this, she simply stood, her head serenely turned away in profile, cradling an armful of immature palm fronds from her yard. His sweet muse deserved a break from the complicated poses.

"Why is this pose so static?" she asked. "Mother nature could be more organic."

"You're a myth, the goddess in the garden. Provider, mother, all that."

"It's hardly work. You're sure it's enough?"

He peered around the canvas, eyes sweeping up her graceful lines. Enough? She could do no wrong. "You're giving me everything I could possibly want, Celia. Here, come look."

She set down her leaves and came around. León watched her face eagerly, anticipating her usual wide-eyed look of pleasure from viewing a new work. His gorgeous green vision was Celia but not, a composition of leafy shapes and lush greenery converging into a standing woman at the center. The noble profile wasn't precisely hers, but the neck and shoulders were all Celia.

Would she see the blend of muse and myth?

"This feels remote," Celia said, her voice tinged with disappointment. "I thought providing for someone would feel personal, but she's looking away."

A tightness clenched in León's chest as her surprising reaction sank in. "She's a garden personified," he explained. "Maybe that makes her a little reserved. She's not offering anything. She *is* the bounty."

"So, I'm just taking...her? She doesn't get to enjoy me eating from the garden? That's the best part of feeding people."

"It's just a story," he said gently. "You don't have to judge whether it's good or bad, just show that it exists."

Her brow slowly furrowed. "I feel bad for her."

León watched her surreptitiously, paintbrush still poised near the canvas, his breath held. As her eyes shone and she gulped a hard breath, he felt an answering rush in his chest.

"You're getting feelings from a painting," he said softly. "My painting."

She nodded.

He reached out to touch his fingertips to hers. "That's wonderful, *mi cielo*."

"I don't want her to be remote," she sniffled.

"We could paint another one after," he offered. "But she's not sad, Celia. This is what she's meant to be."

"We'll make a better story for her," Celia insisted.

• • •

Once Celia introduced León to relaxing in the pool after dusk, he began looking forward to their peaceful hour in the glowing water. She was right—you could think there. Something about floating in the quiet blue freed the mind; maybe because you simply couldn't do other tasks until you got out.

"What's your favorite food to make?" he asked her as they draped next to each other on the side of the pool, both gazing at the remote city lights. He rested his chin on his hands, enjoying the cool weightlessness.

Her happy sigh gratified him.

"Do you want the long answer or the short answer?"

He laid one wet cheek against his hands so he could look at her, not replying. He didn't care. Whatever she said, he learned something about her.

"I guess I like curing meats best," she mused. "Turning a brisket into pastrami is fun, like science. Oh, I'll make you gravlax! Cured salmon. It's delicious. You bury it raw in salt and sugar and fresh dill, wrap it tight and put a weight on top, then flip it every twelve hours...." She trailed off, watching his face. She was better now at reading distraction in him.

León's gaze had shifted to the shimmering reflections on the water's surface, his mind drifting from her enthusiasm to the nagging guilt over how little he contributed here.

She created such elaborate dishes. And posed. And let him stay in her place, and share her bed. He certainly couldn't say he was supporting himself.

León pushed the thoughts away, trying to be present. "Go on," he encouraged.

"Would you like to try gravlax?" she asked. "I haven't

made you any seafood since...you know."

He pursed his lips. "It sounds like so much work, Celia."

He'd wanted to feed her questions and listen to her talk. Asking about cooking had been a misstep. Hearing about her efforts made his feel paltry.

"I don't mind doing it," she said stoically. "I like it."

"You should do it, then," he said. "I just haven't been sure if...I mean, I don't want you to do these things just for me."

"It's for both of us."

"Us." He smiled, seeing his way to a better topic. "That's a nice word, us."

He reached out to touch her arm under the water, so gently that he didn't even rouse ripples.

Celia smiled, lulled by the touch, but León suspected she wasn't done musing on it. She always seemed hesitant when she served him food. It made him feel worse about giving her nothing but art. Her talent was cooking, and his was painting. She wouldn't limit herself for his sake, would she?

• • •

The week before the exhibition, León was painting her sitting cross-legged, cocky and defiant. The memory of her sitting on his cot, telling him off, was begging to be painted in reds. Celia had to stand often to relieve the strain on her knees and back.

"Come tell me what you feel in this one," he said. Getting her impressions was more intriguing every painting.

She approached and considered. Did she see the how the deep red triangles, improbably balancing on each other, resolved into anger, irreverence, and a seated woman? Her spiky face echoed in the pink triangle between her wide-spread knees.

"It's about sex," she said. "But also teasing. You can't have it. All the thorns mean 'stay away.'"

León looked at her, blinking. She kept noticing elements he hadn't intended. It was okay, but he somehow forgot while he painted that she saw things from different angles.

"Did I miss the point again?" she asked.

"No, no. I just was going somewhere else. Somewhere

close," he amended as she looked anxious. "This is your righteous anger at me for being inconsiderate that one day. Your power, refusing me right when I realized I needed to paint you."

"I can see that," she said, leaning close to inspect the jagged red face.

"Why do you feel she's teasing?" he asked, genuinely curious. He hadn't meant it to be teasing.

"Well, it's such a sexual posture. She's spread out, inviting you to see, but the face and all the sharp ends say stop. So, it's...it's about denial." She looked pleased to have found the right word.

León paused, looking again. Had he accidentally painted what she saw? Instead of her wrath and authority, had he been painting something he felt at the time but didn't realize?

Maybe.

He'd wanted her then, for sure. Maybe he was painting his own unseen anger at her rejection of him that day. Their conversation had been entirely different then, but...damn.

"*Mi musa*, you're a prize."

. . .

Celia leaned back in the corner of the sectional couch after dinner, stretching her legs. These days she was either on her feet or sitting in an uncomfortable position. It was a far cry from the empty days before, when she didn't have enough to do to tire her out. It felt good, even with the pain.

León came out of his studio room, having finished his nightly cleanup. He gravitated to her on the couch, sitting and patting his lap so she would put her feet up on him.

"Who was your first crush?" he asked, rubbing her feet absently. She let her head fall back, cheeks turning pink.

"Don't laugh! Mario Lopez." She peeked to gauge his reaction. He didn't laugh.

"Not a boy at school?" She shook her head. "What was it about him?"

She had to think. "He was cute, of course. But I guess I liked his confidence. He acted like everything would go his way, and it did. On TV, I mean."

León nodded along.

"I think that's why I first went out with Andrew," she continued. "He has that same vibe."

This time León laughed.

"When was your first kiss?" she asked back.

It was his turn to redden.

"A girl in elementary school. She was hanging upside down on the monkey bars. I kissed her, then ran away." He saw Celia's eye roll. "I knew she liked me, though. Her friend told me."

"Male aggression," she deadpanned. "Kissing her when she couldn't stop you."

His eyes got that roguish look again, and before she knew it, he had pulled his feet onto the couch and climbed toward her on all fours. Did he never run out of energy? In seconds he was straddling her, leaning close, pinning her under him. She took one quick shaky breath, looking up at him eagerly. He lowered himself until his lips were inches from hers.

"You like a little aggression, though, don't you?" he asked, confident of her answer.

He wasn't wrong. She did like it. She worried that she shouldn't, but every time he got masterful, she felt a deep thrill.

He bent his head and kissed her hard, pressing her into the cushion, one hand coming up to roughly grasp her shoulder where it met her neck. She brought her hands up to his chest but was too confined to reach further.

"Celia," he said against her cheek, breathing hard. "You're mine."

She froze. This again.

"Say it for me," he growled low, running his hand up her neck.

She stayed silent too long. He withdrew a little to look at her. The moment stretched out, him waiting and her refusing to say the words. Finally, he closed his eyes.

"Celia, what do you want?" He shook his head. "I can't just guess. You have to at least react."

She looked down, her chest still rising and falling too fast.

"I don't want to react," she finally said quietly.

He slowly sat back onto her thighs, creating space between them. Frustration was written across him. "You have to, though," he said. "Honesty, remember?"

He presumed her wants mirrored his. How could she say he would never own her, that it was too far?

"I need to know if you like it," he continued, apprehension growing on his face the longer she went without speaking. "Especially if I'm being a little rough, you have to respond. Tell me, touch me back."

Comprehension struck. He just meant reacting when he touched her! Well. She could do better at that.

He swallowed roughly. "You could touch me first, even," he said. "I'd like that. Do you...ever want to?"

Had she really never reached out to him first? She saw worry etching deeper into his face. Why—

Good lord! He was insecure! Arrogant, entitled León, always acting so sure of himself. He was uncertain, just like her.

Relief flooded her. She might not have León's skills or talent, but this she could fix. Celia had spent her life making others feel important. Reassuring León would be easy now that she knew.

She reached for a fistful of his T-shirt, pulling. His eyebrows rose sharply.

"I do like this, León."

She gazed up at him through her lashes, then leaned forward to kiss him. His face when she finished radiated satisfaction.

"I like you, León."

He nearly purred as he melted down onto her.

• • •

With two days to go until the exhibition, León was forced to make tough decisions about what was finished enough to show.

"There was no way I could get them all done," he said, "but dammit, they're done in my head. I wish there was more time."

"There will be other shows."

"I know. It's just so exciting. I want everyone to see. I want to see everyone see."

Celia hovered as he chose and re-chose which paintings to include. The deadline to deliver them was the next day. He finally settled on the purple, the yellow, and the blue. She helped him package them for transport using the supplies she'd ordered.

She was amused to see that he'd added a faint dark spot to her neck in each of them.

SIXTEEN

"The car will be here in three minutes!" León called from the hallway.

Celia adjusted her neckline one last time before joining him there. His reaction was marvelous, mouth falling open as his eyes devoured her.

"Oh, my god. That blue dress. Let's stay home."

Andrew had wanted another group hangout, pre-celebrating everyone being represented in the exhibition in some way. Celia had redirected his plans to a nearby bar. She wasn't ready to break the new spell cast on her place. Their place.

The ride-share was slow, evening traffic glutting the roads. León couldn't sit still in the back seat with her, predicting wild reactions from their friends when they saw their paintings. He played with her hair, petted the soft knit fabric over her knee, ran his hand down her arm to clasp and squeeze her hand.

His flashing eyes warmed her, inviting her to share his cavalier glee. Funny. He'd cleaned up for this too, and she sort of missed the faint roughness of paint on his hands.

León and Celia were the last to arrive.

Celia saw Kelsey at a table near the back of the bar as soon as they walked in. She had an eye on the door, her profile lit beautifully by the nearest wall sconce. A number of men were checking her out already, but Andrew and Trevor were absorbed in a private topic, leaning close again. Poor Kelsey. She brightened when they walked up.

"Damn, Celia, you're looking good," Andrew said, looking up.

Celia glanced at León, who simply beamed at everyone.

"Drinks are on the ladies!" Kelsey said. She rose and dragged Celia back to the bar, leaving the men at the table. The order was simple, four beers and a ginger ale, but the bar was busy and loud, and the wait afforded them time to talk.

Kelsey fluttered, avid. "How's the honeymoon going?"

Celia looked back to the table. León was turned in his chair, watching her from across the dark room. The crowd blurred into murky scenery, the din fading. His eyes were the only real thing in the room, bright and warm and alive. They shared an intimate smile across the distance.

Kelsey laughed, bringing Celia back to her at the bar.

"Wow, that good?" she smiled. "You two have been closeted up for weeks."

Celia nodded, enjoying the warmth filling her up inside.

"He's painting," she responded, turning back to her friend. "All he wants to do is look at me and talk and…well, you know. Everything's changed."

"Are you happy?" Kelsey grinned as Celia smiled shyly. "He's not being grumpy?"

"Oh no," Celia said, "he's bouncing like a kid at Christmas. He's up at dawn every day, ready to get back to work."

"Dragging you out of bed behind him?" Kelsey actually winked.

"Well, yes." Celia ducked her head. "He feels so much pressure to get it all done."

"I'm more interested in how you are, actually. Remember how you said you'd be honest?"

"I can't even describe it." Celia looked back to León, but he was laughing with Andrew now. "He's non-stop. Silly questions all day, painting for hours and hours."

Kelsey shot a considering glance at the men. "Are you painting?"

"Posing and cooking, mostly. We'll do my lessons after the exhibition."

"Girl, you better."

"Don't worry," Celia said. "Really, Kelsey, everything's perfect."

A man deftly bumped Kelsey's shoulder as he stepped up to the bar, just as their drinks arrived. Kelsey took her own but let Celia gather up the beers as she turned to view this contender.

• • •

"I haven't seen you in weeks," Andrew said, moving into

the chair next to León. "You really landed on your feet, huh?"

León tore his eyes from his blue-clad muse and turned back to the table. "Yeah, I never dreamed things would work out this well. I can't believe my luck."

"Hell, it wasn't all luck. I contributed. Trevor contributed." Andrew glanced at Trevor across the table from them. "He got you into the exhibition, and I introduced you to my best girl."

León rolled his eyes. "You weren't dating. Come on."

"No, but I thought maybe we'd get back together eventually."

"Maybe, eventually," Trevor chuckled. "Just what every woman hopes for."

"Well, if people can be stolen away, she's stolen," Andrew said. "We're even now, León. Hope you're enjoying the spoils."

"Dude." León shook his head, hand over his heart. "Literally all I do is paint her. I've never eaten so well in my life. She folds my clothes, she takes care of everything. She ordered the packing materials for the exhibition." That twinging guilt sneaked up again, and he wrinkled his nose. "I basically do nothing."

"You're teaching her how to paint," Andrew said.

León lowered his hand, his thumb starting its tapping. "I think the lessons are over. I tried, but she's just not a painter."

Andrew grimaced. "I'd hoped she'd do better with you to help."

León shook his head. "Her best work so far was throwing paint against a wall."

"Guys," Trevor said.

"She always was better at cooking than art," Andrew said. "Lucky son of a bitch. All you do is paint, eat, and fuck."

"Dude, I'm sleeping with the model," León grinned back. They exchanged fist bumps.

"Guys!" Trevor said.

León finally looked over as Trevor stood. "What?"

"Celia!" He pointed past them, and both turned. Kelsey was rushing toward the exit, but Celia wasn't in sight.

Where...?

"She was right here with the drinks, listening," Trevor said. "She left."

"She did what?" León jumped from his seat, then took off after where Kelsey had just disappeared.

He caught up as she came back in the front door.

"Where's Celia?" A wash of frigid air hit him.

"She left."

"Left? No, she didn't." He pushed past Kelsey through the door, looking up and down the street. His stomach dropped as the empty sidewalks registered.

Kelsey joined him. "What did you say to her?"

"I didn't...." He clutched at her arm. "Where did she go?"

"There was a car parked here, a ride-share." She waved at the one empty parking space in front of the bar. "She just got in, and it drove off."

A sudden void swallowed León's breath. There was some mistake. Celia wouldn't have just left him.

He pulled out his phone and texted Celia. A numbing breeze coursed past as they waited for a response.

He called, on speaker. The taut silence while they waited grew more strained with each failed ring.

"It wasn't a ride she ordered, just a car sitting here?" he finally asked.

Kelsey nodded, eyes wide. "What happened? I was at the bar and she came past, looking...well, really upset. She pushed the beers at me and rushed out."

León clamped his mouth shut and strode back into the bar, Kelsey trailing behind. At the table, Andrew and Trevor still stood, tense.

"She's gone," León reported. "What the hell?"

Trevor shook his head at him. "Dude, she was standing right there when you said she couldn't paint, and all you do is paint, eat, and fuck."

"I didn't—"

"You did! Well, Andrew did. You joked about fucking the model."

León felt an icy numbness wash over him. No.

"That's just an old joke of ours," he said, exchanging stricken looks with Andrew. "I didn't mean it in a bad way. Our setup is perfect."

"Is it, though?" Kelsey asked.

"She's happy!" León said with a scowl. "I know she is." The iciness kindled into an angry heat. Celia couldn't have misunderstood. She knew him better than that.

"We should find her," Kelsey prompted. "It's not safe to get in a random car like that."

Andrew finally snapped out of his silence. "She did what?"

Kelsey explained. Everyone exchanged grave looks. León turned back to his phone, staring in disbelief at unanswered texts.

"Look," he finally said, eyes scanning the anxious group. "I'll go back to the house. Trevor, you drove, right? If I can find out where that car was going, could you go there? And Andrew and Kelsey, stay here in case she comes back? I'll keep calling her."

Kelsey shook her head. "I'll call and text. She's more likely to answer me."

León shot a frown at her. "Come on. Was it that bad? What we said?"

Trevor sighed wearily. "You basically called her your maid, a slutty maid."

"There's no way it sounded like that," León snapped, then glanced at Andrew, who returned a worried look.

"You were crowing about how much she works," Trevor said, "and how she can't paint! It sounded bad, man."

León bristled. "She's happy!"

Kelsey put a hand on León's arm. "Celia might not say if she wasn't."

"She would to me," he fumed.

God dammit, Celia.

León shoved his phone into his pocket, head throbbing. "Okay, I'm going. Let me know immediately if you find her, okay?"

Andrew and Trevor nodded, but Kelsey shook her head again. "I'll drive you there. You'll have a way to get around if you need to."

León nodded curtly. "Thanks."

Andrew had his phone out. "I'll try to find out where the car went. I have as much chance of finding out as you."

• • •

The driver had been willing to take Celia if she ordered the ride immediately, and she punched her home address in the app for time's sake.

Run. Hide.

She held a fist to her mouth, struggling to draw choked breath.

How could he joke like that?

She turned off her phone when the first text came in. It wasn't until the car turned up the twisty canyon roads that silent tears started rolling down her cheeks.

He wasn't putting off her lessons. He was just done with them.

She'd lock the doors and never come out.

The driver dropped her at her front door, but Celia couldn't go in. She stood in silence, staring at her dim moonlit entryway, mocking whispers of wind in the trees behind her.

This was no sanctuary now. León would follow her here. He lived here!

She saw herself sitting on the couch, listening for the click of the door, for the questions and recriminations.

She couldn't do it.

Instead, she went through the side gate to her backyard, past the pool, to stare at the city lights. She wrapped her arms around herself, the chilly wind biting more in the open.

Nowhere to hide, nowhere to run. This was as far as she could go. The world dropped off in front of her, with no path forward.

The quiet tears started again. Despair, at least, was a familiar place. It was a tiny feeling, not enough to fill the empty air over the canyon, the city, the blank dark sky.

She'd known the whole time but had hidden from that too. She couldn't make art. Her only use was cooking and cleaning.

And León, telling Andrew about the paint on the wall?

Laughing about screwing the model! Casually confirming her fears. It wasn't even what he'd said—she knew he'd been thoughtlessly joking. It was that he was right.

Her breath catching painfully, Celia stepped up onto the retaining wall. Her toes poked between the bars of the wrought iron fence, the top of it pressing cold against her thighs as she leaned on it.

He knew she was only good enough for a supporting role—that was all he'd asked for. And she'd rolled over and given him everything like only he mattered. Worse, she'd liked it!

Idiot! Stupid, ridiculous fool!

A dry leaf skittered past her through the fence, powered by the full-throated wind. She leaned over the fence to watch it fall.

Why am I never the one who matters?

A biting pain in her chest curled her up, knotted her. She grasped the railing hard, feeling the sharp cold edges in her damp palms.

You don't have to live like that.

Dad had burdened her, Mom had demanded and beaten. León had seduced her into doing what he wanted.

Was that why she liked him so much? He felt familiar?

She was back to acting like a child, muting herself.

Celia looked down the canyon again, the gritty retaining wall under her feet pattering tiny chips downslope as she shifted her weight. The palm fronds high above her rattled.

Was this rushing din in her head, or was it the wind too? How could she not know?

What had happened to the silence inside her?

A lone airplane appeared over the palm trees, its lights silently gliding over the basin. It flew steadily, despite the wind.

Celia raised her arms out to each side. What if she flew away too?

No. No! That was still just running.

Think! She could only go down or back to try again. She didn't want to give up, but what could she do?

A low gust sent the pool behind her to lapping, the sound washing wide behind her.

I could tell people about it—I've been practicing. Kelsey. Andrew, when he's not being flippant. Trevor.

León.

His name rang in her like a bell.

That infuriating intoxicating man, with his grand honesty and fancy art! He said he'd be nothing if he didn't paint, but she was different. She'd find something else!

The cold faded, and her heart knocked harder.

He'd made her feel these things, the bastard. Incessantly! His surprising questions in bed at dawn. The honeyed harmony when their wondering eyes met. The electricity of his hands on her, gentle and tender or fierce and wild.

Warmth flooded up her skin. So, her body didn't care about his treacherous jokes?

Look at me, feeling.

I will find my own way.

She stepped back, down, planting her feet on the flagstones.

A noise at the house made her jump, then melt into the shadow of a palm tree.

Kelsey and León came in the side gate and went in the back door. She could see everything inside, the white wall of windows like a movie screen. León stalked through the house, looking in doorways, then sat on the dimly lit couch, beaten. Celia's heart melted as always, but she stayed where she was.

How could she explain this to him?

She was going to make some changes.

• • •

León stared at his hands, stomach twisting. Was there anything to do but wait?

"I've sent her a lot of texts," Kelsey said. "She knows we're worried about her if she's checking her phone."

Who knew what kind of driver was in that car? She just jumped in! There was no record in any app about who she was or where. Would someone take advantage of that?

"León, she's probably fine," Kelsey consoled. "She probably decided to not come here yet because she knew we would."

He hung his head, leaning forward. "Was what I said so bad?"

"I wasn't there, I don't know. Trevor said you made her sound like a slutty maid."

"I didn't!" León said. "I mean, technically, it could sound that way, but...she knows how grateful I am for what she does! Yeah, I could have kept my mouth shut about her painting. But she knows—"

"Hey, don't keep telling me what she knows." Kelsey sat on the other end of the couch.

León clenched his teeth, looking away. Celia's kitchen island sat bare and tomblike. He'd never been in here without her being just a shout away.

He took a deep breath. "I respect what she does. I respect her. How could she not know that?"

"Ask her." Kelsey shook her head and rechecked her phone.

• • •

Celia watched them debating on the couch. The urge to stay behind the tree, to put off the confrontation, lost out to learning what she'd be walking into. Was León angry she had run? He was turned away from the window, but his back looked tense.

As they talked, Kelsey kept checking her phone. They must have been trying to reach her. Obviously.

The wind sighed again, needling through the thin dress. She wasn't ready, but the cold would win. There was nothing left to do but climb up to the house and the consequences and the look on León's face when she said she wanted something else, something more.

She turned her phone back on with chilled fingers, delayed notifications trilling one after the other. So many texts and missed calls. The top one was from Kelsey, saying she just wanted to know if she was safe.

Oh, Kelsey. She hadn't intended for anyone to worry. She hadn't intended any of this. She at least had to let them know she was okay.

• • •

"It's her! She's safe."

León sighed hoarsely, dropping his face into his hands. *¡Ay bendito!*

The giddy relief lasted only moments.

Safe all this time and making him go through that! How dare she over such a small thing?

Kelsey flinched as he jumped up to pace, fury radiating.

"How could she make us worry like that? *¿Y para qué?*" His outrage erupted. "*¿Cuál es su razón? Esa aniñada—*"

"Hey!" Kelsey said, "León, she's okay. This is how she reacts, and you might have to get used to it if you're here for the long haul. She may never be different, not even with you teaching her better ways."

He stared at her. Blunt.

"It's childish! Running out, really?"

She twisted her mouth. "Oh please, you did the same thing to her."

"What?"

"That one time, you remember, you disappeared, and she waited around all day?"

He froze. Shit.

"Yeah, okay, but this isn't the same. She wasn't worried that I was hurt."

Kelsey stood. "No, she just thought she wasn't important to you. She hadn't even been rude beforehand."

"I wasn't...that rude." It sounded weak even to himself.

She shook her head at him. "You're not going to win this one, León."

He stared, stuck.

"I highly suggest you work through this, fast," she said, blue eyes like ice. "Be cool when she gets here. You'll get nowhere if you're mad. She'll shut right down again."

He ran his hand through his hair. "Hell. I'll try, but...is she coming back? Did she say?"

"She didn't. But I think she will. She communicated— she's coming out of hiding."

"Will you let Andrew and Trevor know?"

He took a deep breath. This was going to be hard.

• • •

Celia huddled behind the tree, wide-eyed at León's hot-tempered dramatics once she sent the text.

How could she go in now?

Kelsey seemed to be quieting him, speaking with soothing hand gestures. Thank god. He was calming down.

She could go in if Kelsey was there.

Veering behind the pool house, Celia shivered as she slipped through shadows up to the side gate. She would at least come in her own front door.

SEVENTEEN

The first thing Celia saw when she walked in was Kelsey slipping out the back door and heading for a patio chair. What, now she decided to give them privacy?

It was too late to retreat. She walked through the long dark entry hall, dread thick in her throat, memories seeping from each closed door she passed. Studio. Craft room. Bedroom.

León hovered just inside the bright kitchen, hands shoved deep into his front pockets. She saw his deep inhalation when she rounded the corner, then he lowered his shoulders and exhaled.

"Hey," he said softly, his dark eyes grave as he looked her up and down.

Celia tried to reply, but nothing came out.

"You look scared," León said, his voice low. "It's okay. Please don't be scared."

Sharp relief coursed through her, and her face crumpled. She covered it with her hands before he could see, but León was there before she knew it, collecting her into a rough embrace, his face buried in her hair.

"I'm sorry, I'm sorry," he crooned as she wept. "I didn't mean it. I shouldn't have joked about it."

"Oh, León," she finally got out. He just held her, stroking her back, until she began to calm down. His warm body was a familiar comfort, his voice a soft rumbling against her. "I'm sorry I ran," she finally mewled.

"It's okay. We can talk about it. Tomorrow or whenever."

"Now," she said, face tight against his shoulder. "I want to talk now. I'll just worry until we do."

"Okay. Okay. Let's sit down." He walked her to the couch, guiding her to the nearest spot, then securing himself tight against her side.

• • •

León's anger melted at her first sob. Was this what she kept so tensely guarded all the time? He hadn't known his stupid words could do this to her. He hadn't meant a one.

She let him hold her close on the couch, tucked inside his arms but aimed her gaze steadfastly across the room.

"I'm sorry I ran," she repeated, her nose red, cheeks glossy with tears. "I know I'm supposed to be honest and talk, but I panicked."

Thank you, Kelsey. "I panicked and took off once before, remember? But we're okay now."

She swallowed, face turning down. But León saw that sink in, felt some tension leave her shoulders under his arm. He brushed some damp hair off her cheek.

"I've been worried," she finally gulped. "Cooking, posing, it's not important. I like it, but I'm afraid I shouldn't."

He rubbed her arm gently. She hadn't said she forgave him, but she would. "What you do is important," he insisted quietly.

She wiped her cheeks. "It's not art. It doesn't take talent. I'm more than a...a caretaker."

He drew little circles on her shoulder with his fingertips, leaning his head against hers. "I shouldn't have laughed about it, *reinita*."

"You weren't wrong, though. You paint, and I do laundry."

"Maybe we have different talents, but we both do what we're good at."

Motion outside through the glass door caught León's eye. Kelsey. She'd clapped a hand to her forehead, eyes closed, clearly lit by the lights inside.

"No," Celia said quietly. "Being good at laundry isn't a talent, León."

He pressed his lips into a tight line. "I don't mean it like that. There's a lot of organization in making a home. It's comfortable here. You have skill, and it shows."

"Millions of women can do that," Celia said. "But tomorrow, you get to show your work to a bunch of people who will talk about emotions and honesty. No one does that for a clean house."

What was she after here?

León reached for her chin to turn her face to his, but she resisted, shaking her loose curls so they hid her face.

"*Cielito*," he fumbled. "What if I told you more often what I like about it?"

"It's not you." She pleated and unpleated the belt on her dress with limp fingers. "I need something else, something I'm really great at that tells people who I am."

"Not everyone gets that, Celia."

Outside, Kelsey dropped her head in her hands. That sliding door wasn't completely closed! Eavesdropper.

"I can't settle," Celia insisted, her body shivering against his, her voice creaking. "I don't know how to explain. It's too big."

"What do you want me to say here? You're talented, your cooking alone—"

"I can feed the people with actual talent, but...León, listen, I need more! I can't just keep a stupid house!"

"There is nothing stupid about that!" He loosened his arms, turning toward her. "My mother worked hard to make a home and support her kids, so we could go out and do more than she got to! It's...it's noble!"

Outside, Kelsey groaned, "Oh good god."

León shot a glance toward the sound as Celia stiffened in his arms.

"No wonder you feel so comfortable here," she spat.

What?

León released her and bounced to his feet. "What's wrong with that?"

Her frustrated face, red and naked, turned up to him. Her eyes finally met his, flashing mutiny.

"I don't want to be noble!" she cried. Her spine went painfully straight. "It's true. The only thing you have to do is paint and fuck the model!"

"I didn't say that!" The edge in her voice slashed through him.

She stood to face him, hands curled into fists. "I have to make art. I have to do something!"

"Celia," he said carefully. This was going incredibly wrong. He reached for her, but she backed adroitly out of range. "You don't have to make art to be special. You are special. You are art." He waved his hand at the paintings stacked in the hallway. "You literally are the fucking art!"

She crossed her arms across her stomach. "It's not mine. Something has to change."

No. No!

"I knew you wouldn't like it," she said. Angry tears brimmed in her eyes.

Raising a hand to his forehead, he heaved a painful breath. "All because I made a stupid joke?"

She winced. "It's not about you!"

"But we're happy, we've been...you're happy, aren't you?"

Her eyes pleaded with him, but she said nothing. Unbelievable!

"Aren't you?" he insisted.

Her lips parted, then slowly closed.

Her silence broke him, the rejection a shattering blow. A change? Why? If the paintings weren't enough...he had to get out. He'd leave on his own before he let her tell him to go.

He lurched for the door, then stopped and spun around to face her again. She was still paralyzed, sorrowful and mute. He pointed a fierce finger at her, leaning in, eyes burning.

"You belong to me!" he shouted. "You remember that! I'm not playing! I am not done with you!"

He stormed to the front door and out, slamming it behind him.

• • •

Celia sank to the couch, reaching for a pillow and crushing it to her face.

He didn't understand. She couldn't explain.

Standing up for herself always ended in an argument, shouting, fingers pointing at her. How did other people get their way so easily?

The pillow made it hard to breathe. Good.

A touch on her shoulder made her jump and look. Kelsey. Her light eyes were worried, her hand tentative.

"You okay?" she asked.

Celia took a deep breath, hands gouging into the pillow as she lowered it to her lap.

"He left," she croaked. "If I'd just said I was happy, he would have listened."

"It could have gone better," Kelsey agreed softly. "Maybe next time, it will. He said he's not done."

"Not done pushing me around! I belong to him, did you hear that too?" The pillow slowly somersaulted to the floor as Celia gave up her grip on it, and she watched it go. A sickly weight churned deep in her stomach. Was what she wanted so impossible?

"I did all of this wrong," she said. "I ignored my worries until I exploded."

"He needed deflating, honey," Kelsey said as she gently sat close to Celia. "When they're so cocky that they start making jokes, you have to get loud." She leaned over for the pillow, smoothing it as she set it back in place.

Celia scrubbed at her hot cheeks with stiff hands. Her neck hurt, tight and rigid. She felt...anger? Fear? Her insides ached, but with what?

"I don't know how to do this," she choked out. "How do you speak up without making them mad?"

"You didn't 'make' him anything. You don't have that power." At Celia's skeptical stare, Kelsey shook her head. "His reaction isn't your fault."

Celia flexed her painful fingers. "It ended with him mad, either way."

Kelsey tilted her head and patted Celia's knee. "You want to tell me about it? Get some practice for when he comes back?"

Lord no! She'd never said her true fear aloud, not even to León. *Art might save me*, she'd said, but not from what.

Kelsey was looking at her, waiting.

She had to tell, didn't she? Or nothing would change.

"Maybe we could have something to drink?" Kelsey asked.

Celia jumped up, grasping at delay. "Of course, I'm so sorry. I have wine in the fridge."

"Just ginger ale, please."

Celia's head was deep in the fridge in a moment. The cool air soothed her raw cheeks. "Women drink wine when they talk about men, right? I think you brought this bottle, actually. Months ago." She was chattering. Distraction. The mundane task helped.

She returned to the couch with bottle, soda, and glassware, proffering the wine as she approached. "You sure?"

"Ginger ale has like half the calories," Kelsey said.

Celia poured, and Kelsey waited patiently.

Do you have to let every single thing scare you, Celia Rose?

Her chest began pounding again. Okay. She'd been putting off the confession. She took a huge swallow of wine, the glass trembling against her lower lip despite her concentration.

"So," Kelsey said. "I may have heard you two arguing. What's this change you're going to make?"

Celia took a deep breath. *Tranquila.* She would try.

"Growing up was bad," she said carefully. "Only Andrew knows. He was here a lot. He saw me sometimes get really...low about it. He helps when it happens."

"He's not judgy. I like that about him." Kelsey leaned to bump her shoulder against Celia. "I'll be cool too, I promise."

Celia fingered her wine glass, watching the liquid lap gently at the sides. "None of you ever press me or ask questions. I think it's why we're friends." She swallowed hard. "León asks. He presses. It's hard for me."

Kelsey sipped, patient.

"Growing up..." Celia looked down, pulling her hands into her lap. "My dad jumped off a bridge. I was eight."

Kelsey's sorrowful gasp hurt to hear. Her hands reached over, fingers chilled from her drink, and she squeezed Celia's hands hard. "Oh, honey. How awful."

"My mom, she was violent after. I think Dad protected me, but once he was gone...." Celia risked a glance up to see the reaction.

Revulsion curled Kelsey's lip, her eyes narrowing. "She hit you?"

Celia nodded, feeling the familiar shame crawl up her back. "She tried to control it, but she would lose her temper. It was bad for her too when Dad died."

"Oh, that's bullshit," Kelsey said. At Celia's flinch, she shook her head. "I'm sorry, I don't mean you. I mean, hitting your own child? It's disgusting! And after your dad.... Oh, honey!"

Kelsey flung her arms around Celia's shoulders.

Strangely, no tears threatened. Maybe it was the wine, but Celia felt a warm easing in her stomach. Was that relief? "I'm okay," she murmured, surprised.

Kelsey released her but looked skeptical. "I know you don't get along with your mom, but I get it now."

"Her dad spanked her," Celia explained. "She didn't know any other way."

"Oh, that's crap. There's spanking, but you said 'violent.'"

Lips pressed tight, Celia fought to be honest. "She'd beat me. Only where bruises wouldn't show. She broke wooden spoons on me. She felt bad after, but...she bought replacement spoons."

Kelsey goggled. "How?! Going into a store and picking out—oh my god!"

Celia watched Kelsey's face flush with righteous anger and all for her. How could talking feel bad and good at the same time?

"León brought it all back out in me," she said.

Confusion flitted across Kelsey's face. "Wait," she said, tensing. "He doesn't hit you, right?"

Celia shook her head vehemently. "Oh no, he would never!"

"Then, I don't follow."

"I only just saw it, tonight. I always tried to keep my mom happy, so she wouldn't.... I never talked, kept the house clean, and my grades up. I watched her for clues, to anticipate what she wanted so I could make sure she had it."

Kelsey slowly nodded. "Okay, I get that. You do that with us too, you know. But you're not scared of us, right?"

Celia felt a warm blush creep up her cheeks. "No. It's just

how I am now. When I like someone."

"So, you catered to León," Kelsey said, almost to herself. "This is all making sense." She looked back up, eyes shrewd. "Honey, the way he barks at you sometimes, no wonder you responded that way. But, really, he's nice to you?"

A quick flare of joy was instantly doused by ice-cold memory. León had stormed out.

"He was." A lump rose in Celia's throat. "You saw, he doesn't want me to change. I have to, though."

"Good for you. He can do his own laundry."

"Oh no," Celia almost laughed. León, domesticated? "I mean, the art list. I gave up on it to help him paint. I can't do that. It's dangerous."

"Dangerous?"

Celia took a deep breath. This was the hardest thing to admit—it felt so selfish.

"My dad, Kelsey. Sometimes I feel like his way is an option for me."

Kelsey stood in alarm, scattering pillows. "Oh no, it's not!"

Celia raised her face, apprehensive. "I know that, truly. There's something wrong with me, though. I go into a spiral sometimes."

"Wait, how does the art list stop you from...that?"

"Being stuck in my head is bad for me. I need to learn to express myself. Get it out. I thought art would be the way, but I'm not good enough."

"You can keep trying," Kelsey said. "León's lessons didn't help?"

Celia shook her head. "Not with painting. But he makes me admit when I feel things, he's always digging. I was learning to talk. Like this." Her eyes fell. "I messed it up tonight."

"Well, you made a start. It's not fair for him to trigger you into giving him everything."

Celia sighed unevenly, weary. "He didn't know. And I trigger him too, I think."

Kelsey finally sat again, rubbing her forehead and reaching for her ginger ale. "I knew it. Mister Artist has issues too. Well, spill."

How to explain this part? "León thinks his talent is the only thing people like about him. When people help him, like his parents or me, he pays them back by painting well."

"Convenient," Kelsey said, sipping her ginger ale.

Celia nodded. "I'm not sure he knows how to deal with people when art isn't involved. When I started helping him, he sort of homed in on me. I was speaking his language."

"No wonder you two gravitated together so fast," Kelsey mused. "Your dysfunctions match."

Celia felt a chill. Was that all this was?

"So, you see all his baggage," Kelsey continued, "but he has no clue about yours. Typical."

Kelsey's hand rubbing her shoulder felt nice. When had she put an arm back around her?

"That's my fault," Celia said. "I never tell him the important things, my real fears. I didn't want to think about it myself."

"It is absolutely not your fault. And you're changing it now, right?"

Celia let her head rest against Kelsey's shoulder. Hearing that felt surprisingly good. "I'll probably still do his stupid laundry," she said. Amazingly, a giggle almost escaped her. Definitely the wine.

"Celia," Kelsey said, "I'm going to tell you something. Taking care of someone isn't stupid. It's one of the kindest, hardest things you can do. My mom handled everything, so I could just be a kid."

"Noble," Celia murmured and felt Kelsey chuckle.

"I hope I'm a little like her," she continued. "I'm going to find out soon."

Celia was silent, not following.

"I'm going to have a baby," Kelsey said.

Celia sat up in shock, grabbing at Kelsey's hand with a yelp. "What? When? Oh, Kelsey!"

Kelsey's sunny grin transformed her. "I'm about three months in. I was going to have to tell you soon anyway."

"Oh my god, this is why you won't drink wine anymore!"

"I thought for sure that would give me away," Kelsey beamed.

Celia couldn't contain her questions. "Who? Is it Charlie? Will you get married?"

"It's the twenty-first century," Kelsey laughed. "No, if Charlie and I wanted to be together, we would have done it by now. But he'll be involved. So will my mom. I'm going to move in with her, and she'll help."

Celia shuddered. The very thought! "Are you happy about it?"

Kelsey simply glowed. "I'm thrilled! I mean, I am now. It was killing me to not tell you all! A baby, can you imagine?" She eyed Celia thoughtfully. "You could still have a baby, you know. You're good at taking care of people. You'd rock it."

Celia recoiled. "No. I can't have a family."

"Of course, you can. You do! We're your family, me and Andrew, and Trevor. Maybe León if he can get his act together."

"No, I mean—" Celia paused, then plunged ahead. "I won't ever have kids. Someone has to stop my family from going on like they have."

Kelsey's eyes brimmed, saddened. "Oh, Celia." She hugged her friend tightly. "You stopped them by not being like them."

"Is that enough?" Celia said, muffled up against her friend's shoulder. "How do I undo it all?"

Kelsey finally let her go. "The thing you have to do," she said fiercely, "is what's good for you. Undo it that way! If you want your art list, work on it. If you like taking care of León, do that too."

Celia held her breath, feeling almost hopeful. Kelsey made it sound easy.

"Just play to your strengths more!" Kelsey said. "Organize something. Start another business! Just don't let León keep calling all the shots. Take your own shot, girl."

Celia drained the last of her wine. Feelings were exhausting, even the good ones! "For now, just tell me everything about this baby."

Kelsey plunged into the details, to Celia's relief. Part of her searched gingerly inside, though, for fear or anger. It didn't seem to be there anymore.

Telling Kelsey hadn't been as difficult as she'd expected. Maybe she couldn't paint, but talking didn't take talent. Only courage.

Maybe she could tell León, someday.

One thing was for sure, she would not let today's roller coaster send her into a spiral. No backlash from revealing too much, not this time!

She was getting better, dammit!

EIGHTEEN

She was not getting better.

Kelsey stayed for a few hours, Celia finishing all the wine as they talked about the baby. It had seemed like a fine idea until she was alone, trying to fall asleep.

To keep the room from whirling, she stared at the full moon hovering over her skylight. A giant eye watching her. It cast a leaden light over her wide, cold bed.

No texts. No whisper of the back door sliding open. León hadn't come back.

You drove him away, Celia Rose.

Her stomach ached, empty.

The lows tonight had been too low, the highs too high. She was meant for baby steps, not fights and confessions.

Don't be so dramatic, Celia Rose.

Fleeing the bar in tears, standing on the wall in the chilly wind. Realizing that everything had changed in her life but herself. Her voice failing her when she needed it.

You're always feeling sorry for yourself, Celia Rose.

León's gentleness when she came in. Kelsey hugging her, saying Celia had a new family. The baby!

Don't look so pleased with yourself, Celia Rose.

León shouting. The door slamming behind him. The proof that asking to be heard meant abandonment.

You're the reason he's gone, Celia Rose!

She couldn't shut out the voice. Its familiar dismissals were better than being truly alone.

• • •

Tossing on Andrew's sagging couch, León cursed himself for leaving. Why had he run? If he'd stayed, talked with her...he should have explained better or gone over to hold her. She'd been so upset the last time he ran, and now he'd done it again.

She said she wanted a change. What change? She liked

what they had. He knew it! He saw it when he touched her skin, and that reserve of hers melted away. He felt it when she went all soft-eyed over something he'd painted with her.

He could see her looking up at him tonight with those grave eyes, hear the things she'd been about to tell him. She wasn't going to pose anymore, she'd say. She wasn't going to let him stay.

He'd stopped that! It bought him time to change her mind. He'd apologize for leaving. He'd explain. He'd find out what this change of hers was and get it for her.

She belonged to him. He'd fix this.

• • •

Celia awoke to a pale dawn. Her head was muzzy and thumping, a dull fog shrouding the room. Her sinking thoughts had outlived the moon, the circling insults draining her back to the bottom. She'd spent black hours in familiar recrimination. The sleeping pill she'd finally scrounged up must have done its job, but she opened her eyes now to the same rock bottom.

Why swim at all when she always found herself sunk to this well-known depth? It never, ever, ever stopped happening.

That thumping came again. No, knocking. The front door.

They'd come for León's paintings. They had to be delivered today. She had to let them in.

Celia dragged on her robe and shuffled through the hall. Take them away. What did it matter now?

She opened the door.

León stood there, anxiously hopeful in the crisp pale morning. His weary eyes, ringed with bruise-like shadows, widened. His hand fluttered up, then slowly fell away.

She felt nothing. She didn't, she couldn't, she wouldn't. "Take the paintings," she mumbled.

"What?" He squinted at her. "Are you okay?"

She faded back into the bare entry hall, and he followed.

"What's wrong?" he asked from behind her. "I'm here. Let's fix it."

The paintings sat stacked in front of them, leaning on the

wall, hidden in their blank white wrapping. Ready to leave.

He overtook her with a quick step and caught her hand, halting her in the echoing hallway. "Hey. Are you feeling okay?"

Feeling? Never again. She was better off numb than living through another drowned night like that.

León's brows drew together, and he fixed her with searching scrutiny. The longer she went without reacting, the more alarmed his inspection. Silly boy, all those feelings running naked across his face.

"The blank stare?" he asked. "Why?"

Lord, don't make me talk. "I can't," she said.

"Can't what?"

Her hand wavered toward a door—craft room, studio, one of them. "Can't paint, swim—can't anything."

His head lowered, and he inched closer. Couldn't he just let her be?

"Come here," he said quietly. His hand tightened on hers, pulling, and she didn't have the will to pull back. He led her to the black-spattered craft room, watching over his shoulder to see if she'd resist. She didn't.

Her little easel was still set up. Dully, head pounding, she closed her eyes and listened to León sorting brushes and uncapping paint. She knew the sounds too well to need to watch. Then he was urging a palette into her limp fingers, moving behind her, and guiding her forward with firm hands on her shoulders.

"You can do anything," he said.

Ah. Whine like a child, nag like a shrew, and get your third painting lesson. Easy.

He would stand at her back and give prompts like before. She was too empty to paint but too dense to walk away.

"*Tranquila*," he said, squeezing her shoulders. "Breathe."

No. She was tired of this. So tired of flailing toward the sunny surface above her. The peace of giving up, of wallowing in her depths, felt right. She was stupid and ridiculous and laughable, but at the bottom, it didn't matter. The bottom was comfortably terrible, and she fit in. The one place she fit.

No feelings. No trying. Please.

León's arms wrapped around her waist from behind, holding her with care, his chin slipping over her shoulder to rest there.

Celia tried not to feel, but his solid body holding her close was…. Why couldn't he just leave her alone?

"Paint a line, *mi cielo*. You, right now."

The brush was too heavy. She just closed her eyes. Numb. Be numb.

"Are you red?" His voice, low and soothing, rumbled into her body from his. He tightened his arms around her. "Show me," he murmured.

Show him.

She lifted the brush. Red was easiest. One listless stroke, a stuttering line on the canvas. That was her.

"What next?" he asked.

The same thing that always came next. A horizontal line above, in black, the red smearing through it. The arch above, black. Black bars connecting them.

She set the brush down.

"What did you paint?" he asked.

She took another brush and made a blue line at the bottom.

"Is it water under a bridge?"

She shook her head weakly. The pool.

There wasn't more to paint. She existed, the bridge existed, the pool existed. Conflict in the picture but no story. No resolution. She never progressed.

He gently nuzzled his unshaven cheek against hers, the rasp of stubble rough and familiar.

"I know it's scary," he said. "Honesty is hard. I struggle with it too. But it's just you and the canvas. You can tell it what you're thinking."

Thinking? She was done thinking.

You're such a quitter, Celia Rose.

"Can I be in the painting with you?" he asked.

She still had blue paint in the brush, so she painted a line for him. Tight up against her washed-out line.

"Am I blue like the water?"

She nodded.

"How?"

How? They'd first kissed with the pool's waves ringing them, lay together for the first time in its reflected light. It was her safe place, the water supporting her when she floated. Didn't he know?

A tiny painful spark fluttered inside her. The bridge loomed, but the pool underneath might catch her.

How was León like the—oh.

Oh.

She painted another blue line horizontally above the pool. Kelsey. Another line, Andrew. The third, Trevor, threatened to engulf the tops of her line and León's, the level of the water now nearly reaching the bridge. The fall wouldn't be bad, the landing survivable.

"The water is rising," he said. "You're telling a story, Celia Rose. Keep going."

No, she was done painting. Her art list had utterly failed, but what if she didn't need it?

It hurt to care, to feel a crack in her steely numbness. It terrified her, thinking about trying, hoping, one more time. She'd failed so many times before, isolated and helpless.

León squeezed his arms around her, solid. She wasn't alone right now.

She didn't have to be good at painting to see it right in front of her. Even if she fell again, it wasn't the end. The water was there, the support. Opening up to people didn't require talent, just courage.

Could she find courage?

"I'm done," she said. Setting down the tools, she turned into his arms, resting her head against his chest.

"Okay," he murmured softly. "Did it help? Will you tell me what you painted?"

Falling. Floating.

She shook her head against him.

"Why did the water rise? Are we going to drown?"

Him and his questions.

"You don't have to tell me," he said. "But painting helps, right? I should have seen you needed to do it too. I'll do better."

"It's not about you," she murmured against his chest. She felt him chuckle under his breath.

"You keep saying that, but you put me in your painting."

So she had. Oh, how familiar he was. The soft thump of his heartbeat against her ear, the scent of his skin, the steely harbor of his arms. León wasn't easy to push away.

A flood of gratitude and comfort washed through her. She could feel it flow from her chest outward, filling her skin. Bubbling light sluiced through the numbness, leaving her floating and weak. No matter. León would shore her up.

"*Reinita*," he said, "tell me what will help."

Falling in love felt nothing like she'd expected.

"I want to tell you," she whispered. "About the bridge, about everything."

She felt his chest swell against her.

• • •

There was no more painting that day nor the next. Celia had spilled out her story, fidgeting in a desperate little ball as León cradled her on the couch. He calmly collected each new layer and texture, filling in her picture. The flood of colors dammed inside her broke like a wave, hundreds of paintings there for him.

As her story stilled, he'd vowed to help her find this outlet she wanted. Anything to put some warmth back in her eyes.

At midday, his paintings were picked up.

After sunset, they swam quietly in the dark.

By morning, she was more herself.

When the next afternoon shone its great temporary orange triangles on her walls, it was León's turn to feel vulnerable. His colors already lived outside him, and they'd be on display tonight.

They drove to the exhibition gala at dusk, walking into the lofty gallery, lights infusing artworks on warm brick walls and low white plinths.

León tucked Celia's hand firmly under his arm. She'd

resisted coming tonight, not adamantly, but enough to make them late. Her eyes were still a little sad and somber, but she hadn't put on her public mask. Good girl.

A muted throng glided through the converted warehouse, soft words being exchanged as couples flowed from one spotlighted artwork to another. He breathed it in. These people cared about art. They felt it.

He squeezed Celia's arm with his and looked down at her. His quiet little muse. He'd show her the entire creative world.

Celia silently gestured to the far corner of the front room, where the blue painting glowed. His heart hung on that wall. A small knot of people stood nearby. Did they like it? Would they understand?

León bounced just a tiny bit.

Andrew rounded an interior corner, his face lighting up when he clocked them near the door. He threaded his way through the crowd.

"Hey!" he said. "I didn't know if you were coming."

"And miss my LA debut? Please."

"Celia, girl," Andrew took her free hand in his, "I'm so sorry."

León nodded. Good, she was owed an apology from this quarter too.

"Are you better?" Andrew continued, uncharacteristically anxious. "I want to explain."

The group near the blue painting was moving away, but two more couples were approaching. León watched wistfully. What were they saying about it?

"Go look," Celia said to him quietly. "I'll catch up."

"Really?"

Her faint, fond smile said yes. Resisting the urge to sprint, he left her in Andrew's hands.

• • •

With that eager gleam in his eyes, there was no way León would have lasted long. Celia regretted each step he took, but wouldn't cling. Andrew squeezed her hand, frowning fretfully as she turned back to him.

"I'm so ashamed, Celia."

"I shouldn't have run off," she demurred, disquiet filtering through her. She and Andrew had always been at ease together, but he looked agitated.

"No, this one is on me," he said with a decisive shake of his head. "I was teasing León, egging him on. I'm so sorry." His shoulders were actually slumping.

León had explained. "I know it's an old joke you had." She looked across the room but couldn't spot him through the crowd.

Andrew's mouth twisted, and he let go of her hand. "A sexist joke. You're not just a model."

"I'm no artist," she said.

"You are," he protested. "Your art is seeing what people need and making it happen, so naturally that we don't even notice."

She felt her cheeks heating. "That's not art!" Good lord, did she have to go through this with everyone?

"It's a talent," he insisted, leaning in. His eyes on hers were different, direct and keen, almost like León's. "I had time to think about this. We talk about our work all the time, and I realized how it must feel for you not to be a part of it. My joking excluded you."

She stared. Being seen by Andrew was unexpected.

"I forgot how being excluded felt," he continued. "I was always too bi for my gay friends, too black for my white friends, I didn't quite qualify for any one group. I decided a long time ago to stop honoring the rules. Everyone is in my group, just as they are." His pained frown deepened. "I messed that up, Celia."

It was too strange, seeing him so earnest. What was the antidote to Andrew's concern? "You're good at spotting when someone needs to step up," she said. "Yourself included."

He looked more relieved than she'd expected. "You don't have to flatter me while I apologize."

Andrew, rejecting flattery? This *was* serious.

"I'm sorry," he said, sighing as he wrapped her in a firm hug. Wow. She made a change and everyone else had to change too?

As he let her go, she saw him gazing past her shoulder and turned to see Kelsey waiting patiently.

"My turn," she said.

Celia paused. "Wait," she said. Oh, hell. "Do you take turns hanging out with me in public? Because of my anxiety?"

Andrew's face went blank. "Um."

"Did you never notice that?" Kelsey asked.

Celia shook her head, unsure if she should be annoyed or touched.

"Trevor's here, by his pictures," Kelsey said. "Come look, say hi."

Celia cast another searching glance to León's corner, still not seeing his dark head. He would want her there. But Kelsey took her elbow, and so she went along. Trevor first, quickly.

The vast front room had open archways along the back wall, inviting lights burning within each. Trevor awaited in the nearest antechamber, his photographs—many of Kelsey—mounted on a softly-lit plaster wall. He sat, sipping a glass of red wine, on one of the little plinths that doubled as stools. He brightened as the women approached.

"Hey, you're out! Feeling better? Andrew's been in a state."

"León sent a text," Celia said. "He told everyone we're good."

"Yeah, but it's better to see in person."

Kelsey placed herself between the two of them, her expectant air palpable. "I have some news," she said, "but first, I wanted you two to talk. Trevor, you should tell Celia about your parents."

A chill struck Celia. Would she have to tell her story again so soon? And in this crowd? Seeing people's faces when the worst came out was awful enough, but in public?

"Really?" Trevor said. "Celia, you always avoid talking about parents."

She braced herself. "I'm changing things."

"It's not a fun story." He took off his glasses and polished them absently on his shirt. "There was this boy, you see."

Celia stood quietly, watching his gaze soften, his face

growing a little dreamy.

"Jacob," he said like a sigh. "He was older than me. Beautiful. Golden curls. We would skip classes and steal an hour or two in an empty house while our parents were at work. Lying in bed just looking at each other, sometimes."

His blue eyes were so far away.

"In class," he said, "in public, we never even made eye contact. I thought those hours were a secret just for us, and letting others know would break the spell. I thought it was love."

Oh no.

"We were caught—of course we were. He denied everything. Said he wasn't gay, just wasn't allowed to touch Mormon girls, and succumbed to what was available. He'd sinned for pleasure, but he wasn't *that way.*"

Oh, poor Trevor.

"I fought, I proclaimed. I was in love. And the wrath came down on me, not him."

Celia held her breath.

"I spent two months living with an Elder who tried to berate it out of me." His face fell. "My parents were punished, I saw them suffer too. But they didn't stop it. They wanted me cured. For my sake, I'd like to think, but really...they wanted their church back more."

Trevor didn't look dreamy now. He looked hurt.

"I caved. I wanted my life back too. I tried to hide it until the prayers fixed me."

His eyes hardened, a muscle jumping in his jaw.

"And when I was eighteen, my dad took me aside and said it was time to move out. I thought I must have slipped up somehow, but he said he'd always known I was gay. He'd done his duty but knew I wouldn't change, and now it was time to go be gay somewhere else."

"Oh, Trevor, no."

"I moved here to LA, met others like me, and made my own way. My parents didn't want to know me, were never proud, and one day I just let them go too."

Kelsey shook her head, her face echoing the disgust she'd

shown when she heard about Celia's mom.

"You don't talk to them? Ever?" Celia asked. "Does that help?"

"Yeah. I protect myself better than they did. I'm sticking with people who lift me up."

Celia swallowed hard, her throat tight. "I never knew, Trevor."

"See, saying things out loud can change things," Kelsey said. "You might find out other people understand."

Trevor stood to give Celia a hug. "You don't have to talk about your family, not here. But you can when you want."

Kelsey waited until he released her, then turned to Trevor. "Okay, now my news."

Nineteen

León had found a plinth to sit on, near enough to his paintings to eavesdrop but not so near as to give off mother-hen vibes. The yellow and purple canvases hung together on one wall, singing in counterpoint. Sun versus shadow. Solid versus ghostly.

The blue painting, though, on its wall alone, outshone everything in the room. The watery hues rippled across the canvas, that black line of Celia's waist a fluid tendril of ink swirling up the center. It gleamed in aquamarines, the brush marks like wavelets of textured motion. It was a visual love letter to that night.

He almost felt naked each time people approached. He rocked on his seat, head turned away, thumbs tapping. Please, please, really see it.

"Well, this is just stunning. So fluid!"

"This piece could anchor a whole room."

"I've never heard of this artist. Get one of the cards, will you, dear?"

The sample cards in their brochure holder, mounted to the wall between his paintings, were emptying fast. Why hadn't he had more printed? He could have found the money.

He gripped his hands tightly to keep them still. He had more people around his work than anyone else in sight. They liked it!

Andrew approached, grinning at finding León on his perch. "Hovering, are we?"

"Obviously." León looked past Andrew but saw only swanning patrons. "Where's Celia?"

· · ·

Trevor sat back on his plinth, mouth open as he eyed Kelsey's stomach.

"Wow," he mused, taking it in. "Pregnant? Back with Mom at forty? How do you feel about that?"

Kelsey's back straightened. "I am not forty!" She poked Trevor's shoulder as he chuckled.

"So, will you keep working?" he asked.

"Oh yeah, for most of it. Mom will help, and she said she won't charge rent, but I'll want to contribute."

Trevor shook his head. "At least some parents do it right."

"León's parents supported him when he was getting started," Celia said. "He feels really obligated to them still."

"I'll bet they don't want him to," Kelsey said.

"Good for them, though," Trevor said. "Starting as an artist is tough. You're broke and still learning, but having a regular job takes so much energy! You need time to improve your technique, find your creative voice."

"That happened to me," Kelsey agreed. "I wanted to try fashion designing. But I needed money, and before I knew it, I was just working at the shop. I was too tired to try and start another career in my free time."

"I wonder how much art we've lost to poverty," Trevor said, shaking his head. "It's tragic."

"I wasn't in poverty," Kelsey said, pursing her lips.

"No, not you, just in general. Kids out there right now, there could be some great art we'll never get because they have to work."

Celia thought guiltily about the money sitting unused in her bank.

"Well, not my kid," Kelsey said. "She'll get every opportunity. My mom couldn't afford that for me, but we'll pool what we have. That'll make it easier. And multi-generational living is very trendy."

None of them could hold back their chuckles.

"It's brave, Kelsey," Trevor said. "A kid at your age."

"Oh, stop teasing. I'm only thirty-seven. That's also very trendy, waiting until later to have kids. I won't be the last of us."

Andrew's head poked around the corner. "Hey, León's asking about Celia."

Kelsey lifted her head. "I haven't even seen his stuff! Let's go."

Trevor reached out to Andrew, who took his hand to pull him from his seat. Kelsey followed as they moved away, then looked back to see Celia lingering in the corner.

"I'll be right there," Celia said. At Kelsey's raised eyebrow, she smiled. "And I'm okay on my own."

They left her there.

Celia fingered the phone in her pocket. Slowly, she pulled it out and scrolled.

Don't you dare, Celia Rose!

Exhaling deeply, she blocked her mother's number, then followed after her surprising friends.

• • •

León jumped up, jubilant, as the gang finally joined him. They were going to love the paintings, right? Celia would— where was Celia?

"Wow," Kelsey said, drawing the word out into multiple syllables. "Oh, wow! It's Celia in the pool, right?"

"They're all Celia," Andrew said, moving close to the yellow painting. "Look at those big serious eyes."

"They're gorgeous, León." Trevor cocked his head at the purple image. "This one is...wow."

León laughed and bounced on his toes, turning his head to where Celia must be lagging. Where was she? He'd waited long enough!

A steel-haired woman joined the group around León's work. "The raw emotion just leaps off the canvas, doesn't it?" she said. "I see they're all of the same model."

"His muse," Kelsey agreed. "They're the best paintings here, right? I already heard two people say they're going to buy this one." She gestured to the blue painting as Andrew snickered.

There! León finally saw Celia in the middle of the gallery. She was standing alone, though, not looking for him.

"Are there no sample cards left?" the woman asked. León turned, to see she was right.

"Guess not. Here, take mine." Kelsey dug into her purse and pulled out a business card.

"Stylist? The artist needs a stylist?"

Kelsey chuckled. "No, I just know him."

Celia was still stopped in the center of the gallery. León couldn't take it. He loped to her.

• • •

On her way to León's corner, the import of what she'd done hit Celia. Blocking Mom? Oh, the fury once she realized! The last twenty-four hours crashed down, setting her trembling, too full of highs and lows and revelations and feelings.

Celia stopped, trying to control the storm inside. Throbbing fear and relief over Mom. Pain for Trevor, wonder over the change in Andrew. Kelsey's pregnancy! And León, a sweet, constant hurricane of pride and tenderness and want. She could scream right now and still not get all the new feelings out! She could paint this for León, purge it that way, but it would just be one big scribble of every color.

If only she'd had enough talent.

Talking worked, though. She knew things about everyone that she hadn't, just last week. Being vulnerable and honest in person did make things change.

Was this the final end of her art list? She still loved art and could keep it in her life by helping León. Everyone had said in their own way that her support was valuable, a worthy role. Maybe that was enough. Maybe she could support more artists, like the kids Trevor talked about. She had the money.

She looked around the gala again.

She'd wondered, last time she was here, about running a gallery. She liked the building. It was the industrial loft style she'd always loved, an old airy warehouse with high brick walls and concrete floors. It was clean, well built.

What if she bought this space? The current owners hadn't made a success of it; it might be a bargain. They were moving to a more exclusive location, tired of fighting locals who claimed they were gentrifying the neighborhood. Maybe she could do something less elite with the building. Something that involved the community.

She knew how to run a business—that was just organization and planning. And she could afford it.

She started to feel excited.

León was suddenly there, pulling at her hand, eyes quizzical. "Celia?"

She nodded, barely hearing him.

If she had a gallery, she could show León's paintings. Then he'd be free of the extra work of getting his paintings shown, giving him the time Trevor talked about to just create.

She could do that for new artists too. In the community, right here. Gift them the time and space to grow.

A crashing storm broke over her, a blinding electric arc blanking away vision, thunder rolling through her veins.

León planted himself firmly in her line of sight, taking both of her hands in his. "What's wrong?"

"Let me think, please," she begged, eyes screwed shut.

The young artists. The money. Seeing people's needs, supporting them. Running a business. It was all right in front of her! It was worthwhile! It was something she was good at, something that would make a difference!

"Celia?"

Her head swam with too many ideas. Ears ringing, she took a stumbling step toward León, pulling at his hands.

"I need to go look. Come on!" She took off for the front door, heels clicking on the concrete floor. León followed her outside into the darkened street.

The gallery lights through the front windows spilled gloriously onto the pavement, just like her wall of windows at home. She could practically see young artists in there, creating. Safe. Provided for. Uplifted.

A wave of certainty washed over her. She spun in glee. "This is it! This is what I can do! This is my thing!"

"What are you talking about?" León's voice behind her was utterly confused, and a touch anxious.

"The kids! The artists!" She whirled to look at the other buildings on the street and jumped up and down for literal joy. "Businesses on the ground floor but residential on top! And the warehouse is three stories! Look at the windows!"

She'd never been so awake!

How much could a building in this part of town cost? She

could get a mortgage. She had more resources.

"Celia! What are you talking about?"

A final spin brought her around to León's baffled face. "I'm going to buy this gallery and make a studio space! For artists just starting out, to live here and work. Free food and beds and laundry and showers, and they can have the time they need to make art!"

She could barely catch her breath as the possibilities piled upon each other. León gaped at her, transfixed.

"I know how to run it!" She bounced in the street. "I'd finally be using that stupid money for something real! The front can have a little gallery, so they can sell their work. I could invite important people to view what they make. That's networking! Trevor can help with that! And promotion, Kelsey! And Andrew can teach classes here if he wants. We could have other teachers...." A little squeal escaped her. "This is it. This is everything!"

Oh, look at how stunned he was! She laughed out loud, filling the whole street with joyful echoes.

"You want to build an artist collective?" he asked, disbelief written across him.

"I didn't invent it? I don't care," she babbled. "I can cook for them all. And I can live above it! There must be room. I don't need very much space."

León finally broke into a smile. "It's a big idea. Is this really what you want?"

"It's everything," she beamed. "It's all my skills, my way to matter. It's finally it, my idea I was looking for. Oh god." She hugged her arms around her body, blurring vision creating faint halos on the streetlamps. "Is this what inspiration feels like? It's wonderful."

León's grin widened as he watched her, his eyes softening.

A weight, a mantle around her of black and blue tension, wisped away into nothing. The bone-deep burden had gone unnoticed until now, its absence dizzying. Disorienting—a lightness unlike falling, different from floating. She might slip upwards into the sky.

The relief of it.

She ran and threw her arms around León's waist, pressing her face against his chest. As his arms closed around her, she burst into loud sobs.

"I know," he said, stroking her hair. "I know."

She was capable of it. Inspiration.

She'd been so afraid she wasn't.

TWENTY

León quietly navigated the dark kitchen, stopping to lean against the dining room doorway. "Celia?"

Her face, hovering in the darkness, turned up to him immediately. She sat at the dining table, lit from below by only her laptop screen.

"It's late," he said. "Come to bed."

"I'm sorry," she said. "I thought if I could write enough of it down, I could sleep."

"I'll help you sleep." He let his hand slip down the door frame, the whisper of his palm against the wall curiously louder in the dark. She smiled.

The sudden urge to paint washed through him. He saw charcoals and midnight blues around her and Celia's face softly illuminating the night like the moon. For a minute, she was the source of light, not the computer.

Then she closed the lid, winking the image away.

"Big night for both of us," she sighed as she rounded the table, guileless in her sweats, and slipped her hands around his waist.

"We're just getting started." He reached up to brush back her hair, tucking it behind an ear. He could barely see her face, the moonlight outside filtering in to trace its curves.

She leaned her hips against him, and he felt that rush start in his blood. His Celia.

"Did you enjoy your opening night?" she asked, those wonderful eyes of hers looking up at him through those wonderful lashes. "I'm sorry if I stole some of your attention."

"No more sorries." He planted a soft kiss on her forehead. "We were there for hours. It was plenty."

She nestled against him. "It felt like minutes."

"I know." He stepped back, reaching up to capture one of her hands as she released him. "Make no mistake, tomorrow I'll gush about being in this show. I thought you'd want time tonight to make your lists." He stepped back again, pulling on her wrist so she'd follow. Then he paused and stopped pulling. He wouldn't like it if she towed him around, would he?

She followed anyway. "Things really will change now, won't they?"

He turned for the bedroom, draping an arm around her shoulders. "Not everything."

• • •

The leasing agent was eager to show the warehouse, and Celia met him an hour before the gallery opened. She'd wandered the first floor, of course, but never explored it with an eye to ownership. A tiny fear kept buzzing in her; could she find another building if this one was wrong?

But it was perfect.

The open main floor smelled of art—pine wood and stretched canvas and varnish and oil and clay. She hadn't noticed last night, the scents too fragile to compete with the perfume and wine of a gala. The old brick walls soared over a dozen feet to iron rafters and sprinklers and a constellation of halogen light fixtures. Fan blades moved a mild breeze of clean air, their simple white noise masking the sounds of the city street outside.

When the artworks went home to their makers, the room would again be a ready sanctuary, a simple brick shell waiting for creation to refill it. Celia felt the room's potential like a tangible thing, a shiver, a caress.

Across the smooth cool floor, long crosshatched paths of sunlight fell from tall paned windows, and Celia could envision her fledgling artists working there. Fed and bathed in sunlight, their art would be born into the world.

The arched alcoves along the back could be small classrooms. To the left of the front door, gallery shelves could be built. The whole warehouse could blossom with colored oils, ring with welded metal, flow with curves of clay. And Celia herself could finally contribute, leaning into her real talents to organize and feed and house her residents.

She stopped to look at León's paintings in their warm little corner. They were a touch of home, welcoming her to the building. They'd just moved in before she had.

An original iron staircase on the southern wall led to the

second floor. It had been painted many times over the years, its handrail cool under Celia's palm, imperfectly ridged with layers of glossy black paint. The stairs opened onto a new wide bare space, twin to the floor below. It held desks and filing cabinets and racks upon racks of art. Here, practicality and dreams met; the backbone of Celia's plan. She could wall off small offices for the staff she'd need, then fill the center of the room with dormer-style beds and cubbies. By this floor's front windows, she could build a communal living space with a kitchen and couches. Creation would thrive below, but this floor would be for the mess of living.

Celia's footsteps on the next flight of iron stairs set it ringing quietly. The third floor, in unused disrepair, was brilliantly lit and dry. Dust stirred by Celia's feet floated into columns of sun from the domed skylights. She could live up here, after walling off most of the floor for the storage she'd inevitably need. She didn't need much space herself.

A smaller final stair led to the mottled tarpaper roof. Stepping out into the open air, Celia looked over the stuccoed buildings and businesses of the neighborhood. Downtown LA rose behind palm trees and bridges, only the tops of the buildings visible through the hazy autumn morning light. The air sang with the burr of cars and trains, pops of music from a distant market square, the bark of a dog on the sidewalk below.

She turned in a slow circle, breathing in the possibilities. This was a different kind of sanctuary—no pool, no distant view down the canyon. Instead, this building cupped her in full hands, embracing her purpose and potential. A wind rustled nearby palm trees, their tops almost at eye level. She was up high! She'd be giving up floating to start flying.

Trailing back down the stairs, head filling with lists, Celia knew. She could feel deep in her bones that this was her place.

There were a million tough decisions ahead of her, and it felt heavenly. She didn't mind if she lost every penny failing as long as she got to try. With the agent locking up behind her, she pulled out her phone. Next stop, her financial planner.

• • •

León heard her close the front door, returning home. It

had been strange, alone in the house without her quiet presence. He'd touched up all the paintings he could work on without her and desperately wanted her to sit more, but he should let her rest tonight. She'd been out on her project for most of the day.

Meeting her in the hallway, seeing her face lit like sunshine made the whole quiet day worth it.

"It's going to work," she said, blissful.

She beamed when she saw he'd cooked supper. Why hadn't he thought of doing this before? They ate the grilled cheese sandwiches—his specialty—at the kitchen island, her planning already taking over the dining table.

She laughed and chattered about her warehouse. Look at her glowing!

"I couldn't get my mind off you all day," he said, and she glowed even brighter. Seeing her this happy was new. He loved it.

She followed him after their meal to the studio room to see the work he'd gotten done. Paintings lined the room, leaning against the walls, too wet to stack.

"Do you want me to pose?"

He shook his head. "That's too much for one day, Celia. You still have some lists to make, I'll bet. Maybe tomorrow around lunch?"

She nodded assent, looking closely at the nearly completed green painting.

He picked up a brush from where it'd been buried in yellow-green paint, keeping wet, and looked around for his cleaning gear. He hadn't finished putting his things away before starting to cook. Celia found his jars sitting on a dining room chair he'd brought in. Paint stained the seat. His stomach sank.

"Oh no. I forgot to cover that."

She waved it off, careless and smiling. He handed her the brush, turning to reach for a rag. In the scant moment before he turned back, she lit up with an impish energy. He couldn't help but stare, her eyes alight and a mischievous curl on her lips.

She reached out and painted a stripe of green on the back of his hand. Surprise jolted through him.

"Paint gets everywhere," she said with a barely straight face.

Who was this new woman? "You're going to do me like that?"

She giggled and dabbed green onto his cheek. That paint was cold!

"You'll make another mess," he said, surprise fading into fascination. "Be careful."

"Then stand still."

He instantly complied. She drew a wobbly line down his nose, another little laugh spilling out.

"Spontaneous expression," she said.

A shiver tickled down his spine as she drew a line down his neck. Look at her, so playfully intent, her glee so different from his usual somber girl.

She paused, scanning him for another likely stretch of bare skin, and he eagerly pulled off his shirt. "Here, you need more canvas."

"I need more paint, too."

He was quick to hand her the closest tube, and she squeezed a huge glob of yellow into her palm. What?

Lowering her face and looking up at him through her lashes, she painted a stripe across each of his collarbones. "Beautiful," she teased.

That spark under his skin ignited. He'd never imagined that night would lead here, and certainly had never pictured her so confident. She was incredibly exciting this way, lit up with whimsy! Had he ever seen her unreservedly happy? She was mesmerizing.

He needed to paint her like this, but first—he reached for her. She stopped him with the paintbrush, fending him off and leaving paint across his knuckles.

"No. I am the painter tonight. I direct you."

His heart skipped. Jesus, look at the light in her eyes.

She held the brush high, like a magic wand, a conductor's baton. A new giggle escaped her.

"Lay on the floor," she said. "I will pose you."

He scrambled down into her usual spot, the drop cloth rough against his palms. He leaned back onto his elbows, waiting.

She ducked behind his canvas a few times, popping her head out to look at him cheekily. Finally, she stopped and stared, her eyelids lowering lazily as her gaze slowly roamed every inch of him. Ha ha.

"Do I—"

"Shhh." She pretended to consider him, amusement shining from pink cheeks. The little crinkles at her eyes were adorable. He could stare at her like this forever.

"Lay back."

He did as directed.

"Arms out to your sides. Leg slightly bent. Back arched. Neck back."

Like he was floating.

She left the canvas and brush, bringing the tube of paint. Devilish, imperious, she loomed. Then she slowly removed her blouse and bra with her clean hand as he watched from the floor, trembling with the effort of staying still.

Jesus, she was beautiful.

She lowered herself to the floor, sitting atop him, straddling his thighs. She squeezed more paint into a hand, then considered him. She chose to draw stripes up his ribs as he squirmed. The pleasure from her tickling touch might shatter him.

"*Reinito*," she murmured. León couldn't help it—a snort escaped him. "What?"

"It's not right."

She leaned forward, reaching to drag a stripe of cold paint onto an outstretched bicep. "How do I say it? I want a cute Spanish word to call you."

"Traditionally," he teased, "you'd call me *papi*."

She sat up laughing. "Oh no! I am not calling you daddy!"

He had to smile along with her joy. The expressions on her face! The emotions! She was lovely, just goddamn radiant.

"How do I say 'masterpiece?'" she asked.

"*Obra maestra.*"

She shook her head, then painted dots on his stomach with her fingertips. Each touch made his muscles tremble.

"No. How about 'my painting'?"

"*Mi pintura.*"

She shook her head again. "'My canvas.'"

"*Mi lienzo.*"

Her eyes burned. "That's it. León, *mi lienzo.*" She bent close over him and stroked paint up his side. "*Mi lienzo.*"

León had no words. To hear her purr that in his ear...she was everything. He loved her this way.

Shock hit him like a sucker punch, knocking the air out of his lungs, his vision blurring around the edges as he saw the honest truth.

He was in love with Celia.

Of course he was.

He forced himself still as she, still playful and unaware, painted a long thick line down his chest onto his stomach, stopping only when she reached his jeans.

"Unbutton yourself before I ruin your clothes," she said with a coy glance. The realization, the touches, and the cold paint all compounded. León found his fingers trembling almost too much to undo his jeans.

"Look," she said as she stroked paint low across his stomach, eager to cover each bare inch of skin as it was revealed. "We found art I'm good at."

Still shaking, he reached up to her cheek. He wasn't going to be able to control himself much longer.

She surprised him once more by moving first, wrapping herself around him, and kissing him fiercely. This time it was her holding a wrist to the floor. This time it was her mouth on his neck, nipping and sucking, marking him. He was too dazed to contribute, lost in the feel of his woman taking the upper hand for the first time.

Her paint-covered hand fumbled to push his jeans away, and he raised his hips to assist, senseless at her unusual aggression. Anything she wanted! She palmed him, already hard, over his briefs as she explored his mouth with her tongue, panting. When her fingers began slipping under his waistband, though, she paused, pulling back.

She had yellow and green paint all over her face from where she'd pressed it against his. He almost laughed. She was gorgeous.

"The paint, is it safe? If I touch you there? It won't sting or...?"

He shook his head. "Bad idea," he said, breathless.

She grinned. "Rinse off first?"

He nodded mutely. If that's what she wanted, then yes. Anything.

He barely made it to his feet before she grabbed his wrist and led him across the hall, through to the master bathroom.

He'd been wrong. He didn't mind her towing him at all.

She tugged open the glass shower door, threw the water on, and hurriedly pulled off the rest of her clothes as it heated. León followed suit, watching her greedily. Her coppery skin was striped in war paint from having embraced him. Her breasts, daubed with gold...his next painting swam in his eyes.

He followed her into the white-tiled shower under the stream of hot water. She wasted no time, slipping wet arms around his hips and pulling him closer. God, she felt perfect, her smooth skin gliding against him. As their bodies finally pressed together, he reached to kiss her, water running down both their faces, washing the paint away.

Her lips parted, her insistent tongue eager in his mouth. She pressed him back against the tile, kissing hungrily. Both panted shallowly, hands roaming freely across each other's wet skin.

"Jesus, *mi cielo*," he breathed into her. Her knee rose, her thigh sliding up his leg, his stiff length pressed hard against her. His hand slipped down to hold her leg, and she reached down to grab his wrist tightly. Her new intensity had him reeling.

The hot water splashed noisily onto her shoulders and back, spattering them both. He had to close his eyes, and the world became only touch and sound. The hard tile at his back and Celia's slick skin sliding past his...her frantic breaths fighting his...he was lost.

"Here," she whispered between kisses. "I want you right

here."

He was beyond responding. Her mouth moved down to his jaw, then she bit lightly at his neck again. Pain, pleasure, he didn't know what he felt. He didn't care.

Then she was disengaging, her body leaving him. He opened his eyes in alarm, water dashing into them. She moved backward, arm extended, until she stood against the far tiled wall. He nearly slipped in his rush for her, frantic to be enfolded by her body again.

His impact smacked her shoulders against the wall, and she raised her face, laughing toward the ceiling. This joyous goddess of his, this vital gold-skinned siren—he wrapped himself around her, beggared, in the steam and heat.

Her hands slid down his bare back, over his hips, pressing her mound against him. His mouth was on hers, fierce, trying to pull her slippery body closer. Words tumbled from him, but he was beyond knowing what he said.

She put one foot on the shower seat, tilting her hips up to him. His arm slid under her knee again, hand grasping at her hip.

He slid the tip of his cock between her lips, bringing gasps from both. Their eyes locked. Pressing her against the wall with his full weight, he pushed into her deeply. Her cry, her arms clutching at his shoulders, felt as good as her slick hot body taking him in. He sucked in a harsh breath, slowly stroked back out, then in again.

"*Cielito*," he breathed, "*mi amor*, yes." His hand squeezed her hip, holding tight so he could thrust inside again. He whispered her name with each stroke, fucking her fiercely under the pounding water.

His mouth found hers again as the pleasure built to new heights. His free hand scrambled over her, roughly finding her wet breast. He whimpered brokenly, small gasps being torn from him as he kissed her hungrily, thrusting harder.

Under his hand, her hip muscles bunched and slammed into his. "Yes, god, yes," he panted, his whole body tense. He bent his knees to thrust even harder, lifting her to her toes each time he filled her.

Her rhythmic gasps became mewling cries, matching their motions. The sensations grew too intense, too close. As he buried his face in her neck, thrusting hard, her body exploded against him, her head knocking back against the tile. He felt her shudder and writhe against him, supporting her weight as he could, slowing his pace to let her release subside. But he couldn't stop. He cradled the back of her head to him, his ragged breaths muffled against her skin.

With slow, deep, final thrusts, the world erupted, his body shuddering with pleasure. He clutched at her desperately.

For long moments they just clung to each other in the water, breathing hard, nearly in unison.

Incredible. Perfection. She was everything.

Finally, León slipped himself out of her. He kissed her again, his mouth everywhere in the water, on her lips, then her ear, then her neck. "My girl, my amazing girl," he murmured. "Tell me you belong to me. Please, *reina*."

She gently reached to touch his neck where she'd marked him, and he flinched.

"*Mi lienzo*, this time I claimed you."

TWENTY ONE

"*¡Wepa!* Celia! Celia!"

She looked up from her laptop, alarmed by the edge in León's voice from his studio room. They raced to each other, meeting in the kitchen.

"I sold one!" He waved his phone at her.

"Oh, León! Congratulations!"

He shoved his phone in his front pocket and picked her up by the waist, beaming as she laughed with him.

"The first sale! I can do it. I can make it out here!" He let her slide back down, then planted a firm kiss on her lips, bouncing her in his arms. His elation was contagious.

"Which one?" she asked.

He sobered. "The yellow." The bouncing stilled. "I love that one. I'll miss it."

"She's going out to see the world," Celia consoled. "Her new family will love her."

His mouth twisted, trying to smile, but she saw real pain lurking in his eyes. Then he took a deep breath. "Worth it. I can afford a few more months out here now. Three thousand dollars, how's that for one painting?"

Her eyes widened. "That's wonderful!"

Afford a few more months?

He paid no rent and ate for free. He did have expenses—and pride—but she could so easily give him whatever he needed. Would he really leave if he couldn't sell more paintings?

"I'm so proud of you," she said, instead. "This buyer is just the first."

"It feels so good to know someone appreciates the work," he replied, smiling again. "I hate losing the painting, but that's why I do it, so they can go out and be seen." He buried his face in her shoulder. "Thank god, this is going to work."

"The first of many," she said, holding him tight.

He pulled away to look at her. "You'll help me make more? I know you're busy now, but I still need you."

"Of course I will."

He could stand still no longer and released her so he could jump just a little, laughing. "I'm a successful west coast painter! How do you like me now?"

"As much as I liked you yesterday."

He returned her grin.

. . .

Cash could speak loudly. Celia's financial agent liquefied millions as they made the offer to buy the warehouse. It cost six million, much less than she'd feared. She asked for two million more in a renovation account and set about choosing a contractor.

The current gallery would vacate in two weeks after its final exhibition ended. The title would take two more weeks, a month to process, but her contract let her begin applying for permits. That would save so much time.

She pored over the provided blueprints, measuring and planning. The most work would be putting in two kitchens, a large one on the second floor and a smaller one directly above it, for herself. They would go near the large windows at the front. Bathrooms and showers at the back wall would also be work but not as costly. An old dumbwaiter, shown on the blueprints, could be replaced and made useful. As construction went, it wasn't a heavy lift.

She lined up an architect and contractor. Her calendar filled, listing the earliest deadlines she could prepare for. She wasn't in a rush and would make sure everything was done with appropriate care, but Celia lived to organize. She hadn't enjoyed herself this much in years.

She hummed as she cooked, danced as she cleaned. The color-coded folders aligned neatly in holders on the dining room table filled her with a lovely warmth. She indulged in a bouquet of flowers, delivered to herself, and set them behind her laptop where she could see them.

"Celia, it's four!"

León's voice carried faintly through the kitchen from his

studio. They spent more time in different rooms now.

"Coming," she yelled, scrambling to add a few more numbers to her master spreadsheet. The projected costs weren't ballooning as she'd feared, even with plenty built in for unexpected setbacks. She might even spring for a grant writer early, starting the search for possible funding. That cost would go into this column—

"Celia!"

She jumped. "Sorry!" Reluctantly she saved her work and pushed back from the table. She'd been on a real roll this afternoon.

She tried to banish the plans and figures from her mind as she went to León's room. Sitting took a different focus, and she hadn't been as present as she could have been the last few times.

Surprised, she saw that one of her overstuffed armchairs was in the studio, ready to be posed on.

"When did you move that in?"

León's glance at her was impassive as he poked through paint tubes. "Around noon. You really didn't hear me moving it? I could see you through the kitchen."

She shook her head. "I missed it. I'll be comfortable posing, huh?"

He smiled, finally meeting her eyes. "Maybe. I hope so."

Relief spread warmly through her chest at his smile. She began pulling off her clothes.

His blank canvas told her this was a new painting. He directed her to lounge insolently, sprawling with her arms across the back of the chair, one leg crooked over the arm.

"What are you going for?" she asked.

"Wanton, defiant, a little weary. I want eye contact in this one, please. The focus will be on your expression."

She rolled her shoulders, getting into the right frame of mind, as he returned to his easel. He snapped a few photos on his phone before picking up the palette. He'd been doing that now that she couldn't always sit right when he needed her.

"Okay, look at me and think about the night you painted me," he grinned. "That's the energy, that predatory aggression."

"But also weary?"

"Yes, please. Like you're considering round two."

Their eyes met, smiles growing the longer they looked.

Focusing on eye contact was tricky, with him disappearing behind the canvas every few minutes. She froze her expression into a lascivious glare, but let her mind wander, just a little, into types of grants. He painted, but his eyes kept coming back to her face, growing stony.

"Celia."

"Yes?"

"Emotional honesty."

"I know!" She concentrated again, and he went back to his broad sketching strokes. So soothing, the familiar sounds of the brush against the glass, bare feet rustling against drop cloth, the scent of paint.

"I saw you in this, that night when you painted me," he said from behind the canvas. "War paint, I thought. Now you're a warrior queen on her throne."

It was a soft throne. She had to remind herself not to relax back into it.

"Remember?" he asked.

"Yes."

This would be easier once construction was started. She'd have more time then. But she still had two weeks to get through.

"There's something I've wanted to tell you, *reina*."

"I know."

His voice was sharp. "You know?"

She focused her eyes. He was leaning out past the easel, looking at her darkly. Um. She hadn't really heard him.

"I mean...I'm sorry, León, it happened again. There's just so much to think about."

His lips compressed to a thin line. "I'll just paint your body tonight. Your face is too distant."

Her eyes widened. "I don't mean to!"

He shook his head. "It's fine, I can do it. Just...just sit still. I can do it." He disappeared again, brush tinkling in the water glass like an angry bell.

"This is why you have to belong to me," he muttered behind the canvas.

She did hear that but didn't speak. Saying no didn't work when he was happy with her. It would just make things worse to speak up now. Instead, she focused on her pose, stomping down the urge to fidget like a guilty child.

• • •

"What's that smell?" León's shouts could definitely travel.

"Beef stew," Celia called back, stirring by her stovetop. "Andrew and the rest are coming tonight, remember?"

He surfaced in the hallway, relaxed and loose. The painting must be going well. She glanced at the floor behind him to see if he'd stepped in any and tracked it out. He saw and checked as well, but the floor was clean.

He leaned on the kitchen island and tilted his head side to side, stretching his neck. "We won't get sitting time tonight, will we?"

"We might, once they're gone. Do you need it?"

"I always need it," he said, his eyebrows cocking at her.

She grinned. "Then yes, of course. Is it still the chair painting?" The colors across his hands, gold and orange, were usually a reliable indicator.

"Yes." He went behind her to wash his hands, then stepped up to put his arms around her waist, resting his chin on her shoulder to look at the golden batter she was stirring.

"That's not beef stew."

"I'm making cornbread, too."

"Are there feet in it?"

"No. The feet are in the stew."

He chuckled and nuzzled his mouth to her ear. "It's nice to have you home today."

A shiver ran through her as his breath tickled. When things were good, they were very, very good. She almost couldn't bear the happiness that suffused her. He made her feel safe, alive...loved?

Could this be the right time to tell him? He was relaxed.

"How long has it been since we swam in the pool?" he asked. "We could get in tonight after everyone leaves. Or just you, if you want. You've been so busy."

She leaned her head against his briefly. "I'd like to swim with you."

"That's a date, then." He gave her a squeeze and a quick kiss on the cheek.

She watched him amble back down the hall to his room. His pulled-back hair had orange paint in it.

She loved that. She loved him.

. . .

At the firepit, Celia held court, explaining the details of her plan. Having everyone focused on her, listening to her, wasn't as uncomfortable now that she had things to tell. She'd gotten a lot of practice talking to people lately.

"The kids can live there for free, at least at first. I want rents to be a last resort. I'm trying to think of revenue streams, something more stable than selling art."

"What are you going to call it, Celia?" Trevor asked.

"Well. It's an artist colony, really, if a commercial one. But I keep thinking about an incubator. A place where little ones can develop safely. León says it would be *incubadora* in Spanish."

Andrew paused before pushing a square of cornbread into his mouth. "Why Spanish?"

"The neighborhood. I want to fit in, to be welcoming. And, I'm half Filipino. Spanish could be more a part of my life." She looked toward León fondly. "I've had help with the translation of my literature. *Incubadora de Artistas*, what do you think?"

"It's a mouthful." Kelsey stretched her feet to the fire, resting her hands over her slightly rounded belly. "You could do eggs in the logo."

Celia grinned. "No eggs! I've got a company ready to work on a logo once I decide on the name. I need to get moving."

"Get moving?" Andrew asked incredulously. "Has it even been a month since you started? And you already have construction going?"

"Not until next week. But I've bought a lot of beds and worktables."

Kelsey looked at Andrew. "Are you really going to teach there? What about the college?"

"I can do both for a while, but Celia will let me set my own curriculum and schedule. Can't get that from a college. I could fit in more classes each week."

"So, teaching is your focus now?" Trevor asked. "What about your own pieces? I always thought the classes were just temporary. You're falling into that trap, working instead of creating."

"Teaching isn't easy, Trev. It's a skill like any other, and I'm good at it. I like it. Why not show these kids how to work clay and see what they can make? I still do pieces and can sell them in Celia's gallery. It's sort of perfect for me."

"And me," Celia said. "I hope we can find more teachers."

"You'll sell your pieces there too, right, León?" Andrew asked.

"Probably. I actually sold one at the exhibition."

"Hey! Congratulations!"

"Celia, how will you get the word out to artists that they can live in your place?"

She heard León's sigh, but he slouched down in his chair, chin on his chest as he stared at the fire, and she answered Kelsey instead.

• • •

The brisk, lapping pool was refreshing after an evening by the fire. Downslope, León heard the sing-song yips of coyotes. The waning moon peeked from behind a palm tree.

He hung against the wall, supposedly looking down over the city lights but repeatedly viewing Celia over his shoulder. She floated in the center, aqua light wavering on her skin. Her chest rose and fell, serene and weary, her vulnerable edge gone.

He had inherited her edge. She was busy, now! How could he delve into her on a schedule? She was still posing nearly every day, but what if that changed?

Dammit, I need my muse.

She turned in the water, opening her eyes to find him looking at her. Her smile radiated satisfaction. What a sight, her hair slicked back wet, droplets running off her shoulders.

His chest ached. Why couldn't he be with her like this all the time?

She stroked over to hang on the wall with him. "This was a good idea. Thank you."

"You should take more breaks."

"So should you."

He scooted along the wall until their shoulders touched. For a long moment, they both just looked out at the lights.

He wasn't a selfish prick for wanting her to spend more time with him. He was in love with her, that was all. If he told her, would that be selfish?

"León," she said next to him, still looking out. "I've been wanting to say something."

His heart launched into his throat.

Her shoulders were tense, her jaw tight. Nervous! Could she...?

"I'm so proud of you," she said, gazing outward. "Selling a painting. But when you say you can afford to stay here longer...."

Oh. Well, damn.

"I know you'll sell more," she hurried, "but even if you didn't, I don't want you to go back to New York. You can stay here no matter what happens."

He swallowed. He wanted that too, but he couldn't fail. He simply couldn't.

At his silence, she continued gingerly. "I just want you to know there aren't any conditions. I want you to stay. That's all."

His sweet girl. She was taking a chance. Not as big as he'd hoped, but maybe he had to be the one to say it first. Assuming she'd say it second.

"I want to stay, *cielito*. I can't fail, though." When her eyes fell, he reached under the water to put his arm through hers. "I'm not saying I'll go if I can't sell more. I just have to succeed, is all. There isn't anything else."

She controlled her face—the way he hated. "There's us."

His eyebrows lowered. "I'm going to have both. My muse and my career, I'm going to have everything. Just like you're

228

going to have your *Incubadora*. And that's the end of it." He softened the words with a wry smile.

She struggled to return it. "I'll help. I just wanted you to know."

"I do know." He squeezed her arm against him, opening his mouth to reassure her with the thing he wanted to say. Then he shut it again. It was surprisingly hard to say aloud. Instead, he turned to pull her close for a kiss. He'd show her for now.

TWENTY TWO

Celia awoke to León's usual antics. He was already stroking her side, snuggled close, his unshaven cheek rough against hers.

"I'm waking you," he whispered. "Is it working? Say yes."

Celia stretched, wishing for a snooze alarm, but those hands felt nice. "Bring me tea, and we'll talk," she yawned, knowing full well he wouldn't be distracted.

His fingers tickled their way down her bare hip. "You haven't said yes yet. Say yes." Her smile said yes, but he enjoyed the convincing. "Say yes," he whispered into her ear, sliding his other hand over her breast, teasing her nipple. She turned to face him. "Say yes," he murmured, his lips an inch from hers.

This man. "Yes."

He took it easy with long slow kisses, caressing and petting her, teasing every inch of her skin. Then, slowly, he woke her with sensitive fingers and kisses in unexpected places. The comforter was soon discarded, and he spread her out in the fragile morning light, kissing every inch downward until her very nerve endings were glowing.

When he brushed that unshaven cheek against her inner thigh, Celia was ready to beg. He flashed his charming grin, teasing with kisses between her legs, no tongue, no fingers, but only for a few minutes. He was too focused to wait long.

His tongue was warm on her folds, lavishly stroking and exploring. He was tender and wicked, sometimes sucking, sometimes teasing with the tip of his tongue. He had her hips off the mattress in no time, helping to support them with his hands as he buried his mouth on her.

Celia thrashed and shivered, waves of pleasure surging in her from his silky tongue. It was heavenly torture. All too soon, she felt that flood of rapture and cried out his name, lost.

He climbed back up the bed to wrap his arms around her shoulders as her breathing started returning to normal.

"Good morning." He teased some sweaty curls off her

temples.

Celia was pleasantly exhausted, but of course he still had energy to spare. León kissed and coddled and placed her hand on his stiff member, encouraging her with specific directions. He could be persuasive.

"I'm going to fuck you," he kept whispering but didn't make it that far. Her hand stroking him felt too good, and every time she slowed, he took her wrist and directed her back. She knew he wouldn't climb atop her when the Spanish began—words she now knew meant 'good' and 'faster' and 'queen.' He came in her hands quickly, shuddering against her, his face buried in her neck.

They drowsed together, entwined and sweaty and spent, until León's energy rebounded. He hitched himself up to lean on an elbow next to her, cheek resting on a hand, and tickled her face with a lock of his hair until she giggled.

"I need to paint you today, Celia Rose. Maybe something blue," he said, jiggling a foot against hers. "The blue shadows in here are so pretty. You're so pretty." He was in his playful morning mood.

"Do I get to pose in bed, then?"

"Would you? Sometimes I imagine a painting of you here." He brushed her hair back. "I see you under me, or over me, or next to me. I love that. I want to see you like that all the time."

"Well, here's your chance. Live, not a picture."

He teased her cheek with a fingertip. "I'll take it." He took a deep breath. "Damn, I am bought and sold."

She felt a cold stirring of alarm. "What does that mean?"

"I'm off the market." He grinned.

She smiled in relief and touched the fading yellow mark still on his neck. "You kind of have to be."

He mock-pouted at her. "Aren't you too, *cielito*? Off the market? I say something romantic, and you just say, 'you have to be.'" He paused, looking at her more seriously. "You could tell me you're mine."

Again? Would he never get the hint?

"You belong to me, *mi cielo*," he said with a confident

smile. "I'll capture your soul in paint and keep it. Will you finally say it?"

She looked away uncomfortably, and he went still. Oh lord. Deflect.

"Like, put my soul in a jar and seal it away? You don't actually want that."

He took her chin in his fingers, turning her face back to his. His eyes narrowed. "I do want that."

"You can't own a person!"

"Well, not legally!"

She laughed at the distinction in spite of herself. "You're not being serious."

Disbelief and annoyance twisted his features, his forehead furrowing. "I'm dead serious. I've been asking for it this whole time."

"And I've been saying I won't say it." He reached for her wrist, but she evaded. "Don't get masterful," she said. "I will be with you, but you can't own me."

He stared for a moment, then got up to sit on the edge of the bed.

She looked at his back, turned on her. She'd hoped desperately that he was joking or talking about painting. She'd always known he wasn't.

"You said last night you'd help," he muttered to the wall. "That didn't last long."

She sat up, staring at her folded hands on the comforter. Guilt, really? "I can't give you that, León."

He bent, snatching his jeans from the floor in a fierce move, swiped roughly at his face, and left the room.

She sat in shock. How had that gone downhill so quickly?

She wasn't dumb—he obviously meant he wanted some sort of commitment, though he sure never said what kind! Were her actions not enough? Was he so insecure that he needed to hear specific words he chose?

God, he could be exhausting. He didn't mean to be controlling or manipulative; he was just so blinded by his grandiose ideas. But the anxiety, the pressure to give in, it was too much. He had to learn that she had ideas of her own.

She got up, pulling on her robe and following. León stood at the back door, buttoning his jeans, every line of him angry. His bare shoulders tightened in the pale morning light when he saw her. His eyes were red. It broke her heart, but she had to stay strong.

"Please," she said. "Can't we—"

"Just let me think, okay!" He held out a hand, warding her off. A muscle jumped in his jaw as he raised pained eyes to the ceiling. She remembered one of the nicest things she'd ever heard him say.

"It's okay, don't be scared."

He pinned her with an anguished stare. "It's not okay, and I am scared! You said you'd help, Celia! I finally found my muse, and we were going to outdo Frida and Diego, move back to New York in a few years, and...." He trailed off, hearing himself.

"*Incubadora* is here," she said.

He grimaced. "You said taking care of me wasn't enough, but what do you choose instead? To take care of people you haven't even met! What about me? What about the art we were making?"

Unfair! "You're still painting! I pose! And you know that *Incubadora* is going to be my art!"

"Why are you never honest with yourself?" he railed, balling his hands into fists. "It's just a project, the big one that will finally fulfill you, right? You're doing the same thing as always, working instead of feeling. I'm right here, and you're...you're abandoning me for them."

Celia could feel tears stinging. "It's not just a project! It's my purpose!"

He pointed an angry finger at her. "You're fooling yourself, Celia Rose!"

She reeled back, the words a punch to her gut.

A bitter, wounded snarl twisted his features and he stomped past her toward the front door.

She didn't flinch. Betrayal crackling in every limb, anger a raw flame in her chest, Celia hit her limit. If he ran out now, she would lock that door behind him, permanently.

But as she seethed, he stopped at the hallway, bare back taut, sucking in a noisy deep breath. He steeled himself and turned back to her, a silent tantrum blazing on his face.

Fierce indignation torched through her. He wasn't going to trample her this time. "I belong to myself," she said carefully, tightly. "Fighting me on it, that's a deal breaker for me."

"Deal?" He threw his hands into the air, eyes wild. "You're the one who keeps changing the deal! First you gave me everything, and now you can barely pose."

"That's not true!"

"It is! You were honest at first, a mirror for me! Then you needed this warehouse...Celia, don't you see, the paintings are suffering!"

"I wouldn't care if you never painted again!"

He ran his hands through his hair, leaving it wild and standing. "But you agreed! I told you being a muse was hard. Trust, commitment, emotional intimacy! I need you to promise. I need you to—"

He stopped, stricken.

. . .

He stared. Celia eyed him coldly, warily, from across the room.

Need. He needed *her.*

Jesus.

He had it all backward.

"I had it wrong," he whispered.

His pulse quickened as he saw faint hope in her, hesitant but listening.

"I belong to you!" he crowed.

She drooped and sighed, shaking her head. "That's the same thing, León, just reversed."

"No, don't you see?" He bounced, pointing at the faded mark on his neck. "You claimed me. It felt right, didn't it? I'm the one that needs you. I'm yours!"

"I will not own you. No." She crossed her arms.

He laughed. "You already do, Celia! It's not a choice we made. It just...happened!"

"Haven't you heard a thing I've said?"

"I fought it too, but I see now," he said, heart pounding with relief. He gravitated toward her, but she held up a palm, retreating until she pressed against the tall window at her back. "Saying no doesn't change the truth, *reina.* I'm at your feet." He stepped closer, eyes locked on hers.

He knew her, knew that fluttering pulse in the hollow of her neck, her pink-stained cheeks, the tempest inside her waiting to be unleashed. He advanced until her hand, still raised to ward him off, pressed against his chest. He covered it with his own. Let her feel his heart beating as hard as hers.

"Celia, I love you."

A deep, shaky sigh escaped her, but she didn't move.

"You love me back, don't you?"

Her hand trembled under his, but she stayed silent. The tension was too much—he pounced, knocking her against the window with his body.

"Why do you always hold back on me?" he growled, mouth taking hers roughly. His free hand reached for her shoulder, sliding under the collar of her robe, fingers curling at the base of her neck. He felt the hitch in her breathing, heard a whimper.

She gave in as always, her resistance snapping. She melted into him, reaching to thread fingers through his hair, pulling him close and kissing back frantically. He groaned into her.

He pushed the robe off her shoulder, nipped at her mouth. "*Mi cielo,*" he breathed. "*Soy tuyo.* I'm yours."

She stiffened. He instantly felt the tension and eased back an inch, then swam in shock as she wrenched her hands back and pushed him away.

"No!" She was panting hard, her lower lip bruised. No, bloody. Just a little. Whoops.

Her tongue darted out, tasted the blood. Then she raised two fists to her chest and lifted her chin.

"You have manipulated me for the last time!"

What?

She was shaking, face beet red. "This is over."

His mouth fell open. She wasn't serious!

She stared at him, angry tears starting. "Get out." Her voice was flat, final.

A chill washed over him. She couldn't reject him—he needed her! Had she not heard anything he'd just said?

"You don't mean it."

"No means no!"

Fury rose. He stabbed at her with a finger. "This isn't over!"

"Oh yes it is!"

Stumbling backward another step, León stared as an iron coldness stiffened her whole body. Her eyes were glacial, her mouth rigid. She marched toward him, and he retreated backward, chased into the hall. As she passed their bedroom door, she leaned in, one leg outstretched behind her as she leaned down. She reappeared with his hoodie from the floor, balling it up and throwing it at him. He caught it as it bounced off his bare chest.

"Get out!" she shrieked.

And so, he ran.

. . .

Stunned and frightened, León ran straight to Andrew's, heart hammering for the entire car ride. Andrew knew them both, he'd know what to do. He took Celia's side more than León had expected, though.

"Dude, that is a new kind of stupid," Andrew said, mouth open in amazement. "No woman is going to agree to belong to someone. None."

"She knows what I mean." León's footsteps echoed as he stomped his old pacing path from window to kitchen. "My paintings are there, my gear. She'll have to let me in to collect it. I can talk to her then."

"And say what? You're sorry, and you'll never bring it up again?"

León stopped at the front window, looking down at the empty pool below. "Fuck!" The word bounced off the close walls.

Andrew moved a pile of clothes off the couch. "How about you sit down, huh? Calm down a little."

León wiped cold, clammy hands on his jeans. "I should just go back. I'll apologize. She'll listen."

"Man, you are not as good at predicting Celia as you think."

"I know her!"

"And yet here we are!" Andrew sat and patted the couch. "Come sit."

León stalked into the kitchen.

"Celia can be a hard-ass," Andrew said. "She bought that bitch mother a house a long way off."

Back to the window. "So what?"

"So, you're demanding things she won't do. And now who's banished?"

León bounced on the balls of his feet, prickly with adrenaline. A sickly cold weight was growing in his stomach. "Shit, Andrew. What do I do?"

"Grovel? Ask her to marry you? Is that close enough to owning her?"

"This is about painting!"

Andrew gave him a disgusted look. "Jesus. Stupid."

León rubbed a hand over his hot face. The small apartment was closing in like a vise. He needed to get out.

"The painting is over," Andrew said quietly. "You know that, right? She's not letting you back in there."

No. She couldn't....

The room spun in on him. He had to go, catch his breath outside. "Why did I come out here?" he shouted. "I wish I'd never met her!"

Andrew frowned. "You're in love with her, stupid."

"I know!" His throat tightened, nausea swirling up. "I screwed up. Bad."

Andrew looked sourly at his friend. "You don't say."

• • •

Celia sank onto her couch and stayed there, like a stone in water.

Over.

Tears surged within her. Clutching a pillow to her face, she smothered the storm's voice, her sobs soaking into the fabric in a muffled flood.

It felt like hours passed before she ran out of tears. She lay like a wet rag, limp and empty. Then, sniffling, hiccupping, she wiped her face.

She'd always known something would ruin this life with León—probably something she did. And she'd been right. She'd never given him all of her trust, not the way he wanted. She wasn't capable of it. But then, he'd never listened to her. He'd always wanted what he wanted and pushed until he talked her into it. That was over now.

Her tongue probed the small cut on her lip that had shocked her back to her senses. It still tasted of copper.

To claim he loved her, right then! Even if it were true, it wasn't fair to drop that bomb just to win the fight. And how dare he kiss her like that? She could still feel the heat of his mouth, his hand pushing her robe away, baring her. Her skin prickled at the memory of her body betraying her. She'd wanted madly to be manhandled, to relent and submit.

Too bad for them both—she was done being trampled on.

He'd have to come to get his stuff. He had boxes and boxes of gear, so much more than he'd moved into the pool house with. She'd watch it all be carried out, final, gone for good. Her heart ached at the thought, the hollow echo of his absence in every corner of her home. Her bed would be empty, her floors free of paint.

Now she only had *Incubadora*, named by someone who'd probably never set foot in it. She'd ruined everything with her new backbone. What good was 'no' if it lost you so much?

How can you be so selfish, Celia Rose?

Because no one fights for me like I need them to. It's up to me.

Her phone began quietly chiming as Kelsey and Trevor checked in on the group chat. Word was out. Celia said she would talk later, when she was ready.

The sun slowly set, the room's shadows growing long and then merging into uniform darkness. She didn't eat, turn on lights, or move from the couch.

She sat in the darkness, and she didn't spiral.

Andrew called after sunset. She felt more ready now, and heard surprise in his voice when she picked up.

"Hey, are you doing okay?"

She swallowed, her voice a raspy shadow of itself, throat thick from wallowing in tears. "I'm surviving." She couldn't help asking. "Is he there, listening to this?"

"No." His unsettling pause went a fraction too long. "Celia, he's gonna be gone for a while."

"Until late?"

"No, for a while. Like, a few days. Maybe weeks, I'm not sure."

"What?"

"He got a plane this afternoon. He flew back to New York."

The chilled hole in her heart, the empty vacuum in her house, exploded to blanket the whole city. The whole continent.

"This hit him hard, Celia. Scary hard. I think he could have run there, he was so manic."

She'd lived through this before. *He's gone, they told her.*

"Why didn't you call me?"

"So you could chase him to the airport? You told him to get out. Did you not mean that?"

"I meant it." A sharp pain twisted in her chest. It hurt. Bad. "I didn't want it, but I meant it."

"Maybe it's better that he went."

The stillness of the room seemed to hold its breath with her. She didn't have any tears left, but for a moment, her throat was too tight to speak. "Thanks," she whispered. She put her phone back on the table.

León had left everything behind, his biggest panicked escape yet. That stupid, dramatic artist.

She hated it, but she'd been right.

Twenty Three

León arrived empty-handed on his parents' doorstep, and they made up the guest room. It was pure luck that no uncles or cousins were visiting. Space would have been found, regardless. León, the family's artistic itinerant, had turned up before when sales didn't keep up with rent.

He told his parents that Los Angeles was great, that he'd already been in one show. The painting had been going well. He'd sold one. He had six completed pieces that were some of his best work. More were in progress. Andrew said hi.

He said he was back in New York to see some friends, and they didn't ask questions. By day he stayed out of the apartment, and nights, he spent in his room. He could hear discussions about himself if his mother didn't have music playing.

"He's too thin. He barely eats."

"He brought no paints. He must plan to go back."

"No paints? He brought no clothes! I think he's run from something there."

"Surely not, *mi vida*. Surely he's outgrown that."

"It's a girl."

"Probably, yes."

A girl, ha! He'd lost everything he wanted in life. Muse, career, love, identity.

He spent the first week trying desperately to not think at all, walking the length of the city.

The city was wrong, different. He saw only grays in the sky and pavements and river. Thin muffled crowds, faces hidden by scarves, veered past him with winter boots echoing. Even in the parks, lingering leaves fell in isolation, drifting slowly to the cold earth one by one.

No one made eye contact as they did in Los Angeles. Sunsets were invisible behind low clouds and looming buildings. Here, a layer of sooty grime climbed up. There, a dusting of dun spread wide.

He'd fled back to the familiar, but it was all changed because he was changed.

He tried to exhaust himself on his walks. The more mind-numbing, the better. It was futile, as he thought of everything in terms of painting, and now painting meant Celia. He could ignore the gray and the cold, but too often, a stab of color reminded him of his loss.

Mannequins in store windows held clean-lined poses. Black graffiti on a white wall sat waiting to be painted over. A woman on the subway wore a coat of bronze and green.

Just walk on by, look at the next thing, don't think.

In the evenings, his mother's music was all about new love or lost love. The sight of her stirring a pot in the kitchen tore at him. He'd never cooked for his mother either.

His father's desk, laptop open, papers piled high, was begging to be organized and tidied. Paintings he'd made when much younger still hung on the walls. They were awful juvenilia, rife with self-conscious technique but no soul.

Even his own face in the bathroom mirror reminded him of her—blank, frightened, trying desperately to not feel.

In bed at night with the lights out, he was a child again, with no idea what the future held. Painting was finished for him. What else was there that he could do? He terrorized himself with ideas he knew would never work, imagining his failure at each. Nothing was right for him, not if he couldn't have Celia to paint. And she'd told him to leave.

• • •

Construction began at Celia's warehouse. Daily, she descended to the site, prepared for queries large and small. She was politely professional but knew the workers avoided her, this employer who'd memorized the precise measurements of each task they were doing and would correct them if they were off. Her obsessive touch was in everything.

Her general contractor, Carlos, was sometimes frustrated by her phone calls, always starting with "I need." Tough. Her *Incubadora* had to be done right.

Her schedules had to be met. Not because she insisted but because she'd coordinated things so tightly. If cabinets weren't installed on time, the appliances being delivered sat in the workspace, getting in the way.

At home, she filled notebooks with research, scheduled every blank space in her calendar with another task, and sifted through resumes submitted for her job postings.

She didn't cook. The pool lights were turned off. She pushed off all overtures from Trevor, Andrew, and Kelsey, finally silencing notifications on the group chat.

Everything of León's was closed away in his old room. If there had been a lock on the door, she would have gladly bolted it. Floor refinishers and painters were brought in to restore her craft room to its original white state while she continued working in the dining room.

When she had nothing left to organize, she sat alone at her dining table in the dark, looking up local artists and school websites, searching for people who needed a place like *Incubadora*.

At night, she itched for the new day to start so she could keep working. Her feelings sometimes almost got away from her, but she could fall asleep if she recited tomorrow's list of tasks enough times. She just needed to work harder. The exhaustion was getting her through.

• • •

Two weeks into León's stay, his father finally had a go at him. The guest room door opened and in his father marched, leaning against a chest of drawers with arms crossed.

"Why don't you paint?" he barked.

León shrugged, sitting on the twin bed, looking down to finger some T-shirts waiting for him. His mother had bought them, unhappy with her son wearing oversized shirts left by a cousin.

"I've never seen you go so long without a brush in your hand, not since you were a child."

León didn't look up, didn't speak. The futility, his missing future, sat like a stone in his stomach.

"Your mother thinks you are sad. I think sulky."

Silence stretched out, but his father waited. He wasn't accepting the brush-off this time. León finally spoke. "I'm just not painting, Dad."

"When you have lots of emotions, that's the best time to

paint."

León looked toward the door and escape. It was effectively blocked. "I'm just doing a lot of thinking, okay?"

His father leaned down, ducking his head to try and catch his son's eyes. "You're trying to not think," he said. "We both see it. Is it helping? No."

"Dad, come on." León hunched over, dropping his forehead into his hand. Go away!

"So, you give up. I'm surprised at you. What in Los Angeles has robbed you of your heart?"

León looked up sharply, clenched his jaw, then breathed out slowly. *Tranquilo.*

His father stabbed a finger at him. "Is our home a place to hide from this?"

"I'm not hiding."

"Of course, you're hiding. You think I don't know you?" Exasperation was thick in his voice.

León knew what his father was doing. The goading and provocation weren't going to work this time. His feelings were too raw to let out.

His razor-thin control wavered, though.

"Okay, I'm hiding." he confessed. "I can still come here, right? I'm your son even if I'm not a painter?"

His father straightened, eyes wounded, and covered his heart with a splayed hand. León wished he could take back the words. Celia had asked that once, trying to be reassuring, and he hadn't meant to turn the words around into an accusation.

"Of course, you are welcome," his father said, softening. "But you are a painter even if you refuse to paint."

León cringed inside. No, a painter who didn't paint was nothing.

"I'll bring you supplies. If you try once, you'll see. When you're hurting, that's the time to paint more, not less."

León bit his tongue. There was nothing to say, and it hurt to try defending a choice he didn't want.

"Son, why don't you fight? You've never been one to give up."

León looked down.

"It's when you give up that you are beaten."

León closed his eyes. He was obviously beaten.

"If fighting doesn't work, try the opposite. Be gentle and go quietly around this thing that stops you."

León snorted.

"You think that doesn't work? You wait and see."

Dropping his head in his hands, León listened to his father leave and quietly close the door.

• • •

The knocking started as Celia pulled delivery schedules out of their colored folder. It was already dark outside. Who would show up at her place at this time?

When the knocking persisted, she realized. That languid pattern, the way the knocking went a little too long...Andrew.

Sure enough, he stood there when she opened the door.

"Hi," she said, her lips pursed at his audacity. "I'm a little busy."

"You can spare a few minutes for me, right?"

Not really! "If I said no, would you listen?"

His eyes widened. "Of course."

She sighed, relenting. "Come on."

She led him through the dim house to the only fully lit room: the new nerve center. The dining table was covered with folders in various vertical holders, and her laptop was surrounded by neat piles of papers. She sat down in front of it as he pulled out a chair of his own. She lowered its lid, but not all the way.

"How's it been going?" Andrew asked.

Incubadora. The fire in her belly never smoldered out, and she let it flame up now.

"It's going to work, Andrew. I can open just before Christmas. There are only a few more weeks of construction, and I've hired an administrative assistant already. Dolores, she's wonderful. If you want to see your classroom this week, the main floor is almost done. I'll need a list of supplies from you, so I can have those ready." She reached for the laptop, then stopped herself. "We need to test the dumbwaiter and kiln. The signage will be installed next week, and then they're delivering the furniture for my loft, up top. I don't want anything from here."

Andrew swallowed. "I meant, how are *you* doing?"

Her eyes flickered down. "Ah."

"Girl, we're worried."

"I'm just busy. I'll have more time after the grand opening. You and Trevor and Kelsey can come see it, come hang out. After I move—"

"We just want to see you," he interrupted. "You stopped replying to us. I was worrying about you hiding away again. We're still here. You don't have to bury yourself in this."

"I do, though. I want this. I have to make it work!"

"You sound like León," he said.

Oh, that hurt!

"This isn't picture painting," she scowled. "This is my whole future."

His eyebrows cocked at her. "You're doing it alone?"

Celia's lips compressed into a line.

"Look," he said. "You two broke up, and then both disappeared. I'm worried about you."

León had disappeared? Not just to New York? He'd left the group chat. Had he not talked even to—stop. Stop.

"I have to focus on *Incubadora.*"

"You can't do that forever."

"I can right now."

"León—"

"I don't want to talk about León!" she snapped, standing to glare down at him.

Andrew spread his hands. "Okay. Maybe later. I just...okay."

She struggled to calm herself. *Tranquila.*

"Come by later this week and see your classroom," she said stiffly. "Tell me if you need anything else in there. I've only got a few weeks to get it ready for you."

He twisted his mouth, disappointed. "And I'm dismissed until then. Okay, girl, I give in. You better text Kelsey, though. She's been frothing to come over."

Good lord. She wasn't up to that.

TWENTY FOUR

León tired of walking all day. The sights were starting to blur together, not offering the distraction he needed. It was harder to stay numb. It took a lifetime of practice he just didn't have.

Sitting stagnant in his parents' home wasn't better.

His mother sat in the living room, alone. León drifted from his room to lean against the wall in the hallway, watching her resting on their couch, listening to one of her old Tito Rodriguez albums. The scene was so homey and familiar that he wanted to cry. He didn't dare.

Instead, he solemnly joined her and let her put an arm around his shoulders. They sat and listened wordlessly, letting the old songs drift and sway behind them.

"It's good to have you home, Leónito," she said quietly.

He rested his head on her shoulder.

She gave him a gentle squeeze. "What's her name, this girl who broke your heart?"

León wasn't even surprised. He'd have come to the same conclusion if he saw himself moping around. "Celia."

"A pretty name."

"Yes."

She waited, but he didn't volunteer more. "What's she like?"

Tender. Luminous. Sad. "Quiet."

"A quiet girl for you? She'd be the first one."

"She's not for me," he mumbled. "She doesn't understand me. She thinks I'm crazy."

"Well, and so you are sometimes, *lolo.*"

The heartsick lyrics of *Qué Te Importa* mourned behind them.

"I was painting her," he finally offered.

"Ah, so she's pretty, a model."

"Yeah."

"These are the paintings you said were your best ones?"

"Yeah."

He dropped his chin to his chest, playing with the hem of his shirt. He couldn't go on this way, too beaten to speak but too hurt to keep it inside any longer. How could he tell his mother any of this story?

"I wanted her to...agree to something," he said, his voice halting and tight. "Something I felt strongly about, but she didn't. I wouldn't leave it alone, and she told me to go."

"You must have felt very strongly. But so must she, I think, if she made you leave over it. You must be fair."

"Fair?" he croaked, turning to her. "I just wanted to be closer! Why wouldn't she agree to that?"

"Maybe she's not the one for you."

Oh, she was the one. She never left his mind, the soft warmth of her presence his constant companion. Her skin, bathed in the morning's gold, haunted him. Her silhouette against the light, curves and lines he longed to trace with brush and fingers alike...he just wanted her near again.

The rejection, the need, the injustice of it came welling up, and the story tumbled out frantically on its own.

"She's my muse. I could paint her for the next fifty years! She agreed, she was helping. She gave me a place to stay. She cooked for me. She's so good at cooking, *Mama*. But she didn't get how much I needed her! I couldn't explain it right. And then she started her own work, and I saw her slipping away to it."

His mother smoothed his hair, but it couldn't calm the desperation writhing under his skin.

"She was too busy to help then?" she asked.

León's cheeks burned with shame. "No. She helped all the time, every day. But I pushed her. I wanted more. I wanted her to be mine, more than a girlfriend, more than a wife. I wanted her to say she belonged to me."

"She said no?"

"She wouldn't even listen."

His mother waited. The music flowed behind them as he stared at his hands in his lap.

"I finally realized I am hers," he said, "not the other way

around. Then she kicked me out."

"This is what you wouldn't let go? When she said no, you didn't listen?" He grunted assent. "Well, then, you have some work to do."

He saw Celia's glacial eyes pushing him backward, felt his hoodie hitting his chest. "I don't think she'll talk to me again." He stifled a catch in his throat. "I can't paint without her. I lost her and my art on the same day."

Sadly, his mother shook her head. "You gave them up, I think." She gave his shoulders another squeeze as he grew still and sullen beside her. "You had her and your art, but you demanded more until you have neither. It's not better this way, is it?"

"It was important, *Mama*," he growled. "To me, at least."

She stroked his head, trying to soothe. "We always encouraged you to be honest and fight for what you want, but you can't win everything." When he couldn't disguise a sniffle, she patted his shoulder. "Why not accept what she will give you?"

"Hide how I truly feel just so she'll take me back? No."

"Not hide, but change. Don't demand she feel as you want, be happy she gives you everything she can." He snorted, dubious. "Do you demand money from a poor man? Or can you feel blessed he gave you a humble thing he can afford?"

León sat up. "That's not the same!"

"It is the same," she said gently. "She gave, and you said it was not enough. I would tell you to leave too. Instead of telling her, 'I want everything,' you say, 'I want everything you will give freely.' That shows respect, *lolo*."

"She knows I respect her."

"Does she? You rejected her gift."

"She rejected mine!" León felt the wildness inside start to crest. He wouldn't be able to control it if it got much closer to the surface.

His mother sighed. "Ah, *mi lolo*, you always demand the moon. Maybe we should have talked less of fighting and shown you how to sacrifice. You need both." She smoothed his hair again to remove the sting of her words. "Can you apologize?"

"No." She'd had it with his apologies. She'd finally called him on it. If she didn't agree that they belonged together, what could he do?

His mother clucked her tongue. "León, *mijo, te amo*. I wish I could give you something to make you happy."

León's shoulders trembled as he leaned into her again. "She loves me too," he said haltingly. "I know it."

"Yes, she was very giving to you. That's a way to show love." She turned to him. "You could go now and be giving to her, give her patience and respect and maybe a little more silence." She chucked him under the chin, and he ducked his head.

"I doubt she'd even see me."

"You'll have to ask," she said. "Some girls will give you twice what you give them. Give her something. See what she'll do."

"She's not a girl. She's a woman. Older than me. Not much," he quickly said as his mother's eyebrows lifted. "She has her own life, she doesn't need anything from me. I don't know what to give her."

"Give her your time, then. Help her with what she wants because she is important to you. Find joy in her joy. Why not try? This is no way to live, Leónito."

She smiled. He had to smile weakly back. He leaned in for a hug, which she gave him, stroking his back as she had when he was a child. The music quieted, the album coming to an end.

In the hallway behind them, the front door sounded. León's father had returned.

Muffled against her shoulder, León spoke softly. "She does love me, *Mama*."

"Of course, she loves you, *lolo*. Who wouldn't?"

He got up off the couch, averting reddened eyes as he passed his father. He headed for the kitchen, a little hungry for a change. His parents' hushed words in the living room came through the doorway.

"So, what's the girl like, *mi vida?*"

"Sensible. And she cooks."

• • •

Kelsey texted Celia without warning. "I'm pulling up. Got

some news."

Celia gritted her teeth. First Andrew, and now Kelsey? She was busy! She heard knocking at the door before she'd even set her phone down.

Fine.

She opened the door to Kelsey, fresh and breezy in an indigo silk jumpsuit. The outfit flaunted her baby bump. She was so much bigger! How long since she'd seen Kelsey in person?

"Celia," she said, her dauntless smile wide. "You're not going to believe this."

Celia didn't feel like believing anything. She'd been scheduling delivery of the furniture for her apartment on the third floor. Construction should be done there in three days, with only some final painting—

"Hello? I've got news!"

They were all determined to drag her head out of her project. It wouldn't work. It was safe in there.

Kelsey traipsed down the hallway, kicking her taupe flats off toward the nearest couch as usual. "You haven't been reading the group chat, have you? We need your help. Someone wants to buy a painting of León's."

Celia stopped dead at her bedroom door. Kelsey turned to continue talking despite the distance.

"A woman at that exhibition asked me about León. I gave her a card because she seemed interested. Well, she went back to the gallery to buy a painting, but it was closed. Because you own it now." Kelsey grinned. "But she kept my card, so she tried me. Andrew's texting León, but we need to get the painting from you."

Celia's heart lodged in her tight throat. She didn't want to be involved in this. She didn't want to know it was happening.

"It's that blue one."

Ears ringing, Celia finally came into the room, feeling blindly for the couch rather than looking before she sat. She wasn't hearing Kelsey. She was impassive, made of stone.

"Celia, honey…" Kelsey sat next to her, solicitous but giving her space.

Would he sell? Would he come back for that? Would she

have to talk with him? See him?

"Hey. Celia." Kelsey touched her shoulder, her brow furrowed. "Listen to me."

Celia's dazed eyes lifted, trying to focus. "What?"

"You're better than this."

Stiffening, Celia sat up straight. "You don't—"

"You took a risk with León, and it didn't work out," Kelsey said. "Why did you take that risk?"

"I..." Thinking about León was dangerous. Her whole body was thrumming.

"You wanted to learn. What did you learn from him?"

León.

He rose up in Celia's memory as though he were standing before her. Those intense dark eyes focused on hers. The smell of paint as he threaded his fingers into her hair. His rough cheek brushing hers as he murmured, "*Mi cielo*, my good girl."

The vision was so clear that her heart pounded and her breaths came faster.

Kelsey still waited for an answer.

"He made me feel things," Celia finally said. The stabbing grief in her chest threatened to crumple her.

"You wanted that, Celia. And you wanted to share what you felt. You and I, we were getting closer. We confided things, we could support each other. Right?" Kelsey leaned in, intent and resolute.

Celia nodded, her head throbbing.

"Good things came out of that risk. Don't go back to how you were before. You have to keep feeling and sharing, or it was all for nothing."

Kelsey laid a gentle hand on Celia's arm. It felt nice, soothing. She hadn't touched another human in weeks now.

Kelsey was right.

It hurt like hell but hurting was feeling. She was better than this.

Celia reached out slowly and returned the touch.

"I took a risk," she said slowly.

Kelsey squeezed her arm. "Aren't you proud of yourself, Celia?"

It was close to something her mother would have asked. But, somehow, she wasn't hearing that voice now.

Could she feel proud? "Not yet," she admitted.

Kelsey smiled. "We'll get you there." She tilted her head, eyes shining. "Come lean on Andrew and Trevor and me. Let us help with your warehouse. No more hiding out here."

• • •

It took León a few more days of thought before he started to understand what his mother had told him.

It was hard to admit, but she was right about one thing. Celia had told him no, and he'd refused to allow it. No wonder she'd sent him away. He hadn't given her a choice—he'd demanded she agree with him, all-or-nothing. But she did have a choice despite his best efforts, and she'd chosen nothing.

Could he change the way he thought?

He began walking again, but not as frantically. Sometimes he even rode the subway, staying on the move and not punishing his feet.

He knew that he would go talk with her. The possibility of getting her back was a heady thought, far better than facing a future with no art, no Celia. It surprised him how easily he slid from avoiding the topic to furiously debating different ways he could fix things.

How could he convince her if she was tired of being convinced?

He had to be a different person, somehow. Less pushy. Maybe, he might avoid painting her. At first. If he could just get her back, he could work on the rest.

He'd deleted the group chat after he left LA, but Andrew had texted a few times since. A new message popped up as he left the subway at 181st. Someone wanted to buy the blue painting. The amount being offered was more than he'd ever made.

Absolutely not. Never.

Then Andrew said Celia had agreed to hang it in her building and to help with the sale if he wouldn't come. The opportunity was too sweet to pass up.

"Do you think she'd be there if I did come?" he ventured

over text.

"I don't know. There's not a zero chance."

León paused, wondering how exactly to word his next question. He typed it a few times, pausing and deleting.

"She's fine, man."

Ah.

"Think she'll talk to me?"

"Don't know. She's super busy now."

"Maybe she's not as mad. Maybe I'm not as crazy."

"Good luck proving that."

"I'll get a flight tomorrow."

So. He was going back.

TWENTY FIVE

León was coming back.

Celia had to take a moment after reading the text. Actual nausea swept through her, sweat prickling at her hands and temples. She couldn't trust him. She wasn't sure she could trust herself.

But good god, she wanted to see him again.

She looked around her nearly finished loft space. She'd been assembling a nightstand when the text came, watching the crew paint the long back wall a cheerful apple green. Glossy black doors for the bathroom and little guest room had been hung this morning. Near the big front windows, new open shelving waited to be filled with her art supplies.

Construction. Decor. Planning. It was hard to break the habit of burying herself behind it.

He was coming back!

She was different. She could talk to new people without freezing; her contractor Carlos and the other hundred people she'd had to speak to had given her practice. She'd stepped outside of her comfort zone and taken charge. She wouldn't be a fool this time, caving in to his charm.

Or was he different too?

She read the texts again. Kelsey had told the buyer to come tomorrow evening. León would be back by then, staying at Andrew's. And tomorrow night, he would be here, in *Incubadora.*

She had to prepare. She abandoned the nightstand, went downstairs, and found Carlos to tell him the crew could have tomorrow off. A paid holiday, in thanks for getting so much done so quickly. She'd have to scramble to fix the schedule later, but she didn't want drills whining while someone considered buying one of León's paintings.

She barely slept that night, trying and failing to distract herself with thoughts of her project. She decided around dawn to hang all of León's finished paintings, one after the other, down the length of the long central brick wall. They looked more impressive when seen together. Maybe it would help the sale. Okay, it was a bit much, but she couldn't keep the canvases in her house forever.

Early in the morning, she carefully dressed up, did her hair, put on makeup. She drove all of the paintings to *Incubadora*, her nerves buzzing. León would be here in mere hours.

The shiver every time she thought that!

She wore white wool pants and sweater, so pulled out one of the just-delivered aprons, slipping it over her head and tying it behind her. She brushed her fingers over the embroidered *Incubadora* logo with a small smile. Protected, she lugged a ladder and laser level from the crew's equipment on the second floor. Hanging the canvases would be easy, the rosy brick gallery walls already equipped with hangers and lights.

Before climbing up the ladder, she paused and looked around the hushed expanse of the ground floor. Closing her eyes, she breathed in the peace, the safety of sheltering brick walls on the precipice of transformation. She soaked in the moment, alone, the only expectations and voices her own. This was her place.

A lovely upwelling of joy filled her, a tingling rush like the softest brushstroke along her spine.

Then she stepped up on the first rung of the ladder. There was work to do.

She hung León's paintings one by one in the order she remembered them being painted. Each one pricked her senses, reviving the time she'd posed for them.

The tender, vivid blue one that started it all.

She could clearly see León's awestruck face when he saw her getting out of the pool, the silly way he'd darted back into the pool house as though to hide, then popped right back out to face her. He'd been frantic about her ever since that night.

The yellow painting should have come next but was already in someone else's home.

She remembered León's dance when celebrating his first sale on his new coast and his pained eyes as he realized he was giving it up. That sunlit girl with a geometric face like a sunflower, maybe powerful, maybe submissive.

The shadowy purple image of her reaching for the lamp.

He loved this one almost as much as the blue. He said it was supposed to be her inner self, untouchable, but she just remembered that first night together, turning out the light so he'd stop looking and start touching. He was always seeing things in her that she would never have thought of on her own.

The red painting, her seated cross-legged and telling him off.

It had been one of the first times she'd pushed back on his infuriating way of thinking of himself first. Oh, her irritation as he sat outside on her patio for hours! Not his first apology nor his last. He always seemed to know what he'd done badly but never did better the next time.

The leafy green goddess rising from the garden.

Had he seen her like this, then? A provider that offered herself but didn't ask anything in return? The nobility in the profile wasn't hers, she knew. Maybe this one had shades of his mother.

The orange painting of her lounging in the armchair, predatory, weary. Contemplating round two.

He'd finished it despite her head being full of plans and figures. He'd managed to give her the expression he'd described, somehow. She knew she hadn't given it to him the way he'd wanted.

Five paintings, six if he'd still had the yellow. They made a rainbow of memories, a kaleidoscope of the changes she'd gone through.

Maybe he hadn't changed. Most people didn't. Maybe he would always bulldoze then run away when scared. Maybe it was better to look fondly at this art and let León go.

But she'd see him tonight!

Her caution was no match for the burning excitement in her veins. For a moment, she tried to banish the nerves, then laughed aloud. Tamping down feelings again? There were things she might never unlearn too.

She was ready for the next step.

• • •

The potential buyer arrived on time. León did not.

The daylight had long since faded, the brisk December nights as long as they got in Los Angeles. From outside, the warehouse must have looked ablaze with light.

"I'm Jaime Cook," the steel-haired woman said with a polished smile, reaching to shake Celia's hand as she entered. Celia introduced herself, not sure how to proceed without León. Andrew said León hadn't said yes to the sale, much less mentioned price. Should she explain the paintings, tell the stories behind them? It seemed too personal.

"The artist isn't here yet, obviously," she said. "He should be coming, though."

Ms. Cook didn't look bothered, letting her gaze wander around the new interior. "The gallery moved out. Do you know what this place is now?"

"It's a home for artists," Celia said. "They can live here and work on their art without having to waste time on jobs. We're hoping to help them get started in their careers."

"We?"

"I'm the owner."

The woman's eyebrows raised. "But you're the model for these paintings too, right? You were pointed out to me at the exhibition." Her gaze lingered on the canvases. "His muse, I was told."

The word tightened Celia's suddenly dry throat. "I was his model."

"I think he's got a serious career ahead of him," Ms. Cook observed, still absorbed in the artwork.

"Can I get you a drink?" Celia offered. Lord knew she needed one. Was León coming?

Ms. Cook waved a hand, dismissing the offer. She leaned close to the blue painting, inspecting the brush strokes. "The way he captures you," she said, "it's sophisticated, but raw and intimate. Intense." She looked at Celia. "It's clear you had a profound connection."

Celia blushed. "You know how artists are."

"I do. They're often late like this too."

There was no sign of the confounded artist, though the street outside was too dark to see his arrival. Celia decided she'd talk about the paintings after all, leaving out the personal details where she could. She headed for the far end to leave the blue painting for last.

Ms. Cook stopped at the green, though, arrested.

"Is there a story behind this one?"

"It's a goddess of bounty, a provider."

"It's very serene. Not at all like this spiky red one."

"He has range. He was always clear about what he wanted to portray."

Celia looked at her watch. Come on, León!

• • •

León was outside on the street. He'd been rushing to get to the warehouse but stopped when he saw inside the windows.

Celia.

She was wearing white and it stopped him in his tracks, arrested by the long-missed sight of her, glowing in the vast room like a beacon.

As always, he longed to paint her, to remember this moment so he could recall it later. He'd vowed to not paint her at all, not until he could be sure he could do it without the possessive feelings. But seeing her, now...he would paint her in blacks, grays, and whites. Darkness around her, but the world lit up by the woman standing, shining, in the center.

Slowly he became aware of the room around her. The buyer was there, and all of his paintings were hung for display. She hadn't needed to do that. Celia, his radiant Celia, was gently speaking about them in turn, more relaxed than she usually was in public. She had more confidence.

He had to go inside, but he just wanted a few minutes to drink in the sight of her. He was dreading seeing her expression when she saw him. What would it be? Happiness? Anger? Or worse, nothing at all?

By the time they stopped at the blue painting, he had himself more under control. The sight of her selling his painting to this stranger made up his mind. He had to stop it.

• • •

"This one was at night, floating in a pool."

"So, it is water? There are a lot of possible interpretations. I think that's why I like it so much. It feels honest, like the artist really felt each stroke."

"He was describing this one to me before he even started."

"That's usually a good sign."

Celia's heart hitched at the sharp metallic click of the door latch, spinning to face it. With a whispered whoosh, the doorway swung out, its opening almost like a drawn breath, filling the room with an anticipatory silence.

León walked in.

She drank in his familiar form—a little thinner, maybe, a little more ragged. His black hair was tucked behind his ears, his jaw unshaven. He wore the same black hoodie and faded jeans, had the same way of leaning forward and stalking toward her. His serious eyes had the same riveted focus, seeking out hers and trying to read everything she was thinking and feeling.

Her heart was going to burst.

• • •

León watched her come secretly alive. She'd look composed to most, but he knew her. The slight hopeful upward tilt of her eyebrows, the slow intake of breath, that minute baring of her neck in his direction. She wasn't angry. The knot in his throat faded, only to be replaced by a pounding rush from his heart.

He saw her cheeks redden and felt a fierce heat on his own. As he closed the distance, Celia waved a hand to the buyer, still watching his approach. "León. This is Jaime Cook."

He managed to look at the other woman briefly as he joined them at his paintings, but his eyes were drawn back to Celia's far too quickly. His heart lurched as she reeled him in, electricity flowing through the few feet between them. His Celia!

His? The familiar cold pain stopped him. She wasn't his. The gulf between them was real.

"It's nice to meet you," Ms. Cook said. "You have something special here."

"Thanks," he said, throat dry. He'd like to get this done so he could talk to Celia. He sneaked a quick look at her. She dropped her eyes to the ground.

"I hope you're still working together," the woman said. "It would be a shame to only get five paintings out of this partnership."

"Six," León muttered. He drew a deep breath and turned to the other woman. "One sold."

"I'll give you five thousand for the blue painting."

Celia inhaled in surprise.

León felt a tug in his chest, looking at the tender, vivid blue canvas that held so much of them. "I can't," he said. "Maybe someday."

Ms. Cook shrugged. "Three for the green and two for the red?"

He ran his hand through his hair, looking down the wall at his depiction of the garden goddess. This decision didn't claw at his heart the same way.

"Done."

Ms. Cook's chest swelled in satisfaction, and Celia's proud little smile took his breath away.

"Fastest purchase I've ever made," Ms. Cook said. "Will you keep me in mind if you do more in the series?"

León nodded mechanically, paused, then shook his head. "I will, but it'll be a while. I'm not painting right now."

Celia's mouth fell open.

Her eyes dropped to his hands and widened as she realized they were clean, no streaks of color. She inhaled slowly. As her gaze lingered too long, her surprise rippled into a lovely, delicate flush that spread up her neck. Did she realize it meant he could change? Should he explain?

León realized how close he was to blurting out everything he felt, right in front of this stranger. Jesus, he'd been here for five minutes.

A knot tightened in his stomach. What would he even say? 'Hi, I'm back, and I've changed.' Ha! Why should she believe him? He needed time to show her. He had to get this right! Anxiety spiking into a sharp, sudden jolt, he forced himself to breathe. Flee, buy time, but be casual.

He shoved his hands in his front pockets, then swallowed.

"Do you have the contact details, Celia?" It was the first thing he'd said to her since walking in.

"Kelsey does," she said, clutching her hands together.

"You can take the painting straight off the wall. There's no packing or frame." He watched confusion and uncertainty growing in her expression. "I'll ask Andrew to help you deal with the others."

Her cheeks were growing pale.

"Right, thanks," he said to both women and turned on his heel, making the long walk back to the exit. His steps echoed in the wide silent space, and the door slammed behind him like defeat.

The chilly night seeped into him as he crossed the darkened street, away from the brilliant windows. He stopped and turned there, sure he couldn't be seen. Pulling up his hood and burying his hands in his pockets, he shivered and stayed, watching Celia climb the ladder to take down the green painting.

He should have done that himself. He'd botched every decision tonight! How was it possible that after all his hours spent planning the right things to say, he'd barely spoken to her? Worse, within moments of seeing her, he'd envisioned her on canvas. Was he capable of control around her at all?

Inside, Celia handed down the painting. A light behind her head winked out as she moved on the ladder, the backlight igniting her hair into a halo. She was a flame lighting the room, graceful and dazzling in white. Her eyes on him tonight, her little blushes and quick breaths, gave him hope that she'd give him a chance to show he could be better.

Idiot that he was, he'd walked out, panicked and escaped again. He was really, really bad at this. He didn't even have an excuse to talk with her after tonight.

Forget having a solid plan. He just needed to see her again.

Celia looked up in genuine surprise as he opened the door and leaned in.

"I'm coming back here tomorrow."

He heard her squeak as he ducked out. The door shut with a clarion clang, and this time he left.

TWENTY SIX

León rambled the empty dark streets of Boyle Heights, seeing only Celia's face. That rush of exultation he'd felt tonight, seeing her bathed in light! He'd felt so hollow without her in New York. He couldn't—wouldn't—return to that emptiness.

He stopped walking. Quit that!

This all-or-nothing way of thinking was always his downfall. He couldn't force this. She had to genuinely want him, so he had to be the kind of person she could want.

His stomach knotted. How was he supposed to manage that?

Shoving his hands in his pockets, he walked on, directionless.

His mother's words echoed in his mind: help her with something she wants. That meant *Incubadora*. Their friends all had roles in her new world, but he had barely helped at all, back when he could paint her.

Laughter and trumpet-filled music startled him, blossoming as a bar door swung open across the street. A lively couple nearly fell out, draped over each other. "I got you, *mami*," the man said, the woman giggling as her heels clicked on the sidewalk. Her tipsy, uninhibited voice clamored for dinner, a melody in Spanish as they wove their way downhill under the orange street lamps.

León scuffed his feet as he walked on, rejecting idea after idea. The next corner opened into a deserted public square with an ornate bandstand, *papel picado* strung from it and fluttering in the chilly breeze. Mom-and-pop storefronts boasted vibrant murals and window signs in Spanish. It reminded León of home, though here the murals celebrated Mexico, not Puerto Rico or the Dominican Republic. He didn't know where he was, but he recognized the art.

As León passed a narrow alley, a hissing of spray paint rose. It abruptly stopped as a young man crouching between the buildings looked up, startled, his tagging interrupted. León nodded and walked past, the smell of aerosol enamel trailing behind him. His pulse quickened with the urge to paint, but he quashed it with a sharp pang. He had to help Celia, not himself.

Help her with what she wants. Easy to say, but what help could he offer? It was hopeless. She already had everything, her new building in her new neighborhood—wait.

He stopped walking again, breath hanging in the air.

Her neighborhood, he understood it. He understood its art. Maybe he could go out and meet her neighbors, get them interested in *Incubadora*, as a sort of liaison. Maybe he could find artists to live there!

A buoyant wave of hope lifted him and he spun in the street, then loped back to that corner bar. He was overdue for a little warmth.

. . .

Stepping into *Incubadora* the next morning, León felt the changed energy wash over him. Hammering rang out from the back alcoves, workers navigating the grand room with ladders and tools. The contrast to last night's deserted silence was striking.

A short, well-padded Latina stood behind the front desk, a phone to her ear and papers arrayed in front of her. Did Celia have staff already? The place wasn't even open. The woman covered the phone with a hand and leveled a questioning glance at him.

"I'm here to see Celia," he said.

Crisply, the woman flagged down a passing crewman. "*Para la jefa.*"

"*Sí,* Dolores." The crewman, walkie-talkie in hand, relayed, "*Necesitamos la jefa, jefe.*" Dolores shot León an assessing look as he rubbed sweaty palms on his jeans.

León averted his gaze, looking past the swarm of activity, then landing on the far brick wall where his paintings still hung. The glaring gap where the green and red canvases used to be felt like a blow. Mixed feelings surged in him—pride, loss, longing. Her figure, revealed in colorful facets, tightened his throat. His Celia, his muse! He ached to go back to those times, to make more paintings to fill the gaps.

No painting! Not until he could see her and not think the word "his."

He clenched his hands, trying to anchor himself in the present cacophony of construction. This place was transforming, and, maybe, so was he.

A feminine voice bounced down the stairs. Celia! León sucked in a quiet breath as he saw her unmistakable ankles on the top step, descending. He'd know any part of her, anywhere. Another step revealed jeans, a new look for her. Then a T-shirt in—wow! Yellow! Colors, huh?

His eyes skipped over the tall man walking next to her until she turned her face to him and spoke. Suddenly the man sprang into focus; lean, muscular, dark-haired. He put a hand under her elbow, steadying her until she looked back at the stairs.

Huh.

The pair approached. Watching Celia walk into the light from the dimmer recesses was like seeing the sun rise. The vision of her slowly grew brighter, the yellow more vibrant, every part of her beautifully illuminating as she approached him. She shone, her light refilling him. He held his breath, not trusting himself to speak.

"León." She cleared her throat, and her eyes flickered to the man beside her. "This is Carlos."

The man reached out a dark hand, so León grudgingly accepted a firm handshake, making brief eye contact.

"If this is another delivery, I can tell you where to go."

Huh.

"It's not," Celia said. "León and I...I know him."

"Oh! Well, then, what is your priority today? How about that bed in your loft?"

León clenched his jaw.

Poised, Celia nodded at the man. Either she knew him well, or her social anxiety was better.

"I'll get someone to finish putting it together." he said. "Nice to meet you, León." And back he swaggered up the stairs.

Wow, fuck Carlos.

Celia's deep breath brought his attention back to her. Her hair was longer, he realized. Her tan had faded. Trivial details, changes made without him to witness, pierced him one by one. She had the freshness of a new butterfly, a dappled fawn. Her lips were perfect, the small cut long healed. Her coppery neck had no mark. There was no trace of him left on her.

She didn't say anything, just giving him that somber waiting look of hers. There was a strength in her gaze that was also new. But her shoulders were too far back, her spine too straight. Her eyes flickered to his clean hands. She was nervous too.

He'd planned things to say, knowing he'd screw it up otherwise. "Celia." He cleared his throat, the words coming out rougher than he'd intended. "I was thinking. I want to help here, like Andrew and the rest."

Hazel eyes widening in their old way, Celia raised a hand to fidget with her necklace. It was a plain silver chain, no palette pendant. That was new too.

He swallowed. Jesus, let this work. "I could be a sort of ambassador for *Incubadora* to the neighborhood. I know the culture, the language. I could get people interested, or maybe find residents for you."

Her eyes flickered with interest. She saw it, it could work! Then she hesitated, biting her lip.

"Why?" she asked.

That wasn't a no!

León played the one card he had. "There are artists here who need help."

A phone rang sharply, cutting through the moment. Fifteen feet away, Dolores answered, then held the phone out toward them. "Celia?"

Celia glanced between León and the phone, pulling harder on her necklace. León saw it biting a red line into her tender skin. Then she let it go and the mark faded.

"Okay," she said to him, softly.

León took a step back, relief welling fiercely. She was going to give him a chance! Celia turned her face again toward Dolores and the call, and he decided to quit while he was ahead.

"I'll be back," he said, and beat a hasty retreat to the mild morning outside. He'd opened a door. Now it was up to Celia to decide how far she'd let him in.

• • •

Celia moved mechanically, accepting the phone with unfeeling fingers, her mind feverishly replaying the last five minutes.

León hadn't brought up their fight. Was he going to pretend it never happened? If he wouldn't mention it, she sure wouldn't!

"It's the caterer," Dolores said. "She wants the grand opening date."

Celia took the receiver and heard the caterer's voice, a distant buzz. León's sudden offer to help swirled in her like a brewing storm. She eyed the door he'd exited, his presence lingering in the room like a shadow. What was his game?

The caterer repeated a question, snapping Celia back to the present. Opening day? "December twenty first," she answered.

Dolores' brows arched in surprise as Celia ended the call. "So soon? There's still so much work left undone."

Celia raised her chin, tamping down the butterflies. "I'll risk it."

• • •

León got started immediately, going into each storefront in the block, talking about this new community art place opening soon. He didn't tell them he knew the owner, but talked about *Incubadora* as though he was interested.

The full name, *Incubadora de Artistas,* often got chuckles and jokes about chickens and eggs. Well, it was too late to change it now. Celia had chosen it and what Celia wanted, Celia was going to get.

No one seemed concerned about trouble from a group of poor artists living nearby. Most cared more about whether there would be things for the community, like free art classes for kids. León filed every hope away to suggest later.

It was tiring, but he covered two long blocks on the first day.

As the week progressed, León quickly developed a pattern.

First thing, every morning, he stopped in to see Celia.

She was perpetually the center of choreographed action, directing young men as they brought in beds or took away ladders. Getting fifteen minutes of her attention each day was a feat, but it kept him going.

León focused on his new role, showing her he was helping. He didn't even consider painting her as the beating heart of the room, a steady rosy soul in a swirling flock of sparks. A lithe golden flame burning in a chaotic thunderstorm. A sunbeam of white pirouetting through a tangled green forest canopy. A pearl—okay, quit. He wasn't thinking of painting.

He brought her the suggestions and concerns he'd heard. Bringing up their fight would have ruined the fragile peace, so he never did. Miraculously, neither did she.

At night, on Andrew's couch, León would lay awake, overthinking every detail of their interactions. By day, he engaged with her neighbors, gathering goodwill and answering questions.

"Is it free there, like a museum?"

"Those artists will need a local bar. Point them my way, I'm closest."

"They better not take up all the parking."

At the church, Father Garcia said, "I know of a young artist. I'll send him your way."

• • •

Heads down at the front desk, Celia startled as León bounced through the door. He was followed by a young Hispanic man, slight and shy, his eyes darting around at the noisy construction. She spied paint on the young man's hands and felt excitement bloom. An artist!

León eagerly introduced Hector, his voice laced with that old fervor as he described the intricate murals Hector had shown him. Father Garcia had personally recommended him, a young artist full of potential but held back by limited resources. Hector blushed at the accolades.

Dolores joined them to ask Hector the necessary questions, the conversation alternating between Spanish and English for reasons only Celia wasn't privy to. She managed to follow enough that León's zeal became clear. Hector was a good fit! He admitted he'd need his grandmother's approval before moving out of her home but pledged to speak with her.

"Come and fill out the application," Dolores told him. "I will help." She raised her eyebrows as she turned away, shooting an excited glance at Celia. This could be their first resident!

León moved to follow, but Celia stopped him with a light hand on his arm. He jumped as though burned, those big dark eyes locking on her face.

She almost forgot what she was going to say.

"Thank you," she murmured, then cleared her throat. "Could you help convince his grandmother? He'll know other artists, and he could spread the word about *Incubadora*. He could be the ambassador we need."

Pain flickered in his eyes. "I sort of thought I was the ambassador."

Her heart sank. What a thing to have said!

Jaw set, he moved stiffly to the front desk, and she watched him walk away. Two weeks, and he hadn't said anything personal once. Not even a knowing glance. He was like a stranger now, not a lover who had prodded her about art and honesty and need. They must truly be over.

• • •

León, dropping money on a ride-share, headed to *Incubadora* in the early morning to meet Hector. It was too cold and too early to suffer on what they called public transit around here.

He entered to look for Hector, scanning the room for Celia as always, and finally saw her in the back corner, scrubbing on her hands and knees. The smell of solvent drifted to him. She was getting paint off the floor.

He flashed instantly back to the studio room in her house, seeing the bend of her bare knee as she wiped up a drip of paint. He could feel a brush in his fingers, smell the wet colors on a canvas in front of him, and savor Celia, delightful Celia, real and glowing and warm in front of him.

He could go help her. She shouldn't have to do that

herself, she had other work. She was too good to clean up stupid paint.

He looked away forcefully, closing his eyes.

A tap on his shoulder startled him, and he turned to see Hector, face morose.

"*Abuela contestó.* No."

How could his grandmother turn this down? What a world this could be if the women would just let them paint.

León squared his shoulders. "Can I talk to her? Will she come here?"

"She might come," Hector said. "But what can you say? I've explained already." His thin frame slumped, seeing opportunity slip away.

León pursed his lips. "What would help get her to agree?"

"She thinks art is okay, but having a job is more important."

"Making art is a job. Two weeks ago I sold paintings for five thousand dollars."

Hector's eyes bulged. "For real? But you've been doing this for years. I just started."

León patted him roughly on the back. "Dang, I'm not old! And that's why you need this place. Imagine if your job was just painting!"

"I want to! But she said no."

Celia wanted Hector, and she was getting Hector! "Then we've got to convince her! Show her how important this is!"

Wait. Ah, shit. Help her with what she wants, *lolo.*

León laid a hand more gently on Hector's shoulder and leveled a look at him. "You're going to figure out what she wants and help her get it," he said. Hector blinked helplessly. "Show her you can both be happy with the decision. Like, we'll explain the different jobs you can get as a skilled artist."

Hector's brow furrowed in reluctance. "But she also doesn't like that you...well, you're not from here. We don't know you."

"Only time can fix that one," León admitted. "But, see, that means she's protective of her community. Art is good for communities! What if we showed her that your murals can help it?"

"How?"

"Improve it! Make something prettier. Tell a story about your community for everyone."

"I don't have a good place to make a mural right now."

"I'll find you one."

Hector was wavering, hope struggling to dawn on his face. "I don't have enough paint either."

"I'll get you that too. Show me where you buy it."

. . .

Celia had seen León in discussion and felt a pang as they exited. No morning talk, apparently. Maybe they'd be back soon.

She rose, bringing her cleaning rags to the front desk where Dolores was preparing to move her papers upstairs to the newly finished offices. Celia wiped her fingers with the cloth, absently watching the front door. Dolores picked up her box, then paused.

"You know that long-haired boy likes you, right?"

Celia tried hard to stop a smile. If only.

"He does," Dolores insisted. "I've seen him looking at you when you don't see."

"He hides it well, then," Celia answered.

She turned back to her tasks, calling her movers to confirm they would pack and deliver her home goods this weekend. The news predicted stormy weather, but Celia was bent on spending at least one night in her new home before opening. If the movers had to haul boxes in the rain, she'd just tip more.

. . .

Hector and León returned armed with spray paints and tips and masks, and León took Hector to the alley at the building's side, looking for a surface no one would mind being decorated.

"It was illegal to paint a mural on your building until like ten years ago," Hector said.

"Seriously?"

"People painted anyway. My cousin let me help him on one."

"Did you tag, too?"

Hector looked around before answering. "A little. But street art gets painted over. I like to make something permanent."

León eyed the fence in the alley. It probably didn't belong to Celia. He certainly wasn't going to offer the side of her building! However, twenty feet down the alley sat the solution.

A dumpster.

If Celia didn't like it, he'd haul the thing away himself. And what proof for Hector's grandmother! Art beautifying her community!

Hector offered León a pair of latex gloves, but he shook his head.

"This one's all you, *mano*. Do your stuff, then we'll get the women here to see."

Hector began spraying on preliminary shapes, large scallops and circles. León pulled up a box near the alley fence and sat to enjoy the show. It wasn't his style, it wasn't his work, but it was still paint.

• • •

Kelsey came in to finalize the social media calendar. She'd given notice at *La Creche* last week, newly installed as *Incubadora's* official promotions manager. The salary was competitive, a considerable bump up from retail stylist. Celia was just glad Kelsey had accepted without feeling weird about it.

They lined up colored sticky notes across the front desk, debating which posts should go out before others. The first would go live tonight, promoting the grand opening.

Celia leaned on the counter, but Kelsey sat to discuss the posts from memory, leaning back in the office chair, feet up on a box. Her belly was roundly noticeable as she approached five months pregnant.

"Why didn't—" Celia started.

The front door whipped open as León bounded in, and her heart skipped a beat. Would that reaction never stop?

Kelsey didn't even look up at the sound. "I can't believe you didn't know," she said, eyes closed. "They've been off fishing for two weeks. Didn't you notice how quiet the group chat was?"

León broke in, impatient. "Celia, can you come out and look at something?"

• • •

León held his breath as he watched her reaction, heart thumping hard.

Celia's dumpster had been transformed, lively and vibrant. She stood solemnly, reading the story on it. At the bottom writhed a mass of dark green vines. Out of it, a bridge rose, soaring on recurring white arches like wings, flying to the top right where colorful flowers bloomed. The freehand wasn't precise, obviously made swiftly with few paint colors. But the swirls and arcs were graceful, the colors harmonious.

"A white bridge," she said.

León sucked in a breath, his stomach sinking. Damn. How had he forgotten her thing about bridges? But she didn't get that lost look in her eyes; instead she turned a glowing smile on Hector.

"It's beautiful."

Hector stood taller, his slim shoulders straightening eagerly. "It's the new bridge, sixth street."

"*Ya llegué*, Hector."

All turned to see Hector's grandmother at the mouth of the alley, round in her bundled coat and a flowered plastic hood over her hair. Her grandson tripped to her side, their conversation quiet. Hector gestured in earnest, forearms colorful with overspray, his grandmother slowly shaking her head.

Celia watched wistfully, the lines of her body slowly drawing tighter. León felt his own body tense in response, his palms sweating. She wanted this. Let it happen. Let him see her happy again.

Hector led his grandmother closer, describing the swirls of color with hands and voice. She stopped some feet from the transformed dumpster.

"Pretty," she said, then looked at Celia. "What Hector says, it's true?"

Celia clasped her hands at her chest, eyes hopeful. "We have space here, a place to live. Free. So he can make more art like this."

León bounced on the balls of his feet. "Hector has talent! This could be the start of his career."

"There are teachers here," Hector added. "And León made thousands of dollars selling paintings."

"Imagine these streets, alive with Hector's murals," León said.

Hector's grandmother looked at each of them in turn, then slowly nodded. "*Vale*. Okay," she said. The intake of breath from all of them was audible. "But he comes back for dinner on Sundays."

Hector whooped and hugged her, but León turned immediately to Celia. Look at her—the light in her eyes, the lift of her chin, that true glow he'd only seen a few times. His heart swelled as her quiet joy filled him up.

Incubadora had its first resident artist.

TWENTY SEVEN

Celia returned to her front desk, leaving behind the misty day to rejoin Kelsey in the cavernous red brick warehouse. The sound of drilling on the floor above welcomed her back to work, a symphony of sawdust echoing off the lofty ceilings. Hector had gladly promised to move in on opening day—one more puzzle piece was in place!

She tensed as León followed through the door behind her. This was new; he usually lit off to his pursuits after fifteen minutes in her presence. She eyed him cautiously, moving quickly to put the desk between them as he loped up, radiating that energy she remembered so well. She'd seen that beatific smile when he finished a painting, and the heat it ignited in her belly was a warning: look away or bear the futile, painful wanting.

"Hector is coming to live here," Celia told Kelsey, who still lounged in the single desk chair with her feet on a box, waiting to finish the social media plan.

"The first resident!" León crowed.

Kelsey raised one eyebrow at him. "You found one, huh? You're quite the little worker."

He ignored her to watch Celia avidly. His thumb was tapping against his thigh in that old familiar way. "There are a lot of beds to fill," he said.

"One less now," Celia said, blood thrumming at the change in him. His casual friendliness of the last weeks had melted away. This was the spirited León she remembered, eagerly bouncing when she had time to pose, his face alight as he woke her with questions in the morning. *Mi cielo*, he used to say.

The drill upstairs whined to a stop, silence emptying the room as Kelsey lowered her feet and turned the chair to watch the show. The chair's soft squeak and Kelsey's toes tapping against the dusty concrete floor echoed in the charged silence.

León stood on his toes, fingers tight on the edge of the desk, his arms stiff.

"I can't stay on Andrew's couch forever," he said, eyes burning into her. "Maybe this type of group living is right for me."

Oh.

Good lord.

León living one floor below her? There was only one way that could end. One of them would fly a white flag, and it would be all over.

Celia suddenly saw herself at the top of the black stairs, her eyes adjusting to the night-filled room below her, weak with apprehension but unable to stop herself from descending. He'd be awake, waiting for her, hoping. She'd approach as he lay in his dormitory bed, his face serious, eyes dark as he watched her come. He would slide the covers away, and she would climb onto the bed on hands and knees, her skin barely skimming across his, his quiet, shaky gasp welcoming her as—

Kelsey kicked at her ankle.

Celia's held breath escaped in a rush. No. It would kill her to touch him again without returning to what they'd had, and she couldn't go back to being trampled over.

She refocused to see him watching her with poorly concealed interest, so she shook her head, leaning one hip against the desk to steady her tense body. "Maybe there are other places like this, for established artists like you."

He went still, the light draining out of him. "Sure. Maybe."

He wasn't going to fight her?

Muffled thumps shook the floor above and the drill started again, filling the echoing space with the familiar song of construction. Her stomach still in knots, Celia watched as León's casual mantle stole back over him, his shoulders lowering and expressive face softening into a polite mask.

Celia couldn't pretend as easily. For a minute she thought León had finally shown his hand. But if he had come back for her, why didn't he press like he used to?

"If you're done distracting Celia," Kelsey said, "we could

finish this work in ten minutes."

"I'm done for now," León replied, stuffing his hands in his pants pockets.

Kelsey clambered from the chair, one hand pressed to her lower back. "Good."

Carlos appeared on the stairs, juggling an armful of sawn boards. He dropped a short one, which clattered musically down the iron steps. Celia stifled the urge to go pick it up.

"You could help me," Kelsey was saying to León. "I want to post some neighborhood reactions to *Incubadora*. Positive ones."

"Sure," he replied.

Celia snuck a look at him. His attention to Kelsey felt off, artificial. It had been so easy to understand what he wanted before they broke up. Where was that honesty he'd always railed about?

Kelsey moved a sticky note to a new place on the calendar. "Hang out. We can talk after this."

León shrugged, offering a half-smile that didn't quite reach his dark eyes.

He hadn't pushed back at all. Why wasn't he fighting, burning with the same intensity that once defined him? Who was he now? The uncertainty was a vise, squeezing tight around her heart.

Celia looked over her shoulder at the black iron stairs, offering escape up to distracting work, up to her new loft home. For the first time, she saw an echo of her father's black iron bridge; another way of escape. She clenched her jaw. No. She was better than that.

• • •

León stuffed the rejection deep down, ignoring the sinking feeling in his gut. It had been a long shot, and ill-timed due to his pleasure at landing Hector for her. She'd considered having him here, though! He'd seen her body respond, that pink blush creeping up her neck like the slow bloom of a morning rose.

The damned drill noise stopped again, and the board-carrying bigshot Carlos disappeared through a back alcove.

Celia had wanted to go help the tall klutz; he'd seen her stifle a step in his direction. León risked a peek at her.

She still looked toward the stairs, the lovely familiar line of her neck and jaw like the curve of a river, her shoulders inching back as she stood taller and looked back to the front desk.

As if a cold gust of wind had blown straight through the room, Celia suddenly froze, snapping rigidly to attention. Her eyes grew round with terror.

León's skin prickled, a shiver tracking down his spine. What...why? Her eyes were riveted past him, on the front door. Frowning, he glanced quickly too, seeing a short, vague figure outside, a silhouette cupping a hand to the fogged glass to look in.

"Oh no," Celia breathed, her whisper nearly lost in the vast space. She was pale as death, her face suddenly as blank as an untouched canvas.

The figure entered, an older woman well-bundled against the damp weather. She was petite and graying, her champagne-toned anorak beaded with mist as if she had walked through a cloud, her neutral light-eyed gaze taking in the empty brick warehouse.

"Good morning," Kelsey chirped, slipping into her *La Creche* sales voice. "We're not open yet, but do you have a question?"

"A few." The woman smiled absently, her footsteps a soft tip-tap against the concrete floor as she walked to the front desk. "I have been leaving you voice mails for weeks, Celia Rose."

León gasped. No way. No god damn way.

Kelsey still had no idea. "Our grand opening is in two days. Do you live nearby?"

"No," the woman said. "I'm visiting."

She didn't look like a monster. She seemed polite, comfortably social. Sort of like a retired teacher or office manager. She had a competent air, her presence solidly normal.

A glance at Celia was alarming. She was stiff as a ramrod, her posture as rigid as the steel beams that framed the warehouse, but her blank face told him everything. A protective rush flooded through him. He stood at the ready to help, as soon as she gave any hint of what she wanted.

• • •

Mom was here, and she was mad.

Celia could see her anger in the flinty fractional narrowing of her eyelids, the thin creases at the corner of her mouth, the smoothly deliberate restraint in her walk. Celia was dead in her sights. Careful, her trapped body crooned, careful....

"We're not open," León said. He sounded different, hard-edged.

Mom flickered a glance through him, dismissing him immediately. "What is this place?"

Celia's voice, small and cracked, sounded far away. "How did you know about...."

Kelsey's head tilted.

"I thought your phone number might have changed," her mother said. "I put your name in Google and saw this place."

"I said we're not open!" León said louder. Celia wanted to look at him, encourage him to say it again, draw some strength from the steel she heard in his voice, but she was pinned by Mom's gimlet eyes.

"I stopped at your house first, but no one was there." She lifted her hand, bulging purse dangling from her fingers, a loose charging cord hanging out of the top and whipping about as she waved it. "I've got bags. The least you can do is give me a room. And your new phone number."

Kelsey gasped, then stepped sideways to stand next to Celia.

Celia barely felt the lump in her throat, the frantic stutter of breath. The verbal beating was inevitable, her friends here to witness her shame. Cowering wouldn't save her. It never had. She was small and lightheaded, powerless and unlovable, called to answer for her failures. She looked frantically at her black iron stairs but knew escape had never been an option. Her *Incubadora* closed in on her, no beat of activity, no melody of construction.

Cornered and mute, a frantic drumbeat in her chest, she was finally driven to stand.

Kelsey's hand softly touched her back. León stood poised to protect.

From a strength borrowed and built, she chose.

"No."

"No?!" Mom's voice was a whip crack, echoing in the high rafters. She raised a thin hand to her throat in hurt disbelief. "You're really going to turn your back on your own mother?"

Wheedling, Celia tried. "Mom. Please. I'm just...I am doing what's best for me."

"And what about me? I'm just thrown out in the cold?" Mom stinging voice rose, sharp and pointed.

"I've taken care of you! You have the house, everything is paid—"

"I mean, you refusing to talk to me. Incredible!"

Celia's fingernails bit into her palms. "No, you said...."

With a sorrowful pity in her downturned mouth, her mother sighed. "You're confused. This isn't how an adult handles things, Celia Rose."

"Maybe," Celia conceded, a chill sinking through her. "I know I'm confused. That's why I need time on my own to figure it out."

Mom rolled her eyes. "Figure what out? I can't go through your dramatics again, poor little Celia! What did I do? I never thought my own child would abandon me like this."

"Mom," Celia begged, "please don't."

León dropped an arm across the desk with a thump, a barrier between them. "She said no." His voice had never sounded so steely. It rang up Celia's spine like a bell. Kelsey's palm pressed firmly against Celia's back, a warm reminder that it was there.

Mom turned her affronted glare on León and Kelsey in turn. "You're being influenced," she declared. "You would never do this otherwise."

Probably true! Celia's friends...those beside her now, Andrew who knew the antidote, Trevor with his story in the alcove. Her found family.

"I'm sticking with people who lift me up," she said.

Biting back a laugh, her mother raised her eyes to the

ceiling. "Oh, that's rich! After everything I've done for you!"

"Maybe I will regret this," Celia placated. "I don't know."

Kelsey whispered, almost to herself, "Celia, no."

Mom skewered her with a look, brows low, lips set in a line. Her coiled stillness held the promise of a slap. "Is this really what you want, Celia? To hurt your mother?"

Silent dust motes floated through the weight of years. A collective breath was held.

"No."

Her mother raised her chin, righteous.

"I'll get you a hotel," Celia finished. "I'll tell them to call you with directions." She heard Kelsey release a long breath. From León, there was only tense silence.

Mom goggled. "Has your mind snapped?"

"No." The single word was a shield.

"You stop this craziness right now, Celia Rose."

Celia breathed. "No."

León finally took his eyes off her mother, risking a look at Celia. She met his dark, ready gaze and understanding flared between them. He inclined his head slightly to the door, raising his eyebrows. She replied with a barely perceptible nod.

León took Celia's mother by the elbow. She jumped, mouth open, but didn't struggle as he firmly walked her out of the building.

TWENTY EIGHT

León dropped Celia's mother's arm in disgust the second the door banged behind them. The terrible things that had come out of her mouth!

She stuttered to a halt on the wet sidewalk, her feet slapping through the shallow stream crossing the sidewalk from *Incubadora's* gurgling downspout. Rounding on him in outrage, she stepped back out of the water, cheeks fiercely red. She gaped as León planted himself solidly in front of the door.

"What are you doing?" she asked, voice shrill. "That's my daughter."

A young Latina walking on the other side of the street, carrying a sleepy toddler, looked over as the sound carried. León caught her eye as she passed, and she moved on.

"Let me in!" Celia's mother demanded, leaning forward, her bag nearly dragging in the wet puddle in front of her.

León checked inside through a tall window. The overcast sky reflected back, but he could just make out Kelsey with an arm around Celia's shoulder, talking earnestly. She was in safe hands for now.

What would Celia want him to do? Get rid of her, surely.

"Celia will call you if she wants to talk," he said, standing taller and crossing his arms over his chest.

She sneered, looking him up and down. "What are you, her bodyguard?"

He snorted. Celia needed a bodyguard, around her! She'd told him what this woman had done, breaking wooden spoons on her lost little daughter. She looked so normal; nondescript, no horns or pitchfork. Yet she had hurt his Celia badly.

"Why the silent treatment?" she railed, indignation kicking in. "I didn't do anything! I deserve an answer! She can't just pretend I'm not here!"

Not with that screeching voice, she couldn't! A mustached man and his dog, clad in matching raincoats, approached from behind Celia's mother. León wanted this scene over before neighbors started noticing Incubadora kicking angry white women out.

"Celia said no," León said grimly. "That's all I need to know, all you need to know."

The man and his dog passed them, startling Celia's mother. She waited, eyes narrowed, until they passed out of earshot.

"She didn't mean what she said," she hissed.

The negation flared in León's blood. She wanted a fight, did she? "Don't ever come back here," he growled, eyes narrowing. "Ever! If you show up again without Celia's personal invitation, we'll have the police on you."

She stiffened, meeting his glare. "It's not illegal to come to see my own child."

León pointed at her, fierce, his voice a snarl. "This isn't a fucking joke!"

Her eyes bulged as she retreated a step. That shut her up!

"Go home now," he gritted, "and don't come back."

He glowered as she gaped in disbelief, but faced with his immovable stance, she ran out of steam. She watched him warily as she hitched her bag higher on her shoulder, then turned and stalked away, head high.

What a *bicha*! Did she talk to Celia like that all the time? His mother would never dream of using guilt as a weapon. She would never call him crazy, no matter how *loco* he acted.

Oh, Celia.

He clenched a fist. He couldn't fix the past, but he'd fight a hundred demons until Celia had what she wanted. It felt good—right—to fight for someone besides himself.

The wretched woman stopped halfway down the block, her bag swinging. She was a 'last word' type, for sure. "This isn't right," she shouted. "She's *my* child!"

León's blood boiled. How dare she? She had no power over Celia anymore.

"She's a grown woman!" he shouted back.

He watched until she retired around the corner, his breath puffing into mist in the chilly air, his racing heartbeat gradually calming.

Celia didn't belong to that ignoble woman.

She didn't belong to—*idiota.*

He screwed his eyes shut and scrubbed a hand over his face. "God dammit," he muttered, then hastened back inside.

Celia was sitting in the chair, eyes closed and arms crossed tightly around herself as if she were cold. Kelsey was bent over her, whispering. She looked up at his entrance.

"She feels guilty."

León briskly rounded the front desk, dropping to a knee on the cold floor in front of Celia. "She's gone. Are you okay?"

She nodded, opening eyes to him that were shadowed but not shattered. He felt deep in his chest the slight hunch of her shoulders, a curve of containment and self-protection, weary lined from past battles.

He would give anything to be allowed to put his arms around her right now. "What do you want?" he asked instead, in a low voice just for her.

"To go upstairs." Her brimming hazel eyes swept his concerned face, the yellow overhead lights reflecting in unshed tears. "Alone."

León and Kelsey exchanged wary glances.

Kelsey scratched her ear. "Celia, I don't know."

With a tiny shuddery sigh, Celia turned a sunflower face up to Kelsey, a private smile barely touching her lovely lips. "I'm okay. I'm proud of myself."

Kelsey placed a light hand on her shoulder with a sad smile.

León stood, straightened, shoulders squared. "She wants to be alone. Can we stay down here, Celia?"

She nodded, some of the tension melting from her shoulders. *Reina.*

They watched somberly as she climbed the black iron stairs. It felt uncomfortable, but she said she was okay. They had to trust her.

. . .

Hands shaking as the adrenaline wore off, Celia centered herself on her bed, the mattress embracing her troubled weight with a comforting sigh. She wrapped herself in the new blue comforter and exhaled a breath she'd been holding for many silent years.

The quiet of the half-furnished loft cradled her, her home-in-progress, the low buzz of the enveloping city a humming cocoon. She brought fistfuls of blanket up to her chin and stared, unseeing, across the room. She was alone here, safe. She could make the decisions she wanted and no one could judge her. She could feel guilt, or joy, or anything she chose.

Weak sunbeams breaking through the clouds reflected off the polished floor, brightening the warm brick around her. She'd said no! They'd all heard her! She had people who lifted her up now. She was happier! That was proof that she'd done the right thing...wasn't it?

She wasn't finished with her mother forever—she would never be truly finished. But she had chosen to protect herself in the loudest way she could. No! Like a toddler, No! It was selfish and she deserved to say it. For the first time since she was a cowering eight-year-old, Celia had the power to refuse.

It was done.

The wave of relief and empowerment receded as sorrow seeped in, a cold draft sneaking through unseen cracks, a callow trickle that traced the enormity of what she'd done. The walls around her, her safe place named for an incubator, began to crack under the pressure. Sunlight faded again behind the clouds, and sour guilt and sorrow rushed in its wake.

Why, Mom? Why did I have to burn our bridge?

I just want you to love me.

Tears flooded her, wet and messy. Her nose dripped, her eyelids swelled, her throat stuck as she drew a thick open-mouthed breath. Pain warred with pride, relief with rejection. Her gut cramped as a sob built. It burst from her, raw with power and bile and release.

The dampening comforter held her tight as she trembled, her gasps echoing off the soaring ceilings, filling the whole space. She let the storm come. She wracked with each cleansing wave, feeling and feeling and feeling.

She cried out loud. She was getting better.

• • •

"Dude," Kelsey said, fingering her sticky notes. "Her mom

sucks. You know about what she did?"

"I know." León waved an offering hand at the empty office chair, and Kelsey sat, eyebrows raised and face speculative.

León looked at the high beamed ceiling as though he could look through to Celia's floor. "She'll be okay up there, right?"

Slim hand resting on her burgeoning belly, Kelsey nodded, lips pursed. "She's changed, don't you think?"

"Yeah. I do."

She gave him an appraising once-over. "You've changed too. You're way nicer to her."

Kelsey and her bluntness! León set his jaw, a slow wary fire starting in his stomach. "I was an idiot."

"I don't get why you quit painting."

He looked over to the luminous blue painting, still hanging on the far wall, his fingers twitching as though he could feel a brush. Weak sunbeams breaking through the clouds reflected off the polished floor, casting the painting in a soft glow. He hadn't had anyone to tell this to; Andrew had been off with Trevor for weeks. The blue days, the black nights of missing Celia, lying awake thinking up ways to earn a few extra minutes near her....León was near his breaking point.

"I'm an ass when I paint," he admitted. It was tough to say, but... "I want her more than I want art."

"You're here to get her back, aren't you." It wasn't a question, and he didn't feel the need to answer it.

Kelsey's voice behind him softened. "You're going about it all wrong, you know."

León spun on her. If she expected him to take this with good humor...he was sailing too near desperation. "Help me, then! I'm making this up as I go, and Celia's not telling me if I'm getting through."

"Oh, she's telling you," Kelsey replied.

León stared.

"Look, you're an expressive guy. Celia responded to that, it gave her permission to be expressive too. Now you're buttoned up, all casual. It comes off as fake, by the way. But she's retreating to that, copying you. You're cooling things off."

His mouth opened, then closed. "God dammit. How do you see things like that, Kelsey?"

"I just watch," she sighed, slumping back into the chair. "I can't believe you guys need this spelled out! Fine, I'll help. Go be yourself, idiot."

"I am, though. The new me."

"No, stop being casual and boring." Her voice sharpened, and she fixed him with a pointed look. "The guy she fell for is all emotion and drama."

León felt something melt in him. A warmth spread through his chest, the icy shell of his fears beginning to crack. "You think she'd take me back?"

Kelsey chuckled. "I'm not touching that one. Ask her."

TWENTY NINE

Thunder grumbled through the night sky, and up in her quiet loft, Celia smiled.

Golden lamplight pooled against red brick, little amber halos warming places that mattered. The watery blue silk comforter on her bed, way off in the corner, shimmered under a single pendant's warm sunset hues. In the room's center, yellow couches faced off across a low glass table set with glowing punched-tin lanterns. Her artichoke-green dining chairs basked in rows under the modern copper chandelier.

It didn't all match, but she had picked furniture that spoke to her. This was her place.

When she'd needed healing yesterday, a safe place on her first day of official estrangement, she'd had her loft. Her *Incubadora*. Her new life.

Tomorrow was her grand opening, and that would be a first day too.

Lightning strafed the windows like fireworks.

The weather reports had been correct, and Celia's movers had indeed hauled everything in the wet and cold. They finished before the heavens opened, torrential rains snarling traffic and giving Celia another reason to appreciate her new sanctuary. No commute!

She ignored the unfamiliar creakings and tappings, the lashing of water down the big windows. Tonight, she could spend a few hours on her own, unpacking. It was a special treat she'd been looking forward to all day.

She turned on music and pulled a dining chair into the empty space she had yet to address. No closer to being filled with the equipment of a certain painter, it had been the obvious place to stack her well-labeled moving boxes.

Sitting to open the first one, she pulled out the bottle of red wine she'd been looking forward to. Was this what Christmas mornings were supposed to feel like?

No, Christmas Eve. Tomorrow's opening was the main festivity. The work was done, everything was prepared. She wasn't nervous. She was excited.

Then the power crackled off, snuffing out the lights and music and low hum of the heater. In an instant, she was sitting alone in a blackened warehouse.

The streetlights were out too. She had candles and flashlights, but they were still packed in boxes that now looked exactly the same. She had a space heater but no power. She'd unpacked her pantry when the boxes first arrived, but it was just ingredients like flour and vinegar, nothing useful against the dark.

Oh lord, the catered food! The fridges on the second floor were full of appetizers. If the power didn't come back, it might not be safe to serve tomorrow.

She hadn't been less prepared for something in decades. It was unsettling to be plunged into inadequacy.

She used her phone to prowl around tall stacks of boxes, looking for a label indicating something useful, but being hemmed in felt creepy, like she couldn't see something coming at her. The bright light on close cardboard ruined her night vision and threw tall, wavering shadows on the walls.

She gave up and felt for her chair, deciding to reach out on the group chat. Normalcy would help.

Andrew and Trevor immediately offered to drive over, but with this traffic, it would take them hours to get there from Trevor's Los Feliz apartment. Kelsey was even further away in West Hollywood. León, however, was still near, his ride-share from her neighborhood stuck in outbound traffic like everyone else. He called instantly.

"Hey, I'll come back. What do you need?"

It was a relief to hear the offer, but Celia balked. Alone with León in her dark loft? She was already too vulnerable.

"No, I'm okay. The power will probably come right back on, and I'm worrying over nothing."

"Are you safe? Does your security system work with no power?"

She had to think. "I haven't had time to get super familiar

with it, but it has to, right? Otherwise, people could just disable them by cutting power."

He chuckled. "Good point. I could come worry with you, you know."

"No. Thank you."

"Call if you change your mind, then." And he ended the call.

Celia was briefly surprised, expecting more cajoling. She'd said no, and he'd listened. Huh.

She looked into the blackness of her cooling loft, hearing the rattle of wind-driven rain on the large windows. The power might not be back on within the hour. Los Angeles' infrastructure wasn't always the best at handling heavy rainstorms.

León would come back if she asked. He was getting further away by the minute, and the longer she waited, the longer it would take. Not that she wanted him here.

The random hiss of palm trees in the wind kept startling her. And what kept tapping on the black windows? That staircase was so exposed, yawning down into all that empty space.

She made it ten minutes before texting him.

In twenty minutes, he was at the front door. She opened it by the glare of her phone, starkly lighting the water streaming off him. He juggled slick plastic bags from a convenience store, handing her an emptier one.

"Candles," he explained. "And a lot of ice. I thought it might help the refrigerators."

She wanted to give him a wondering glance but concentrated on lighting the stairs. "How did you know I was worried about them?"

"You mentioned the food here this morning. Figured you'd be thinking about it."

She heard him shift the bags again. They must be cold in his arms. "Sorry about hauling it up so many flights."

He chuckled behind her. "New York is nothing but stairs. I've lived in walk-ups higher than this."

They stopped on the second floor to put ice as quickly as

possible into each refrigerator. They were new and still plenty cold inside. It relieved her, knowing that if ice remained when the power came back on, likely the food was still safe.

They climbed the last flight together. Time slowed, and her skin prickled with goosebumps.

She whisked ahead at the top landing, ducking into the pantry, her phone's light swinging unexpectedly along the walls. León was stripping off his soaked jacket when she emerged with crumpled newspaper and a few cans of food.

"Here," she said. "It's all I have to dry off with." She caught a glimpse of amused black eyes and dripping hair before turning to the stovetop with the cans.

"You're not going to try to heat those, are you?"

The rustle of newspaper scrubbing over his head was loud in the darkness.

"No," she said. "I don't have any saucers for candles."

Oh hell. No matches, and her stove was gas.

León, however, pulled a lighter from the bag. It took a few tries as it'd gotten damp, but soon a small forest of candles was stuck to cans of coconut milk and black beans and set out on the dining table.

Celia was less nervous now that he was here. A friend, here to help. But still, her body tensed. They had been getting along, sort of! She couldn't stand a fight with him, not tonight, not with tomorrow looming.

She sat at the long table, candlelight reflecting off its glass top and glowing softly through it onto the floor. León sat at the end, leaving a corner between them.

A loud sheet of rain drummed against the inky black windows, and León looked up at the sound. Celia sneaked an extended glance at him. His skin shone golden in the candlelight, his alert eyes as inky as the windows, tendrils of wet hair stuck to his neck. That sight had always done things to her, and she shivered.

He looked back to her sooner than she'd expected, the force of his eyes on hers like a little kick, that impish twist of his lips giving her a hollow feeling in her stomach. Who was she kidding? They weren't friends.

Through the glass table, she could see his hands resting between his knees, fingers intertwined but fidgety. For a second, she felt his fingertips trailing over her bare skin, with that faint rasp of paint traces so uniquely León. Two minutes sitting with him, and she was already like this? She jumped up, his surprised eyes following her.

"There's not a lot of options," she said, "but I'm sure there's something I could cook for us." She walked to the kitchen island as though to start looking.

"If anyone could pull something together, it's you," he said.

She closed her eyes. If he was going to pull that fake friendly bullshit tonight, she'd scream.

His voice was too casual. "What are you going to do about tomorrow? Is there a contingency plan for no power?"

She gripped the counter out of his sight, tension burning in her, starting to feel angry but not at León. Here she went again, her old mental floundering. When would she know what she wanted? Was casual better than his old forceful, possessive intensity? Was she hoping for comfort or closure?

"Celia?"

What am I feeling, dammit?

She looked at him over her shoulder, seeing his brows lower in concern. The sight set blood rushing through her. This was León. She was sick of pretending he was just a friend like Andrew. She wanted seduction and distance and comfort all at the same time. She wanted to yell until he turned honest again.

The diplomacy was getting old.

Provocation it would be.

"I only have this handy," she said, grabbing the bottle of wine off the counter. *In vino veritas,* right? Caution was about to be thrown to the winds. She walked back to the table and set the wine before him.

"Red so it doesn't have to be chilled, twist top so it doesn't need a corkscrew. I don't have any glasses unpacked, though." His eyes, looking up at her, had turned deadly serious. "It'll warm us, at least." She unscrewed the cap, knuckles white, and set it between them with more clatter on the table than she'd intended.

Never breaking eye contact, he reached for the bottle and took a long swallow, then passed it to her as she sat.

Something was finally going to happen, good or bad.

THIRTY

Celia took a healthy swig from the wine bottle, then rested her hands in her lap. She would remind León how emotional honesty was done.

"I don't know what I'm going to do about tomorrow," she said, finally answering his question. Faint thunder outside punctuated the tight admission. "Probably the power will come back on, the food will be fine, or it can be replaced. It'll go as well as it can go."

"Sure," he agreed, reaching for the wine. Casual.

"This is only the first unexpected twist, the first of many things I can't plan for. Construction has been the easy part, and it's about to get real."

He nodded as she took a deep breath.

The warmth from the tart, fruity wine hadn't reached her hands yet. They pricked with cold. "I'm scared, León," she said. "It could fail. I have no control, no power over what's going to happen."

He pursed his lips, setting the bottle on the glass with a dull clink. "You have some power," he said.

She shook her head, tucking her hair behind her ear. "I can pay to have this place built, but the people, they'll be unpredictable. I have to make rules, and not everyone will like them. What if someone is rude or a bully? Or worse?"

León's solemn dark eyes never left hers, like on that first day when his gaze left her unable to speak. She could dig deeper now, but how deep?

"Whatever goes wrong," she said, "and there will be something, it'll be my fault. I'm in charge. I took that stupid money, and rather than do something useful, I gambled on this—this vanity project! A playground for myself to play patron in. Did I do it for them or for me?"

Her hand fluttered to her lips, trembling. Her stomach churned.

Hell. These were questions she hadn't said aloud, even in her own head. Pretending to be generous, in control, then realizing it was all a farce? The pain was sharp and unexpected.

"Hey," he said, stretching a hand near hers but carefully leaving a distance between them.

• • •

Golden light had always turned her wide eyes that lovely gray-green. León wanted to drown in them.

His muscles ached with the strain of acting relaxed. He didn't want to spook her or interrupt this emotional gift. Look at her, open and engaged and luminous.

"Starting something new is scary," he agreed slowly. "Things can go wrong. You'll just keep doing what you can. A lot of people don't even do that much. You're brave, and you try."

She shook her head, a quiver in her lower lip. "Brave? I knew I could get this built and ready to open. I enjoyed it. But now what? What happens next?"

"Celia, that's what's brave," he said. "You can be proud of this!" He swallowed as she looked down at her twining fingers. "I'm glad you didn't settle for just helping me paint. This is more."

A flash of silent lightning strobed in, capturing her still image in a frozen moment. Celia, listening.

"I was wrong about *Incubadora* being just a project," he said. These words, he'd rehearsed late at night. "You invested yourself fully in something you believe in. It shows who you are."

She closed her eyes. "Giving the cash straight to artists would have helped just as much. Instead, I built a place for myself. It's so selfish."

"You committed everything you have. How is that selfish?" he asked. "Your time, your money, even where you live! If they can't be grateful to you for giving them literally everything you can...." He paused.

His mother's words flooded through him, and he dropped his face into his hands.

"What?" Celia asked, her wary voice close.

Heat flushed slowly through him. *Idiota.* Slowly, he lowered his hands, finding her gaze on him, unwavering. Even the candlelight was still in the moment.

"That was me," he said, his pulse a drumbeat in his head. "I did that. You gave me everything, and I asked for more. How could you feel like it was enough? I'm so sorry, Celia."

She sat mute, giving away nothing. He could count his heartbeats, waiting for her to move. Then she reached carefully for the wine and took a slow drink. There, the slightest proud curve to her neck, finally a reaction.

"I felt like I gave enough," she said, and his heart stopped.

Felt? Gave? Past tense? What else did he have to offer her if his long-overdue apology was passed over?

She fixed him with a straight look. "Why did you come back like this?"

Her unexpected question was punctuated by another growl of thunder. His mind blanked, and suddenly León could only see her fingers curled around the bottle, the delicate goosebumps on her coppery forearms. He swallowed, fumbling for any thought.

"Really," she pressed. "Why are you helping me like we're just friends?"

His knee began bouncing as he averted his face, pretending to look at the windows. Rehearsals for this question had never gone well in his head, and this one counted.

Truth, just give her the truth. "I couldn't think of any other way to be near you. I hoped I could show you I'm different."

He looked back. Even in the dim light, Celia's cheeks burned with bright red spots.

León reached for the neck of the wine bottle, and she pulled her hands away to give him space to take it. He tipped it up to his lips, partly for courage and partly to stall. Still, she sat silent.

"I know," he said, painfully aware of what was at stake. "I promised it before. 'I'll do better, one more chance.'" He snorted. The audacity he'd had! "But I learned. I'm listening. You see it, right? No more ego or demands about posing."

A light slowly dawned in her eyes.

"That's why you're not painting." Her forehead creased. "You think it was about the painting?"

"It was about me getting my way," he said, leaning forward in his chair. "I know that. But the painting is part of it. I thought…Celia, I thought if I could make art, authentic art, it excused everything else. My parents' help, your work, I would deserve it if I could really paint."

Her face swam in his eyes, dizzying adrenaline plunging through him. Please, Celia. Please.

"León, your art never had anything to do with it," she said softly. "The posing, the cooking, it wasn't for the paintings. It was for you."

He groped for his chest, fingers splayed, and drew a breath as the world regained its dark balance.

She'd looked at him with that gentleness before, across the kitchen island, in the pool. His shoulders actually twitched as he stopped himself from reaching for her. Wait. Breathe. *Tranquilo.*

• • •

His corded forearms and tense neck didn't frighten Celia. They were familiar signs, this coiling León did before pouncing. She watched him restrain himself but not relax.

The heat spreading through her had nothing to do with wine. He wanted her still. Could it be up to her to say yes? Was she the one to decide?

"Painting clouded everything," he said low. "I stopped so I could see, and the picture was rotten. I was so entitled. Now I'm just, I don't know, some guy on your crew. But a better guy, maybe."

His chin drooped, fingers balling into fists in his lap. His breathing was shallow. Hers matched it.

"You were always a good guy, León," she said. "That first painting lesson you gave me, I'll never forget how kind you were that day." She waved toward the black room. "You came back here tonight and listened to me whine about being scared. I do know that my feelings matter to you."

"Matter?" he exploded.

She sat back in surprise as his chair squawked back and he shot to his feet. He pointed that damn finger at her.

"I've begged to know your feelings! I kept telling you, I want to paint everything inside you! I've at least been clear about that!"

She stood as well, breaths coming harder, but not wary like in the past. She knew him. This was León at peak expression, all his whipcord drama frustrated. That illicit thrill ran up her spine. Finally, truth.

"You always held back on me," he gritted. "Always."

"I know." There. Some truth back.

He clutched the back of the chair, knuckles white. "Why? What did I do?"

"It wasn't about you."

A broken, mirthless laugh escaped him.

"First, I couldn't speak at all," she said. "Then I could barely tell you the bad things. But I always held back the good things, and the more you pressed, the harder it got to say them."

He frowned ferociously at the floor, jaw set.

She lifted her chin. "If I showed you the worst and you left, I would know why. I expected it."

"If I left?" he scoffed, fingers working tightly on the chair.

"León, I couldn't be your muse."

He spun to pace, a few desperate feet back and forth before her and the candles. "I know, I pushed too hard, that stupid argument about belonging. I was wrong. I wanted to be closer to you and didn't care how I got it." He stopped, his eyes beseeching, the distance still gaping between them. "I still want that, and if that means never painting again, well...I quit painting."

"It's not that, León! I'm the one that failed!"

In his confused silence, another slice of lightning split the room.

"You said we needed trust, and I didn't trust...." Her throat choked unexpectedly.

She couldn't even say the words! Staying silent was the only power she'd ever had. She drew a stuttering breath, the air too thin.

She felt herself standing on the edge again, the world dropping off before her. Did she jump this time?

Slowly, she rose and walked to him. His eyes burned with that old terrible hope.

He joined her in the dark, stopping only before they touched. Their eyes met, their breaths mirrored, but the bare handspan between them lay deep as a canyon.

"*Reina*, I want one more chance."

"And if I say no?"

He took a ragged breath. "Please don't," he said, low.

"What if I say no?"

"Then, I just keep trying to be someone you want to say yes to."

Her heart felt like it might tear open and pour out all her words.

She jumped.

"León, I love you."

His expression only grew more sorrowful.

"Don't you dare say that unless I can stay," he said, voice breaking.

She choked on a laugh that was half sob.

"Yes. Stay."

He reached for her, and the world lit up; music soared.

• • •

León buried his face in her neck, breathing in her longed-for scent, hands wrapping around that beloved curve of her waist, crushing her to him.

"*Cielito, reina*, my Celia," he repeated against her skin, words cascading like the rain that battered the world outside. Electricity hummed between them, his eyes squeezed shut against a painful radiance, the thrum of their joint heartbeats echoing through his bones.

"León!" she gasped, and he withdrew by inches, eager to see her face—

Jesus!

The loft had burst into color and life. Light blossomed around them into the fathomless dark, the rain outside reduced to rushing by the swells of music. Every jeweled hue glowed, rich red brick warmly surrounding pools of blue, flares of goldenrod, lush shocks of green.

"The power!" she squealed.

Overwhelmed by the boundless spectrum, León closed his eyes. The chaos of color and form he wanted was already cradled against his chest. He couldn't help the joyful, relieved amusement that bubbled up, though, and it sent her into giddy peals, arms twining around his neck.

He couldn't stand still, lifting Celia by her waist and spinning her around, their laughter rippling through the melody surrounding them.

THIRTY ONE

Incubadora officially opened its doors in the damp gray morning. Waiting on the sidewalk, bundled up and chatting, were Dolores and Hector's *abuela*. Hector stood behind them, thin arms wrapped around a stuffed duffel. He bounced when Celia opened the door, welcoming them into the warmth. Hector's *abuela* handed her a covered plate of food as she entered, and Dolores removed her wrap to reveal a festive white blouse with turquoise embroidery. The little signs of celebration put a happy lump in Celia's throat.

"I'm taking Hector upstairs," León said to her, coming close. His glance took in her fidgety excitement, then he reached for her hand and leaned his shoulder against hers. She leaned back with a deep breath. "*Tranquila*," he murmured, and she squeezed his hand. He let go with a beaming smile and headed for the stairs, Hector and his *abuela* following.

Dolores was left standing, her eyebrows as high as they could go. She looked pointedly to León's retreating back, then to Celia's face. Feeling the heat on her cheeks, Celia shrugged with a smile, and Dolores clucked to herself as she headed up to her office.

Celia stayed to bask in her newly opened haven.

Rich red brick climbed to the lofty ceiling strung with multi-colored flags. Tall silvery windows fogged by the cool weather diffused the morning's gentle gray light. Polished concrete floors reflected long tables laden with literature and platters of bright finger food. Easels stood ready, paints and oil crayons awaiting their first use. Low mariachi music filled the room, *Deja Que Salga la Luna* playing quietly. The faint earthy smell of fresh clay trailed from Andrew's classroom.

Now, to fill her space with people.

Trevor's car passed outside, so Celia went out to meet him. Traversing the block, she stopped to view *Incubadora* from this angle. No rain fell, but the wet sidewalks reflected the golden light inside. She didn't know about her new neighbors, but to her it was the most inviting thing she'd ever seen.

Andrew waved at her as he exited Trevor's car, parked in her alley. She watched as Trevor opened his trunk and loaded bag after bag of gear onto both of their shoulders. Today, Trevor would photograph the entire opening, and Kelsey would post the best online. Celia saw Trevor steal a kiss before he and Andrew met her.

"How was the fishing trip?" she asked. She caught them blushing as they went through the front door she held open.

"We stayed in the hotel for most of it," Andrew said. "It rained like crazy." He set down some bags.

Trevor put an arm around his waist. "He did better than expected, sitting outside and doing nothing."

"I'll give anything a chance," Andrew grinned. He looked eagerly toward the food table, and swiped a pastry on his way into his classroom. Anyone who came in today could create clay masterpieces with a free teacher at their disposal.

Kelsey fluttered in, wearing her version of an artsy caftan and littering the front desk with her purse, phone, and tablet.

"You're wearing the blue dress," she said with a grin. "You gonna make León regret what he's missing?"

Celia looked down at the thin turquoise knit, warmth spreading through her at his name. "He's not missing anything."

"He's blind, then."

Catching Trevor's eye, Kelsey moved off to where he was getting shots of the awaiting easels. They were instantly heads-down over screens again.

The first members of the public filtered in. They looked around, tried some food, then wandered back out. Well, the next ones might ask questions.

León trouped back down with his group, and Hector agreed to paint something at the easel by the window. Trevor crouched down to take photos, making sure to include Hector's *abuela* watching in the background.

Celia savored the sight of an artist in her front window, finally! León hovered avidly, watching Hector set up.

Look at him.

He stood on his toes and ran eager fingers through his dark hair when Hector's first color went on the canvas. It was no surprise when he turned his head, eyes wide with longing, seeking her out. When he realized she was already watching him, his smile outshone every light in the room.

Kelsey came up behind her. "Oh ho, did he finally stop playing?"

Celia shook her head, unwilling to look away from her love. "We talked," she said.

León's smile drew her like a magnet, and she was walking to him before she realized. He met her halfway, sliding arms around her waist and beaming as he leaned in for a kiss. Celia felt the room melt away.

Kelsey shrieked.

Trevor turned at her squawk, then chuckled and snapped a few photos of the couple. Andrew poked his head out of the classroom, hands covered in wet clay. He grinned.

"Good god, it's about damn time!"

• • •

Celia had never been this happy in her entire life. Week after week, new joys were added.

Their loft could have become a creative clutter, but León and Celia worked together to contain the inherent messiness of inspiration. His studio space by the windows blossomed with colors and textures while her kitchen bubbled with simmering aromatics and nourishment. The two hearts of their apartment wrestled and danced in beautiful chaos. He cleaned when paint strayed outside its confines, and she accepted that art was messy. Across their bare brick walls, their story unfolded as one painting at a time was added.

Three more residents moved in, giving Hector his first roommates. Howard, a musicologist down from San Francisco, fused hip-hop with Chinese traditional melodies. Shmuel was a young local man who made multimedia installations. And Sengdaloune, a local Laotian woman, welded metal sculptures piece by tiny piece. The electrical system was put to the test by her equipment and passed.

People walking by began to notice the art being created in the large windows, the welding, in particular, attracting attention. The small sales gallery in the front grew slowly, and one metal sculpture was sold.

The following week, Andrew had his first full classroom. Suddenly, small round pots took over the back of the space as they dried. The kiln on the top floor ran daily, and everyone was glad for the dumbwaiter to take the pieces up three flights.

Hector began inviting friends in for impromptu painting sessions, then asked if he could officially teach a class. He knew his style and could show anyone how to try it themselves. Celia sat in on a session so she could make something awful.

León tried to keep a straight face when he poked his head in. "You can do everything but paint," he teased.

She swiped up a drip of spray paint with one finger and drew a stripe on his wrist. "You just don't get my style, *mi lienzo.*"

His laugh distracted the whole class.

In the next month, five more residents moved in. Celia cooked dinners when she could but found the residents taking over the job on their own. They enjoyed the sense of community when cooking and eating together. Celia and León sometimes joined them, the communal table barely able to seat everyone. Conversations flew, jokes peppered with words in different languages. Food and stories were exchanged, and some nights León had to hold Celia afterward as she cried, overwhelmed by happy tears.

Two more classes started, led by residents who discovered that guiding others in the creative process sparked inspiration for their own pieces. Hector had initiated the tradition, and although Celia attempted to dissuade residents from shouldering extra responsibilities, the classes unexpectedly amplified everyone's work.

León's parents were invited to come visit.

Celia had one of her rare panics, trying to make everything better than perfect. She failed, but they were still impressed, being led over the warehouse from top to bottom. León was bursting with pride, his father teasing him about his luck.

Dinner simmering on the stove, Celia sat on a yellow couch next to León's mother, sweat pricking at her palms. It was harder to make conversation when there wasn't a task she could retreat into, but surely she could do this.

León's mother studied Celia for a moment before speaking. "León has changed since he met you. He seems to have found his place in the world."

Celia smiled bashfully, feeling the edges of her anxiety soften. "He changed me a lot, too."

As if on cue, León's laughter, accompanied by his father's, floated from the other side of the room, and Celia felt her heart swell with affection.

"I'm glad you forgave him," his mother continued. "Leónito can be dramatic."

Celia chuckled at the understatement, her tense back starting to ease.

His mother smiled gently. "It was past time he learned to think of someone besides himself."

As if on cue, León's eyes sought Celia from across the room. His beaming face started a warm flush up her neck and into her cheeks.

"And I see that now, he does," León's mother continued. "Our family is always close, even when distance separates us. Now we include your place, your town, in our hearts."

The approval unlocked something astounding deep within Celia. She had no words for it. Feeling the pull to straighten a couch pillow or go check the food, she started to rise. Then she paused and sank back. She couldn't be so unkind as to run off after that.

"Thank you," she said, clasping her hands to hide the faint trembling.

"Estella, *mi vida*," León's father called, "come see this painting of your son's!"

The visit flew quickly, and plans were made for the new couple to visit New York in a few months.

León did his best not to pester her to sit for him, but there were days he couldn't resist. She couldn't work all the time, and he craved having his muse in front of him.

"Here, this will be an easy pose," he begged, pulling her to the bed by the hand. "Pants off. Underwear too." She complied quickly. "You can keep the sweater on, I think. Yes, that's gorgeous. Green sweater, blue bed. Lovely." He directed her to lay on her stomach, diagonally across their bed, facing him. "Okay, feet up at the knees. Cross them at the ankles." He moved to pull the sweater down to her waist, bunching it artfully at her left hip. "Right. Pull the sweater cuffs almost over your hands. Lace your fingers. Okay, lower your head and peek at me over your hands."

She followed his directions, then waited as he pulled out his phone to capture a few shots. He had to get these because she just couldn't sit as much now. But when she could...he dragged his easel over, threw a canvas on it, and began painting furiously.

"I'll be fast, *cielito*, promise."

"I have time, it's okay." She held the position without moving a muscle. "I would sit for you more if I could, León. Maybe I can take a day off next week."

"To work for me? Oh no. You rest on your day off." He leaned around the canvas to look at her a little more closely. "Well, maybe a little sitting." He scrubbed more paint on the canvas. She could hear him muttering to himself.

"*Musa encantadora, reina, eres tú....*"

She grinned behind her hands. He did still get worked up.

Spring brought even more residents to *Incubadora*, filling the last of the beds. The entire building, top to bottom, surged with the voices and pigments and scents of art. Celia longed to expand her new family, but her funds weren't unlimited. She cast about for ideas; inexpensive ways to bring in more of the community, or failing that, overlooked sources of money.

Coming down to the front desk one bright afternoon to collect mail, she heard squeals and shouts on the street outside. Children playing. A whole herd of them, by the sound. Sun slanted in the tall front windows, the glare rendering them opaque. As she turned away, the front door wrenched open with a rush of air and Hector tumbled inside, breathless and damp, his ruddy face lit with a wide grin.

"What's going on out there?" she asked.

"Football, Celia! The street's blocked so we're playing."

The shrieks outside rang louder with the door open, and Celia rounded the desk to peek outside at the fun.

Sure enough, a laughing clutch of children, all knobbly arms and legs, flocked around a soccer ball as it rocketed back and forth under their kicking feet. Mothers with toddlers, some Celia had met before, roosted in the narrow shade across the street, watching.

And among the children, a taller figure raced around them shouting instructions, bouncing and pointing at the ball, as loud as any kid. Her capricious, energetic painter. His hair flew, sweaty and loose, his back twisting under the fabric of his t-shirt as the ball shot out toward him. He stopped it with a sneakered foot, face alight as the group turned to him.

"*Tío* León! Here!" they shouted, waving hands in the air, begging that the ball be sent their way. "*¡Tío, aquí!*"

He kicked it squarely back, bubbling with laughter as he tried to direct them, any of them, to aim for the goal.

The sun on Celia's face couldn't rival the warmth that bloomed inside her. The playful chaos of the children gave voice to the wild love she felt for this man. He'd made friends; he was at home here. They were at home.

Hector joined her in the doorway, gulping down a bottle of water he'd fetched.

"Let's get waters for the kids," she said, still watching the scrum.

"I'll bring some," he said, jogging back in.

Maybe she spent too much time inside with her artists. Maybe it was time to invite in the whole community. The classes at *Incubadora* paid for a lot of expenses, but if she had more funds, she could offer free classes to the kids, just like León had said the neighbors wanted, back before they opened.

It wasn't a hard decision. It was time to put her canyon house on the market.

• • •

Celia's house sold in record time, furnishings and all. While she didn't miss rattling around her empty white house, she couldn't say goodbye without a last look. She invited the gang back for one last night of hanging around the firepit.

Between the full day and heavy traffic, everyone beat León and Celia there, including the pizza delivery driver. They just missed the April sunset, the city sparkling under a clear indigo sky as they came through the side gate. The patio looked so bare without its cushioned lounge chairs, her wall of windows mirroring back only the first stars.

León walked her down the sloped lawn, his hand warm in hers. Andrew already had the last fire cheerfully leaping, crackling and warm. Her familiar little pool glowed a still, luminous blue next to the silent, dark pool house. Celia stopped where the old food table had stood, more saddened than she'd expected. She looked down the canyon to the constellation of yellow city lights.

"I'm going to miss this view of the city," she said.

Palm fronds whispered above them as León squeezed her hand. "It's beautiful," he agreed. "But you're looking at it from a distance. I like our place, down in the heart of it. It's more exciting, hearing the sirens and crowds and traffic."

"Says the New Yorker," Andrew said from his folding chair.

They joined their friends around the fire, León handing her a full paper plate before sitting too. Celia's gaze roamed around the circle, a gentle warmth spreading through her as she observed each of her friends lit by the flickering light. Kelsey sprawled low in her chair, her yellow sundress brushing the grass below, rounded belly like a beach ball filling her lap. Trevor sat at ease, an ankle crossed over his knee, eating slowly as the fire reflected off his dark-rimmed glasses. Andrew leaned forward, elbows on his knees, beer bottle in one hand and a slice of pizza folded in the other, disappearing quickly in large bites.

And next to her, León, with hair pulled back from his gold-washed face, eyes black in the firelight. Her heart fluttered at his gaze, looking up through his lashes, his bouncing knee nearly dumping his plate on the ground. She reached out, steadying his plate with a reassuring smile. As she relaxed, so did he, his shoulders easing as he picked up his slice with paint-smudged hands.

Sitting in her old backyard, gutted and changing, brought up more feelings than she'd expected. Celia retired back into her chair, letting the fireside chatter wash over her as she used to.

This house had been an uneasy sanctuary, a place to hide. She'd needed a place to be small and alone.

The past would always be a part of her; Mom was still out there, and Dad's choices, and her tendency toward spiraling anxiety.

But she couldn't be small anymore. There were too many new people, too many changes, even in her friends.

She watched Andrew's sensitive hands slipping around the curves of the beer bottle as he turned it. As he glanced sideways at Trevor, she recalled the charming glee on his face when he told her they were moving in together. She wasn't the only one with a new home.

Kelsey's yellow dress fluttered as she poked at Andrew with a bare foot, and Celia thought of her voice last week, talking sweetly at her round stomach. "Stop kicking, Ruth. Soon you can come out and meet me and Grandma and *Tía* Celia."

Her family was growing. Through the fire, she saw Trevor taking off his glasses and cleaning them on his shirt. He'd been so pleased to announce a new addition. "I hired an assistant, finally," he'd said, pride bright in his smile. "A queer kid new to LA. Boy, does he need help getting around."

León reached absently to take Celia's hand, holding it low between their chairs, stroking his thumb over her knuckles. She looked fondly at his profile, glowing in the firelight as he listened to Andrew and Kelsey tease each other. She could see again León's red cheeks when they'd surprised him with a dinner at the gin bar on the first night of his new show. Six paintings in a Hollywood gallery, running much longer than the last exhibition. His career was coming alive on his new coast.

The fire blazed in gold, the sky deepening to dark blue.

León felt her gaze and met it, squeezing her hand. If she could paint, he would be a golden light to her aqua waters, the sun to her sea.

It's okay to move on to something new, Celia Rose.

"Hey! Celia, wake up!" Andrew was suddenly standing over her, holding out an open hand. "We're getting in the pool."

"We're what?"

Kelsey trilled a laugh. "Didn't you hear a thing we said?"

Celia inhaled deeply, watching them all stand one by one. León dropped her hand to stand too, unzipping his hoodie. Andrew was already stripping off his shirt. "There aren't any towels," she said, struggling to come back to the present. "The pool house is empty."

"It's warm tonight," Trevor said, kicking his shoes off under his chair. "We'll dry by the fire."

Celia watched wide-eyed as clothes were shed, a laugh tickling up inside her, warmth spreading from her belly to the tips of her fingers. Andrew was the first undressed, his white briefs gleaming against his dark brown skin in the firelight. Kelsey lay her sundress over the folding chair, one graceful hand supporting her unwieldy belly, the other adjusting a bra strap as it slipped low. Trevor folded his clothes carefully, setting his glasses atop them as Andrew vaulted up the two steps to the pool surround, his muscles flexing with the motion. He cannonballed into the pool before the rest made it onto the flagstones, the lights under the water shattering into a riotous chaos, the roaring splash echoing through the backyard.

Celia turned to León, pulse quickening as he straightened from pulling his jeans low, his dark boxer briefs familiar but somehow new by the fire. He raised playful eyebrows at her as Trevor jumped into the deep end, and Kelsey shrieked as she stepped down the stairs into the cold water, her laughter ringing clear and joyous. Celia grinned and pulled off her sweater.

There was no room for diving, no still surface to disturb. León held her hand, his grip reassuring and warm, and together they leapt into the splashing and laughter.

The shock of chilly water faded quickly, and León stroked along by her through the deep end, following her to the side of the pool where they'd spent so many nights hanging on the edge, looking at the city.

The familiar yip-yip of coyotes sounded below in the chaparral, but the sparkling city lay distant and silent. León was right; this perch of a house wasn't for her any longer. The city streets below called to her, cradling her *Incubadora*, full of art, where they lived in the heart of it.

A tickle along her cheekbone surprised her—León, tracing a finger down her skin, his touch as gentle as moonlight on water. She turned to him. His brown eyes held that focused heat that turned her insides to fire. His wet hair streamed back to his shoulders, one black curl plastered against his neck. That had always done electric things to her too.

"Aqua green with turquoise," he murmured. His finger trailed across the bridge of her nose. "A highlight here in cerulean with titanium white." He traced along her jaw, then down her neck. "Bronze and burnt sienna for your shadows. And—"

She put a finger to his lips. "*Tranquilo*," she said.

He tucked a wet lock of her hair behind her ear, a content smile curling his lips, his wet body drawing closer to hers. "*Eres tú, mi amor.*"

It's you.

"*Eres tú*," she replied gently.

León raised a dripping hand to cup her cheek and touched his soft mouth to hers.

"Hey!" Kelsey shouted. "No making out in the pool!" She laughed at Celia and León as they startled and broke apart. Andrew splashed water at Kelsey, the water droplets catching the firelight as they flew. Then he stuck out his tongue at her and hauled a grinning Trevor in for a wet kiss.

"So unfair," Kelsey groused. She hauled on the waistband of her underwear, twisting in the hip-high water. "And my granny panties are falling down!"

León pushed a wave of water at her. "Who made you boss?"

"You call that a splash?" Kelsey retaliated with a wide swing of her hand, sending a cascade toward everyone. Andrew pulled his legs up in front of him and kicked furiously, adding to the maelstrom.

Ducking the airborne water, Celia laughed aloud, joy bubbling up uncontrollably. As León joined in the water fight, she pushed off the wall and dove under the water, a brief, pure quiet enveloping her. She surfaced in the middle of the pool under the cascade of splashing, then lay on her back, floating in the center one last time.

Laughter lapped at her from all sides, water pattering on her skin like rain.

She relaxed and let the water hold her up.

Maya Bairey lives on the banks of the Columbia river in Portland, Oregon, with her husband and their old cat, Dory. Turning from corporate writing to storytelling, Maya was surprised to find she had a lot of passionate stories inside her, where stuck people learn to live out loud.

Her debut novel, *Painting Celia*, explores the way honest art and love can heal and embrace us. Maya invites readers to enjoy a fun escape but also to look inward, discovering their own creative and emotional depths.

For a deeper dive into the world of *Incubadora*, visit bairey.com.

ACKNOWLEDGEMENTS

This first novel of mine spilled out over the course of three years, a cascade of story that wouldn't let me rest until it was told correctly. I can't name all of the people who helped, for fear of leaving some out, but some rode the currents with me on the whole journey.

My husband, Peter, has believed in me every time I say I'm going to do something big, then picks up the slack so I can get down to work. He once called me the most important person in the world, a compliment that remains my highest honor. To date.

Rascally poet Sulima, my friend and mentor, read every single draft and soothed my angst over telling the story right.

Dancer Lavinia was the first I told of my secret dream to write, and the first to suggest art could heal me.

My nieces Jaime and Jess remain the cheerleaders who understand me best.

Friends whose support I deeply value: Kay and Devon and Kate; Gamble and Andrea; Daniela and Loune; Karen, Joana, Connie, Sheryl, Megan, Kathy, River, Denise, Natalie, and Robin; Editor Christine; Writing Coach Joey; and Willamette Writers.

To New York City and Los Angeles, cities whose immensity never diminishes me, I vow to return.

And to the artists whose work I consumed on an endless loop as I wrote, thank you for the inspiration and aspiration to be as authentic, clever, and dedicated.